The Experts Praise Jacob Stone and His Thrillers

"Whether he's writing as Dave Zeltserman or Jacob Stone, you can expect the best in suspense writing."
—Max Allan Collins

"Dave Zeltserman is one of the best suspense writers in the business, and his Jacob Stone thrillers are not to be missed."
—Steve Hamilton

Unleashed
"A roller coaster ride between covers! A skillful blend of psychological and investigative thriller writing, *Unleashed* brings back the great Morris Brick and his crew, who have to stop a horrific series of murders in L.A. Rarely is an author so skilled at portraying such unremitting evil and the poignant, human side of his characters in a single tale."
—Jeffery Deaver

Malicious
"A killer with a penchant for Rube Goldberg devices has been leaving calling cards for Brick as he slaughters Hollywood actresses one by one, with the goal of destroying all of Los Angeles. Zeltserman's writing is smart, witty, and edge-of-your-seat thrilling."
—*Ellery Queen Mystery Magazine*

Crazed
"Moves fast and makes for entertaining reading…Great stuff if you like serial killer thrillers and highly recommended."
—*Bill Crider's Pop Culture Magazine*

Deranged
"*Deranged* is a dark and different serial killer novel that will haunt the reader long after the book is closed and back on the shelf. Author Jacob Stone transfixes us with dread, and something more. He has the rare capacity to startle. Read if you dare."
—John Lutz

Also by Jacob Stone

Unleashed

A Morris Brick Thriller

Jacob Stone

LYRICAL UNDERGROUND
Kensington Publishing Corp.
www.kensingtonbooks.com

LYRICAL UNDERGROUND BOOKS are published by

Kensington Publishing Corp.
119 West 40th Street
New York, NY 10018

All Kensington titles, imprints, and distributed lines are available at special quantity discounts for bulk purchases for sales promotion, premiums, fund-raising, educational, or institutional use.

Special book excerpts or customized printings can also be created to fit specific needs. For details, write or phone the office of the Kensington Sales Manager: Kensington Publishing Corp., 119 West 40th Street, New York, NY 10018. Attn. Sales Department. Phone: 1-800-221-2647.

First Electronic Edition: March 2019
ISBN-13: 978-1-5161-0640-0 (ebook)
ISBN-10: 1-5161-0640-7 (ebook)

First Print Edition: March 2019
ISBN-13: 978-1-5161-0641-7
ISBN-10: 1-5161-0641-5

Printed in the United States of America

To Eric Sockol

Chapter 1

Morris Brick woke up with the sound of a key unlocking the front door, which was quickly followed by the heavy thumping of his bull terrier, Parker, scampering down the staircase. He didn't have to look at the alarm clock on the shelf next to him to know it was seven o'clock. That was the time he had arranged for their twenty-five-year-old occasional dog walker, Kat McKinty, to pick up Parker, and Kat was not only cheerful and dependable, but always punctual enough to set your watch by. Last night he'd decided that he and Natalie could use a late-morning sleep-in, so he'd arranged for Kat to take the bull terrier to Laurel Canyon dog park, which just might be Parker's favorite spot in the world that didn't involve food.

Although the bedroom door was closed, he heard Parker at the front door letting out several excitable grunts, and Kat shushing him. He knew she was trying to be quiet, but he still heard the door clicking shut when it closed. What could he say? He had ears like a bat. At least they were big and nearly stuck out as much as a bat's.

Natalie had been sleeping on her stomach, but she must've woken up too. She rolled onto her side and scooted over so that she was up against Morris. She rested the side of her face on his shoulder and placed one of her small, delicate hands on his not-so-small belly. Morris's hand found the curvature of her slender, pajama-covered hip.

"Kat must've collected the little guy," she said in a soft, throaty whisper, her eyes cracked slightly open.

Morris turned his head so he could kiss her on the forehead. His voice was not much more than a croak as he told her that Kat wouldn't be bringing Parker back until ten. "We can actually sleep late for once."

Nat smiled wickedly and nestled in closer to him. "Not too late," she said. "I have other ideas for how we can spend the time."

"Cooking bacon without Parker mooching all of it?"

She laughed at the suggestion. "That wouldn't be bad," she admitted. "But I've got other ideas and none of them involve leaving the bed. But a little more sleep first."

Morris soon felt the rhythmic rising and lowering of her chest and heard her light breathing as she drifted back to sleep. Life was good, especially in the wife, daughter, and dog department. Even though he and Nat were approaching their twenty-fifth wedding anniversary, she could still make him feel weak in the knees with a smile, and at times he had to pinch himself over his good fortune at not only finding her, but the fact that she seemingly fell as much in love with him as he did with her. Their daughter Rachel was a beautiful young woman who fortunately resembled Natalie more than himself, although she did have his hard, slate gray eyes. She had just started her last semester of law school while also working ten hours a week as an intern in the district attorney's office, with plans of being hired by them once she passed the bar. And then there was Parker. The bull terrier was six now and was beginning to slow down a bit, but as far as Morris was concerned he was the best dog in the world and any runner-up would be a distant second.

Morris had no complaints about work either. His company, MBI, was flourishing with all the corporate and insurance-fraud cases they could handle, and thank God, no serial killer work since the Nightmare Man terrorized Los Angeles. But it was more than that. When Charlie Bogle left MBI, things didn't seem quite right at the investigative firm, like they were out of balance. Since Charlie's return six months ago, things were back to normal again. Better yet, Morris had been able to reduce his workweek to fifty hours, and it had been over two months since he had had to work over the weekend, which meant more late Saturday and Sunday mornings with Nat—at least the rare times when he remembered to call Kat McKinty the night before.

He closed his eyes and focused on the sound of Natalie's light breathing, and soon drifted off also.

Chapter 2

Duncan Moss bought coffee at the counter and took it outside so he could sit at one of the patio tables. This was a nice, upscale downtown LA neighborhood, and the people walking by all looked nice and upscale. Or at least clean, fit, and well-off. Quite a contrast from the boarding house he was staying at half a mile away. That area could best be described as dingy and downbeat. More than that, a heavy oppressiveness seemed to hang in the air like a bad stench that just wouldn't go away, and the people living there carried an unmistakable hopelessness. Duncan much preferred that neighborhood. He could barely stand to see all these happy, privileged people who thought nothing bad could ever happen to them. They were so wrong. *So very wrong.*

On the same block as the coffee shop there was also a bakery, a café advertising Los Angeles's best breakfast, and a diner, and across the street a small park with neatly arranged flower beds and benches. While it wasn't quite 9:30 yet, it was one of those near-perfect early spring days, and all of that was enough to bring out a small parade of people. Duncan sipped his coffee and watched as fellow millennials walked past him. Older people were also in the mix, but it was the millennials that he focused on. They were the ones who stirred up a toxic and suffocating mix of rage, jealousy, and psychotic need to cause pain. All of them trying so hard to look hip and cool with their tattoos and piercings; the dudes with goatees, soul patches, and man buns, the women with brightly colored dye jobs. There was barely a pound of body fat among them. They kept themselves in shape by dieting and CrossFit-type training classes. Duncan was also as lean as a rail, but he accomplished this the old-fashioned way: Survival.

And while he had never in his life stepped into a gym or taken an exercise class, he had a wiry strength that few of them would've been able to match.

Of course, most of them had their noses stuck in their cell phones. Some sort of strange sixth sense kept them from colliding with each other as they crisscrossed on the sidewalk. Jesus, what a bunch! Most of them were so oblivious to the world around them that Duncan could've gotten up and punched them in their smug faces without any of them having a clue what was happening until they hit the pavement. As tempting as it was, he stayed seated. He had a plan, after all. Soon he'd be unleashing his rage in a very specific, controlled way. Besides, none of them were what he really needed.

While he remained invisible to most of them, one of them noticed him. A blond woman walking a little four-legged fuzz ball that was supposedly a dog. She was in her early thirties, maybe five years older than him. Slender, yellowish hair that fell past her shoulder, cute heart-shaped face, a short dress showing off long, thin legs. She smiled at him. An invitation of sorts. Why wouldn't she? He was a good-looking guy with dark features and at the moment was impeccably groomed and dressed smartly in slacks, sports jacket, and boat shoes. He was also making a concentrated effort to show only a carefree, pleasant expression. If this was four months ago, she wouldn't have smiled at him, and not just because he lived 3000 miles away in the Jamaica Plain neighborhood of Boston. If she had caught sight of him then, she would've fled to the other side of the street. Back then he was a mess. He had gone over a month without showering or shaving or changing his clothes, and almost six months without getting a haircut or even combing his hair, but more than his ragged, disheveled appearance, it would've been the craziness shining in his eyes that would've frightened her. He had reached rock-bottom and was consumed with dark, suicidal thoughts. He no doubt would've ended his life had he not received the postcard when he did. It had been mailed from Los Angeles, and at first it nearly sent him out of his mind with rage and homicidal fury, but later that postcard allowed him to see as clear as day what he needed to do. After that, he came up with his plan.

Once he had the plan, everything was okay, at least as okay as it could be. He cleaned up his act—first clipping off his beard and cutting his hair short, then making sure to shower and shave each day, and taking care of other personal hygiene issues. He also made it a point not to glare with homicidal rage at the lucky, happy people he would see, and instead hide his true self behind a pleasant façade. It took effort and concentration, but it became easier once he had his plan. And while the sight of the happy, lucky people made him feel like a heavy stone was crushing his chest, at least he no longer felt like he was on the verge of suffocating. Because he had a plan...

He couldn't come out to LA right away. He was broke and he needed to raise enough cash to bankroll his plan. It had been almost five years since he had burglarized any homes or rolled drunks or robbed anyone at gunpoint, but certain skills come back quickly, and these were skills that he had always excelled at, and it didn't take him long to raise the money he needed. After that, he bought a 2002 Cadillac Eldorado for 500 dollars at a police auction, and a week ago hit the road. He drove almost nonstop for two days, drinking enough coffee to keep himself awake, and arrived five days ago in LA. Since then he'd been getting the lay of the land and making plans for where to go hunting. He also bought himself an appropriate wardrobe so he could fit in with the happy, privileged people. Money wasn't an issue. He had the necessary skills to always get more.

The blonde walking the fuzz-ball dog slowed down a step, her smile turning more hopeful. Duncan smiled back, but in a noncommittal way. He had no intention of inviting her to join him. She wasn't what he needed. She tried to maintain her smile as she walked past him, but it cracked, the hurt weakening her mouth and betraying her. He looked past her toward a couple holding hands half a block away. So happy, so much in love. But they weren't what he needed either. While they were privileged and charter members of the Beautiful People's Club, they were in their fifties and Duncan needed them to be younger. He needed them to have their whole lives ahead of them, so that the loss and pain would be all that much more profound.

He tilted back the cardboard cup and finished off the last few sips of coffee, then got up, crushed the cup into a ball, and tossed it into a trash can. He didn't come here to hunt, at least not exactly. If he had seen exactly what he was looking for, he would've gotten on their tail. But today was Saturday, and if a person like Duncan wanted to find a young, well-off couple who were oh-so-in-love, why not go directly to the source and crash a wedding?

Chapter 3

Right before waking up Alex Frey was having a delicious sex dream involving Jill. Cruelly interrupted, he lay on his back, disoriented, struggling to hold onto any last remnants of the dream and to get his bearings. His disappointment was further compounded when he reached over and found that Jill was no longer in bed. That was a shame, as he'd been hoping to immediately turn his sex dream into reality.

"Jill, where are you?" he shouted out.

"In the bathroom."

Okay. Still a chance, then. "The honorable Willie Winkie needs immediate attention!"

"You mean *wee* Willie Winkie?"

Alex looked down at the pitched tent that had formed in his pajama bottoms. *Wee* certainly wasn't the right adjective to use, as Jill knew perfectly well from experience!

"Come on," he pleaded, desperate. "The more-than-adequate Willie Winkie isn't going to blow himself!"

He heard Jill laughing. "I'm sorry, love," she called out. "If he wants to get blown, that's the only way it's going to happen. At least this morning. I'm getting ready for later and I don't have much time."

Further disappointment! How much could one man take? Alex peered over at the alarm clock. It was only few minutes after ten and their engagement party wasn't until two. Well, he'd have to use his smooth-talking skills to change her mind and remedy the situation. His health was in danger, after all!

He carefully maneuvered himself off the ridiculously expensive king-sized Swedish-made bed that Jill's parents had given them as an apartment-warming present. Brett, his future father-in-law, had told him at the time that nothing was more important than a good night's sleep. Alex murmured something in agreement, but in his mind nothing was more important than going through life with Jill at his side.

Thanks to his current predicament involving the aforementioned tent pole, he shuffled in a hobbling gait to the bathroom located outside the bedroom. His gorgeous fiancée was seated in front of the mirror, tweezing her eyebrows—not that they needed any tweezing. Jill really was gorgeous in a blond, wholesome cheerleader sort of way. He groaned, seeing that she had already put on lipstick, eyeliner, and blush. She had also slipped on silk stockings and her recently purchased and very expensive designer dress that was quite stunning on her, although almost anything she wore would've been stunning. Jill could've grabbed the first dress she saw off the discount rack and still turn heads. Alex knew immediately the situation was near-hopeless but not impossible. Clothing could always be taken off and put back on. While she was also wearing her flawless one-and-a-half carat engagement ring, a strand of pearls, and a pair of matching earrings, none of that would be an issue. They'd made love plenty of times in the past while she was wearing jewelry. It was the makeup that was going to cause him problems.

"How long have you been up?" he asked.

"Since eight." Without losing her focus, she yanked out a blond eyebrow hair. "This doesn't just happen all by itself, you know."

"Jill, darling, your eyebrows are already perfection, as is the rest of you. In fact, you'd be every bit as stunning without a drop of makeup. I like the au naturel look on you. Why don't you wash it all off?"

"Nice try, buster, but no dice."

Alex grimaced noticeably. "Can't you see I have a dire situation happening?"

She glanced at the pitched tent in his pajama bottoms, her eyes opening wide, as if in shock.

"I see that I have grossly underestimated Mr. Winkie," she said, straight-faced. "But unfortunately, my love, I'm on a super-tight schedule and have to leave in ten minutes. And I'm not smudging my makeup, especially not my lipstick!"

Sulking, he asked, "Why ten minutes? The party isn't until two."

"I have an appointment with Roxanne to blow-out my hair. And one of us has to be at the hotel by noon to make sure all the arrangements are handled properly."

"Let's talk about being handled properly…"

"Sorry, sweetie, I'm not risking you leaving a stain on this dress. You'll just have to wait until tonight."

More exaggerated sulking. If there was a rock nearby, he would've kicked it. "You might be asking the impossible here."

Jill reached up and touched Alex's cheek. "I have faith that you'll find the strength, somehow. Or take a long, cold shower."

"You're not being at all helpful. And you realize this is your fault."

She arched one of her recently tweezed eyebrows. "How's that?"

"You're the one I had an erotic dream about. And quite a lovely one, at that. It involved you lying naked on the bed, a gallon of hot fudge, a large tub of whipped cream, and a jar of maraschino cherries." His sulk turned into a frown. "It was a messy dream that tired out my tongue. It also got me both horny and hungry."

"I'm flattered, of course," she said with a wicked grin. "But my hands are tied."

"Not yet, but they could be."

Jill rose from the seat and reached over to kiss Alex chastely on the cheek, being careful not to disturb her expertly applied lipstick. "I must get going. I can't help with the horny, but I can help with the hungry. There's quiche lorraine from Madeleine's in the fridge. Heat it at three-fifty for seven minutes in the toaster oven. And don't use the microwave. You'll ruin it!"

"What a gyp," he complained, hating that he was sounding like a five-year-old about to throw a tantrum. "I don't even get to see you naked!"

She patted him on the spot on his cheek where she had kissed him. "Tonight, my love, I promise. And I'll take extra-special care of Mr. Winkie then." She started to turn away, but stopped to give him a stern look with hands on her slender, but beautifully curved hips. "You'll shave, right? And you'll wear the suit that I picked up at the cleaners yesterday? And the shirt and tie I left on the bureau?"

Alex nodded sullenly, knowing that he was beat. "Yes, dear," he said obediently.

Jill squinted at him as she tried to make sure he'd do as asked. Satisfied, she left the bathroom so she could finish getting ready. Alex grudgingly accepted his fate and squeezed his eyes closed and forced himself to think only about the marketing plan he was working on for the Hillsborough condominium project. Once his penis had shriveled and the pitched tent in his pajamas was gone, he emptied his bladder into the toilet, quickly washed his hands in the sink, then headed to the kitchen for some coffee and quiche. He caught Jill just as she was about to leave. She blew him a kiss, her face glowing with excitement. He waved back, forcing a goofy smile and trying to hide his earlier disappointment. He waited until the apartment door closed behind her before walking into the kitchen.

What a jerk he was being, pouting like a spoiled brat just because Jill was too enthusiastic about their engagement party to have a tumble with him this morning. She really was a wonderful person, and one of the many things he loved about her was how enthusiastic she got about things. She and her mom had been running around like nuts over the last month planning this engagement party, making sure to get every detail just right, and he was going to complain because she didn't have time to blow him this morning? Part of the problem was he didn't want an engagement party or a fancy wedding, for that matter. He would've been quite happy for the two of them to just drive to Vegas and elope. But he kept quiet about that. Their engagement party and wedding were important to Jill, and it wasn't for the presents and attention (although there was nothing wrong with either of those), but because she wanted to celebrate their love. How could he fault her for that?

Alex poured himself coffee from the pot Jill had left warming on the coffee maker. He had wanted to buy a single-cup brewer that used different flavored pods, but Jill insisted those were bad for the environment. That was something else that mattered dearly to her that he never would've bothered thinking about. After a long sip, he moved to the refrigerator and retrieved the quiche she had left for him. He took it out of the paper bag (Madeleine's used plastic containers for takeout, but Jill would always insist they put her orders in a paper bag instead—again, the environment) and laid it on a tray so he could reheat it in the toaster oven. Jill really was a wonderful person, thinking of every little detail to make their lives better. His life, really. He was ashamed to admit that he had considered briefly extorting her this morning. That if she didn't have sex with him, he'd skip the engagement party. Gawd, what an asshole he was to even think of that, even though he had dismissed the idea almost immediately.

He grimaced over that thought.

That would've been the biggest dick move of all time. He adored Jill. How could he even have had that impulse? All because he was so damn impatient. So he would have to wait until tonight to enjoy Jill's lovely nakedness. Not the end of the world.

He'd live.

The timer dinged, indicating the quiche was ready. He grabbed an oven mitt, removed the tray from the toaster oven, and slid the quiche onto a plate. He took a bite of it. Delicious. Once again, Jill was thinking of him, since she wasn't touching quiche or anything else fattening, not willing to risk gaining as much as an ounce before the wedding. He took another sip of coffee and smiled as he thought about his future wife. Soon his thoughts involved peeling off her dress and panties, but he forced that image out of his head. He didn't want a reappearance of an alert and erect Willie Winkie.

At least, not until tonight.

Chapter 4

Duncan brought a gift-wrapped box with him when he returned to the hotel, so he wouldn't be crashing the engagement party empty-handed. To give the box some heft, he packed it with two coffee mugs decorated with a cartoon drawing of a young boy and girl kissing, surrounded by a flurry of hearts and the caption WORLD'S CUTEST COUPLE. Yeah, it was a tacky and incredibly cheap engagement present, but as far as Duncan was concerned, an appropriate one. Anyone catering an affair at this ritzy Bel-Air hotel already had enough money without needing an expensive gift from someone like him.

Earlier that morning, he had driven to a half-dozen luxury hotels in the Bel-Air area and studied their daily event boards. Each of them had weddings that night, but this one had an engagement party starting at two. Duncan figured he had nothing to lose by checking it out.

He parked on the street and walked up the drive to the hotel's entrance. While the Eldorado was a Cadillac, it was worth less than five grand and was hardly a classic. A noticeable difference from the Mercedes, BMWs, and Jaguars that other guests were bringing to the valet station, and if he left his car with the valet it would draw the wrong kind of attention. Before stepping inside, he saw a Rolls-Royce driven by one of the beautiful people pull up to the hotel. Yeah, he'd made the right decision.

He checked his phone. Twenty past two. The Alex Frey and Jill Kincade engagement party was scheduled to start at two, and he figured they'd have a half hour or longer for cocktails before a sit-down lunch, which would give him enough time to pop in and see whether they were the ones he needed. Whichever way it was, he'd leave right afterward. He had their names and it wouldn't be a problem to track them down if it came to that.

A sign had been placed in the lobby to direct guests for the engagement party toward the back of the hotel and to a large outdoor patio. A man wearing a tuxedo, who was either a hotel employee or private security, was guarding the door to the patio. He gave Duncan a quick look, but if he was suspicious that Duncan didn't belong, he didn't show it.

Duncan asked, "Is this the Frey-Kincade engagement party?"

"Yes, sir." The man nodded toward the gift-wrapped box. "I'm safeguarding the presents for the couple."

Duncan handed it over, glad he wasn't handing over an empty box. The man brought it into a small room off to the side of where he was standing, and Duncan continued on to the patio area. That was the first time in his life he'd been called *sir*. The novelty of it wore off quickly as he saw all the food and bartender stations and the flower decorations. Tables had been set up, each with antique linen tablecloths, vases stuffed with red roses, and some seriously solid-looking glistening silverware that must've been the real thing, but nobody was seated at any of them. The guests, maybe as many as 150, were instead milling about in groups, all of them looking well-heeled, most of them with either wine, champagne, or cocktail glasses in their hands. A classy affair that included a quartet playing jazz, the music muted and unobtrusive. If Duncan had come to rob the place, he would've done nicely. But that wasn't why he was there.

A waitress carrying a tray of appetizers appeared and asked if he wanted one. Why not? he decided. He hadn't eaten anything since breakfast and he could feel his stomach rumbling. The waitress showed some interest in him with the way she smiled, but he wasn't there to flirt or have anyone remember him, so he grabbed what turned out to be a piece of grilled lobster wrapped in bacon, and then headed to a nearby food station, where a chef was slicing up prime rib. After that, he grabbed a glass of champagne from a waiter, which he emptied quickly. He'd had champagne a few times in the past with Julia, but nothing like this stuff. But eating gourmet food and drinking champagne that was far better than anything he had ever had wasn't why he had crashed the party. He did, though, need a drink in hand so he'd appear less conspicuous. He worked his way to the front of the line at one of the bartender stations, and when he asked for bourbon, the bartender handed him a menu. A quick count showed over twenty choices, and he picked one at random and asked for it with ice. It didn't matter to him which one he drank, as long as he would look like he fit in. Whichever one it was, it would be a far cry from the bottom-shelf brands he usually drank.

It didn't take him long after that to spot the engaged couple. Two of life's privileged most-lucky people—Alex Frey looking like he could be a *GQ* model and Jill Kincade a movie star. Not necessarily one of those glamorous stars, but instead a blond, bubbly pretty one that guys secretly daydream about. They were making their way through the patio area, chatting with guests, beaming in their happiness—or at least that was true of Kincade. Frey seemed to be trying to project a ho-hum, nonchalant affectation, as if this was just a typical day for him. When Duncan caught a look the two of them exchanged, he knew he had found what he needed. It was the type of look that spoke volumes. The type you'd only see from two people who were deeply, madly in love.

He found himself mesmerized by them and couldn't leave after that. It was partly a compulsion to keep feeding the rage that was now burning so furiously inside his chest, and partly a growing obsession to learn more about them. The thought of walking out, as he had originally planned, no longer seemed possible. And so he stayed, making sure to always keep a drink or a plate of food in hand as he stood near different groups that had coalesced, so he could listen in on their conversations. He'd wander over to the next group whenever necessary to make sure he kept a good distance between himself and the oh-so-in-love couple.

He was good at blending into the background and eavesdropping. While he had never crashed a party like this, it was still a skill that served him well when he used to hang around bars and racetracks so he could find targets with money to burglarize or rob. Now, as he eavesdropped on conversations, he learned about how Frey and Kincade met, their bright futures, and the spectacular apartment they shared in Marina del Rey. He even learned the address of their apartment, which saved him the trouble of having to discover it on his own.

He had moved over to a group of rich frat boys who had to be Alex Frey's friends and was listening in on their crude frat-boy talk when a hand clamped down on his shoulder. He turned to see a thick-bodied man in his fifties offering him a plastic smile. The man extended his hand to Duncan. He took it.

"I'm Brett Kincade," the man said. "Jill's dad."

Duncan said, "Your daughter and her fiancé seem very much in love."

"Yes they do. How do you know them?"

"I don't."

Kincade's eyes dulled, his suspicions confirmed. Duncan had been expecting this since catching Jill Kincade giving him a puzzled look five minutes earlier.

"Why are you here, then?" Kincade demanded.

Duncan had worked up a story earlier in case anyone confronted him: He was a guest at the hotel and when he saw there was party on the patio he thought he'd crash it for a drink. He had even decided to offer a hundred dollars for the happy couple. An innocent-enough story, but it was no longer needed after his earlier eavesdropping. He nodded toward a plump, but cute, redhead on the other side of the patio who was engaged in a heated bit of gossip with her friends.

"I'm Marci's boyfriend," he said. "Well, not really her boyfriend. We hooked up three weeks ago after her breakup with Brad, and four more times after that. She asked if I'd come here with her, and I didn't have the heart to say no. Anyway, really great party. Thanks for having me."

Kincade's expression softened as he bought Duncan's lie. He smiled apologetically and confided, "If you can believe it, I've already kicked out three scumbags who thought it would be fun to crash the party."

"The nerve of some people."

"It takes all kinds," Kincade agreed. He lowered his voice and his tone turned confidential as he added, "Marci has been one of Jill's best friends since high school. A sweet girl with a lot going for her. You could do worse. Just saying."

"Yes, sir."

Kincade clapped Duncan on the back before walking off, his gesture far friendlier than when he had earlier clamped down on his shoulder. Duncan watched as Kincade joined his wife, no doubt explaining to her that it was only a misunderstanding. Kincade would be wondering about him later, but Duncan wasn't worried about it. First of all, the police wouldn't be convinced that the perpetrator was someone who'd been at the engagement party, even if there were suspicious people like Duncan seen there; and second, Kincade would be in a state of shock when the police came to him, and he'd have a hard time remembering much of anything at first. When he started remembering about this afternoon, Kincade would first think about those three others who admitted they had crashed the party. Duncan had also made it a point, when he switched his drink from his right hand to his left before shaking hands with Kincade, so that the older man would notice Duncan didn't have a tattoo on his wrist, and certainly not one of a snarling wolf.

No, there was no need for worry. Still, Duncan decided it would be best to leave. The rage that had ignited inside him had become something icy and barren. He searched the crowd and spotted the happy couple, and he gave them one last, long look before heading for the door. He'd have plenty of time with them soon enough.

Chapter 5

Morris often daydreamed about lazy Saturdays like this when he was on the force. As they had arranged, Kat brought Parker back at ten, which allowed him and Natalie to stay in bed until then. Since all three of them had worked up an appetite that morning and he had planned ahead, he played chef and prepared a bacon, cheddar, tomato, and spinach frittata from a recipe he had clipped earlier in the week from the *LA Times*.

He had never attempted anything more advanced than scrambled eggs before, and Nat offered to help, but he insisted that she relax while he cooked up the frittata, and she only half-heartedly fought him on it. So, while he peeled and diced an onion, chopped up a tomato, cooked a pound of bacon in a cast-iron skillet, and beat the eggs into a frothy mixture, Natalie sat at the kitchen table, drank coffee, read the paper, and repeatedly bit her tongue to keep from offering advice. While the end result might not have looked exactly like the picture in the recipe, Morris thought it was tasty, Natalie claimed the same, and Parker nearly inhaled the slice Morris slipped into his dish.

After what had to be considered a successful brunch, they lingered over coffee before Morris again insisted that Natalie relax, this time while he took care of the dishes. She didn't put up a fight this time, not even a token one.

"You're spoiling me," she said.

"Not nearly as much as I'd like to."

From out of his peripheral vision, he caught the contented way she looked at him, and that made him smile.

"It's a nice, sunny day," she announced. "I'll be pottering around in the garden."

He watched as Natalie got up and headed out the patio door, with Parker trotting along after her. Once he had the kitchen cleaned up and everything put away, he joined her out in the yard and spent the next two hours pruning shrubs and filling up two green recycling bins with the trimmings. While he did this, Natalie weeded flower beds and Parker did his best to get underfoot. Now that they were back inside the house, all three of them went to the den; Morris lounging on a recliner with the newspaper, Natalie sitting on the sectional with her feet tucked up under her as she read a book, and Parker lying like a lump on his side in front of the same sectional. The book Natalie was so engrossed in was a Frankenstein-retelling from an obscure Boston author. She'd become a fan of this author after reading another of his novels, the earlier one about an odd type of weed that might or might not bring about the end of world.

Morris heard a jingling from Parker's dog collar, and saw that the bull terrier had raised his head, his ears perked up. Parker made several excited grunts, pushed himself to his feet, and took off in the direction of the front door, his ropy tail whipping back and forth. Morris got up and followed along after him. Even before he heard a knock on the door, followed by a key turning in the lock, he knew who it had to be. He was at the door in time to greet Rachel. He gave her a hug and a quick kiss on the cheek, then took the box from Maxine's Bakery that she had brought so she could get on her knees and wrestle Parker. Morris didn't know the bakery, but whatever was inside was heavy.

"This is a pleasant surprise," he said.

Rachel was too busy at first keeping Parker from licking her face wet to respond. Once she had the dog corralled, she asked with a grin, "My visit or the dessert from Maxine's?"

"Both."

Parker had calmed down enough so that he was only wagging his tail and panting happily. Rachel hugged the bull terrier tightly and kissed him on top of his cement-hard head before getting back onto her feet. By this time Natalie had joined them, and she and Rachel embraced.

Morris interrupted them to show Natalie the box from Maxine's. "Our daughter came bearing a gift."

Natalie gave Rachel a careful look. "Is everything okay?" she asked.

"Things couldn't be better. How about we head to the kitchen, make some coffee, and have some dessert?"

Morris had been an LAPD homicide detective for too many years not to pick up on clues. For example, from the size of the box and its weight, he was pretty sure there was a cheesecake inside. And given the cat-who-ate-the-canary grin on his daughter's lips and her concerted effort to shield the ring finger on her left hand, he had a good idea why she was really there and what she was planning to tell them. It added up. She'd been dating Doug Gilman for a little over a year, and a week ago when they had dinner together Morris could see how relaxed they were with each other. It was more than just that. He saw the looks and smiles they exchanged, as if the two of them shared a secret code that only they knew. But he kept his suspicions to himself, even though he could tell from how tensely Natalie was now studying Rachel that his wife was expecting the same news.

They headed back as a group to the kitchen, all of them too deep in their private thoughts to speak. Parker, who had recovered from his excitement at seeing Rachel, noticed the box Morris was carrying, and tried unsuccessfully to stick his nose into it. Morris, for his part, was trying to come to grips with what was coming. He didn't want to show any of the uneasiness he felt when Rachel announced to them her engagement; and he also couldn't understand why he was feeling this way. Gilman was a good man. He knew that.

He had first met Gilman when, in Gilman's role as the mayor's deputy assistant, he'd arranged for Morris and MBI to take charge of the Skull Cracker Killer investigation. At the time, Morris thought this was a purely political move by an astute and ambitious young politician who hoped to gain influence in the mayor's office, but he later came to understand that Gilman's only motivation was that he wanted to see the killer caught before any more lives were taken. Morris liked him a good deal more after that. He also knew Gilman cherished his daughter, and although Rachel kept her feelings close to the vest, he suspected that his daughter felt the same way about him. So why was he feeling so anxious? Because they'd only been dating for a year? That made no sense. He had only known Nat a week before he knew he wanted to marry her. Could it be only a selfish impulse because he didn't want to lose his little girl? Rachel was twenty-four and as independent as they came. If that was his reason, he better get over it damn quick!

When they got to the kitchen, Morris started a pot of coffee while Natalie and Rachel set the table. With that done, it was left to Morris to open the Maxine's Bakery box and as he suspected, it held a cheesecake, one that was decorated with cherries and blueberries.

"Maxine's is famous for that," Rachel said.

Morris had never heard of the bakery, but he nodded as if he had. He smelled a whiff of bourbon. No wonder their cheesecake was so famous! When he picked up a knife to slice the cake, Rachel offered to do the honors. It was only then that she let them see the ring finger on her left hand, and as Morris expected, she was wearing a diamond engagement ring. Natalie must've been looking for the ring also, because she burst out into tears, and she and Rachel met for a tight embrace.

Morris felt his own eyes tearing up, but he played dumb. "I don't get it," he said.

"Men," Natalie said with a smile of pure joy once she separated from her daughter, her face already wet with tears. Rachel grinned from ear to ear as she pointed out the engagement ring. Morris continued to play dumb for several more seconds, only because a lump had formed in his throat and he wasn't sure he could talk right away. When he did talk next, his voice came out as a hoarse croak and he whispered "Mazel tov" to Rachel, then moved in and kissed her on the forehead. He used the back of his hand to wipe away the wetness from his eyes. The anxiousness he was feeling before was gone. Now he only felt happiness for his daughter.

Natalie was bursting with questions for Rachel, and so Morris took the knife, cut the cheesecake into slices, put three of them on plates, and got the coffee together. As he did this he half-listened as Nat asked about the wedding plans and tried to convince their stubborn daughter to let them throw an engagement party. Later, as they were sitting at the kitchen table sampling the bourbon-soaked blueberry and cherry cheesecake, Morris asked why Rachel didn't bring her fiancé along.

"Doug wanted to come, but I thought it would be better if it was just us when I told you the news." Rachel's slate gray eyes slitted and her lips tightened into a hard smile. "I didn't want you digging out your old baseball bat."

Morris had played third base for his high school team, and scouts thought he was good enough that he could've played pro ball someday, but he'd decided early on that he wanted to follow in his dad's footsteps and be an LAPD homicide detective. He did, however, keep his bat from his senior year's state championship game—a game in which he had hit two home runs. He thought he might someday pass the bat along to a son, but he only had one child—Rachel, and while she played soccer and basketball (at four feet ten inches as a high school freshman, she was an undersized point guard, but still a starter) she never had any interest in baseball. He still kept the bat and he used it when Rachel brought home boyfriends. He'd show the boys the bat and he let them know what would happen if they ever disrespected his daughter. While he never showed it to Doug Gilman, he still told Gilman the same story a year ago when he discovered Gilman was dating his daughter.

"The bat's been retired," Morris promised between bites of bourbon-infused cheesecake.

Chapter 6

"You look as tired as I'm feeling," Alex said.

His fiancée showed him a weary smile. "I'm good," she insisted.

He didn't argue the obvious. It made sense for Jill to look wiped out. She had spent weeks running around to make sure that every detail of their engagement party would be just right, and once the party started she was on like he'd never seen before as the two of them spent the entire time making the rounds and chatting with guests.

They returned back to the apartment a half hour ago, and their plan had been to put on more comfortable clothing and head straight out to their favorite Santa Monica bar for burgers and beer—something they hadn't done since Jill accepted his marriage proposal. But he had worn her down earlier, insisting that since she had eaten almost nothing that day, she could break with her pre-wedding diet this one time. Fortunately, she was too hungry to argue and so she agreed. Even though they had all that ridiculously delicious-looking (and expensive) food at the party—food that they had so carefully selected—they ended up being too busy to eat even a bite of it. But thanks to the security firm Jill's parents had hired, their plans were quickly shot once she saw the piles of gifts that were left stacked up in the bedroom. Of course, she wanted to open one or two of them before they left (and truth be told, so did Alex). They started with the gift cards, but those soon became like potato chips—it was impossible to stop after one.

After a mad frenzy of ripping open the gift cards and tallying up an impressive amount in cash and checks—enough to pay for their planned Paris honeymoon, as well as upgrade to a suite at the Four Seasons—they were now sitting cross-legged among the wreckage. At Jill's urging, Alex had opened three additional gifts, unveiling a high-end cappuccino maker from Jill's sister, a chef-quality German knife set from one of his uncles, and a Baccarat crystal bowl from one of Jill's sorority sisters, but his stomach was rumbling and he knew Jill had to be even hungrier since, unlike himself, she hadn't eaten any quiche lorraine that morning.

"The rest of these gifts will wait," he said. "If we don't get burgers in our bellies soon, we'll be passing out."

"One more," she pleaded. "After that, we'll get going. I swear."

She gave him that puppy-dog look she was so good at and was impossible for him to resist. What else could he do but take one more gift-wrapped box from the pile? He chose a smaller one—a cube-shaped box that was ten inches by ten inches.

"I'll open this one, but if I have to put you on my shoulder and carry you out afterwards, I will," he threatened.

Jill looked quite pleased with herself. Alex used one of the German-chef knives to cut through the wrapping paper and slice the cardboard box open.

He pulled the flaps apart and frowned as he looked inside. "There's no card," he said. He reached inside and took out a heavy tissue-paper-wrapped object. There was a second one just like it. He gave the wrapped gift a puzzled look.

"I think it's a coffee mug," he said, his voice showing his disbelief over that prospect.

"Give it to me."

He handed it to Jill while he took the other one from the box and ripped away the tissue paper. He had guessed right: It was a coffee mug. A cheap, cheesy-looking one with a cartoon drawing of a chubby little boy kissing an equally chubby little girl with pigtails. Underneath the cartoon drawing were emblazoned WORLD'S CUTEST COUPLE, and above it were a bunch of hearts.

"You've got to be kidding me," he said.

Jill, who was the most positive person he had ever met, seemed amused by it. "It's a gag gift," she said. "I bet it's from Todd. But I like it. I'm bringing it to work with me on Monday."

Alex thought it over. Yeah, it made sense that Todd would give them these. His brother had a perverse sense of humor, to put it mildly, and he was probably laughing his ass off right now, knowing that Jill would insist for sentimental reasons that Alex use one of them, which meant that he'd have to look at this ugly-as-sin mug every day, at least until he *accidentally* broke it.

Enough of this. "I kept my end of the deal," he said. "Let's get going before we pass out."

He could see that Jill was about to beg that he open one more gift. He knew the argument she was going to make. *That a gag gift shouldn't count.* But before she could say anything, their intercom buzzed.

Saved by the bell, he thought.

He got up and headed to the hallway so he could answer the intercom. Jill joined him. When he pressed the intercom button and asked who it was, a man's voice said, "Roma's Pizza. I have a delivery."

He wondered whether Roma's could've found out about his and Jill's engagement, since Roma's was their favorite pizza place. "I didn't order anything," he said.

There was the sound of paper rustling over the intercom, then, "It says here the order was paid for by Todd Frey."

That made sense. Sending over a pizza was exactly what his brother would do. He might be a smart-ass at times, but he also had a good heart, and he'd know that the two of them would be worn-out after the party. Still, knowing Todd, there was a chance he'd send over something like broccoli and anchovies, which Jill would like but he'd hate.

"What type of pizza?"

"A large fig jam and prosciutto."

He raised a questioning eyebrow toward Jill. He'd had his heart set on a burger, but this was their favorite pizza. She leaned in close to him and wrapped a thin arm around his waist.

"Why not?" she said. "We'll be getting to bed earlier this way. And I made you a promise this morning."

Well, that settled it! Alex pressed the intercom button and told the guy to come right up. While they waited, Jill nestled in closer to him and whispered in his ear all the things she'd be doing to Mr. Willie Winkie, assuming he was able to make a return visit. Her hand crept down to feel that that wasn't going to be an issue.

"How about we eat one slice to keep up our strength, and then head to bed," Alex suggested. "We could keep the rest of the pizza warming in the oven and have it when we're done."

She smiled naughtily. "Or when we need to replenish our strength."

Thank you, Todd, he thought.

There was a knock on the door. Alex gave a quick look through the security peephole and saw a guy his age wearing an LA Dodgers baseball cap pulled low over his forehead and holding a large Roma's Pizza box. He wrestled his wallet out from his back pocket so he could give the guy a twenty-dollar tip. The pizza might've already been paid for, but it had been a perfect day so far and he expected it to only get better, so why not pay it forward? With the twenty in hand, he opened the door. Before he could say anything, or even reach for the pizza, the box was slammed into his chest. He stumbled back, and out of the corner of his eye he saw a foot-long club swinging at his head. Whatever it was hit him in the left ear and knocked him woozy. His feet slid out from under him, and next thing he knew he was tumbling to the floor.

The room spun crazily around him as he lay sprawled out in the hallway. Nauseous and desperate, he fought to push himself to his knees, but his muscles had become rubbery and there seemed to be a disconnect between his brain and body. While his thinking remained jumbled, he still had enough wits about him to know his attacker had rushed past him. A cold horror filled him, realizing that Jill was defenseless. If she screamed, there was a chance that could bring help, but he didn't hear her scream. Instead, he only heard the sickening sound of something hard smacking flesh. This caused him to fight harder to get to his feet so he could save Jill. The spinning had slowed down enough so that when he lifted his head he could see that Jill lay crumpled on the floor. A second later he was kicked in the jaw and the world disappeared on him.

Chapter 7

When Alex woke up, he couldn't remember where he was or what had happened. The only thing he knew was that his head throbbed, his jaw ached; his shoulders also. Something was wrong with his tongue. It felt unnaturally fuzzy, the same with the inside of his mouth, like it was stuffed with cotton. No, not cotton: something scratchier. It also hurt when he tried opening his eyes. Almost like tiny little slivers of glass were cutting into his eyeballs. He remembered then about opening the door for the pizza-delivery guy and being attacked.

Oh, Jesus, Jill!

He forced his eyes open enough so he could see that Jill was sitting naked in a chair across from him, maybe six feet away. His vision was blurry and the room ebbed in and out, but he could still see that duct tape had been wrapped around her mouth. The brightness in the room made him squeeze his eyes closed. When he could open them again, he saw that it was far worse than her being stripped naked and gagged. Her ankles were bound tightly to the chair legs by duct tape and her arms pulled back behind her. Something was very wrong with her right shoulder. It sloped downward and was bent unnaturally. He forced his gaze upward and saw that her eyes were wet with tears and her face rigid with fear. It was like a punch in the heart seeing her like that.

Alex tried shouting for help, but something had been stuffed into his mouth, gagging him also. A wool sock. Somehow, he instinctively knew that's what was used. Like Jill, duct tape had also been wrapped around his mouth. He also understood why his shoulders ached. His arms had been yanked back and his wrists bound together behind the chair with duct tape. He blinked several times, hoping to clear his vision. They were in the living room. The blinds were closed, but the lights were set to their brightest, making it torturous for him to keep them open more than a crack. While Jill was naked, he was still in his clothes.

A shallow breathing noise had him looking to his right. Their attacker was crouching beside him. The man was no longer wearing a baseball cap. Instead, he now had a ski mask covering his face. That had to be a good sign. If he was hiding his face from them, that meant he was there to rob them and that he planned to let them live. Alex only had a vague sense of what the attacker looked like. The assault happened too fast for him to see the man's face, and when he looked through the peephole, he only paid attention to the baseball cap and the pizza box. This man had to know they represented no threat to him. Still, a cold dread seized him. He couldn't think of this person as anything other than a savage animal who had been let into their apartment.

The man straightened out of his crouch. Alex saw then that he was wearing latex gloves and had a tattoo of some sort on the underside of his right wrist, but he was unable to focus enough to see what it was. His blood chilled when he saw that the man was holding a thin and very sharp-looking carving knife from the set that he had unwrapped earlier.

He's just trying to scare us, Alex told himself. *He knew about our engagement party and he's here to rob us. And he wants to scare us first so we give him more money.*

Mission accomplished. He was terrified. There was over 6000 dollars in cash sitting on their bedroom floor, another 7000 in checks. He'd let this man empty out their bank account as long as he didn't hurt Jill again. If he'd just remove his gag, Alex would offer him whatever he wanted.

"Just so you know, I'm not going to kill you," the man said, his voice flat and muffled somewhat by the ski mask. "I'm not even going to hurt you again, as long as you don't misbehave. But your fiancée is sadly a different story. She's already in a great deal of pain from a broken collarbone, and it's going to get so much worse for her. The simple fact is she's going to die tonight after hours of torture."

The man turned his back to him and casually strolled over to Jill, as if this was all a game to him. He stood to her side so Alex could see what was being done. Jill had small, but beautiful, pert breasts with perfect pink nipples, and he watched in disbelief as the man squeezed Jill's left nipple with his index finger and thumb, pulled it, then sliced it off with the knife as if he were slicing off a button from a shirt. Alex screamed and fought to break free as the man did the same to her right nipple, but only a faint, inhuman sound made its way past the gag and his efforts to escape the chair were beyond futile. He collapsed in the chair, panting heavily, his head feeling like it was being squeezed in a vise. He struggled again to break free when the man stabbed Jill in the side, but there was nothing he could do. Jill's skin color had turned sickly white, and it tore him up inside to see the pain flooding her eyes and the way she was silently pleading with him to save her.

The man took his time as he repeatedly cut and stabbed her. She was so slender that there just wasn't that much of her, but the man found places to use the knife so he'd hurt her without killing her. There had to be something Alex could do. He tried rocking his body from side to side, thinking if he could knock himself and the chair over that he'd make enough of a racket for their downstairs neighbor to investigate. The problem was he was bound too tightly to the chair and he couldn't generate enough momentum. Their tormentor noticed what he was attempting and he left the knife buried deep in Jill's thigh while he came back to Alex.

"You want to save her, huh, champ?" he asked.

Alex nodded furiously.

"You want me to kill you instead?"

Yes, dear Lord, yes, Alex pleaded silently, the throbbing in his head becoming something unbearable as he violently nodded affirmatively.

"Sorry, champ, but that's not going to happen. I will, though, let you save her from hours of agony, if you're up for it. All you have to do is give me the old say-so and I'll let you choke her to death. It's the best I can do."

Alex could only stare at this maniac, not believing what he was hearing.

The pale blue eyes behind the ski mask were merciless. "Think about it, champ," he said in a taunting tone. "It's the only way you're going to be able to save her from all the pain that's coming. But I have to warn you that if I cut you free and you change your mind, or try something stupid, I'll break every bone in your body. I'll still keep you alive, though. No matter what, you're not dying tonight. And your girl over there, you don't even want to think about how much worse it will be for her if you piss me off."

The man waited to see if Alex would accept the offer, but Alex refused to, and so the man moved back to Jill and continued to stab and cut her. Every few minutes he'd look back at Alex to see whether he had changed his mind, but how could he? Someone might send the police to check up on them. It was almost a certainty that Jill's mom would be calling, and she'd definitely freak if Jill didn't answer her phone. So how could he possibly do what this maniac was suggesting when there was a chance Jill could be saved?

While Alex couldn't save her, he could bear witness to what was done to her while he prayed for them to be rescued. They'd always been able to say so much with a single glance, and he concentrated to do that now, as if he could psychically tell her how much he loved her. That she needed to stay strong and that someone would soon be saving them. The maniac took his time, but the cutting and stabbing didn't stop, and the psychic messages Alex was desperately trying to send Jill began feeling hollow and false. Worse, he found himself growing numb to the atrocities being done to her. It became hard for him to think of her as the Jill he had fallen in love with, and instead she became something less than that. He hated himself for that, and even more so for wanting this to just end. Her eyes had grown glassy and he knew she was lost somewhere deep inside of herself. But even so, she whimpered each time the maniac used the knife on her.

The maniac kept doing worse and worse things to her. Disfiguring her in sickening ways, as if he were carving her up like a jack-o'-lantern. Alex knew that she wouldn't want to live even if she could be saved. He also accepted that ending her suffering would be the kindest thing he could do for her—really, the last act of love he could show her. But he couldn't do it. The maniac would turn around at times and give him a questioning look, but Alex lacked the strength to even nod his head.

He saw the moment when Jill died. Even before her head dropped to her chest, he knew she was dead. He wanted to cry out, to feel anguish, but all he felt was numb. The maniac grabbed a handful of her hair and lifted her head before letting it drop again. He turned to give Alex a damning look and then left the room after that without saying a word. Soon Alex heard water running in the bathroom. This went on for a while. When the maniac returned, he was still wearing a ski mask, but had replaced the latex gloves with leather ones. The maniac crouched in front of him as if he were searching for something in Alex's eyes.

"I bet if I were to take that gag out of your mouth you'd have something you'd like to say to me, huh, champ?"

Alex squeezed his eyes shut. He just wanted this man to go away, but he could feel his presence and knew the man hadn't moved and was continuing to stare at him. In an odd way this became the most unbearable part of everything that had happened. After the horror Alex had been forced to witness, this was what was going to send him out of his mind.

"Or maybe you don't have anything to say," the maniac finally said, his voice dripping with contempt. "Maybe you just want to hope I disappear and when you open your eyes again, this all turns out to be nothing but a bad nightmare. Sorry, champ, that's not going to happen."

The maniac used his thumbs to force Alex's eyes open. It seemed like an eternity while the maniac continued his searching. Finally he nodded to himself, as if he found what he was looking for.

"Now you have yourself an especially wonderful rest of your life," he said.

The maniac got out of his crouch and walked out of view. Shortly after that, Alex heard the apartment door being opened and closed. Only then did he begin sobbing, the pain racking his chest, becoming something excruciating.

Chapter 8

Duncan popped out the cosmetic contact lenses, changing his eye color from blue to brown. After that he used a washcloth and baby oil to scrub away the temporary tattoo of a snarling wolf's face from the underside of his right wrist.

He was beyond famished when he left the couple's apartment in Marina del Rey, like he had a hole in his stomach that no amount of food could fill. He'd thought about taking the Roma's pizza with him, but he couldn't risk someone seeing him leaving the building with it, and he wasn't about to sit in the couple's apartment and eat the pizza after what he'd done—he'd learned long ago nothing good can come from hanging around after finishing a job.

Although he couldn't remember ever being that hungry before, he showed enough forethought to wait until he drove back to downtown LA before stopping at a twenty-four-hour market and buying a couple of turkey and cheddar sandwiches and a liter of orange soda. He was shaking like a drug addict by the time he got back into his car, and he wasted no time ripping off the wrapper and devouring one of the sandwiches along with half a liter of soda, but it did little to satisfy his hunger. Somehow he showed enough willpower to put away the other sandwich for later.

Now was as good a time as any. He pulled his backpack out from under the bed and fished inside for the remaining sandwich, being careful not to cut himself on the carving knife he had taken from the Marina del Rey apartment. He hadn't planned to take knives from any of his victims, but inspiration struck earlier. Why not let the police see that the same knife was being used in all the murders? Even better was the idea he had of what he could do with the knife when this was all over. Besides, he'd be hard-pressed to find a better knife. This one was a finely crafted tool; the blade thin and sharp enough to cut through cartilage and bone, the balance and handle perfect.

He found the turkey and cheddar sandwich and tossed the contact lens case and baby oil into the backpack. Aside from the lens case, bottle of baby oil, and knife, the backpack also held a baseball cap, ski mask, eleven-inch leather sap, materials for making a temporary snarling wolf tattoo, and a whole lot of cash—1800 dollars he had remaining from what he had saved up to bankroll his plan and an additional six grand he took from the couple's bedroom. He shook his head, thinking about anyone getting six grand in cash from an engagement party, and that wasn't even the half of it! There was another a pile of checks for even more money and all those other presents. The way some people live! A harsh smile tightened his lips as he thought about how if he and Julia had had an engagement party, they would've been lucky to get a can opener out of it. Maybe they would've gotten a set of dishes if he and Julia had gotten married.

He finished unwrapping the sandwich, but letting himself think of Julia dulled his appetite. The one blemish to what had so far been a perfect night. And it really had been perfect. The first step of his plan had gone off without a hitch, in no small part due to the time he invested that afternoon. Crashing the engagement party and eavesdropping on conversations allowed him to learn useful tidbits, such as the name of Frey's brother and the pizza the couple were always raving about, and that helped him to gain quick entry to their apartment.

When he had charged into the apartment, he was afraid at first that he'd hit Frey too hard in the ear with the leather sap and the guy wouldn't be waking up that night, but even that worked out just right. Frey was out of it just long enough to give Duncan time to get Frey and his girlfriend ready and to search the apartment, and that was when he found the money, which turned out to be a nice little bonus.

Things could've also gone wrong quickly if the girl had screamed when she had the chance. The apartment door was still open and a neighbor might've heard her. But she froze, too much in shock at seeing her fiancé crumple to the floor. When she finally reacted it was to try running to the bedroom, and Duncan felled her with a single crushing blow, the leather sap striking her flush on the collarbone. It was all over for her then. She was in too much pain to scream for help or to fight off Duncan. Thinking about what happened next brought back his appetite. He picked up the sandwich and took a bite, and unlike earlier when he wolfed down his food, this time he made a concerted effort to chew slowly so he could savor it. As he did this, he closed his eyes and replayed in his mind what happened inside the Marina del Rey apartment.

If he could have, he would've used the knife on Frey and left the girl untouched. Frey was the one he wanted to hurt. Not just hurt, but destroy, and so he had to use the girl for that purpose. That was what the plan needed, but it was so much more liberating than he ever would've imagined. Each time when he looked back and saw the anguish flooding Frey's eyes, he felt just that much better. Like he could breathe easier. As if a little bit more weight had been rolled off his chest.

After the girl was dead and he forced Frey's eyes open, all he could see in them was shock. Eventually, though, the shock wore off, and he found what he was searching for. Deep, profound shame. It was more than just cathartic seeing that. He experienced what had to be something close to ecstasy. He wished he could've held onto that feeling, but it proved fleeting and now it was barely a memory.

He took another bite of the sandwich and washed it down with more orange soda. What surprised him most that night was how he felt when he used the knife on the girl. He had expected it to disgust him and fill him with loathing, maybe even mental anguish. After all, she wasn't whom he wanted to hurt—at least he hadn't thought so. But he didn't feel that way at all. Instead, he discovered he liked it. Each time he stuck her with the knife and saw her react in pain, all he could think was: *Good, let's see if I can make you suffer even more.* That really did surprise him, because he didn't think of himself as a sadist, but he came to accept that there was nothing wrong with him feeling that way. Why shouldn't he enjoy seeing both of these privileged, beautiful people suffer? The plan he came up with had him waiting a week before finding another oh-so-in-love couple, but he no longer wanted to wait. He badly wanted to feel that same euphoric lightness again that he had felt with Frey, even if it only lasted minutes.

The doorknob rattled softly, knocking Duncan out of his thoughts. This was followed by a slight metal-against-metal scraping sound. Someone had tried the doorknob, found the door locked, and was now using a lockpick. A clicking sound confirmed that the person was successful with the lockpick. Duncan didn't have time to retrieve the sap from the backpack. It didn't much matter. It was after midnight, and whoever was breaking in was expecting to rob him in his sleep. He couldn't imagine any of the human jackals he'd seen hanging around this skid-row boarding house being a serious threat to him. He got off the bed and moved quickly to the door. The person on the other side was carefully inching the door open and Duncan yanked on the doorknob, speeding things up and revealing his intruder, who turned out to be a man in his thirties with a ravaged face, dirty, greasy long hair and beard, and clothes that were even dirtier. Duncan had seen him before lurking around the hallways, as if he were looking for someone weaker than himself to rob.

"Let me guess," Duncan said. "You got confused and thought this was your room?"

The intruder showed no reaction to being confronted. "Yeah, man, a rough night, you know?" He smiled, revealing brownish and rotting teeth. His twitchy movements, cystic acne, and ruined teeth were enough to show that he was a serious meth head. He sniffed and swiped a bony thumb across his nose, then showed Duncan the lockpick. "I lost my room key so I've been using this. My name's Stevie."

He switched the lockpick to his left hand and held out his right, as if he expected Duncan to take it.

"Very resourceful of you," Duncan said, ignoring the extended hand. "So we'll call it an honest mistake, then."

He started to close the door, but the meth head named Stevie stepped forward, putting his shoulder in the way. He sniffed again and made another twitchy swipe at his nose with his thumb.

"How about helping out a fellow brother in need? Meth, smack, crack, anything. It's going to be a long night if I don't get something to take the edge off."

"Sorry, but I don't use drugs."

Stevie made no attempt to back away. Instead, he looked past Duncan so he could take in the room in a glance, which could easily be done since there wasn't much to it. Most prison cells were bigger. Just enough space to hold a single bed that was really more of a cot, a small desk with two drawers to hold clothing, a matching wooden chair, and a coat hook. Not even a closet, and the residents shared a bathroom at the end of the hall. No doubt in that quick half-second glance he saw Duncan's duffel bag shoved between the bed and the wall and the backpack under the bed. When he shifted his eyes back at Duncan, they had the glazed look of someone contemplating violence. In a way Duncan understood it, but in another way it surprised him. From Duncan's well-groomed appearance and preppy, clean clothing, Stevie must've thought Duncan was slumming it at this boarding house and was someone who could be victimized. Still, a predator should be able to recognize a far more dangerous one if he meant to survive long, and this meth head should've been able to sense who he was dealing with.

"You sure you don't got anything in that backpack that could help me?" Stevie asked, his eyes half-lidded, violence imminent. Duncan showed no indication that he noticed Stevie slipping a switchblade out of his back pants pocket.

"How about you leave before someone gets hurt?" Duncan suggested.

That brought a vicious smile from Stevie. "How about you give me that backpack before I hurt you real bad." The five-inch switchblade was snapped open. Stevie poked it toward Duncan's stomach, trying to get him to step back into the room. Instead, Duncan turned sideways so that his left shoulder faced Stevie, and in a quick, fluid motion his right hand circled under and around the meth head's knife hand so that he could grab the wrist. Before Stevie could put up a fight, Duncan had the arm twisted so that the knife pushed into Stevie's lower back and drew blood.

"If I push the blade in another three inches you lose a kidney. How'd you like that?"

"I wouldn't like that at all," Stevie admitted in a strained voice.

Duncan would've gotten no satisfaction from killing this pathetic lowlife. And even if he could claim self-defense, all he'd accomplish would be putting himself on the police's radar. It would be even worse than that if one of them insisted on looking inside his backpack.

"You better drop the lockpick, then."

Stevie did as he was ordered and the lockpick and tension wrench clattered onto the scratched and battered oak floor. Duncan twisted the wrist enough to make Stevie both drop the switchblade and cry out in pain. After kicking the knife into the room, Duncan let go of Stevie's wrist and smacked him hard enough with his palm to send the man tumbling onto the hallway floor.

"It would be a good idea if I never see you again," Duncan warned before closing the door to his room.

When he had found the six grand earlier, he thought about leaving this skid-row boarding house and checking into a decent hotel, but realized he couldn't do that. He didn't want to use any credit cards while in LA and allow the police to track him here, and it would be too suspicious if he used cash at a hotel, especially since the authorities would soon be learning that Jill Kincade's killer stole all that money from the couple's apartment. Like it or not, he was stuck in this boarding house. He knew that meth head was going to be trouble. The guy was intuitive enough to know there was something of value in Duncan's backpack. Now he also knew that Duncan was someone he had to be careful with, but that wasn't going to stop him from trying again. Duncan wasn't too concerned. As far as the predators he'd had to deal with in his life, Stevie would be low guy on the totem pole. If he became too much of a nuisance, Duncan would take care of him. Just not anywhere near this boarding house.

He fitted the wooden chair under the doorknob, and tested the door to make sure it couldn't be opened. Satisfied, he sat back on the bed and finished the rest of the turkey and cheddar sandwich.

Chapter 9

Dammit! Matt Kammer caught the way his wife was eyeing his plate. He knew what was coming.

"Your French toast looks so scrumptious," Hannah said innocently enough. "How about we change plates for a few bites?"

They were sitting at an outdoor patio table at a Santa Monica restaurant located on the Third Street Promenade. He had ordered brioche French toast in a brandy strawberry sauce and an order of homemade sausage patties, while Hannah chose an arugula salad. No kidding that his brunch looked tastier. A piece of cardboard drenched in maple syrup would've looked tastier also. He gave his wife a sour look.

"I ordered this because I wanted to eat the whole thing," he complained.

She smiled sweetly at him, even batted her eyelashes. "Just a few bites. Honest."

Ha! She'd end up eating at least half of his brunch! And they both knew it!

"If you had ordered the brie and bacon omelet instead of a salad I'd be happy to trade bites."

"You wouldn't want me ordering that and getting fat, would you?"

The logic of that escaped him. Hannah could've ordered something equally fattening as the French toast, eaten half of it, and gotten the rest packed away to go, which would've left Matt an enjoyable breakfast for tomorrow morning. They also both knew there wasn't much chance she'd get fat, no matter what she ordered. Hannah had some sort of supercharged metabolism and still possessed the same toned, trim body as when they were married three years ago. God, he loved her body! Every Sunday morning since they'd first moved in together four and a half years earlier, he had shown her just how much he adored her body. And not just Sunday mornings. He was thirty-two and Hannah was twenty-nine and they still made love as often as a pair of randy teenagers. Just thinking of how Hannah had wrapped her slender thighs around his neck after he had stripped off her pajamas that morning made him hard all over again. He handed over his French toast and grudgingly accepted her salad in exchange. What could he say? Hannah could play him like a fiddle and she knew it. And truth be told, he didn't mind all that much.

Matt dejectedly picked at a piece of arugula. "If you have more than three bites, I'm ordering dessert," he threatened.

"As long as it's the apple crumble," she said with an impish smile.

Hannah ate five healthy bites of the French toast and two good-sized bites of sausage before trading back plates, and Matt ordered the apple crumble pie for dessert, even though he would've preferred their dark chocolate crepe with vanilla ice cream. The waiter placed the apple crumble in the middle of the table along with two forks, and Hannah kept pace with Matt as they polished it off.

"You could've ordered your own dessert," he grumbled.

"What would've been the fun of doing that?" she said, straight-faced, before a smile cracked her expression. "Besides, one of us has to keep you from getting tubby."

He knew there was more than a little truth in what Hannah said. Not that he was at all tubby, but he had put on a few pounds since they got married, and he also went to the gym less often, sometimes only once a week. It's what happened when you were content and happily married, and despite his sullen act at that moment he couldn't possibly be happier. He adored her, and he knew the reason she ordered salads instead of what she really wanted was so that he'd eat a little healthier himself after she finagled him to switch plates.

"Tubby, huh?" he said, making a harrumphing noise as he played up the insult he had just suffered. "I'd like you to know I haven't completely traded in my six-pack for a keg."

She laughed. "Not completely," she agreed. "But last time I checked, I only counted four abs."

He made the mistake then of looking into her gorgeous blue eyes, and he broke out into a grin, forcing him to give up his act of being so egregiously wounded. Even though they'd had a marathon session that morning, he wished right then they were back in their bedroom ripping off each other's clothing. How many couples together almost five years could still say that? But any further lovemaking would have to wait until tonight. The weather was perfect, and Hannah loved spending time at the pier and walking the boardwalk to Venice, and he didn't want his own selfish desires to interfere with their plans.

They lingered over coffee before Matt beckoned their waiter over so he could pay the bill. After that was taken care of and they got out of their chairs, Hannah's hand found his and her fingers interlaced with his own. Matt wasn't one for public displays of affection, at least not much more than holding hands. In fact, they made him extremely uncomfortable. But at that moment he was so overcome with affection for Hannah that he reached down and kissed her gently on the lips. She looked quite pleased with herself as he pulled away and the half-smile she showed was enough to tell him that she felt exactly the same.

They left the restaurant's patio area without ever noticing Duncan sitting two tables away. He waited until their backs were turned to him before dropping twenty dollars on the table to cover his bill. After slipping on his backpack (he learned his lesson last night that it wouldn't be safe to leave it alone in his room) he left the half-eaten breakfast burrito on his plate, walked past Matt and Hannah's table so he could surreptitiously read the name on the credit card receipt, and then followed the couple.

Duncan had woken up early that morning, anxious to see whether there were any stories in the *LA Times* about the home invasion and brutal murder last night in Marina del Rey, but it was too soon for that. He next walked four blocks to the parking garage where he kept his Cadillac so he could turn on the car radio, but nothing was being reported yet, which surprised him. He would've thought that Frey would've been found by now and that this would be the type of sensationalized story that would dominate the news. He got the car on the road and started toward Marina del Rey, thinking he'd drive by the apartment building to check whether the police were camped out there. Fortunately, he still had enough wits about him to stop once he reached Santa Monica. He couldn't afford to have a cop outside Frey's building think he looked suspicious, not with him having the backpack in his car.

He'd originally planned to find a wedding to crash tonight to see if he could find his next privileged, beautiful, madly-in-love couple, but he had time to kill and he needed to eat, so why not do a little hunting here? When he spotted Matt and Hannah Kammer, he picked up a certain vibe and decided to follow them. The guy was an ordinary-looking schmo with a somewhat doughy face, but the woman was very pretty. She reminded him in a way of the one last night, although not as curvy. Blond, petite, stunning blue eyes, an even more stunning smile, and thin, lovely legs. Even though there were no outward signs they were madly in love with each other, he could see a guy like that being ruined for life, having to watch a woman like that being cruelly tortured and murdered, so there was at least some promise that they could be what he needed. After he watched them get seated at the patio table, he waited ten minutes and then sat down at a nearby table so he could eavesdrop.

Duncan lost enthusiasm quickly once he heard the couple bicker over inconsequential matters. What guy in his right mind could be married to an adorable, sweet thing like that and get upset because she wanted to taste some of his food? He pretty much gave up on them as being candidates—if anything, he was considering getting the guy alone so he could work him over with the leather sap as a matter of principle—but then he saw them holding hands and caught the look they exchanged after they kissed, and that was enough to put them back into contention. It was also enough to start the rage bubbling once again in his gut. Not a full-out boil—if that were happening, he'd know for sure they were the ones he wanted.

For now, he'd keep following them and make up his mind later.

Chapter 10

Morris was feeling too restless to hang around at home. He wasn't sure why, but he didn't think Rachel's bombshell from the other day was the cause. While at times it seemed mind-boggling to him that the skinny little seven-year-old girl he had taught to ride a bike was all grown up and engaged to be married, he had mostly reconciled himself to that fact. He knew Doug Gilman would treat Rachel right and, for reasons he couldn't quite understand, the two of them appeared to be a perfect fit for each other, like interconnecting jigsaw-puzzle pieces. But he didn't need to understand. He trusted his daughter, and he saw the way Rachel lit up when she was with Gilman. No, it wasn't Rachel's engagement. There was something else making him feel antsy. Maybe it was just something in the air.

Natalie was planning to spend the day looking for a place to hold the engagement party, so when he suggested taking Parker somewhere so she could focus on that task (his actual words: to get the two of them out of her hair) she told him that would be a splendid idea. He didn't need to be told twice. He whistled for Parker, and the bull terrier flipped himself on to his feet and trotted along after him. Once they were in the car, Morris mentioned a few places they could go for a hike, and the dog responded by yawning so fully that he almost unhinged his jaw.

"I hear you, buddy," Morris said. "Today seems more like a day for strolling than hiking."

Parker let out a grunt, his tail thumping on the passenger seat. Morris pulled the car out of the driveway and headed to Santa Monica. Traffic on I-10 West from West Hollywood was surprisingly light and in just under thirty-six minutes he had the car parked in one of the downtown garages and was walking Parker toward the pier. The bull terrier let out an excited, pig-like grunt once he realized where they were going and what would be waiting for them.

"You're making an assumption there," Morris said. "I could surprise you."

If Parker was worried about that, he didn't show it, and he had good reason not to be worried. Morris was a creature of habit. Whenever he went out for Chinese food, he'd always go to the same restaurant and order his favorite dishes. The same with deli, Italian food, Indian, and all other varieties of food. He saw no reason to venture out of his comfort zone and risk a less-than-satisfactory meal.

When they got to the pier, Morris did what he always did when he brought Parker there, and that was buy two hot dogs, slathering his with mustard and leaving Parker's free from any condiments. Like every other time he had ordered hot dogs at this pier restaurant, he first struggled over the idea of ordering the bacon and cheese dogs, and like those other times, decided they'd be too gluttonous. He could stand to lose ten pounds from around his middle and he was trying to be more careful with what he fed Parker. Parker, though, was more than fine with a plain hot dog, and the bull terrier's attention was laser-focused on the paper bag holding the food while they walked further down the pier and sat on one of the benches overlooking the water. He broke Parker's hot dog into three pieces and fed them to his dog as he ate his own.

Morris said, "I didn't disappoint you, huh?"

Parker seldom barked, but he did then to show his appreciation.

A woman's voice asked, "Would it be okay if I pet him?"

Morris turned to see that the request came from a very pretty blonde in her late twenties. He noticed the wedding and engagement rings and also the man standing next to her, who was looking somewhat uncomfortable. This man must've been her husband, and Morris felt an immediate rapport with him. While the man wasn't necessarily funny-looking, he had a similar beauty-and-the-beast thing going on that Morris had with Natalie.

"Most people ask whether he's friendly," Morris said.

The woman showed him a brilliant smile. "I can already see he's a sweetheart," she said.

That was true, at least as long as the person wasn't a serial killer trying to do Morris bodily harm. In those cases, the bull terrier would turn ferocious.

"He's certainly that," he agreed. "And of course, go ahead. Parker will enjoy the attention."

"Parker?" the husband asked with one eyebrow arched. "Like the criminal from the Richard Stark books?"

"Very good. Most people think he's named after that fictional Boston PI. Or the wine critic."

The wife didn't just pet Parker on top of his head, but instead got down on one knee and petted the bull terrier vigorously behind his ears. Morris found himself strongly liking this woman. Parker, for his part, acted shier than he usually did, but by the end he was licking her face. The woman laughed at that while her husband watched on with an embarrassed grimace.

"I love this breed of dog," she told Morris. She turned to her husband. "One day..." she threatened.

"Maybe a cat," he said with little enthusiasm.

The woman rolled her eyes, but chose not to argue the matter. If Parker felt any insult, he kept it to himself. The woman got to her feet, thanked Morris for indulging her, then she and her husband continued on toward the end of the pier. Morris watched them for a moment before turning back to look out over the ocean. After several minutes of quiet contemplation, he got off the bench. Parker had gotten comfortable lying in the sun, but he let out an old-man groan and got back onto his feet.

Morris was still deep in thought when he almost lost his balance as Parker strained suddenly against the leash. The bull terrier's head was down and a deep-throated growl rumbled out of him. The source of Parker's agitation was a man about Rachel's age. Medium height with a wiry build, the man was clean-cut and dressed in a sports jacket, button-down shirt, slacks, and boat shoes. Nothing overly suspicious about his appearance, but something about the dead-eyed look he gave Parker and his thin, bloodless smile made Morris wonder about him and also about the backpack the man wore. What was in it? Drugs? The man had no visible tattoos or piercings, but what did a drug dealer look like these days? While Morris and the other investigators who worked for him at MBI had all been deputized by the mayor and could be hired by the city as needed, he had no probable cause to look inside the man's backpack no matter how much Parker was growling.

Morris shortened his hold on the leash until he had Parker almost by the collar. He got down on one knee and used his free hand to clamp Parker's muzzle shut to quiet the growling.

"He's making me a liar," Morris said with an apologetic smile. "Only a few minutes ago I told a young woman that he's usually friendly."

"Strange. Dogs typically like me," the twentysomething millennial said.

He walked past them and Morris kept Parker's muzzle clamped shut as the dog's growling came to a stuttering halt. Morris considered taking a photo of the man and giving it to one of the LAPD detectives he was friendly with, possibly Annie Walsh out of the robbery-homicide division, although someone in narcotics would be a better fit. There had to be something of interest in his backpack. Morris looked back and spotted the guy thirty yards away and already mingling in with the crowd. Parker brought back his attention as he snorted out an angry noise that was halfway between a grunt and a whimper.

"Yeah, I know," Morris agreed. "Something's off about him, but nothing we can do about it. You can't win them all."

He gave Parker a good-natured thump on the side and grimaced as he got back to his feet and straightened his creaky knees. He thought once more about walking down the pier and taking a picture of the twentysomething with the backpack, but decided he didn't want to agitate Parker again. Besides, maybe the guy just had a roast beef sandwich in the backpack and Morris misread the vibe he picked up from him. He led Parker off in the opposite direction, thinking he'd take the dog along the Santa Monica State Beach trail before heading back home.

He squinted as he peered up at the sun and felt the warmth of its rays on his face. It was too nice of a day not to take advantage of it.

Chapter 11

Matt Kammer's phone rang. He considered ignoring it, but his conscientiousness more than his curiosity got the better of him. When he saw the caller ID, his face contorted as if he were suffering a toothache, and he told Hannah that it was Kent Sangford from work. It was never good when his boss called him on a Sunday, and he knew Sangford was going to tell him something he didn't want to hear. He considered again ignoring the call.

"I could tell him my battery ran down?" he suggested.

Hannah, being the voice of reason, said, "You should answer it."

Another idea came to him. He held the phone over the railing. "How about I drop it into the ocean?" he said. "If Kent wants to give me a lie-detector test to prove that I didn't really lose my phone, let him. I'll pass it with flying colors!"

"Now you're being ridiculous."

Matt had to agree that his wife was right. Reluctantly, he did as she suggested, and his expression grew increasingly despondent as he listened to what Sangford had to say.

"There's no one else who can go?" he finally asked when given a chance. He listened some more before muttering in a defeated tone, "I understand." Once the call ended, he showed Hannah a bleak smile and informed her that he had to fly out that night to Omaha.

"The company has me booked on a flight leaving at nine-ten," he said. "Nothing I can do about it. According to Kent, the account's in jeopardy, and I need to be there to support the sales team."

Hannah looked as disappointed as he felt. "How long will you be away?"

"I'm not sure yet. Possibly the whole week." He made a disgusted face, like he had swallowed a fly. "Omaha! They couldn't send me somewhere decent, like Vegas, Seattle, or San Francisco? Goddamned Omaha!"

"I see," Hannah said. "That's why you're upset. Because you have to go to Omaha instead of someplace fun."

"That wouldn't be the only reason," he conceded. "I don't sleep well when you're not next to me."

"So I'm only useful as a sleep aid?"

"No, that's not entirely true either. You have other uses."

She elbowed him lightly in the stomach. "Thanks!"

The look she gave him forced a grin out of him, but it quickly faded.

"The truth is I worry about you when I'm away," he admitted.

"Finally, the truth." She took hold of his arm with both of her hands, and bumped his hip with her far more slender one. "I'm a big girl, you know. I can take care of myself."

"I know," he admitted, although the truth was he worried about her all the time when he was traveling. She was so trusting and the world was such a damn violent place. Hannah was only five feet one and couldn't have weighed more than ninety-five pounds soaking wet. How could he not worry about her? How could he possibly want to live if anything were to ever happen to her? But enough of such morbid thoughts. "Whatever preparations I need to make for the meeting tomorrow will have to wait until I'm in the air. We won't let this ruin our day."

He draped an arm over her shoulder and she moved in close to him.

"We'll walk to Venice and find a nice place for an early dinner," she said. With a straight face, she added, "After all, I only had a salad for lunch."

As tempted as Matt was to correct her, he swallowed it back. The two of them headed off the pier so they could get on the boardwalk that would take them to Venice.

Duncan watched them from a distance, making sure to keep far enough back so they wouldn't notice him. He wished he could've overheard Kammer's phone call, but he had little difficulty reading their body language and seeing how the call had temporarily dampened their moods. He also saw that this was short-lived, given the affection they showed each other afterwards, and it left him both simmering in his rage and knowing they were exactly what he was looking for.

He kept an eye on them the rest of the afternoon, first following them as they walked the boardwalk to Venice (and wishing he had dressed differently—he was sweating through his shirt before he made it a mile), then having drinks at the bar while they ate dinner at a table, and finally following them back to Santa Monica. Once he figured out which parking garage they were heading to, he ran and got his car so he could be waiting for them when they exited. There was no missing them. They drove out of the garage in a new BMW convertible, and Duncan had little trouble recognizing Kammer's doughy face behind the wheel and the man's very pretty wife sitting in the passenger seat.

Duncan knew his Cadillac would be conspicuous, so he made sure to keep at least three car lengths back. He almost lost them at an intersection after he got stuck behind a progression of cars taking left turns in front of him, but he caught sight of them before they got onto I-10 East, and after that it was smooth sailing to Pasadena. When they drove into a palm tree–lined cul-de-sac, he slowed down so he could see which driveway they pulled into, then continued on to the next block before turning his car around and parking so he could watch the entrance to the cul-de-sac. He was guessing that Kammer and his wife were in for the night, but if they were to leave again he'd see them and be able to follow them.

The house he had parked in front of had its lights off and its driveway was empty. He figured the owners were out, and chances were good that no one else on the street would notice him parked there. It would be unfortunate if someone did and called the police. If that were to happen, it would mean he'd have to give up on Kammer and his wife, and he didn't want to do that. The more he thought about them, the more he wanted them to be his next victims and he wanted to do it that night. It was almost like he needed to do it to relieve the pressure squeezing his chest. He made a disgusted face, realizing he was acting like a damned drug addict needing his next fix. He had a reason for what he was doing and a plan that he needed to follow. He couldn't let himself be swallowed up by this compulsion. If it ended up being tonight, fine. If it turned out to be a week from now, that would have to be fine also. That was what he had to keep telling himself. He wasn't a homicidal maniac. As cathartic as it might be, there was still a purpose to what he was doing.

He took a few deep breaths, but it didn't help him. He would just have to keep at it. Maybe if he meditated. Of course, it wouldn't be what most people would consider a holistic, life-affirming meditation, but one where he'd visualize what he'd be doing to Kammer and his wife when he got them alone. He'd have to try that later in the rare event that things didn't work out that night. But why wouldn't they?

He checked the time. He'd been parked for almost twenty minutes. He couldn't risk much more than that. Originally he thought he'd wait until it was darker before breaking into their home, but why wait any longer?

If he knocked on the door, the odds were good that one of them would be clueless enough to answer it, and it wouldn't matter whether they kept a chain on the door—he'd be getting in.

When he drove to Kammer's house, he had passed a school four blocks away. Nobody would see it if he left his car there. He had his kill clothes in the trunk and everything he needed in his backpack to add the snarling wolf's-face tattoo to his wrist. With the stencil he had carefully constructed before he left Massachusetts, it would take five minutes, no more than that, and then he'd be ready to walk back to the cul-de-sac. If he wanted to hide in some shrubs by Kammer's house until it got dark, he could do that. He'd decide later.

He was just about to turn the key in the ignition when he spotted Kammer's BMW driving out of the cul-de-sac and heading in the opposite direction from where he was parked. That was a surprise. He would've given odds that they were in for the night. Now he had a decision to make: Break into their house while they were gone and wait for them or follow them. He decided to err on the side of caution. He started the car and drove off after them.

Chapter 12

Philip Stonehedge filled everyone's wineglasses with the sangria he had prepared that afternoon. Morris took a sip and showed a puzzled frown. "Is there gin in this?" he asked.

"There is," Stonehedge admitted. "I was given the recipe last month when I was shooting *No Prior History* in Barcelona." He lowered his voice and added, "The *sangria master* swore me to secrecy, but I'll admit to gin being one of the ingredients."

Morris doubted there was such a thing as a sangria master, and that his actor friend was embellishing the matter and that he must've instead gotten the recipe from one of the many bartenders he schmoozed with while in Spain. From the way Brie Evans rolled her eyes, she must've thought the same thing. Before Morris could comment further, Natalie told Stonehedge that the sangria was simply delicious.

Stonehedge winked at her. "Wait until you try the Catalan paella that I've been slaving over for hours."

"With an assist from these," Brie said as she wiggled her famous fingers—which were famous not only because she was a major star in Hollywood, but because they were attached to the person who topped *People* magazine's most-beautiful list two years running.

"I couldn't have done it without you, my dear," Stonehedge said with an intentionally wry smile. He took a healthy drink of his sangria and then used a ladle to refill his glass. They were all sitting around a patio table at Philip Stonehedge's Malibu estate. Also joining them was Parker. Earlier, the bull terrier had been running around the grounds, chasing small critters who had ventured out after dusk, but now he was lying by Natalie's feet. He wasn't snoozing, though. Both his eyes were open and his ears perked up as he listened to sausages sizzling on the grill.

The temperature had dipped down into the low sixties that evening, and Stonehedge earlier turned on a heat lamp. He got up so he could flip the sausages, and when he sat back down he was about to tell them about one of his adventures in Barcelona when he did a double take on Natalie.

"You're bursting to tell us something," he said.

"Big news," Morris agreed. "At least for us."

"Rachel's engaged," Natalie said, beaming.

"That's wonderful," Brie said. She was sitting next to Natalie and she reached over to take hold of Natalie's hands. "It's still so hard for me to believe that you could possibly have a daughter old enough to get married."

"Nat was only six when we got hitched and seven when she had Rachel," Morris said with his best poker face.

Natalie gave him a stern look. "Behave yourself," she warned.

"Yes, ma'am."

"Mazel tov," Stonehedge offered. He absently stroked the vivid scar that ran down his right cheek, his eyes distant as if he were trying to remember something. "Her fiancé is that fellow from the mayor's office?" he asked Morris.

"That's right."

Stonehedge nodded to himself. He had met Gilman after he had used his studio connections to force his way onto the SCK investigation, which was also how Morris got to know him, and indirectly the reason that he got the scar on his cheek—although it didn't come from SCK, but rather when Stonehedge was slashed with a gun barrel after he tried to play hero during a Beverly Hills jewelry-store stickup that he and Morris stumbled upon. He also got shot in the thigh during the robbery and if it hadn't been for Morris's actual heroics, he would've died.

The actor raised his glass for a toast, and the others followed suit. "Is there going to be an engagement party?" he asked.

"Nat's trying to get one together," Morris said.

"No matter what, there will be one," Natalie promised. "Even if it's at the house."

"Let me throw it here," Stonehedge said. "A Malibu location overlooking the ocean. It would be hard to top that."

"That's such a generous offer," Natalie said. "But only if we pay for the catering and all other costs."

"Uh-uh. It will be on me. I want to do this and besides, it will give me a chance to rub elbows with people in the mayor's office and see if I can impress the heck out of them."

Morris leaned back in his chair, his arms crossed over his chest. "I can't let you pay for something like that," he said.

Stonehedge smiled thinly. "How about we bargain, then? You've got something you could offer me that would be worth a whole lot more to me than whatever I could spend on a party."

Morris sat patiently and waited to hear what that would be. While Stonehedge rarely showed his theatrical side to him, the man was still an actor and so he attempted to build suspense by using that moment to retrieve the sausages from the grill. Parker pushed himself to his feet and followed after him, and with barely any mooching was hand-fed a generous piece of sausage, which he gratefully chomped on. The actor waited until he was seated again and had sliced the sausages into pieces before telling Morris what he wanted in return, which was to play detective for two weeks.

Morris sampled a piece of sausage and nodded his approval before asking, "Why would that be worth anything to you?"

Stonehedge made a face as if he were about to sneeze. "I'm shooting a crime thriller in Montreal in six weeks where I'll be playing a police detective, and I'm having a hard time getting a handle on the role."

Another eye roll from Brie. "You'll be fine," she said.

"I won't be," Stonehedge insisted, his usual carefree façade gone as his insecurities showed through. It was a painful thing to see. "I'm completely lost about what motivates my character."

"Philip, darling, you always go through this before filming, and you always find your center."

"Not this time," the actor groaned miserably. "Unless Morris bails me out, I'll be bombing badly. My career will be over."

"I can't let that happen," Morris said, somewhat tongue-in-cheek. He didn't quite roll his eyes, but he came close to doing so. "You can tag along with me for two weeks. I can't offer you anything as exciting as hunting a serial killer. The work will mostly be dull corporate stuff, but we just started working a missing-person's case that you might be able to help out with."

Stonehedge's face melted into a relieved grin. "You're the boss," he said. "A lifesaver, also. Whatever I can do to help, I'll do it."

"You'll be at MBI eight sharp tomorrow morning?"

"You can count on it."

"I'll need you incognito."

"No problem. I'll use the same disguise I did with SCK."

"Good enough." Morris held out his hand and Stonehedge took it.

"Isn't it nice when they get along?" Brie asked with an amused smile.

"Yes it is," Natalie agreed.

"One more condition," Morris said. "We pay the cost for the party."

"Definitely not," Stonehedge insisted. "Morris, I'm being completely serious about this. I'd gladly pay five times what this party will cost for what you're offering me."

Morris didn't like the idea of taking that type of generosity from anyone, regardless of the circumstances. He gave Natalie a sideways glance and caught the tension straining her face. He knew she also wouldn't feel comfortable having Stonehedge pay for something like that, but he could see that she was hoping he wouldn't blow this up. Their daughter was as down-to-earth as anyone Morris had ever known, and wasn't one to normally care about things like someone's celebrity status, but having her engagement party at the Malibu home of one of Hollywood's biggest stars would still have to impress her. Sometimes you just have to live to fight another day.

"We can talk about this later," he said.

"We can always talk about anything," Stonehedge agreed. "It won't change anything."

Stubborn bastard, Morris thought. His friend might even be more stubborn than he was. There was even a chance he was more bullheaded than Parker.

"Another day," he said.

"Of course."

Stonehedge whistled for Parker, fed the dog another piece of sausage, then pushed himself away from the table so he could get the paella.

* * * *

Duncan followed Matt and Hannah Kammer to LAX and watched their somewhat tender and awkward goodbye. From what Duncan could tell, Kammer felt uncomfortable kissing his wife in public, and he tried to usher his wife to a more private spot before embracing her and exchanging spit. How a guy like that ended up with a dish like his wife was beyond Duncan's comprehension. However it happened, the two of them might just have won the lottery that night without ever realizing it. Or maybe not. It all depended on how long Kammer was away and whether Duncan found other victims.

Duncan didn't bother following Kammer to his gate or trying to find out which flight he was on. It didn't much matter. Odds were that Kammer would be home within a week. If Duncan got impatient and wanted to find out when exactly Kammer was due back, he had ideas of how he could do it. Or maybe by then Duncan would've moved on and found other victims.

Time would tell.

Chapter 13

At eight a.m. on Monday Dennis Polk was drinking coffee and leaning against the desk of MBI's office manager/receptionist, Greta Lindstrom, as he complained about the Dodgers' loss the other night and ignored her hints that she was busy and needed to focus on her work. The office-suite door opened and Polk looked back to watch Philip Stonehedge walk in. Stonehedge was dressed in a cheap, ill-fitting suit that had been bought off-the-rack at the same store Polk bought his suits, and he wore thick-rimmed eyeglasses, a fake prosthetic nose, scruffy blond wig, and an equally scruffy fake mustache and beard. Even with his thick scar, he would've fooled them all except for the fact that they'd seen his disguise before.

Polk gave him an inscrutable look. "Look who's here," he said. "Mr. Hollywood. Nice suit."

"Thanks."

"You were told that the new guy is supposed to bring the doughnuts, right?"

Stonehedge was well aware of Polk from his earlier involvement at MBI. While maintaining a stone-faced expression, he took a fifty-dollar bill from his wallet and handed it to Polk. He further brought a smile to Greta's face by telling Polk, "Knock yourself out with all the jelly-filleds you want."

"Don't think I won't."

"I never would've thought that."

If Greta had been drinking coffee, she would've burned her nostrils snorting it out her nose. As it was, she had to bite her tongue to keep from bursting out laughing. Stonehedge asked her if Morris was in.

"Yep, he's waiting for you in his office."

The actor nodded thanks to Greta, and as he turned from them Polk called out, telling him in his honor he'd be going to one of those froufrou doughnut shops now populating Los Angeles, the type that make their jelly-filled with organic fruit and basil. "I know that's all you sensitive actor-types can tolerate these days!"

"In that case, get me a chocolate-caramel-salted," Stonehedge said.

Morris stepped out of his office to see what the commotion was about. He raised an eyebrow at Stonehedge.

"Polk's taking doughnut orders," the actor said, straight-faced.

"How about getting me a Bavarian cream," Morris said.

"If you go to the shop on York Boulevard, could you pick me up a lemon poppy seed?" Greta chimed in.

Polk stood speechless, trying to come up with a snappy comeback. Sensing that the moment was lost, he left MBI grumbling under his breath how he liked it better when they didn't have to deal with pampered actors. Stonehedge didn't give any indication of having heard him, and after he was settled in Morris's office and realized it was free of bull terriers, asked about Parker.

"Nat's got the little guy today."

Stonehedge was surprised by this. He knew Natalie worked as a therapist and had a private office downtown. "Her clients don't mind?"

Morris made a face at the idea of that. "That butterball with fur? Not a chance. Today's one of the days where she schedules only clients who respond well to him." He handed Stonehedge a photo of a model-thin woman with haunting eyes and long, dark brown hair framing her face. "Grace Warren, twenty-eight, missing since June eighteenth."

Stonehedge studied the photo before handing it back. "A drug addict?" he asked.

"According to her parents, Grace is a recovering heroin addict. From what I've been able to find out, she also likes coke, weed, and hard liquor, with tequila her favorite. A hopeful actress who in the past has worked as a waitress and bartender, but didn't have a job for over four months before disappearing. No known address either."

"Homeless, then?"

"Technically, but she wasn't living on the streets. Instead, she was staying with friends, moving on to the next one before wearing out her welcome. Her parents are used to Grace disappearing for a month or two at a time, then showing up at their door to hit them up for money. After ten months of no contact they got worried enough to hire me. And I think they have a good reason to be worried."

"Why's that?" Stonehedge asked. "Beyond the obvious reasons."

"Because of the guy she was last seen with."

Chapter 14

The wildfires that recently broke out in northern California dominated the first three pages of the newspaper, and Duncan had to search through half the paper before he found a story about Jill Kincade's murder. He was surprised by that. He would've thought the story would've been horrific enough to have made the front page, even with the wildfires devastating several of the northern towns. A beautiful, blond girl from a financially well-off family butchered in her apartment only hours after her engagement party, and the newspaper buries the story? Even after the fiancé was forced to watch and the Faustian deal he was offered? But this was Los Angeles and maybe it wasn't such a big deal here. After the next victims, it would become a big deal. Once the city realized they were dealing with a depraved serial killer, it would be the only story!

Duncan became increasingly bewildered as he read through the article. It mentioned how Kincade's fiancé, Alex Frey, was beaten and had suffered a concussion, and there was quite a bit about how Jill Kincade led an exemplary and caring life, and how everyone who knew her adored her, but there were no details about what was done to her, and there was nothing about the snarling wolf's-face tattoo on the underside of her killer's wrist. He read through the article a second time, this time more carefully, and he understood what must've happened. The dead girl's family used their influence to bury the story and keep all the gory, sensationalized details out of it. He could picture Jill Kincade's dad doing something like that, thinking he was protecting his daughter's memory.

His thoughts were interrupted by the waitress, who brought over coffee and a plate of fried eggs and corned beef hash.

"Here you go, hon," she said. She smiled sweetly at him. "Good choice. The hash and eggs are my favorite here."

Duncan hadn't paid attention to her earlier, but the tone of her voice caused him to give her a quick look. About his age, skinny, a dark, tangled mess of curly hair, nose stud, lip ring, and both thin arms covered with colorful tattoos.

"Good to know," he said.

The disinterest in his voice should've sent her walking away, but instead she lingered. "Are you from around here?" she asked.

"Missouri, originally."

"Really? St. Louis?"

"No, a small town. Look, I don't want to be rude, but my eggs are getting cold, so let me make this easy. One of the few things that turn me off more than lip and nose piercings are tattoos. And maybe the only thing that turns me off more than tattoos is when a gal's too stupid to realize when a guy's not interested."

Her dark eyes burned and anger flushed her cheeks. "What a sweet thing to say to someone," she said in a very different tone than earlier.

Duncan smiled, showing his teeth. "Timing is everything in life. If I had told you that earlier, you would've had a chance to spit in my coffee or do worse to my food. Too bad for you, huh?"

The waitress stood, staring at him, her lips squeezed into a tight oval and moving in and out as if she were chewing something. Duncan wondered whether she was going to spit on his food, and he was prepared to use his hands to shield his plate if necessary. The moment passed and she turned and stormed away without adding any bodily fluids to his breakfast. He watched her. A nice, tight ass, which was really quite lovely in the way it was squeezed into her almost obscenely short leather skirt. A lot of passion in her also. It wouldn't have been the worst thing in the world if he had gotten naked with her for an hour or so.

But he reminded himself that he wasn't there to admire some tattoo-freak waitress's nice ass, or read the paper or have breakfast. He was hunting that morning and he had followed a couple into this restaurant that was all lovey-dovey with each other, and he'd been surreptitiously watching them as they sat two tables away. He was still paying attention to them while reading his paper, and also when he was having his chat with the waitress. He caught the guy leering at the waitress's cute ass as she stomped her way back to the kitchen, and he also saw the hurt look forming on his girlfriend's (or wife's?) face when she caught him doing this. Her expression quickly changed from injured to fuming.

"You got to be kidding me," she said in a low enough voice that Duncan had to strain to hear her.

Her partner gave her a confused look, as if he had no clue what she was talking about.

"You've got me at a disadvantage," he said.

"You're drooling," she said.

The idiot actually wiped several fingers across his lips to see if she was right. Then he showed a stupid grin to act as if he were only joking.

"I still have no idea what you're talking about," he claimed.

If looks could kill, the guy would've dropped dead at that moment.

"Screw you!" She pushed her chair back from the table and stood rigid. "And you might as well screw that freak show of a waitress, because we're done."

She didn't waste any time after that fleeing the restaurant, all the while her boyfriend (or husband?) stayed seated at the table. The guy had no intention of following after her and he caught Duncan looking his way and returned an embarrassed smile, mistaking Duncan's disappointment for sympathy.

Oh well, Duncan thought as he dipped a forkful of hash with egg yolk and shoveled it into his mouth. It wasn't as if he had invested all that much time in that couple. Really, less than an hour. If he kept hunting, he was sure he'd find another one who'd be exactly what he was looking for.

As he chewed his food, he wondered about the vagaries of life. If he hadn't been such a prick to his waitress, Ms. Freak Show wouldn't have stormed off the way she did, that guy wouldn't have broken his gal's heart, and she'd be dying in a terrible way later that day. Now she was going to live. Or at least if she was going to die today, it wasn't going to be by Duncan's hand.

He took another bite of his food and found himself thinking back to a time when he wasn't such a mean-hearted bastard. It wasn't all that long ago, and it didn't take a Mensa candidate to figure out what had caused him to become the way he was.

Chapter 15

Jack Readinger kept his eyes squeezed shut while he groped blindly along the floor, but it still felt as if the sunlight was piercing into his brain. Finally he found his cocaine stash—or at least the baggie that used to hold his stash. He opened his eyes a crack and saw the baggie was mostly empty. Not at all deterred, he wiped a finger along the inside of it and picked up enough residue, so that when he rubbed the finger over his gums he felt a jolt. Not much of one, but enough to get him going for a few hours.

Moaning, he sat up in bed. A grimace tightened his jaw muscles as he checked the boot-sized bruise along his right side. Two weeks ago it had been a vibrant purplish-blue color, but now the cracked ribs were mostly healed and the bruise had faded to a more muted yellowish-brown. He tested the bruise with his fingers and winced, still finding it tender to the touch. His lips twisted into a hard smirk as he thought about the beating he had taken two weeks ago.

That night he had walked into a dive bar in East Hollywood with the thought of picking up some spending money from rolling a drunk or ripping off a sucker, and that was when he spotted a potential honeypot—a woman who was young and attractive enough to entice most other men, but filled with enough self-loathing, insecurities, and masochistic tendencies that Readinger would be able to exploit her and mold her to suit his purposes. He was good at spotting a honeypot; it was like he had a special sixth sense. Not that all the potential honeypots he approached fell under his sway, but the ones that did he would milk dry before he'd cut them loose. He preferred the scams he could run with a honeypot than the ones he had to do solo. And of course, he thoroughly enjoyed the side benefits of having a honeypot under his thumb.

This one was a redhead with the type of soft, red lips that would give any man ideas. A little plump, but still, she had a nice, luscious body under her loose-fitting dress. He had her sized up before he'd taken more than two steps into the bar, and the look she gave him was better than an engraved invitation. It was always exciting when he came across a honeypot he knew was ripe for the picking. Usually when this happened, he'd be coy when he approached the woman, only hinting about what he was after, and he would wait until he got them drunk and alone before letting them know he was in charge from now on. With this one he went straight for the kill, joining her at the bar, and after introductions and a round of drinks, laying it on thick, letting her know that he was exactly what she needed.

"Is that so?" she asked.

She didn't say this as a challenge, but more because she wanted to hear why that was. He couldn't help laughing, seeing the desperate plea in her eyes.

"You better believe it, darling. You need a guy like me who'll keep you in line and hurt you when you need to be hurt. And you especially need me to make the hard decisions you're too weak to make."

If she wasn't a honeypot, she would've either laughed in his face or told him to get lost, but instead she accepted it. He nuzzled in close to her after that, getting handsy and whispering in her ear what he was going to do to her later, and how he would punish her if she didn't sufficiently please him. Somehow, he knew that he needed to take this direct approach with her and from the way she responded, he also knew he'd hit the jackpot. It would take a few days, maybe a week, to completely break her spirit, but after that he'd have exactly what he needed. As he continued to work on her, he was too caught up in his scheming to notice the dude who had snuck up behind him, at least until he was nearly yanked off the barstool.

He twisted his neck and got a good look at the dude then. Forties, skinny, and dressed like a hipster. The guy had a long, heavily-lined face and a ridiculous pompadour, almost like he had come out of a nineties Billy Joel video.

"I don't appreciate you making time with my girl," the dude said.

Readinger smiled, showing all of his cracked and chipped teeth. "You own the lady, huh?"

"You better believe it."

Readinger turned to the redhead. "What do you say? Should I toss out the trash?"

She laughed nervously. "That would be lovely."

The dude was incensed. He raised his hand as if he were going to strike the woman across the face, but before he could do so, Readinger was off the barstool. He grabbed a handful of the dude's pants from behind, and with his other hand he grasped the scruff of the guy's neck and then he rushed the dude toward the bar's front entrance. One of the other patrons opened the door so that Readinger could heave the dude out without losing any momentum. He sent the skinny-assed man airborne and crashing onto the sidewalk. Readinger considered following him outside and kicking the living daylights out of him, but he was laughing too hard from when the man had flailed helplessly in the air before gravity took over, so instead he went back inside and joined the redhead at the bar.

They had a few more drinks after that, snorted some coke in the bathroom, and then did some more serious drinking before leaving together. They were half a block from the bar when the redhead urged him down an alley.

"I want to prove my worth to you," she told him, badly slurring her words. "Let me get on my knees so I can take care of you properly."

Readinger liked the idea of that. The sooner he started debasing her, the sooner he'd have her broken and trained. He joined her down the alley, and as he was unzipping his fly someone tapped him on the shoulder.

Of course, it was the dude. Readinger had been right about the redhead being a honeypot, but he was all wrong about who owned her. This was the game they ran, which was to find a sap to lure into the alley, and that night he was their sap. The booze he drank slowed his reflexes enough so that he wasn't quick enough ducking, and the pipe the dude swung at him caught him in the jaw and knocked him off his feet. As he lay among the garbage, broken glass, and rat feces in the alley, the dude and the redhead stomped him good. After that, they went through his pockets and took his coke and wallet. Readinger was barely conscious when he heard the redhead tell the dude that Readinger was a freak and that she wanted to take his clothing. The dude must've liked that idea, because they left him naked in the alley, not even leaving him his boxer shorts.

* * * *

Readinger's legs felt rubbery as he pushed himself off the bed and stumbled to the bathroom. He spent a minute splashing cold water over his face, then he gripped the sink and leaned toward the vanity mirror. Through the cracks and the grime, he could see that the cuts on his face had healed. The swelling in his jaw had gone down over a week ago and there was no longer any discoloration. Same with his nose. No black eyes anymore either. Bloodshot, maybe, but nothing much more than that. From what he could see, his face didn't show any signs of the beating he took. That was good. It was easier to intimidate people when it looked like you were the one who gave beatings, as opposed to taking them.

If Readinger were a different type, he would've gone back to that East Hollywood bar by now, or at least been asking around about that pair, but he looked at revenge as a waste of time and effort. Not that he wouldn't gut that redhead or the dude if he ever ran into either of them again and it was safe to do so, but he wouldn't go out of his way to look for them. His philosophy: It was better to share the pain. Make the next guy hurt even worse. That way, instead of going up against someone who was waiting for him, he would instead deal with a sap who was clueless and defenseless. It was much easier that way and more profitable also. And what difference did it really make who ended up suffering as long as he made someone suffer?

Pay it forward. That was the way he saw it.

He left the cramped bathroom that was just big enough to hold a sink, toilet, shower stall, and a few dozen silverfish, and went to his studio apartment's kitchen area, ignoring the roaches that scattered. He spooned instant coffee into a dirty mug and filled it with hot water. He took a sip of it, made a face, dumped the rest of it in the sink, and got the last can of beer out of the refrigerator.

The place really was a dump. Not only did he have roaches and silverfish, but he was finding mice pellets on the small counter space and in one of the cabinets. He'd find better living accommodations once he got his hands on the right honeypot and started making some serious money. Sooner or later that would happen. In the meantime, whining was for losers and he wasn't a loser. That was for damn sure.

He took the beer back to the bed and sat and drank. When he was done, he put on a pair of boxers and badly-worn jeans, and slipped on a long-sleeve knit shirt that covered the snarling wolf's-face tattoo on the underside of his right wrist.

He was in the middle of running a scam, but he wouldn't know until tomorrow whether it would pay off. For now, he was nearly tapped out and he needed to raise some cash. If he could cause some pain along the way, even better.

Readinger left the apartment in search of someone to victimize.

Chapter 16

When Stonehedge stepped into the dive bar, the thick-necked bartender glanced his way and gave him a suspicious look, as if he didn't belong there. It was possible the actor was misreading things and that it was simply because of the bartender's craggy bald head and bushy horseshoe mustache that the man appeared more sinister than he really was. Whichever it turned out to be, Stonehedge was glad Morris had taken him to a secondhand store so he could ditch the suit for a pair of khakis and a button-down flannel shirt. Even though the suit he was wearing earlier was bought cheap off the rack and fit poorly, he still would've stuck out like a sore thumb in this place wearing any kind of suit. A quick look at the dozen or so patrons in the bar, and he was especially glad Morris had suggested he rub dirt and grease on the clothing before putting it on. The actor continued to the bar and waited as the bartender took his time to come over.

The bartender gave him a hard, flinty look. "This is a cash-only establishment," he warned.

Morris had earlier given Stonehedge a battered and badly-worn billfold to use so that the actor wouldn't ruin his disguise by pulling out a 500-dollar Bottega Veneta men's wallet. He dug the billfold out of his back pants pocket and removed a twenty-dollar bill, which he put on the bar.

"A Bud and a shot of bourbon. Pour a shot for yourself."

If this impressed the bartender, he didn't show it, his expression remaining as wooden as a tree stump. He collected the twenty, poured a draft of Bud in a glass that had lipstick and other smudges on it, dug a brand of bourbon from the bottom shelf that Stonehedge had never heard of before, and poured a shot, which he pushed in front of the actor.

The bartender showed Stonehedge a screw-you smile. "I decided I'd rather keep the cash than drink this rotgut bourbon," he said.

"No doubt a wise decision." Stonehedge was thoroughly enjoying being in disguise and playing an undercover cop, and this was maybe the most fun he'd had since he got to play detective with Morris on the SCK investigation. That might've been why the bartender's surly disposition brought out a thin, cocksure smile from him. He took a sniff of the bourbon, which smelled worse than kerosene, but he swallowed it down in a single gulp, then chased it with the Bud, ignoring the potential diseases he could be picking up from the glass, comforting himself with the thought that the rotgut alcohol would kill anything short of the bubonic plague. It was all part of the experience he was soaking in.

"I didn't come here to bask in the glow of your delightful personality." Stonehedge picked up the empty shot glass. "Or to drink this lighter fluid, which isn't bad as far as lighter fluid goes. I'm looking for Trey Johnson, and I was told he likes to frequent this establishment."

The actor's manner, confidence, and language had thrown the bartender off-guard. He looked unsure of himself as he shook his head and said he didn't know what Stonehedge was talking about.

"You don't have to." Stonehedge dug a pen out of his pocket and scribbled the number for a burner phone onto a napkin. "Just tell Johnson to call me. That I have a mutually beneficial business opportunity I'd like to discuss with him."

He handed the napkin to the bartender, who peered at it before crumpling it into a ball and tossing it onto the floor.

"That can always be smoothed out after I leave, assuming you didn't memorize the number," Stonehedge said with a wink. He got off the barstool, dug out his billfold again, and left another twenty on the bar. "I'll pay you fifty more if you get Johnson to call me, even if we don't end up doing business together."

The bartender looked as if he was trying to keep his mouth clamped shut, but he couldn't help himself from asking Stonehedge who sent him there.

"Duane Crawford."

Morris had gotten the name of the bar and a description of the bartender to seek out from one of Dennis Polk's sources. The source didn't know the bartender's name, only that everyone called him Tex, even though the guy claimed to be from Washington State originally. Polk's source had also given them Crawford as one of Trey Johnson's associates. Crawford had been in lockup at MCJ for the last two months, and Stonehedge caught

Tex nodding slightly to himself, as if he were thinking that Stonehedge must've just gotten out of MCJ himself.

Stonehedge left the bar without looking back, not wanting to give the bartender a chance to ask him any further questions, because if he was asked to describe Crawford or anything else about the man he would've been stumped. He found Morris parked half a block away on the other side of the street facing the bar, and joined him in the car.

"I had no idea bourbon could taste that bad," Stonehedge said, laughing. "Damn, I used to drink some low-quality stuff when I was starting out as a struggling actor, but nothing like that cat piss. On the positive side, I probably don't need a tetanus shot from putting my lips on the filthiest beer glass you've ever seen. I gotta believe that cat piss would kill any germs. A hundred and ninety proof, at least."

"All part of the job," Morris said. "Sorry, but no extra hazard pay for having to drink bottom-shelf booze."

"Yeah, but I'm not getting paid anything."

"That's true too," Morris agreed. "Such is life for a Hollywood star wanting to slum with us little folks."

"Yeah, well, that was certainly slumming in there!"

"No doubt. What's your gut telling you?"

"That I'll survive that shot of cat piss."

Morris peered over at him, his eyes half-lidded as he saw that the actor had said this completely straight-faced and without the hint of a grin. "Are we on the right track?" he asked.

"I think so." Stonehedge popped a mint in his mouth to get rid of the unpleasant taste. "Crawford's name struck a chord with good ol' Tex. So what next?"

Morris reached behind him so he could offer the actor a takeout bag from the Oak Grill. Stonehedge fished inside of it and selected the roasted lamb sandwich with fennel and herbed tahini on focaccia, and handed Morris back the bag. Inside were three other wrapped sandwiches. Morris had picked up enough so they could have lunch and dinner while staking out the bar, if needed. He also had in the car a supply of bottled water, snacks, and two empty milk jugs so they could return the water when the time came. He took one of the prime rib sandwiches for himself.

"We watch, we wait, and we eat."

Stonehedge crunched the mint he was sucking on into dust. After grabbing a bottle of water and taking a healthy swig, he unwrapped the sandwich, took a bite, and nodded his approval.

"The pay might suck, but at least the food's good," he noted.

"The only reason I've been able to keep Polk on the payroll," Morris said, as he chewed on a mouthful of prime rib, horseradish, onion, tomato, and ciabatta. Maybe they'd get lucky and Trey Johnson would call soon, or maybe they'd spot him heading toward the bar, but more likely they had a long wait ahead of them. Johnson was the last connection Morris had found to Grace Warren, and he didn't like what he saw when he looked at Johnson's sheet: A violent man who liked to rob and pistol-whip tourists.

Morris knew when they found Johnson that the man wouldn't voluntarily tell them about Grace, but that was a problem to worry about later. First things first.

He settled into his seat for what he expected to be a long wait.

Chapter 17

Duncan hadn't lifted a wallet from a mark's pants pocket since he was nineteen, but he'd been quite skillful at it back then. He damn well should've been! When he was nine, Wainwright forced him to practice for hours at a stretch, smacking him hard enough in the head to knock him on his ass every time he failed to meet Wainwright's unusually high standards. At that age he had small hands and thin, nimble fingers, which helped, but the trick to being a successful pickpocket was the same for being a magician—namely, misdirection. Sleight-of-hand skills were important, but you needed to strike when the mark was distracted, and Duncan could see that he was about to have an opportunity.

For the last hour he'd been watching the couple that he mostly decided was going to be his next victims; *mostly*, because it depended on whether they were locals or tourists. At that moment the husband was paying too much attention to his wife and was oblivious to the middle-aged woman walking toward him. The woman, for her part, was loaded with shopping bags, had just dug her phone out of her designer pocketbook, and was seconds away from a collision. Duncan watched as this unfolded, and he picked up his pace so he could make up the distance between himself and the husband, timing it so that he was slipping the wallet from the husband's back pocket the moment the woman smacked into him.

What do you know, he thought. *Just like riding a bike. You never lose it.*

He heard the husband sputtering out an apology, and he caught the accusatory and icy stare that the woman gave him back in return. Neither of them noticed him walking off with the pilfered wallet tucked under his sports jacket.

Well, the temporarily pilfered wallet.

He was going to have to return it. A lot of these Rodeo Drive stores had video surveillance and some of their cameras would be pointed toward the front of the stores, capturing what went on outside. Duncan knew the police wouldn't start pulling video because of a stolen wallet, but they would if the husband later connected the theft to his wife being butchered by an intruder wearing a ski mask.

He went through the wallet and found the driver's license. The husband's name was George Campbell and he had a Los Angeles address. While Duncan had nothing against the idea of killing tourists, and in some ways preferred the idea of it, too many hotels had security cameras in the lobby, on each floor, and in the elevators, and so he was relieved to see that the Campbells were locals. George and Meagan. He had earlier learned the wife's name by eavesdropping on them. They just seemed perfect for what he wanted. Both of them were wearing expensive designer clothing and had stylish haircuts, and both were obviously members of the oh-so excusive beautiful and privileged club. George Campbell was tall, broad-shouldered, and good-looking—the type who would've played quarterback for his high school football team. Meagan was a pretty little thing with shoulder-length auburn hair and sexy-as-hell almond-shaped hazel eyes. They were so into each other that Duncan could almost taste the bile in the back of his throat as he watched them. Yeah, they were what he wanted.

But for now he needed to return the wallet to Campbell's back pocket.

They were half a block away, arms wrapped around each other as they did a little window-shopping at one of the upscale women's clothing stores. When Duncan saw the two of them enter the store, he swore under his breath. He had to get the wallet back to Campbell before the guy realized it was missing, which meant he had to go into the same store, which further meant there'd probably be video surveillance of the two of them together. But what were the odds the cops would search for that? Zero to none. He had to quit sweating the little stuff.

He took a deep breath as he concentrated to relax his facial muscles, and then headed to the same store. Once inside, he spotted the Campbells by the lingerie department. Meagan was holding up a skimpy and mostly see-through nightgown to get George's opinion, and the husband was clearly enjoying himself. Perfect. The two of them were already distracted.

Duncan headed to the same department, picked up a pair of lace underwear that would at best cover only 10 percent of a woman's ass cheeks, and then while examining the underwear he "accidentally" bumped into Campbell, while at the same time slipping the wallet into his back pocket.

"Ah, I'm sorry," Duncan apologized, making his voice higher-pitched and raspier than it normally was so the husband wouldn't recognize it later.

"Don't sweat it," Campbell said without looking back enough to get a good look at Duncan. "It happens."

Duncan caught Campbell freezing, as if a thought had just occurred to him, then a quick pat on his back pocket. His features relaxed after feeling the outline of his wallet and realizing that he was being paranoid thinking he might've had his wallet picked. Duncan flashed the wife an embarrassed smile, who smiled sweetly back in return.

A nice kid, he thought. He also realized for the first time that he must've had a type for the women he wanted to kill. He had run across other happy, beautiful and privileged, in-love couples he could've picked since coming to Los Angeles, but so far he had only chosen couples where the woman was a pretty little thing, like Meagan Campbell. Jill Kincade was a little curvier than this one and Hannah Kammer, but they were all five feet two or shorter, all slender with thin legs and small breasts, and none of them weighed more than a hundred pounds. They also all had very pretty faces. Yeah, he had a type, all right. And even though two of them were blondes, he knew why he was really picking them, although he hadn't realized it until then. In a way, it was startling; in another way, it made perfect sense.

He put the underwear back and then made a show of examining several other pairs so he wouldn't look overly suspicious, all the while keeping his back to George Campbell. Meagan Campbell had gotten a good look at him, but that didn't matter.

Duncan hung around for what he considered an appropriate amount of time and then left the store.

Chapter 18

Morris didn't need to bring the empty milk jugs, since there was another bar two doors from where he had parked, and Stonehedge paid the bartender twenty dollars for bathroom privileges for them. Stonehedge had left the car ten minutes ago to take advantage of those privileges, and Morris sat as still as a granite block, his hands folded over his belly and his eyes mostly, but not completely, closed. Natalie wouldn't have been fooled, and neither would any of the cops or MBI investigators who had ever joined him on a stakeout, but almost anyone else looking at him would've thought he was about to nod off. He wasn't. Instead, he was in a Zen state, fully relaxed, but still watching for Trey Johnson. This was a skill he had mastered after dozens of stakeouts over the years.

Stonehedge left the bar and rejoined Morris in the car. Grinning, he asked Morris how many fingers he held up when he left the bar. Morris moved only his right hand so he could show the actor the same finger that was shown to him.

Stonehedge broke out laughing. "Very good," he said. "I know you've got this Buddha act pretty well perfected, but I needed to make sure you didn't fall asleep while I was gone. Otherwise, who knows? Trey Johnson might've slipped past you and might right now be in the Rattlesnake."

The Rattlesnake was the bar they were staking out. "Very thoughtful of you," Morris breathed out in a soft whisper.

Stonehedge's burner phone rang. Morris opened his eyes and glanced over at him. The only person who was given the burner's number was the bartender at the Rattlesnake. The actor answered the call.

"Yeah? Who's this?" he said.

A man answered, his voice as slick as an oil spill as he said, "The guy you've been asking about."

"Sorry, fella. I've got feelers out with four potential business partners. So how about you tell me your name?"

Johnson sounded disappointed as he reluctantly did as Stonehedge asked. "How much money's involved?" he demanded.

"Two hundred grand, at least. Should be more. We split it evenly."

"What's the setup?"

"I'll tell you that when we meet. How fast can you get to K-Town?"

"Pal, why don't you tell me first how you know Crawford."

"I met Duane while I was sitting in MCJ. A charming fellow."

"Why were you in MCJ?"

"I had a business venture that busted out because I picked the wrong guy for a partner. I'm not making that mistake again."

Johnson didn't sound entirely convinced as he asked, "How'd you get out of there?"

"It wasn't too hard. Costly, though. I paid three grand to make some evidence disappear."

The connection went silent long enough that Stonehedge thought that the man might've hung up on him, then Johnson got back on the line. "Okay. I'll meet with you. But forget K-Town. There's a Travelers Motor Lodge on South Figueroa. You tell me what car you're driving, and when you pull into the parking lot I'll signal you to my room."

Stonehedge gave Morris a questioning look, and Morris shook his head. He'd been a homicide cop long enough to know why Johnson wanted to get Stonehedge alone in a motel room, and that was so he could beat the details of the business venture out of Stonehedge, and then cut the actor's throat and leave him dead. Morris made a cutting motion over his throat to let Stonehedge know what Johnson would do to him if he were to meet him at that motel.

"I'm beginning to think you're more trouble than you're worth," Stonehedge said. "I've got a restaurant in K-Town where they've got a back room I use that's safe. The cops can't listen in with a parabolic microphone and I can vouch that the place isn't bugged. More importantly for me, though, is if you try any funny business there are four guys there with butcher knives who'll make sure you end up as a special ingredient in the bibimbap. If you're going to give me any further grief, tell me now so I can quit wasting my time."

"Forget the Travelers Motor Lodge," Johnson grumbled, properly chastised. "I'll meet you in K-Town in an hour. This deal better be what you're saying it is."

Stonehedge gave him the name of the restaurant, told him to ask for Mickey D. when he got there, and ended the call.

"Impressive improvisational skills," Morris commented.

"Thanks," Stonehedge said, beaming. "We do a small amount of improv with some of the scripts, although nothing like this. Damn, though, that was fun. I felt like I got to stretch my acting muscles."

"It was a struggle not to applaud," Morris said, straight-faced. "Mickey D., though. I don't know. Not the most original name you could've come up with."

Mickey D.'s was the name of the bar where Stonehedge had arranged bathroom privileges.

"We didn't discuss ahead of time what name I should use," Stonehedge said with a grin. "And as an actor, you use the material you're given." His grin faded and he replicated the same throat-cutting gesture Morris had used. "You really think he wanted me in that motel room so he could kill me?"

"Yeah, rap sheets don't lie. This guy's a sadist. Even if he could've gotten you to willingly tell him about your big score, he'd still want to do it his way, which would be to tie you to a chair and torture the information out of you. When he was done, he'd have to make sure you were dead before he left the room."

"Why would he need to do that? He'd know I wouldn't be able to go to the police, at least if I was really who he thought I was."

"He wouldn't want any competition around for the big score."

Stonehedge's expression weakened as he absorbed this. "Wow," he said, swallowing hard. "It just hit me how real this is. I'll be alone in a room with a bloodthirsty psycho."

"It won't be your first time. And you survived Jason Dorsage without any backup. Besides, I'd also say Johnson's more of a violent sociopath."

Stonehedge made a pained face as he thought about his encounter with the malicious serial killer who had hoped to kill thousands in Los Angeles. "Thanks. Should I have a gun?"

"Nah, you'll be fine. He'll be cautious meeting you on your home turf. He'll also be taking your threat seriously. Johnson will be on his best behavior." Morris's flinty gray eyes took on a hard sheen as he added, "If you were to actually partner with him on a robbery, I'm sure he'd double-cross you and leave you dead."

Stonehedge whispered, "This is getting damn real."

Chapter 19

George Campbell waited until the drinks arrived before reaching across the table and placing a small, gift-wrapped box in front of Meagan.

"What's this?" she asked.

"Open it and find out."

She tentatively picked up the box, but seemed unsure what to do with it.

"You really shouldn't have bought me anything," she said, a heaviness in her voice. She looked exhausted all of a sudden, as if her strength had bled out of her. "It wasn't necessary."

George's eyes began misting up. "Meagan, I needed to buy you this. Please, just open the gift."

"Today's been a lovely day," she said somewhat wistfully.

"Like when we first started dating."

She showed him a heartbreaking smile. "Not just like back then, but I was just as happy the first two years we were married."

"I know. But I swear it will be like that again," he promised her. His face convulsed as if he were struggling to maintain his composure. He rubbed a hand roughly across his eyes. "I'm so sorry. I'll never be able to tell you how truly sorry I am."

"I forgave you," she said, self-conscious of the other diners around them. She kept her voice low as she added, "We're moving forward and working past what happened, right?"

"Right," he agreed. His eyes quickly became liquid and he choked back a sob. "You need to know I'll be spending every day of the rest of my life proving to you how much I cherish you and how grateful I am for this second chance."

"Stop it now."

"It was all so stupid," he said, his words rapidly tumbling out. "So ridiculously, insanely stupid. I can't explain why it happened other than I was an idiot, but you have to believe me that Lindsey never meant anything to me."

Meagan stood up, her body shaking. "You were never to mention her name again," she said, her voice like ice. "That was the deal we had!"

Their waiter had stopped to look at them. Other diners in the Beverly Hills restaurant were staring also. George clasped his head with both hands, as if he were going to start tearing his hair out.

"I'm screwing this up," he moaned. "We had such a good day, and I'm screwing everything up. Please, baby, sit down. I'll never mention her name again. I promise."

We're making a ridiculous scene, Meagan thought. *Like we're starring in some badly-written afternoon soap opera.*

She became painfully aware that everyone nearby was staring at them. There was nothing she hated more than being the center of attention, good or bad. No, that wasn't quite true. There was one thing she hated more than that, and that was finding out the man she thought she was happily married to was having a tawdry affair with a coworker. A loudmouthed, pushy woman with big hair, big boobs, and a big ass to match by the name of Lindsey Bushnell. The whole thing was so damn cliché that it sickened her. She sat back down, looking like she had aged a decade.

"You're not screwing everything up," she said, feeling self-conscious and concentrating to keep her voice low so no one could listen in on them. "And we did have a nice day. We'll have more nice days too. You just have to be patient and not force things."

"I don't deserve you," he said. "I really don't."

Meagan didn't argue with him. Instead, she picked up her martini and sipped it slowly.

George rubbed the wetness from his eyes. He tried to manufacture a smile, but it didn't stick.

"I really wish you'd open that gift," he said, nodding toward the gift-wrapped box that Meagan had left on the table. "I'm sure you'll love it. And it cost a small fortune."

"It's not going to work that way."

He gave her a confused look. "What are you talking about?"

She put down her drink and met his gaze. "You're not going to fix things by buying me stuff," she said. "I hope we can get back to what we had, but it will have to be by hard work and you winning back my trust, and not by you spending money."

"I know that, and that's not why I want to give you this. When I saw it in the store window I knew you'd love it. That's my only reason, I swear." He forced a goofy grin. "Maybe I was also trying to be romantic."

"When did you buy it?" she asked.

"Today, when you were in Stefano's trying on clothing." His grin grew wider. "I bet I ran a fourteen-second hundred-yard dash so I could buy that and get back to Stefano's before you left the dressing room. I'm pretty sure I ran even faster to get back to the store. My high school coach would've been proud."

Meagan accepted that he got caught up in the moment, just like she did after they had walked into that clothing store. She only wanted to go in there to buy a blouse for work, but it was George's idea that they look at lingerie, and she went along with it. They had gotten along so well that day, and for the first time in over six months she was feeling comfortable with him again. It was also the first time since she found out about his affair that she'd been able to spend any time with him without being consumed by anger. They still had a long way to go, but she was beginning to believe that they could get back to what they once had. More importantly, she found herself trusting him again, at least mostly. When he started trying to reconcile with her, she was convinced he had an ulterior motive and was only trying to protect his assets and company-stock options, but she now believed he was sincere. That he did love her and regretted betraying her.

She pushed the gift closer toward him. "Why don't you hold this 'til Christmas Eve and leave it under the tree so I can open it Christmas morning?" she suggested.

"I understand," he said. He put the gift away in his pocket. The look on his face showed he didn't understand, but then he caught the meaning of what she had said. He could always be a little slow on the uptake. "You think there's a chance we'll be back together by Christmas?"

"I'm hoping so."

The waiter brought their food. Meagan mostly picked at her wood-grilled sea bass. She knew the food at this restaurant was delicious, but a mix of confusing emotions had left her with little appetite. George also picked at his food. He looked conflicted, as if he were struggling over a question.

"We don't have to wait until Christmas," he said. "You could come home tonight and we could see how it goes."

Her therapist would've wanted her to tell him that it was too soon, but he was looking like such a lovesick fool right then that it tugged at her heart. And it had been a nice day, after all. Maybe it was time for them to take the next step. She had moved out of the house after she found out about his affair and hadn't had sex since then, or even had any desire for it. That was over six months ago. When she thought about how long it had been, it stunned her.

"Come on, baby," he pleaded. "You bought that sexy nightgown for a reason."

She could've argued that she was swept up in the moment, but she knew that wasn't true. For the first time since that awful day she was feeling sexy and desirable again, and would it be so awful if they slept together?

"One night, baby," he said. "We can see how it goes and make a decision after that. Please, baby?"

"I'm not saying yes or no," she said. "We'll see."

He broke out into a stupid grin; the type that always touched her heart.

"That's all I can ask for. Just for you to keep an open mind."

* * * *

Duncan had followed George and Meagan Campbell to the Beverly Hills restaurant. While he would've liked to have eavesdropped on them more, he didn't think it would be safe to do so—that they might've recognized him from the ritzy-ditzy clothing store and found it suspicious if they also saw him in the restaurant. So instead he parked his car half a block away so he could watch when they left the restaurant's parking lot.

He didn't need to be following them any longer. He knew where they lived and he could've gone to their home so he'd be waiting for them when they returned. For a reason he couldn't quite articulate, it seemed important that he continue to follow them so that he knew everything they did on their last night together.

It was more than simply a compulsion on his part, although that was partly it. As Duncan sat and wondered about this, the reason soon became crystal clear. It was so he could work up enough rage for what was coming.

Chapter 20

Philip Stonehedge had seen Trey Johnson's mugshot, so he knew what to expect, but that didn't stop a cold sweat from crawling down his back when Johnson entered the room. He was one scary-looking dude, even though he was three inches shorter than Stonehedge and much thinner. Johnson had the same facial and neck tattoos that the actor had seen in the photo, although the tattoos somehow seemed more sinister in the flesh. What spooked Stonehedge the most was the deadness in Johnson's eyes and a feral quality that emanated from him in waves like a bad cologne. Stonehedge knew he was safe meeting him in the basement of this restaurant. He of course had lied to Johnson about the room not being bugged, and at that moment Morris and Charlie Bogle were in an adjoining room listening in. Also, Morris had arranged for Johnson to see two of the cooks holding meat cleavers and giving him the evil eye as a warning. While he knew he was in no danger, he also knew Morris was right that Johnson wanted him alone in that motel room for evil purposes.

There was a bottle of Canadian whiskey and two platters of dumplings on the table where Stonehedge sat. Johnson took the chair across from him and popped a fried pork dumpling into his mouth.

Stonehedge said, "Those taste better if you use the dipping sauce."

Johnson gave him a dull-eyed stare in return. He picked up the whiskey bottle and instead of pouring some into a glass, he drank straight from the bottle. He was wearing a biker's leather jacket, and when he was done, he wiped a sleeve across his mouth and held the bottle as if he were planning to use it as a weapon.

Johnson leaned back casually in his chair, but any sense of calmness was betrayed by his right leg bouncing up and down as if he were revving himself up to commit violence. A menacing sheen showed in his half-lidded eyes.

"How about you tell me about this opportunity," he said in that same slick voice Stonehedge had heard earlier. In person, his voice made Stonehedge think of a poisonous snake.

"Assuming you do this with me, we'll be hitting a high-stakes poker game," the actor said. "All the players are top film execs and the game's held at a Malibu home. We'll be gaining access disguised as caterers after we leave the real caterers tied up. There will be three security guards inside. We'll need to rush them fast and knock them out. One of them is my inside man, and you need to make sure he never wakes up again, otherwise our two-way split becomes three-ways. While you're keeping the players occupied, I'm hitting the safe. Any questions?"

The plan Stonehedge outlined came straight from a movie he'd shot two years ago that was still looking for distribution. Johnson seemed impressed enough by what he heard that his leg-bouncing came to a stop. His eyes took on a distant look as he appeared to be searching for cracks in the operation.

He wet his lips and asked, "How do you know there will be two-hundred grand?"

"From my inside man. All the games have had at least that much. Last time these fat cats talked about upping the stakes for their next game."

Johnson smiled in a borderline obscene way. "You have no problem double-crossing your inside guy?"

"None at all."

"How do I know you won't be double-crossing me?"

Stonehedge was impressed by how closely their conversation was following the dialogue from the movie. He had to give those writers credit. They nailed it!

"The guy's a sap who's just begging to be double-crossed. You and me, we won't trust each other for a second, which means we'll both take the necessary precautions. Once we get the money, we do the split and never see each other again. Does that satisfy you?"

Johnson's smile became an outright obscenity. "You're one confident fucker."

"I'll take that as a *yes*."

Stonehedge signaled for Johnson to hand over the whiskey bottle, and the man did so without a fuss. Stonehedge refilled his glass and when he put the bottle down, he made sure it was out of Johnson's reach.

He said, "I've heard that you like to crack people's skulls with the butt end of a pistol. That's what I need. Someone who'll go in there like a tornado and wreak havoc. But I need to make sure you can handle doing more than just cracking skulls. My inside guy needs to die in that house."

"That won't be a problem."

"There's a big difference between knocking someone unconscious and killing a man in cold blood. I need to know you can handle it."

"Yeah? You want me to demonstrate?" Johnson asked. "Because if that's what you need to see, get me someone from the kitchen no one will miss."

"This isn't a joke."

"What makes you think I'm joking?"

The actor knew this psycho was deadly serious, but he continued to act as if that wasn't the case.

"I don't have time for this nonsense," he said, exaggerating the disgust in his voice and making sure to curl his upper lip. "You want to act like this is a game, then how about you get lost. Scram, okay?"

Johnson didn't want to leave. That was evident from the way his eyes shined and the tightness in his jaw. Stonehedge had no doubt the guy badly wanted to be part of this fictional heist, and was already scheming about different ways he could double-cross Stonehedge and take all the money.

"Don't get your panties in a bunch, okay?" Johnson said. "You want me to explain why killing some schmuck won't bother me? Your inside guy won't be the first body I've planted in the ground, if you get what I'm saying. There have been plenty of others, brother. A week ago last Thursday there was a fat slob working the cash register at a liquor store on Oxnard that I robbed. I put a bullet right here." He pointed to his left eye. "I had no problem doing that for three hundred and eighteen dollars. What do you think I'm willing to do for a hundred grand?"

Before Stonehedge could catch himself, he asked, "It didn't bother you to kill this man?"

Johnson gave the actor a look as if he were crazy. "Why would something like that bother me?"

"I just want to make sure you're the guy I need for this job."

Johnson laughed under his breath. "The dumb slob had already handed over what was in the cash register. I didn't need to shoot him. I did it for kicks. Are you satisfied yet?"

"I'm satisfied."

Johnson's back was facing the door and he didn't hear Morris Brick and Charlie Bogle enter the room, nor Bogle approach from behind. It wasn't until Bogle reached around him and yanked down his leather jacket so that it acted as a makeshift straitjacket and left his arms pinned to his side, that he realized there was anyone else in the room.

"Hey, hey, hey!" Johnson yelled as he struggled to free his arms.

"Easy there, son," Bogle said.

Bogle took the 9mm pistol wedged in the back of Johnson's pants, and after more searching found a sheathed hunting knife in Johnson's left boot. Morris took the seat next to Stonehedge and faced an increasingly irate Trey Johnson. He placed a digital recorder on the table, introduced himself and Bogle, and then played back Johnson confessing to killing a liquor store employee.

"That's entrapment!"

Morris didn't bother explaining that tricking someone into a confession wasn't entrapment. Instead, he placed a photo of Grace Warren in front of Johnson.

"Trey, all I care about is finding Grace," he said.

Stonehedge was reminded of a cornered rat as he watched Johnson struggling against his restraints, but he saw the moment something clicked in the man's eyes. Johnson settled down after that and took a look at Warren's photo.

"Little Gracie," he said with a hard smirk.

"She was last seen on June eighteenth. You were with her."

A calculating look shined in Johnson's eyes. "If I tell you what I know, you'll get rid of that recording?" he asked.

"I told you already all I care about is finding Grace."

Johnson made a decision. He asked, "How about you fix my jacket and I'll tell you what I can?"

"How about we talk first."

Johnson didn't like that, but the fight had gone out of him. "I remember the last time I was with little Gracie, and it might've been that date," he said. "Yeah, June something seems about right. We were in this dive bar in Inglewood, maybe four miles from the airport, and she ditched me for some other guy. A badass type."

"What do you mean, ditched you? She left with him?"

He made a face as if he'd swallowed vinegar. "I didn't stick around to see. But even a blind man could see that he took ownership of the bitch."

"You were okay with that?"

Johnson might've shrugged if his arms weren't restricted. "That girl had a mouth on her that just wouldn't quit, and I don't mean that in a good way. She was always riding me, always with the smart-ass cracks. I wasn't all that sorry to see her go. And I damn well wasn't going to lose any blood to keep her. Good riddance, you follow me?"

"Tell me about this other guy."

"Like I said, a real hard-ass." He stared at Stonehedge. "Same height and build as this rat, but a much harder dude. I could see in his eyes that he was a stone-cold killer."

It takes one to know one, Stonehedge thought. From the bare trace of smile that had crept onto Morris's lips, he must've been thinking the same.

"Hair and eye color?" Morris asked. "Beard, mustache, tattoos, piercings?"

Johnson thought about it. "I can't tell you eye color. Just rattlesnake eyes, you know what I mean? He had his hair short, like in a buzz cut. I think it was a dirty blond, but I might be wrong, so don't quote me on that. No beard, no mustache, no piercings, at least none that I remember. He had a beauty of a tattoo that made me jealous. A wolf's face on his wrist with the fangs bared, like it's about to rip someone apart. Some real dope ink, man. Much respect."

"Age?"

Johnson looked like he would've shrugged if he could've. "Older than the rat over there. Younger than you."

"Name of the bar?"

"Man, I can't remember something like that. Outside was painted black, with the name of the place in gold letters. Inside it was a real dive."

"Why'd you take Grace there?"

"To get some drinks."

Johnson was lying about that, but Morris didn't press him. Instead, he said, "Tell me someone famous that he looks like, and we're done."

At first Johnson's face was a blank, but then a thin smile crept onto his lips. "You know that old movie *Escape from New York*? He looks like the dude in that."

"Kurt Russell?"

"Yeah. That's his name. Not like he is now, but from that movie. No eye patch, though. And like I said, shorter hair."

Morris took out his phone and called Annie Walsh, the LAPD detective working out of the robbery-homicide division, so he could tell her he had a confessed murderer for her to pick up. "The suspect's name is Trey Johnson. He robbed a North Hollywood liquor store a week from last Thursday and killed an employee." He gave Stonehedge a questioning look and the actor pointed to his left eye. "I've got a witness to the confession and an audio recording. According to the witness, Johnson indicated that he shot the employee in the left eye."

Johnson had been smiling dumbly, as if he thought Morris was playing an elaborate prank on him, but once he realized what was happening his face went white with rage. He tried to stand, but Bogle's hand clamping down on his shoulder kept him in his seat.

"We had a deal!"

Morris told Annie he'd be right back, and he gave Johnson a pitying look and asked him, "Did I ever say I wouldn't call the police if you helped me with Grace?"

Johnson's face fell flat as he realized that never happened. "You made me think you wouldn't!"

"I can't help what you think."

Johnson groaned miserably as he fully understood the situation. He tried to get to his feet, but Bogle put his hand on his shoulder and kept him seated where he was.

"How about you stay put until the police come?" Bogle said.

Morris got back on the phone with Annie.

Chapter 21

Sometimes a gift is just a gift.

Meagan knew she overreacted when George tried to give her that gift. While she'd never admit this to him, she should've accepted the box and assumed the earrings or whatever piece of jewelry he bought was because he wanted her to have it, as opposed to trying to buy her affection. She also knew she reacted the way she did because it touched a very raw nerve, but once they got past their self-inflicted drama, they settled into what turned out to be a quite pleasant dinner. Meagan regained enough of her appetite to enjoy the wood-grilled sea bass and George seemed to do the same with his rib eye steak. When the waiter asked about desserts, George ordered the caramel bread pudding, which he remembered was her favorite. The waiter brought two spoons, and George made sure to eat leisurely enough so that she could have at least half of it.

Later, when George was driving her back to the furnished guesthouse she was renting in the valley—which was really a glorified studio apartment—she asked him why he didn't try again to invite her back to their Echo Park home. He seemed surprised and pleased by the question, and told her that he didn't want to put any pressure on her.

"Don't get me wrong," he said. "I badly wanted to do that, but I kind of blew it earlier tonight and I didn't want to risk blowing it again."

"You didn't blow anything."

He wet his lips, a nervousness tightening his jaw muscle. "Meagan, my love, there's nothing I'd like more in this world than for you to come home tonight."

"Yes," she said. "But I'm not making any promises about moving back. We'll see how tonight goes."

He looked like he wanted to high-five her. "That's all I can ask for," he said.

He didn't say another word as they drove, and Meagan knew it was because he didn't want to risk changing her mind. That was okay. She found herself feeling both nervous and excited. She'd also been missing the creature comforts of their home. The guesthouse she'd been renting for the last six months was advertised as "cozy," and to say it was cramped and tiny would be an understatement. The couple she was renting the unit from were nice enough, and their two-year-old daughter Allie was a little sweetheart, but Meagan missed having a shower with decent pressure and more than two minutes of available hot water, and she really missed their king-sized bed. But that wasn't the only reason she wanted to get back together with her husband. He had proved to her over the last four months that he was willing to fight for her. And it broke her heart a little each time she saw little Allie and realized that part of her life was missing.

George got off at the first exit he could so he could turn around and head toward the Echo Park neighborhood of Los Angeles. After he parked in their driveway, he held her hand, just like when they were dating in college. Once they were inside, he asked what they should do first.

"Can you still make a mean cappuccino?"

He grinned at her. "As mean as any junkyard dog."

George and his clichés. At least there were some constants she could count on in the world. She followed him to the kitchen and sat at the table as he meticulously measured and ground the coffee beans into a fine powder. He was steaming the milk for the cappuccino when a *ding* sounded to let him know he had received a text message, and he absently took the phone from his pocket. For a brief second a look of dread froze on his face. Or was it guilt? He fiddled with the phone before shoving it back into his pocket, then continued steaming the milk as if nothing had happened.

Meagan began trembling. "That was *her* texting you," she said, her voice barely a whisper.

She could see the lie forming on his face. He had deleted the evidence and he was going to lie to her about it. But then there was another *ding* indicating another text message.

"I swear," he said, "I blocked her. But she borrowed someone else's phone. Someone named Samantha Rigby."

"Why would she do that?"

He gave her a helpless, beseeching look. "Meagan, the only person at work who knew I was seeing you today was Bob Doltrice. He must've told her."

There was another *ding* from his phone.

Her voice was surprisingly calm as she asked why Lindsey was still texting him.

"Out of spite. No other reason."

"I want to see your phone."

"Ah, please, Meagan. She's unbalanced. She only wants to sabotage us—"

"Let me see your phone or I'm leaving now!"

A pained look squeezed his face as he dug the phone out of his pocket. There was another *ding* and he stared dolefully at the unread text messages before handing over the phone.

"None of those are true," he said. "She's trying any way she can to hurt me."

Meagan felt like vomiting when she read the texts.

Hon, are you really back with the frigid little princess?

What about all those times you told me screwing her was like screwing a piece of ice?

I guess I can't blame you doing what you must to keep from handing her half your stock options.

When Meagan demanded to know how he could still be working with that woman, her voice sounded tinny to her own ears, as if it were coming from someplace far away.

"What else am I going to do? You want me to throw away twenty million dollars?" he asked angrily as if he were talking to a child. "Because that's how much I'd be throwing away in unvested options if we go public next year as planned!"

"Don't you dare lose your temper at me! I'm not the one who cheated! You are!"

"Why do you keep throwing that in my face? After everything I've been doing to try to win you back! Damn you, Meagan, I keep slicing open my veins for you, but nothing is enough!"

The doorbell rang. George stormed out of the kitchen as if he couldn't get out of there fast enough. Meagan grabbed her pocketbook and followed after him, thinking it had to be Lindsey ringing the bell. She wasn't sure what she was going to do. All she knew was she couldn't spend another minute in that house with him.

George beat her to the door. From the angry way he swung the door open, he must've also thought it was Lindsey and he must've been waiting to lay into her. Before he could say anything there was a sickening *crack*, like the sound of something hard hitting a jawbone, and George flew backwards. Did she really just see teeth flying out of his mouth?

George crashed onto the floor and Meagan saw that it wasn't Lindsey at the door, but a man dressed in black and wearing a ski mask. This stranger must've hit George with a club he was holding in his right hand. It was a foot long and a dull black, like it was made of leather, and the end fishtailed out like a beaver's tail. When he stepped past George's unconscious body and headed toward her, a wild panic took over and she turned and ran toward the bathroom on the first floor.

She almost made it. Her hand was reaching for the doorknob when she was struck on the shoulder. The blow crumpled her and she fell to the floor. The pain was so intense it sucked her breath away, leaving her incapable of screaming for help. Hands grabbed onto her ankles and started dragging her away.

Chapter 22

Duncan couldn't help chuckling, thinking about what happened to George Campbell when that idiot answered the door. The guy was just so damn careless, flinging open the door like he did without knowing who was there and sticking his face out as if he were about to give someone an earful. The only way Duncan could understand it was that Campbell must've gotten so used to living in a tony neighborhood like Echo Park that he had convinced himself the ugliness of the real world couldn't touch him. Well, Duncan showed him just how wrong he was when he swung the leather sap at the man's chin like he was throwing an uppercut. The end of the sap was weighted with lead and it struck Campbell right under the chin, hitting him hard enough to knock out teeth and lift him off the floor. A quick look was all Duncan needed to see that Campbell was out for the count. He then ran after the wife and, just like he had with Jill Kincade, he broke Meagan Campbell's collarbone. That he did intentionally. He wanted to make sure the police recognized a consistent pattern.

With both husband and wife lying helplessly on the floor, he took his time following the same script he had used with the first couple; first dragging them both into the kitchen, then stripping off Meagan's clothing and securing her with duct tape to a chair. Just as he had with Alex Frey, he left Campbell fully dressed when he positioned him, so he'd be facing his wife. Campbell was out cold when Duncan shoved a dishrag into his mouth, and from the unnatural way the man's jaw moved, he could tell that he had shattered it the same as if he had struck a glass vase with the sap.

It was such a rush, obliterating Campbell's jaw. Campbell, after all, was the person Duncan really wanted to hurt, and if it wasn't for his plan he would've beaten the man to a bloody pulp. But he had his plan, and he knew that for it to work he had to follow it to the letter. So he used an ammonium carbonate capsule to bring Campbell back to consciousness and otherwise left him untouched. After that, he followed the same script he used before: First slicing off both of Meagan Campbell's nipples, then cutting and stabbing her dozens of times before offering Campbell his Faustian deal. To Duncan's surprise, Campbell accepted it.

"I want you to think long and hard about what you're agreeing to do," Duncan warned him. "Just so we're clear, if I cut you free and you don't choke your sweet little thing to death, it's going to be even worse for her. We're talking ninth-level-of-Hell stuff. You'll live, but I'm serious about breaking every bone in your body. So champ, what's it going to be? You sure you want to do this?"

Campbell nodded, and so Duncan used the knife to cut off the duct tape. Campbell stood up slowly, rubbing his arms as he took a step toward his wife, but then he tried to spin and duck while at the same time throwing a punch at Duncan. The man had forty pounds on Duncan and while he wasn't bulky, he looked like he worked out regularly with weights. Still, on his best day Duncan would've taken him apart like a loaf of wet bread, and this wasn't Campbell's best day. He had a broken jaw and for forty minutes his arms had been bound behind a chair, leaving them without any circulation. His hero attempt was pathetic and Duncan hit him across his broken jaw with the leather sap. Campbell hit the floor like he'd been shot in the head.

Duncan stood over the man, shaking in his rage. What the hell! He had warned him what would happen if he tried a stunt like that, and the idiot went ahead and tried it anyway? The hell with him! Duncan was going to live up to his word, but first he needed to wake Campbell up. He broke an ammonium carbonate capsule under the man's nostril, but Campbell didn't stir. He tried another one and again got no reaction. The man's breathing was shallow, but he was still alive, and he was stubbornly refusing to wake up!

Duncan grabbed Campbell under his arms and lifted him back into the chair. After he secured him again with duct tape, he waited. A half hour later he tried yet another ammonium carbonate capsule, and again, nothing.

Meagan Campbell's skin color had paled to a sickening white, which was quite a contrast to all the blood on her. During this time, she sobbed uncontrollably, and while most of the noise was cut off by her gag, enough of it leaked through so that she sounded like a wounded animal. That noise was soon hitting Duncan like nails on a chalkboard. He wanted Campbell to witness what was going to happen, but it could be hours before he woke up, maybe longer, and Duncan found himself wanting to get out of there.

Anyway, it didn't matter. Campbell had seen the snarling wolf's-face tattoo on Duncan's wrist and when he finally woke up, he'd find his wife horrifically butchered. That would have to be enough.

He moved back to Meagan and started cutting and stabbing her again, but it wasn't the same any longer. With Campbell unconscious, the actions just seemed hollow, even dirty. Duncan understood that the release he felt with the first victims didn't come from hurting the wife, but only from the agony he caused the husband by making him watch. He cut Meagan two more times, but it just seemed so pointless. Yeah, the husband would wake up to see his wife carved up like a jack-o'-lantern, but Duncan wouldn't get any satisfaction from it.

He backed away and considered leaving her alive. She hadn't seen his face and aside from slicing off her nipples, her other cuts and stab wounds were superficial. He could just walk away from this one.

He sat down so he could give the matter full consideration. Soon, though, he grimly accepted that he had to follow through with killing her. The point of these murders wasn't simply to provide an outlet for the rage choking him almost every minute of the day, but because his plan needed these deaths. If he were to leave Meagan alive, it would screw up everything. She had to die the same way as the other one.

Duncan tried not to look into her eyes as he continued stabbing and cutting her. She lasted a good deal longer than Jill Kincade, but eventually she died.

Chapter 23

When Morris got Annie Walsh on the phone, she was still on the job and she told him she was too swamped to collect Trey Johnson and would send over Detective Ray Vestra. "I'm lead detective on a bad one," she confided. "On a scale from one to ten, this one's an eleven."

"I'm all ears if you want to run anything by me," he said.

Usually that lame joke got a laugh out of her, but not this time. "I'd love to get your take on it, but Hadley already put the kibosh on me doing that. He promised it would be our badges if anyone went outside the department."

The Hadley she referred to was Police Commissioner Martin Hadley. Years ago, when Morris was on the force and made detective, he was partnered with Hadley, and the two of them mixed as well as oil and water. As far as Morris was concerned, Hadley hadn't gotten any better with age.

"What bee flew up his bonnet?"

"The best I can figure out is the victim's family has some political clout, and they're trying to keep the details out of the media, probably thinking they're protecting her memory. I can understand their concern. What was done to her was inhuman. But that's all I can say on the matter. Expect Ray soon. I've got to get back to the salt mines."

Vestra showed up fifteen minutes later with two uniformed officers. He broke out laughing when he saw Johnson looking sorry for himself as he sat helplessly in a chair with his jacket yanked down under his chest.

"Whose idea was that?" he asked, referring to the jacket being used as a restraint.

"All Charlie's," Morris said.

"I think I saw it in a Bogart movie once," Bogle said. "Or it might've been the Three Stooges."

Vestra gave Stonehedge a hard look, as if he were trying to remember where he knew him from. "Who are you?" he asked.

"A lousy rat," Johnson volunteered, his upper lip curling as if he were spitting out something vulgar.

"Mickey D.," Morris said.

The LAPD detective gave Morris a questioning look. "A new hire?"

"I'll explain later."

Morris played back Johnson's confession to the homicide detective. Vestra looked suitably impressed. "All gift-wrapped and with a bow on top," he said. "And it's still months before Christmas."

"They entrapped me!"

Vestra gave Johnson a patronizing look. "And how'd they do that?" he asked.

"They tricked me!"

"They tricked you into robbing that North Hollywood liquor store and shooting the clerk?"

Johnson looked away, his face a sullen mask. "That rat over there tricked me into talking about it," he said.

Vestra gave Morris a look as if he couldn't believe the geniuses he had to deal with, then informed Johnson he was under arrest. Johnson's leather jacket was pulled back up and he was cuffed before he could put up any resistance. When he was led away, he was still complaining about how he'd been unfairly tricked. One of the uniformed officers had to bite his lip to keep from laughing.

Morris, Bogle, and Stonehedge accompanied Vestra to the Wilcox Avenue Hollywood precinct so they could give their statements, and Stonehedge used the opportunity to remove his disguise and change into the clothes he had packed away in a travel bag. Vestra was impressed when he saw him out of his disguise.

"You had me fooled," the LAPD detective admitted.

Vestra was more impressed when he heard how Johnson was tricked into confessing. He put his feet up on his desk and stroked his chin as he marveled over the sting operation.

"That was pretty damn clever," he said. "There's no reason we couldn't use that same approach here."

"You could," Morris agreed. "But not too many times. Maybe once or twice before word of it spreads among the criminal community. It also helped that we had one of Hollywood's brightest actors sell it." He turned to Stonehedge and applauded. "Philip, brilliant performance."

Stonehedge was seated and he bent forward slightly and exaggerated a bowing motion with his right hand.

"I'll save it for when I really need it," Vestra said. "So Mickey D., what do you say? Would you be up for another performance?"

Stonehedge looked pleased with himself. "Anytime I'm in town," he said.

Vestra turned to Morris. "Johnson has no idea Mickey D. is really Mr. Stonehedge?"

"None."

"He'll find out when this goes to trial."

If Stonehedge was worried about a vicious criminal holding a vendetta against him, he didn't show it. "I'm not worried in the least," he said.

"There's no reason you should be," Morris said. "Odds are Johnson will plea to second-degree long before a witness list is made available. In the rare event it goes to trial and he learns the truth about you being Mickey D., all it will do is give him bragging rights that one of Hollywood's biggest stars sent him away."

"That sounds about right," Vestra agreed. "But I'll try to keep Mr. Stonehedge's name out of it anyway." He was stroking his chin again as he looked over at the actor. "I'd suggest you do the same."

Stonehedge smiled thinly. "Mum's the word," he said.

Morris asked Vestra if he could do him a favor in return for closing an open homicide.

"What do you need?"

"The name and addresses of any perps with a wolf's-face tattoo on the underside of his right wrist. The tattoo shows the wolf's fangs."

"Like it's snarling?"

"Yeah, that sounds about right."

"I'll put in a computer search tomorrow morning and let you know what I find," Vestra said.

They ended up sitting in the precinct for a little under two hours before they finished giving their statements. As they were leaving the station house, Stonehedge suggested drinks and dinner at Luzana's, which had the reputation for being Hollywood's most exclusive hot spot. Bogle declined, saying, "Sorry, Hollywood, too rich for my blood."

"I'll be picking up the tab. Come on, guys. I'm on too big a high from what we just pulled off to go home. I need to do some basking!"

Bogle gave Morris a questioning look, who in turn checked the time and saw it was a little after nine. Morris wanted to find the Inglewood bar where Johnson last saw Grace Warren, but it was late and he was hungry, and he decided that could wait until the next day.

"If we go, MBI will be picking up the tab," he said. "Let me give Nat a call."

Natalie picked up on the fourth ring and he gave her a quick summary of what he'd been up to that night. "We just stepped outside after giving our statements, and Phil's suggesting drinks and dinner—"

"You haven't eaten anything for dinner yet?"

"A bag of chips."

"Go," she said. "Enjoy yourself. Wow, though, that was quite a feat. Solving a homicide you didn't even know about."

"We got lucky," he admitted. "I was hoping he'd tell us something we could use to squeeze him, but I didn't think it would be anything more than a robbery or an assault. I didn't expect him to cop to a first-degree murder." Morris lowered his voice and asked about Parker. "How's the little guy? He's not missing me too much?"

"Right now he's snoring up a storm. He'll be fine. You can make it up to him for any hurt feelings by taking him for a long walk when you get home. And hon, please don't bring him back any takeout."

"I'll be good," he promised.

Chapter 24

The radio turned on at a quarter to six, playing Tom Petty's "Runnin' Down a Dream." Morris tried to bury his head under the pillow and ignore it. All he wanted was another hour of sleep. Natalie crawled to his side of the bed and reached over him so she could turn off the radio alarm.

"Hon, don't you need to be at the office by seven?" she asked, her voice heavy from just waking up. When he groaned in response to her question, she took pity on him and added, "If you want, I'll take Parker out. That will buy you another half hour in bed."

Morris accepted the sad truth of the situation. His voice sounded downright froggy when he told her he could use a walk around the neighborhood to clear his head, which was true. He tried unsuccessfully to suppress a second groan as he rolled out of bed bleary-eyed and his mouth tasting like he had gargled with sawdust. His body felt unnaturally stiff as he slipped on a pair of old jeans and a sweatshirt, and he groaned for a third time as he struggled to put on socks and a pair of sneakers. Too little sleep and too much scotch last night. It didn't help that he wasn't a scotch drinker and would've preferred beer, but Stonehedge had insisted and after the actor's performance with the lowlife Trey Johnson, he decided he'd indulge his friend. While Grace Warren was still missing, it was a break in the case that gave them clear-cut threads to pull, and he doubted they would've gotten the information out of Johnson any other way. Charlie Bogle, at least, showed some sense—not only sticking to beer, but packing it in after two hours. Morris had a couple of scotches too many. Well, really a few, if he were honest about it.

He finished tying his sneakers and then stumbled to the door and heard a soft whimper from Parker on the other side of it. He found Parker waiting impatiently, the dog's ropy tail whipping back and forth.

"Tough morning for you also, huh?" he asked as he rubbed the bull terrier's snout. Parker answered with a sneeze and then scampered down the stairs. Morris moved much slower as he followed after him. They went through their usual tug-of-war routine with the leash before Parker consented to let go and sit still long enough for Morris to put the leash on him. Once they were outside, Morris shivered from a chill in the air and considered going back for a jacket, but Parker was straining on his leash, impatient to start his walk, and Morris let the dog pull him forward.

Later in the day it would warm up to the low seventies, but at that early-morning hour it was unusually cold. Probably not even fifty. Morris peered up at the sky. The sun hadn't broken much past the horizon and was covered by thick, purplish-dark clouds. Overall it seemed grayer than most mornings and Morris soon found his mood matching the weather.

His thoughts drifted toward Grace Warren: How she not only latched onto a vicious criminal like Trey Johnson, but ditched him for someone who Johnson instinctively knew was even worse trouble. It wasn't good, to say the least, although it didn't necessarily mean Grace was beyond hope. Someone could still be rescued after diving into a pool of piranhas, but they were going to be damaged by it. The questions would be how much flesh remained on the bones and how deep were the cuts. Assuming that Grace was still alive, God only knew what shape she'd be in when they found her, or what this new lowlife—the one with the snarling wolf's-face tattoo—would be making her do.

Natalie had coffee waiting for him when he returned. While they sat together at the kitchen table, her expression turned increasingly pensive.

"It's more than you being hungover," she said, never being one to mince words. "Something's troubling you."

"I'm not that hungover," Morris argued.

"That might possibly be believable if your eyes right now weren't more bloodshot than the Donovans' basset hound."

"A handsome dog, even with those bloody eyes."

"Nonetheless."

Morris admitted, "You're right about me being preoccupied."

Natalie said, "Your missing-person's case."

"Yeah. It took a bad turn last night."

"How bad?"

"To be determined. There's still a chance we'll find her alive and well."

A tiredness weighed on Natalie's face as she considered that. It could've just been the early hour. She said, "I'm glad you're taking Parker today. He always cheers you up when you're in one of these moods."

The bull terrier was lying by Natalie's feet and he lifted his head at the sound of his name.

Morris forced a grin that he wasn't feeling. "Usually," he agreed. "Although sometimes I pass my funny moods onto him."

"They can be contagious. Good or bad."

Morris could've used another cup of coffee, but a quick glance at the kitchen clock showed that if he was going to take a shower that morning, he'd better do it now if he wanted to get to MBI on time. And yeah, he wanted a shower. While he doubted he was actually sweating alcohol, he felt that he was. He left his chair so he could kiss Natalie on the lips and head upstairs.

He almost asked her if she could take Parker for the day. She was right about the dog usually lifting his spirits when he fell into these darker moods, and he liked having the bull terrier with him when he was on the job—not only was the dog great company, but he helped keep Morris calm. Parker was also handy for stakeouts—with the dog in tow, Morris could stretch his legs and walk around the area he was watching without being conspicuous. Today, though, was different. It wasn't just his mood, but an uneasiness that had wormed its way into the pit of his stomach, and he didn't want it to spread to Parker like some fast-moving virus. But he knew he was being overly paranoid. Parker would be fine. He just wished he could've understood his reason for this gnawing uneasiness.

Chapter 25

Morris had planned to take a cab to Luzana's so he could pick up his car from the other night, but Natalie insisted on driving him and while he didn't want to inconvenience her, he also learned long ago that when she insisted on doing something, she was going to do it. After that, he made a stop for bagels and cream cheese, but even with these detours he and Parker got to MBI by seven.

Stonehedge was waiting for him in the reception area, in full disguise, and champing at the bit to continue the investigation. Parker, like all dogs, relied more heavily on his sense of smell than sight, and wasn't fooled at all by the disguise. Morris had already taken Parker off the leash and the bull terrier let out a couple of excited grunts and scampered forward to greet Stonehedge. The actor, for his part, got into a crouch so he could properly greet the dog.

"There's my buddy," Stonehedge laughed as he playfully wrestled with Parker.

"Be careful he doesn't knock off your prosthetic nose," Morris warned.

Parker did almost exactly that as he tried to grab the fake nose in his mouth, probably thinking that Stonehedge was playing a game with him by wearing it. The actor straightened out of his crouch and consented to instead thump the bull terrier good-naturedly on the side instead of tussling with him.

"That was a close call," Stonehedge said with a tight grin.

"He can certainly keep you on your toes." Morris handed him the bag of food he had picked up from Katz's Bagels. "Why don't you take this to the conference room? I'll collect Charlie and we'll join you."

"A strategy session, huh?"

"That's right. To make up for not having an actual one last night."

"We got distracted," Stonehedge said. He showed a guilty smile. "My fault. I guess Luzana's wasn't exactly conducive to planning out an investigation."

"Just as well. We'd be spinning our wheels doing anything until we hear back from Ray, so we've got time."

Stonehedge scratched above his ear as he thought about that. He was careful not to dislodge his wig. "In case he's able to identify the guy with the wolf's-face tattoo," he said.

"Exactly."

Stonehedge gave that more thought as he headed toward the conference room, and Parker stood as still as a marble statue watching him, undecided about whether he should follow the food or Morris. His indecision didn't last for more than a few seconds before he turned and hurried after Morris.

Morris glanced over his shoulder at the dog. "We both know what you would've done if there was b-a-c-o-n in that bag," he said accusingly.

The bull terrier looked guilty from almost abandoning Morris over nothing more than a bagel.

"Forget it." Morris reached down and scratched the dog behind his ear. "It happens to the best of us sometimes."

His mouth felt drier than it should have—no doubt from drinking too much scotch last night—and he made a quick detour to the kitchen area so he could pour himself a cup of coffee. This would be his fourth that morning, but he needed it, and he mouthed a silent prayer of thanks on finding a fresh pot waiting for him. This also meant that Bogle was already in. Every morning either he or Bogle brewed a pot of coffee, depending on who got to the office first. With a mug of black coffee in hand and Parker tagging along close enough that the dog's thick body bumped against his legs, he continued on to Bogle's office. No Bogle, though. He frowned at that, but stood quietly in the hallway and soon heard a low murmur coming from Adam Felger's office. Felger worked as MBI's computer and hacking specialist and was the lone millennial at the firm. Aside from Greta, he was also the only employee who wasn't a former LAPD homicide detective.

Morris knocked and opened the door to Felger's office. Felger and Bogle were sitting by the computer in consultation. Bogle looked up and commented that it was nice of him to finally make an appearance. Parker squirmed his way past him so he could greet Bogle. The bull terrier was more standoffish with Felger.

"You know what was even nicer of me? I brought bagels and cream cheese," Morris said. "They're in the conference room being guarded by Philip."

"You mean Hollywood."

Morris didn't argue about the nickname the other MBI investigators had given Stonehedge. Instead, he commented about Felger being in early that morning. "I'm guessing Charlie roped you into this?"

"He called me last night," Felger acknowledged.

"You better believe it," Bogle said. "I had an idea that the mystery scumbag we're looking for wanted Grace for nefarious purposes, so I called Computer Boy and asked him to come in so he could help me look for any unsolved crimes in the area that might've been committed by Mr. Scumbag with the wolf's-face tattoo and Grace."

"Any luck?"

"Not yet. We were just about to expand our search to Long Beach and San Diego."

"Not a bad idea," Morris agreed. "I'll leave you two to keep searching. Feel free to grab some bagels. Maybe Philip and I will drive around Inglewood and see if we can locate the bar where Grace met this guy."

That got Felger's attention. "What do you know about the place?" he asked.

"Roughly four miles from LAX. Exterior painted black, name of the bar in gold letters."

"Let me see if I can save you some wear and tear on your car."

Felger brought Google Earth up on his computer. He used another window to create a list of bars in Inglewood, and soon had them entered into a spreadsheet and sorted by their distances to LAX. After that, he went back to Google Earth and used its street view to visit these bars, starting with the ones four miles from LAX. Using this method, he found one named the High Spot Lounge in less than five minutes that matched the description he was given.

"Impressive," Morris admitted. "I need to be paying you more."

"I agree wholeheartedly," Felger said.

Bogle suggested that it was as good a time as any to take a bagel break. All of them headed over to the conference room, with Parker taking the lead. They found Stonehedge and Dennis Polk waiting for them inside. Polk had sliced two bagels in half and was spreading them with cream cheese. Morris was surprised to see Polk in the office. He was supposed to be out that day working on an insurance-fraud case. Morris asked his investigator about it.

"What can I say?" Polk said. "I left some paperwork on my desk that I needed. And lo and behold, look what I found."

"Bull," Bogle said. "Wherever you were, you smelled the bagels and came running."

"Nah, that can't be right," Polk deadpanned. "I don't have a sniffer like that moocher," he said, ignoring Parker's best efforts to mooch a piece of bagel from him. "But who knows, I might have a sixth sense when it comes to tasty food. That could be what sent me here, at least subconsciously."

Morris was thinking about how to best word a crack along the lines of how moochers should be careful about throwing stones at glass houses, when his cell phone rang. Doug Gilman. He'd been planning to call Gilman after the news Rachel had dropped on him and Nat, thinking he'd ask his future son-in-law to join him after work for some drinks. That had been his intention, anyway, but searching for Grace Warren yesterday had kept him off-balance. He stepped out of the conference room so he could have some privacy when he answered the call.

"Doug, I've been meaning to call you—"

Gilman's voice held a cold formality to it when he cut Morris off and told him he'd been planning to call also. Morris had heard this tone from Gilman several times before, and so he was expecting it when Gilman informed him he was calling in an official capacity.

"Detective Walsh told me she picked up a bad homicide," Morris said. "A woman who was murdered in Marina del Rey. Is this related?"

"Unfortunately, yes. We now have a second victim. Or a third. Or you could say a fourth, depending on how you look at it. And to call it *bad* doesn't do it justice. What was done to these women is beyond sickening."

"Doug, you're doing a good job confusing me. Were two women murdered, or were there more?"

"Two women were tortured and butchered, but there are other victims, one of which is expected to make a recovery; the other might not. The mayor wants you and MBI to take charge of the investigation. I'll explain everything after you sign the NDA. Can we count on you?"

"Is Hadley onboard?"

"He is."

Morris knew some arm-twisting must've been needed to get Hadley's approval. Maybe not that much, though. While Hadley would hate the idea of seeing Morris involved, he was first and foremost a shrewd political animal. If these murders were as bad as Gilman was suggesting, Hadley would want the cover that Morris and MBI could provide.

Morris said, "Tell me where you need me."

Gilman gave Morris the Echo Park address where the latest murder occurred.

Chapter 26

Morris found Doug Gilman sitting on the curb four houses away from the Campbell residence. The mayor's deputy assistant was a good-looking man who could easily be mistaken for a Hollywood star, given his bronze tan, perfect head of hair, chiseled features, and slim, fit physique, but at that moment he was looking green around the gills and his face was shiny with perspiration. He looked shaky when he got to his feet so he could offer Morris his hand. Morris took hold of him by the elbow to make sure he didn't fall.

"Are you okay, Doug?" Morris asked. "There's no shame in lying down if you're not feeling well."

"It got to me in there," Gilman admitted. He made a face and gritted his teeth. "But I'm not going to lie down out here and be a joke to the police."

"Let's get you to your car, at least."

Morris took Gilman's briefcase and walked him back to his car, holding Gilman's arm so the man wouldn't fall. Gilman nearly collapsed onto the driver's seat. He leaned forward, holding his head in his hands.

"You really should lie down," Morris said, concerned.

"I'll be okay. I just need a minute."

Morris wished he had brought a bottle of water with him. He searched the inside of the car, but didn't find any. When he popped open the trunk he found a cooler that held, among other things, bottles of organic coconut water. Morris brought one of these to Gilman, who greedily emptied it. His color quickly improved.

"This is so damned embarrassing," he said. "What you must think of me marrying Rachel."

Morris clapped him on the shoulder. "What I know is that you're a good man who'll be treating my daughter right and making her happy."

Gilman clenched his jaw. "I guess Rachel's tough enough for the both of us," he said.

"That she is."

He stared straight ahead, almost like he was ashamed to look at Morris. He said, "Please don't tell Rachel or Natalie about this."

"Tell them about what?" Morris said, as if he had no idea what Gilman was talking about.

The mayor's deputy assistant looked relieved. He dug through his briefcase for the NDA. Morris was surprised he still needed to sign these forms, since he and the rest of the MBI staff had been deputized, but he didn't see any point in arguing with City Hall. He put his John Hancock on the bottom of the NDA, and took extra copies for MBI employees who might get involved in the investigation. At this point, Gilman was looking more like his old self.

"I'm sure when you see what was done to Meagan Campbell you're going to want to take this on," Gilman said. He frowned as he checked the time. "I'm scheduling a press conference for noon. Call me before then to let me know what needs to be held back and what I should emphasize."

Morris was glad to see the more confident Doug Gilman back. He told him he'd do exactly that, even though he hadn't fully committed in his mind to taking the case. He'd been happy over the last six months not having to think about catching depraved serial killers, and he wasn't sure he was willing to dive back into that blood-drenched pool even though he now had Nat's blessing to do so.

Satisfied that Gilman was no longer on the verge of passing out, he gave his future son-in-law a good-natured pat on the shoulder and left the car. He called Annie Walsh on his way back to the prototypical California-style ranch home where Meagan Campbell was murdered. Earlier he had spotted Walsh's car and also Roger Smichen's, who was Los Angeles County's chief medical examiner. Walsh answered on the first ring.

"I'm walking to the house now," Morris told her.

"You'll need to go in through the side entrance. I'll meet you there."

"What do we have?"

Morris heard her on the move as she told him that Meagan Campbell was stabbed and cut over a hundred times and that her husband was found at the scene unresponsive with severe head injuries. "The psycho used a club on him and mutilated her," she said, her voice low and angry. "He cut off both nipples, her nose, one ear, and cut deep grooves into her face like he was carving a pumpkin for Halloween. Roger's here and he believes cause of death was from heart failure due to a combination of shock and low blood pressure."

"Is this the same as you saw at Marina del Rey?"

"With the female victim, yeah. Her fiancé was struck once in the head with a club and kicked in the jaw. He suffered a severe concussion, but that was the extent of his injuries. At least his physical ones."

An olive tree covered the right side of the Campbells' home, and that kept Morris from seeing Walsh until he climbed six of the steps leading to the front door. She waved to him. He waved back. When he got to the top of the stairs, he followed the pathway to the side door. Walsh, with a hard grin, asked where his better half was.

Morris was confused by that. "Natalie?" he asked.

"Your other better half. The handsome devil with four legs and a tail."

"Handsome is right. Devil also, at least at times. Parker's back at MBI."

Walsh seemed to have reached her limit for chitchat. She told Morris that the attack started at the front entranceway, and she'd walk him through it. They both slipped on paper shoe covers before entering the house.

Chapter 27

The side door led into a great room decorated with sectionals, built-in bookshelves, a large, flat-screen TV on a wall, and a portable bar in the corner of the room. Inside the house, a small mob of crime-scene technicians dusted for prints and vacuumed the carpet for hairs and other debris. Morris spotted a technician he knew from his time on the force and nodded to her. He also nodded to Roger Smichen, who was standing by the kitchen, his arms crossed over his chest and an exceptionally dour look creasing his face. Morris soon understood why Smichen was on break. A thick-bodied police photographer had taken over the murder scene. As the man shot photos, he also blocked Morris's view of the victim.

Roger Smichen was a tall, cadaverous-looking man with a head as bald as an egg. Since Morris had last seen him, the coroner had grown a wispy white beard, and if his beard were longer, he might've looked like a wizard from *Lord of the Rings*. Smichen joined Morris and Walsh. He was never one for the custom of shaking hands and this time was no exception. Morris never took it personally.

"Morris, I'd say it was a pleasure if the circumstances were different."

"Same here, Roger."

"This was a brutal one. A true sadist at work. I'll go over it with you once the photographer is done in there."

"I'd like to say I'll be looking forward to it, but I don't think that will be the case."

Smichen's expression grew more morose. "No sane person will want to see what I'll be showing you," he agreed.

Morris and Walsh left him to continue on to the front door. On the carpet was a fist-sized bloodstain, almost as if someone had spat out a mouthful of blood. The stain looked congealed, tacky, as if it would be damp to the touch.

Morris squinted at five small pieces of police tape, three of which were inside the blood splatter and two within inches of it. He asked, "Let me guess: Those are to show where teeth were found?"

"Yep. Five teeth were knocked out of George Campbell's mouth."

Walsh touched her two top front teeth and then three of her bottom incisors to indicate which teeth Campbell lost. "The medical personnel who examined him claimed he was struck with a great deal of force here and here." She pointed under her chin and then to her left cheek. "Forensics are certain that he must've been struck under the chin when he was facing the door."

Morris said, "Because of the way the blood splattered."

"Also because there's no blood on this wall," Walsh said, indicating the wall to their right.

"So the perp is at the door and when Campbell opens it, the perp surprises him, swinging a club upward. A leather sap?"

"It could be. The striking surface is smooth and could be leather. It could also be iron or wood. All we know for sure is it packs a wallop and the blow not only knocked out teeth but demolished his jaw."

Morris raised an eyebrow. "What do you mean, *demolished* his jaw?"

"Four breaks and numerous fractures. His jaw is a mess."

Morris grimaced at the thought of that and absently massaged his own jaw. "Is he down for the count at this point, or is this where he was struck a second time?"

"The second blow happened in the kitchen, so he's probably out cold here. The hospital is going to test for elevated liver enzymes to see if smelling salts were used to wake him up, but I think we can assume that was done. So after the perp dispatches with Campbell, he chases down the wife and incapacitates her."

Walsh led Morris to a bathroom off to the left of the main hallway. Another piece of police tape was attached to the carpet outside the bathroom.

"That tape marks where crime-scene techs found recently dried saliva. Meagan Campbell must've been trying to get to the bathroom to lock herself inside, but the perp struck her from behind, breaking her right collarbone. The same thing happened with the first victim. Crime-scene techs were able to tell from marks in the carpeting that he must've grabbed her by the ankles and dragged her into the kitchen. He did the same with the husband. And this is exactly what he did to the first victims."

"Also breaking the woman's collarbone?"

"Yep."

Walsh led Morris back to the kitchen. The police photographer was done documenting the murder scene, but Roger Smichen still stood off to the side, looking exceedingly glum. He joined them as Walsh explained what happened inside the kitchen and how the husband had been duct-taped to the chair opposite Meagan and forced to watch as his wife was tortured.

With the photographer gone, Morris was able to get a good look at the victim and it sickened him to see what was done to her. She was only twenty-seven. He had spotted a wedding photo earlier where she looked just a year or two older than Rachel. A beautiful young woman whom the killer had reduced to a grotesque mockery.

Morris asked, "Is this the same or worse than the first killing?"

Smichen said, "They were disfigured in the same way, but overall this one was worse. The first victim suffered ninety-three cuts and stab wounds. This one endured a hundred-and-twenty-two, if my counting's correct."

Morris picked up on his use of the word *endured*. "None of the wounds were done postmortem?"

"From my preliminary examination, no. I'll be able to answer that more definitively after the autopsy. It appears that the killer repeatedly cut and stabbed her until her heart stopped working, partially from shock, and partially from a loss of blood contributing to a lower blood pressure. As vicious as these two killings were, none of the wounds by themselves appear to be fatal."

"Do you know what type of knife was used?"

"We have a good idea," Walsh said. "A carving knife is missing from a knife set that the first victim received as an engagement present."

Morris felt a coldness deep in the back of his skull, almost as if ice was pressed against the bone. "The first victim was engaged?" he asked, his voice sounding distant to his ears.

"They'd just gotten back from their engagement party," Walsh said angrily.

Smichen offered, "The coroner's office tracked down that same knife set, and the wounds on the first victim are consistent with the missing knife. These wounds look similar. A six-inch blade. Thin. Very sharp. Solidly constructed."

The grisly remains of Meagan Campbell lay strewn along the marble-tiled floor, as if the killer had carelessly tossed them away after slicing off these pieces of flesh from her. There was also a splattering of dried blood that didn't look like it could've come from her. Morris asked whether the blood came from Meagan or her husband.

"I believe it's from George Campbell," Smichen said. "I'll know for sure when we get the lab results back."

Morris entered the kitchen and walked over to the chair where George Campbell had been found. He stared at it and then at the splatter of dried blood, as if he were trying to make up his mind.

"This blood didn't come from Campbell being struck with the club while he was tied to the chair," he said.

"That's right," Smichen agreed. The medical examiner walked over to a spot on the floor near the blood splatter and faced the empty chair Campbell had been bound to earlier. "He was standing like this when he was hit. The blow most likely knocked him unconscious, and he struck his head here when he fell to the floor."

Smichen touched his long, bony index finger to a spot on the right side of his skull.

Morris was puzzled by that. "How would that have happened?" he asked. "Would he have been able to fight his way free when the perp was taping him to the chair?"

Walsh said, "I can make a good guess what happened." She then told Morris about the offer the killer had made the first victim's fiancé, Alex Frey.

Morris's eyes took on a glazed look as he tried to wrap his head around the killer not following through with his threat, because it must've happened the way Annie suggested it did. The killer would've made the same offer to George Campbell, and in Campbell's case, he agreed to it and when he was cut free he tried to fight back. For his troubles, he was smacked across the face with a club and knocked unconscious. But the killer didn't break every bone in his body like he had promised. He also didn't make it more hellish for Meagan. He stabbed and cut her more times than he did the first victim, but that was only because Meagan's heart lasted longer. He didn't skin her alive or break more of her bones or go out of his way to more cruelly disfigure her than he had his earlier victim, but given his obvious pathology, that was what should've happened. George Campbell's actions should've outraged him, but all he did was strike Campbell once in the face with his club, and then continue on as he would've otherwise. This went against everything Morris knew about serial killers, especially sadistic predators.

Maybe it was because Campbell was knocked unconscious. After that, he would've tried to wake Campbell, and when he couldn't he saw no reason to follow through with his promise. But that didn't make sense. None of the other serial killers Morris had dealt with would've acted this way.

This killer was different. That much was clear.

Morris asked when Meagan Campbell was murdered. Smichen told him that the victim had been dead somewhere between ten to fourteen hours. Walsh added that the Campbells had dinner last night at a Beverly Hills restaurant and their credit card receipt showed that they had paid their bill at 8:17 p.m.

Beverly Hills to Echo Park was a half-hour drive. Morris asked, "How long did the torture go on for?"

"At least an hour," Smichen said.

Morris did a quick calculation in his head. "That means time of death was somewhere between nine-forty-five and midnight last night." He turned to Walsh. "You told me Campbell was unresponsive when he was found. I'm assuming he didn't break free and call the police and then fall back into unconsciousness."

"That's right."

"What time were they found?"

"A call came in at six-oh-three this morning."

Morris was surprised by that. "How'd that happen?" he asked. "A delivery person found the door unlocked?"

A grim smile hardened Annie Walsh's lips. "Something else," she said.

Chapter 28

Duncan Moss ate a dinner of macaroni and cheese with an added sliced hot dog while his dad joined him at the table and drank a beer from the bottle. Duncan knew from the way his dad was studying him that he was trying to figure out the reason for Duncan's sullen attitude. Well, it should've been easy to figure out, and Duncan wasn't going to tell him. As a further act of rebellion, he surreptitiously fed Buster a piece of hot dog under the table. Buster was a stray that Duncan had found in their backyard three years ago when he was six, and he begged his parents to let him keep the dog. At the time there was a big discussion about it, but in the end his dad told him that if no one called about a lost dog, they could adopt him. They put up posters around town, but no one called, and so Buster joined the family. When Duncan asked his dad what type of dog Buster was, his dad told him he was a mix, but he looked like he had cocker spaniel and border collie in him, and maybe some black lab also. And that he had to be part alley cat too. Duncan was only a little kid then, and since his dad said this as if he were deadly serious, it wasn't until later that he realized his dad was joking about the alley cat part.

Duncan knew what a cocker spaniel was from the cartoon *Lady and the Tramp*, which he watched so many times that his mom begged for mercy whenever he asked to see it again. He also knew about a black lab, since the Hendersons had one. He had never seen a border collie, and when he was eight he went to the library in Carthage with his mom and found a picture of one in the encyclopedia. He could see the resemblance between Buster and that breed, although Buster was shaggier and had floppier ears and his color was more like a muddy brown. Buster's tail was like a border collie's, and it made Duncan think of a giant feather duster.

Duncan wasn't supposed to give Buster any food at the table, but since he got away with it, he tried sneaking Buster another bite-sized piece of hot dog. This time his dad caught him. His dad, though, didn't get mad. Instead, he gave him a curious look.

"I thought this is your favorite dinner?" he asked.

"It's not. Mom's meat loaf with mashed potatoes and gravy is my favorite."

"Okay, I stand corrected. But it's your favorite I'm able to cook. Your mom deserves a night off from cooking, don't you think?"

Duncan nodded, since he knew that was true. He could hear his mom rushing around upstairs, getting ready for tonight. She was very pretty, prettier even than most women he'd see on TV. She was also thin and didn't weigh much, but noises carried and magnified in the house, and when she walked around upstairs it sounded like someone much heavier in army boots was stomping about.

"Are you upset we're not taking you with us tonight?"

Duncan couldn't believe his dad was asking him that. He knew this was their big night out and that his mom had been looking forward to it for weeks. How could his dad be so clueless as to why he was so upset?

"I'm nine years old," he said grudgingly, since he didn't think he should have to explain something so obvious. "I'm too big to have a babysitter."

"Come on, Duncan, you don't think I know that? But your mom…well, she worries too much sometimes. She wouldn't be able to enjoy herself tonight if we didn't have a babysitter, even though you and I know you don't need one. Don't you like Ella?"

Duncan did like Ella. She was what he imagined Mrs. Santa Claus looking like: A large, (although not tall) bosomy woman with white hair and rosy cheeks. When she hugged him it was like being swallowed up by a big, fluffy blanket. She baked a lot also, and whenever she came to their house, whether it was to babysit Duncan or to visit Duncan's mom, she always brought something good to eat. Maybe that was why Duncan thought she always smelled like apple pie, even if she brought over her homemade chocolate chip cookies.

Duncan felt better after his dad confided in him the real reason Ella was coming over to babysit. He also got his appetite back and soon was licking his plate clean.

"I wonder what Ella will be bringing over tonight?" he asked somewhat sheepishly.

"Whatever it is, I'm sure it will be freshly baked and I'm sure it will taste good."

Duncan was sure of that also. He then heard footsteps descending the stairs, and seconds later his mom walked into the kitchen. Duncan had never seen his mom dressed up like that before. She wasn't just very pretty right then, but glamorous, like a movie star, and he told his mom that. She blushed and told him he had to say that because they were related.

"The boy's right," his dad said. "You take my breath away just looking at you."

"Hush now," she said, her blush deepening. To change the subject, she started fretting about whether they'd get to their dinner reservation on time. "Traffic to Joplin can be a snail's pace, especially if a truck breaks down on I-forty-nine. It's been known to happen, you know!"

"We've got over an hour and the drive's only thirty-five minutes, even with bad traffic. Sue, honey, you got nothing to fret about."

The doorbell rang almost as if on cue. Ella. Duncan found himself hoping she had baked a cherry pie for the occasion. He could sure fancy a slice of that now!

Buster rose to his feet and trotted out of the kitchen and toward the door, his big feather-duster tail wagging back and forth. Duncan's dad followed after the dog. Duncan's mom came over to him and showed him a lopsided smile—the type that always made him feel good just to see.

"Sweetie, I'll miss you tonight," she said.

"I'll be okay," he said. "Me and Buster will keep the house safe."

"I'm sure you two will."

She reached down, pushed his hair aside, and kissed him on the forehead. His mom usually didn't wear any makeup, but this was a special night and she had put on lipstick. Duncan was sure she had left a smudge on him, but he didn't mind. He reached for her hand.

"Let's go see what Ella brought," he said with a sly grin.

Normally, he wouldn't want to be seen holding his mom's hand. That was something little kids did. Or girls. But this was a special night for his mom, and he was feeling much better after learning the truth about why Ella was babysitting him tonight. And so he walked to the front door with his mom, not caring at all what anyone might think. If any of his friends from school were there he might've acted differently, but it would just be his dad, Ella, and Buster, and he could trust them.

It was Ella who had rung the doorbell. She was chatting excitedly with Duncan's dad, her face flushed while his dad was holding a plate covered with tinfoil. Ella spotted Duncan and his mom and she gushed over both of them, first engulfing Duncan in a hug (and today Duncan thought she smelled like vanilla and butterscotch), and then taking hold of Duncan's mom's hands and talking about what a wonderful time she was sure Sue was going to have.

"Ten-year anniversary! Well, doesn't time fly! I remember when you and Tom moved in here, and Duncan was no bigger than an acorn squash!"

"Ella, I can't thank you enough for making the time to be here tonight with Duncan."

Ella looked shocked at that. "Of course I'd be here tonight!" she exclaimed breathlessly. "Why wouldn't I want to spend the evening with my favorite boy in the world!"

Duncan knew that couldn't be true. Ella had three children of her own. All of them were now older than Duncan's parents, and they had sons and daughters of their own. Still, even though he knew Ella was exaggerating, he liked hearing it. His mouth also began to water. Whatever Ella had brought smelled awfully good. Ella caught him looking at the plate his dad was holding, and she told him to go ahead and have one already.

"I found a recipe for something called blondies," she said, cheerfully. "They're sort of like brownies, but different."

Duncan peeled away the tinfoil and took one of the thick rectangular pastries arranged on it. He found it gooey and delicious.

"It's really good," he said. "Mom, you should try one."

Ella was beaming. His mom said that it smelled wonderful and that she'd have one when they got home later. "You don't want me to ruin my appetite for later, do you?"

Duncan agreed that wouldn't be a smart thing to do, especially since he knew his parents were going to a fancy restaurant, something he couldn't remember them ever doing before. His dad left them so he could put the plate of blondies in the kitchen and while he was gone, his mom gave Ella a piece of paper with the name of the restaurant and a phone number to call, then she hugged and kissed Duncan and headed outside so she could warm up the car. When Duncan's dad came back to the door, he handed Duncan two comic books that he must've hidden earlier. The most recent copies of *Wolverine* and the *Uncanny X-Men*. The *Wolverine* comic book had the Incredible Hulk on the cover, Duncan's favorite comic book superhero.

"I thought you could use something special tonight also," he said, winking at Duncan and tousling his hair. "Just don't tell your mom, okay?"

Since Duncan turned nine, his mom wanted him reading regular books instead of comic books. He promised his dad he wouldn't say a word about it. Ella promised that her lips were sealed also. His dad grinned at both of them as he left the house. Ella and Duncan headed back upstairs.

Duncan shared another blondie with Ella (she warned him that if he ate a second full one he might suffer a stomachache), read both comic books twice, then played Ella in checkers before she told him it was time for him to get ready for bed. He was brushing his teeth when he heard someone knocking on the door. It was a harsh, violent sound. Without fully understanding it, he knew it was a bad omen. That no good could come of someone knocking on a door like that, especially late at night. He left his toothbrush in the bathroom and headed downstairs.

Ella was at the door talking to two policemen. Her back was turned to him, but she was standing funny. Brittle, like she might fall apart. That was what Duncan thought. When he saw the grave expressions on the policemen's faces, his stomach began hurting as if he had drunk sour milk. Ella must've heard him, because she turned to face him. She looked stricken. Like she had just heard the worst news in the world.

"Is my mom okay?" he asked, his voice tinny and sounding like it must've come from a boy much smaller than himself.

He asked only about his mom, not because he didn't care about his dad, but because his dad was tough and powerfully built, and because of that Duncan believed he was invincible. His mom was different. Not that she was weak, but she was so slender and delicate-looking and Duncan didn't think he could stand it if anything bad ever happened to her.

Duncan's question only made Ella look more stricken. She rushed to him, hugging him so tightly she could've almost smothered him. She was crying and telling him how sorry she was. He didn't feel the wetness from her tears or even his small body being pressed into hers. He was too numb right then to feel anything.

Chapter 29

Jasper, Missouri. April 2000

Duncan's parents died when a truck drove into them. The Mosses were heading south on I-49 when the truck driving in the northbound lane drifted into their path. This happened too suddenly for Tom Moss to maneuver his Chevy Impala to safety, and he and his wife were killed instantly, their car crushed like a tin can. The driver in the truck, Arnold Nagly, suffered only minor bumps and bruises, and the incident was later ruled an unfortunate accident. Nagly had fallen asleep due to fatigue from driving nonstop for eighteen hours.

Duncan didn't learn all this right away, and some of it he didn't discover until years afterwards. For the first eight days after the accident he was too numb to pay much attention to what was being said around him. Those were eight terrible days, although he'd have much worse later, but during that time he was too numb to feel anything and whenever anyone spoke to him it was as if they were talking to him through a windstorm and their voices would fade in and out. There were moments also when he'd start to panic and feel like he was drowning. It was a crazy feeling, since he wouldn't be in water, but that was what it was like. Those moments would sneak up on him. They never lasted long and afterwards he'd be left desperately trying to catch his breath, as if he couldn't draw enough air into his lungs.

It was two days after the double funeral for his parents that he finally broke out of the numbness shrouding him and was more like his normal self. Not that he was happy or anything. He was sadder than he had ever imagined possible, but at least he could breathe more easily and was able to understand what people were saying. Things that he heard during those eight days had sunk in, even if he hadn't been aware of it. Fragments anyway, and slowly he began recalling some of it.

Ella and her husband, Mr. Hubble, had brought him to their home and he remembered a woman with short red hair and a long, pointy chin who came to ask him about his relatives. He remembered Ella and Mr. Hubble sitting at the table with him, Ella looking like she was fretting and Mr. Hubble deep in thought. Duncan couldn't remember what he told this woman, but it couldn't have been much. He knew his mom had had an older brother who worked on oil rigs and died in a fire before Duncan was born. He also knew that his grandma and grandpa on his mom's side died when he was little and he couldn't remember much about them. As far as he knew that was her only family. He didn't know anything about his dad's family. When he was seven he asked his mom about it and she told him that it was a subject he shouldn't ever talk about. That it would only make his dad sad.

It was two days after Duncan broke out of his numbness that he overheard Ella and Mr. Hubble talking about him. They thought he was asleep, but he had gotten out of bed for a glass of water and had walked to the kitchen, being extra-quiet about it. It wasn't that he was being sneaky, but he didn't want Ella catching him and fretting about him and asking if he was having nightmares. He didn't much like anyone asking him any questions since his parents died. Buster, who had stuck by his side almost every minute since the accident, followed him to the kitchen, and was also being quiet. Ella and Mr. Hubble were in the living room, and she was talking about how she wanted the two of them to adopt Duncan, and Mr. Hubble said that he wouldn't be opposed to it, but that they had to wait to see if Children's Services were able to locate any of Duncan's family. That surprised Duncan. Mr. Hubble was usually aloof around him, like he didn't much understand him, but since the accident he looked at him differently, almost with a softness, and at times he would put his hand on Duncan's shoulder like he was trying to be reassuring.

"That's ridiculous," Ella retorted angrily. "Duncan wouldn't know any family they might dig up. He knows us! Sue and Tom would want us to take care of him!"

"That might be so, but they didn't arrange for us to be guardians, and so the law has to be followed."

"Blast the law!"

"Now Ella, don't get yourself overheated. They most likely won't find anyone." Mr. Hubble hemmed and hawed then, as if he were trying to find the right words to use so he wouldn't offend her. "But they might also think we're too old to adopt the boy."

Ella made a loud harrumphing noise that would've woken Duncan up if he were still asleep.

"Too old! We still got good years left!"

Mr. Hubble had the good sense not to argue the point any further. Duncan went back to bed without getting his water. He had a lot on his mind all of a sudden. He had been too busy mourning his mom and dad to think about the consequences of what had happened, or even to realize the simple fact that he was now an orphan. As he mulled over the thought of being raised by Ella and Mr. Hubble, he realized that was the best possible situation. They were good people—they had to be, since his parents liked and trusted them. He had also met their grown children and grandchildren, and got along fine with them. If he lived with them he'd also be able to keep his friends and stay in the same school. What happened to his parents was terrible and it would leave a hole in his heart, but he knew his parents would be happy knowing Ella and Mr. Hubble were looking out for him.

For the next three weeks Duncan's life seemed to settle into a new kind of normalcy. He returned back to school and even got permission to bring Buster with him. There were afternoons when he'd need to be alone with Buster, but there would be other times when he would play with friends as if everything was okay. None of his friends mentioned his parents or the accident, and that was fine with him. In the evening Ella would fuss over him and make him his favorite dinners, and Mr. Hubble taught him how to play gin rummy and gave him a sip of beer once, although he had to promise he wouldn't tell Ella about it. One night Ella and Mr. Hubble even asked him how he'd feel about living with them permanently, and he told them he'd like that.

It was after those three weeks that things changed. Ella began to act as if she were distracted all the time, and Duncan would catch her muttering angrily to herself when she didn't realize he was in the room. Five days later he came home from school and heard Ella and Mr. Hubble arguing heatedly in the kitchen. Ella was saying it wasn't fair, that something had to be wrong with this man having a different last name than Tom, and that she'd use a shotgun on him if he showed up at their house. Mr. Hubble soon got just as upset and insisted that she couldn't act crazy like that, and that they'd see a lawyer and do whatever was lawful. When Duncan walked into the kitchen and they realized he was there, they stopped talking and they both looked sick to their stomachs. Mr. Hubble cleared his throat and asked him if he remembered Ms. Frost from Children's Services. Duncan was in a haze when he met the woman with the red hair and thin, pointy chin, but he told Mr. Hubble that he remembered her.

"She'll be coming by tomorrow afternoon," he said. "Best that you don't go to school tomorrow so you're here when she shows up."

Duncan knew what it had to be about. The authorities must've tracked down one of his relatives. He found himself scared and excited at the same time. This relative might be like his mom or dad, and the truth was, he'd give anything to have either of them back, even if it was only a small piece of them. But he was also beginning to feel at home with Ella and Mr. Hubble, and the thought of possibly leaving them made him anxious. He knew if he asked any questions right then he'd make Ella upset, so he simply nodded okay and left the kitchen with Buster tagging along beside him.

The next day Ms. Frost showed up as promised, bringing along with her a man who Duncan knew had to be his grandpa on his dad's side. The man was taller, lankier, and more sinewy than Duncan's dad, and his face was longer and craggier, making Duncan think of a bloodhound. But he had his dad's large ears and a similar look around the eyes and nose and the same hairline. He also had large, knuckled hands that were heavily veined like his dad. He held out his right hand to Duncan.

"Frank Wainwright," he said, his voice sounding like loose gravel.

"Duncan Moss," Duncan said somewhat shyly. "Pleased to meet you, sir."

Wainwright seemed amused by that. "You don't got to call me *sir*," he said. "We ain't in the military and I ain't no officer. Frank is fine." His brow wrinkled as he more carefully studied Duncan. "You don't look at all like Tom. You must take after your mom."

Duncan wasn't sure that was true. He might've been thin and short, but that was only because he was nine. He was sure he'd grow to look like his dad. Before he could argue that point, Ella began talking even faster than usual, suggesting they get this meeting over with so they could all get back to what they were doing. She must've been taken aback by seeing Wainwright, because she didn't offer coffee or her freshly baked molasses chew cookies to anyone after they took seats around the kitchen table.

"I thought you were coming by yourself," she asked Ms. Frost with a forced cheerfulness. "I thought today was to talk about what's best for Duncan. After what just happened, he shouldn't be uprooted. It's important that he stay in the same neighborhood and be in a supportive environment."

"What's important is the boy be with his kin," Wainwright said.

Up until then it seemed as if Ella had purposely refused to look Wainwright's way, but after that she did, and as she stared at him the color bled out of her cheeks and she began trembling.

"Are you going to keep Duncan in his parents' house?" she asked.

"What I do with him is no concern of yours."

Her trembling stopped and her eyes grew small and hard. Duncan didn't think right then that she looked anything like Mrs. Santa Claus.

"In all the years I knew Tom, he never once mentioned you," she said, her voice so deep and harsh that Duncan thought for a moment someone else must've been talking. "How come that is? And how come he changed his name from yours?"

Wainwright didn't answer her. He sat as still as a chunk of granite, his eyes darker and duller than dirt.

Ella turned to Ms. Frost. "Something's wrong with this man," she insisted. "It's obvious just to look at him."

Ms. Frost didn't exactly roll her eyes, but she might as well have. "Mrs. Hubble, I understand your concerns, I truly do. But the law requires us to unite Duncan with a family member, if possible—"

"For Heaven's sake, he's not a family member! For the last nine years he could've been dead, for all Duncan knew. He never once visited or showed any interest in him!"

Ms. Frost appeared unmoved. "Mr. Wainwright is showing interest now," she said. "There's really nothing to discuss here. We appreciate you looking after Duncan like you have, but the adoption rules are straightforward in these matters."

Wainwright didn't exactly sneer at Ella, but his upper lip curled, revealing large, yellowed canines.

The color went clean out of Ella's face. "I see," she murmured. She stood up and without another word left the room.

"This really is for the best," Ms. Frost said to Mr. Hubble, keeping her voice low so Ella wouldn't hear her. "Given your and Mrs. Hubble's ages, it's doubtful an adoption would've been approved, and most likely Duncan would've ended up in foster care—"

Ms. Frost was interrupted by Ella returning to the room carrying a shotgun. She loaded a shell, pumped the shotgun to chamber the shell, and was lifting the barrel toward Wainwright when Mr. Hubble knocked her to the floor and attempted to wrestle the gun away from her.

"Ella, what are you doing! What are you doing!" Mr. Hubble shouted as the two of them thrashed about on the floor. He got the upper hand and was able to yank the shotgun away from her. Ella began weeping.

Ms. Frost goggled at them, too frozen in fear to move.

Wainwright had left his chair so he could dive for cover if necessary. "The old bat's as crazy as a loon," he exclaimed heatedly to Ms. Frost.

"You saw what she just did. Threatened me with a shotgun. I ain't letting the boy stay in this loony bin another second."

Wainwright grabbed Duncan by the upper arm and half-dragged him out of the house. Buster followed along after them.

Chapter 30

Years later, Duncan would marvel when he thought about how Wainwright had picked clean his family's old home. At the time he was too swept up in the upheaval swirling around him and kept too busy by Wainwright to notice, but whenever he thought back about it, he had to admit it was quite something.

Those first few days Wainwright didn't talk to him much, nor did he invite conversation, but he did concede to answer Duncan when the boy asked about whether they were going to stay in Jasper by telling him that living in some hick town wasn't his idea of paradise. Right away Wainwright had Duncan inventorying the family's possessions and packing it away in boxes. He kept Duncan working late into the night and told him there was no point in him going to school, since he wouldn't be there long. Wainwright would disappear for hours at a stretch, at times bringing back men in trucks who'd cart away furniture or the packed-away boxes (after first inspecting them). Wainwright came back one day furious that the house was mortgaged for more money than it was worth. After that, he sold off the appliances and fixtures, and later that night he began tearing up the walls so he could pull out the copper plumbing. With the plumbing being torn apart and the toilets already carted away, Duncan asked him how he was supposed to go to the bathroom. Wainwright, who was straining to yank out a length of pipe, told him to just pick a room he didn't plan to go back into and that if he asked him another fool question he'd knock out a mouthful of his teeth.

Wainwright seemed in a better mood once he got the last of the copper pipes out of the wall. He chuckled to himself about what the bank was going to find when they foreclosed on the house. That evening a pickup truck came by, and Wainwright and Duncan helped the driver load the pipes into the back of it. Money was exchanged and after the man drove off, Wainwright told Duncan to get his suitcase, that they were heading off to greener pastures. Earlier, Wainwright had Duncan pack whatever he wanted to keep into a suitcase, telling him that it was important for a man not to be encumbered by possessions. "Anything more than you can pack in a single suitcase just slows you down," he claimed.

Duncan went back into the house to get his suitcase, and he realized that Buster wasn't anywhere to be seen. As he thought about it, he realized he hadn't seen his dog since last night—that Wainwright had been running him too ragged to notice until now. When he came back outside, he told Wainwright that Buster was missing.

Wainwright had the car's hood popped open and was checking the dipstick to make sure the car's oil level was sufficient. Without looking up, he grunted out, "The dog was scratching at the door last night to get out. Damn thing must've decided to run away. Good riddance, if you ask me."

Duncan realized what happened. Buster must've gone to Ella's to get a good meal, since Wainwright was barely giving the dog any scraps at all, and he warned Duncan what would happen if he gave the dog any of his food—not that Duncan was being given all that much himself.

"He must be at Ella's!" Duncan exclaimed. "We have to go there and get him!"

Wainwright pulled his head out from under the hood and wiped his hands clean with a hand towel. "Uh-uh, boy. We're not wasting time looking for some mangy mongrel."

"We have to—"

Wainwright rapped Duncan across the mouth with one of his large-knuckled hands. The slap was hard enough that it sent Duncan on his butt and had him seeing a burst of fireworks in his head.

"You don't ever back-talk me again. You understand that, boy? Now get in the car now."

Duncan sat stunned. He had never been struck by an adult before. His dad didn't believe in it; neither did his mom. He was never even spanked when he was a little kid, not even a single slap on the rear. He picked himself off the ground, spat out some blood, and meekly did as Wainwright had ordered.

Neither of them spoke during the five and a half hours while Wainwright drove. At times Duncan would doze off, too exhausted to keep his eyes open, but then he'd wake up after only ten or so minutes with an overwhelming sense of dread, and he'd remember about Wainwright. He'd wince from the throbbing in his swollen jaw, and he'd remember the glazed look in Wainwright's eye when the man struck him, and how Wainwright had sold off everything of value his family owned. Worse than just that, he tore apart their home and left gaping holes in the walls. Duncan considered what Wainwright did a desecration, something that would've made his mom cry if she had been alive to see it. Worse than even all that, he made Duncan leave Buster behind! He was only nine, but he'd be damned if he was going to willingly say a word to this man.

He was awake when he saw the sign on the side of the highway welcoming them to Nebraska, and later also the sign letting them know that they were entering the city of Lincoln.

Wainwright pulled into a motel parking lot. After he put the car in *park*, his gaze slid over to Duncan and he broke into a wheezing laugh over what he saw.

"Boy, I thought you were sleeping all this time. You going to give me the silent treatment, is that it?" he said as he wiped away a tear. "That's just fine with me. I'd rather have silence out of you than hear you yapping about anything. Grab your suitcase or don't. I truly don't care. But this is where we're staying tonight."

Chapter 31

Duncan had never seen so many people gathered in one place before. Easily thousands were milling about the fairgrounds as they looked at prized cows, draft horses, hogs, roosters, and other farm animals. There were quite a few other attractions, contests, and demonstrations, as well as carnival rides and games for suckers who thought they were going to win a stuffed animal, but were really just throwing away their money. What amazed Duncan the most was how everybody seemed to be eating something as they walked around. Fried dough. Corn dogs. Deep-fried turkey legs. Cotton candy. Pizza slices. Ice cream treats. Or if they weren't eating something, they were waiting in line to buy something to eat. Or in some cases, they were already stuffing their faces as they waited to buy something else.

If he were here with his parents, Duncan would've liked it. His parents, also. He would've wanted to go on the bumper cars and Tilt-A-Whirl, and he'd be eating a chili dog and soft-serve vanilla ice cream on a waffle cone. But he was already a different person. He'd only been with Wainwright for a year and three months, but that was more than enough to change anyone.

He shielded his eyes as he peered up toward the sun. It had to be at least ninety degrees already. The hot weather wasn't stopping people from coming to the state fair, but it kept them from wearing jackets, which made picking pockets all that much easier. The heat mixed with the humidity also helped distract them. It made them uncomfortable and sweaty, and less likely to notice when an eleven-year-old boy (Duncan's birthday was in June) with small, slender hands lifted their wallets from their back pockets. Wainwright insisted that even if they lollygagged they should be able to hit fifty marks that day, and if they applied themselves, they could take as many as a hundred wallets. If you figured each wallet had at least fifty dollars in it, they should walk away today with between 2500 and 5000 dollars—at least, that was what Wainwright claimed. He called these state fairs gold mines, and promised that if they did well enough over the next three days, they could take the next month off, maybe even rent a cabin by the Lake of the Ozarks. Duncan had never heard of the Lake of the Ozarks before, but he liked the sound of it.

Wainwright was right then engaging one of the "rubes," as he called them: A heavyset man wearing cargo shorts, the outline of his wallet visible in his back pocket. Standing next to the rube was an equally heavy woman, who must've been his wife, and two heavy kids, who must've been his children. Since Wainwright had trained him, Duncan had already lifted hundreds of wallets. He wasn't ready last year for the county fairs, so those thefts were entirely on city sidewalks where the marks were alert and often already had their hackles up, as if they expected every stranger was out to rob them, and because of that it was trickier and Duncan and Wainwright had to be more careful and sometimes they spent an entire afternoon looking for the right pocket to pick.

According to Wainwright, picking pockets here would be like shooting fish in a barrel. That these rubes were all in good spirits and they'd be the trusting types who would naturally think the best of their fellow state fairgoer. When Wainwright and Duncan operated in the city, they'd use the bump-and-run technique where Wainwright would *accidentally* bump into a mark hard enough where he'd almost knock them over—in fact, he'd grab onto them to make sure they wouldn't fall and give them enough of a jostle at the same time, so they wouldn't feel Duncan slipping their wallet out of their back pocket. It didn't always work. Sometimes the mark would react violently enough to being bumped that Duncan wouldn't have an opportunity to take his wallet, and sometimes Wainwright would give him a last-second signal that someone was watching and he needed to veer off. No one yet had caught him in the act of stealing a wallet. The many hours of practice Wainwright put him through were seemingly paying off.

They weren't going to use the bump-and-run today, at least not much. Instead, when Wainwright found a mark, he was simply going to ask them an innocent question, such as where one of the exhibits was located, and then distract them with additional conversation. He figured that these rural Kansas types would be too polite not to engage back. As long as no one was watching, it would be safe for Duncan to walk behind the mark and relieve him of his wallet. He'd just have to do so without breaking stride or acting suspiciously.

No one was watching.

The mark and his family were laughing at a joke Wainwright must've just told. Duncan was impressed that someone as mean as him could turn on the charm when needed. Duncan took a deep breath. Now was as good a time as any. He walked behind the mark and, in a quick, deft motion, slipped the mark's wallet out of his back pocket and tucked it under his shirt. He was walking away when a hand clamped down on his arm. Wainwright had told him what to do if that happened. Punch the guy in the nuts and run as if the devil were after him. Except it wasn't a guy who had grabbed onto his arm, but a woman. It startled him so much to see a woman staring at him sternly without a hint of pity that he lost his chance to break free. She dragged him over to the mark.

"This boy's got sticky fingers," she said loudly enough not only to get the mark and his family to turn around, but for other people to look over also. She took the wallet from under Duncan's shirt and handed it back to the mark. "I believe this is yours," she said.

Wainwright had been noticing this, but so had a small mob who encircled him. The mark at first gave Duncan a puzzled look. Soon his look hardened into something close to disgust. He shoved the wallet back into his pocket and turned to glare angrily at Wainwright. Others were also staring at Wainwright.

"This something you and the boy are doing together?" the mark accused.

"Friend, I don't know what you're talking about." Wainwright held up his hands in a *let's-be-calm* gesture and tried to back up, but a few large farm-boy types had gotten behind him and blocked his path. One of them made a grab for Wainwright, and Wainwright surprised him by turning on his heels and smacking him in the mouth with a hard jab. It didn't knock the man down, but it made him stumble backwards and left him with a bloody mouth. Another of these farm boys moved toward Wainwright, but Wainwright had taken a switchblade from his pocket and began waving the seven-inch blade in a wide arc. This made the crowd back up and when Wainwright lunged at the woman who was still holding onto Duncan's arm, she let go and stumbled backwards. She quickly lost her footing and fell hard on her butt.

Duncan ran then. So did Wainwright. When they got to the car, the two of them jumped in, and Wainwright took off like a bat out of hell, the tires kicking up several pounds of dirt. A mob had chased after them, but they were too far back to stop them.

For a half hour, Wainwright sped along the country roads, too preoccupied looking for any police cars that might be on his trail to pay any attention to Duncan. Once he was convinced that the police weren't after them, he began seething.

"You intentionally trying to get us caught?" he accused. "Is that it, boy?"

Duncan was seething also. Not over Wainwright's accusation, which was too ridiculous to even address, but because it had been Wainwright's responsibility to signal him if there was anyone standing behind him who could've been watching what he was up to. This was on Wainwright, not him!

"If you hadn't been so cheap and bought me cotton candy or soda or something I could've been holding, that's what that lady would've been looking at instead of me taking the wallet," Duncan complained irritably. "It's your fault I got caught and you know it!"

"You better watch your mouth, boy!"

"Or what? You're going to knock my teeth out? You can only do that once."

Wainwright was fuming too intensely to respond, his knuckles white as he gripped the wheel. Duncan didn't much care whether Wainwright hit him or not. He knew Wainwright was to blame for what happened at the fairgrounds, and he was furious about it. He'd been looking forward to spending a month at a lake, and he knew that wasn't going to happen now.

For the next hour they drove in an icy silence. All at once Wainwright broke into a wheezing laugh.

"Did you see the look on their faces when I waved that pig sticker around?" he said. "That was something, wasn't it, boy?"

Duncan knew that was as close to an apology as he would ever hear from Wainwright, so he met him halfway and admitted that it was something.

Wainwright's laugh died down. He wiped a tear that had leaked out from his eye. "The look on that bitch's face when I showed her my pig sticker up close was worth the price of admission. She went paler than a glass of milk. Fell hard enough on her ass that I felt the earth shake."

"I bet she left a big stinker in her pants."

"I wouldn't doubt it. I wouldn't doubt it either if that good ol' boy I popped needs some serious dental work. Ah hell, boy, money ain't everything. At least we got to see that."

They both seemed to relax after that. Wainwright stopped grinding his teeth and began holding onto the steering wheel loosely with one hand. Duncan found himself giggling when he thought about the scene at the fairgrounds. Wainwright might've transformed him into a hardened criminal, but deep down inside he was still only an eleven-year-old boy.

Duncan was soon absently staring out the window and watching as they drove past what seemed like endless miles of cornfields. Wainwright interrupted his daydreaming by telling him that even though they might've had some fun, today wasn't a good day.

"I was counting on that money," he said. "We won't be able to show our faces back at those fairgrounds tomorrow or anytime soon, and we won't be able to make enough money lifting wallets like we'd been doing. We'll have to do something else. But don't worry. I've got some other ideas."

Wainwright had spoken to Duncan more in that one day than the past fifteen months combined. It made Duncan feel better. He even found himself feeling an attachment to this miserable sonofabitch. Wainwright was his grandpa, after all. And if he squinted real hard, he could see his dad in Wainwright's features.

Chapter 32

They were in the Crown Heights neighborhood of Wichita, and the house Wainwright had taken them to looked bigger and ritzier than any Duncan had ever seen. Nothing like it in Jasper, that was for sure!

It was a little after two in the morning and Wainwright had opened a broken window for a first-floor bathroom that was in the back of the house, and he lowered Duncan to the floor inside of it. The reason the bathroom window was broken was a man named Earl Sarkosky broke it when he was at the house a month earlier installing some fancy closets. Sarkosky's side business was sizing up homes to rob, making sure there'd be an easy entry by making copies of keys or breaking window latches, and selling the information to criminals like Wainwright. When he went over the job with Wainwright, he told him where the jewelry could be found, and he also warned Wainwright that the owners had a guard dog.

"A mean mother," Sarkosky had said. "Some sort of shepherd. All black. Big teeth."

"That's all right." Wainwright winked at Duncan. "The boy's got a fondness for dogs."

Duncan wasn't entirely sure that was true. He'd liked Buster all right, but he didn't want to deal with a mean dog with big teeth. Later, when he expressed his concern, Wainwright seemed amused by it.

"Don't worry, boy. That's what the hamburger will be for. You just feed it to that dog and he'll be asleep in no time." Wainwright winked at him. "I been taking you along slow this past year or so, but you'll be poppin' your cherry tonight. Your first home robbery."

All that happened only five hours ago. Now Duncan was in a strange family's bathroom with a small ball of hamburger meat, inside of which were two sleeping pills, and he was worrying. Trembling, actually. Like he had a bad case of the flu. What left his heart thumping wildly in his chest was the thought of coming face-to-face with a big, mean dog with sharp teeth.

The bathroom door was closed. He held his breath and tried to listen for a dog growling. Nothing. But would he have been able to hear anything over the pounding of his heart? He turned around, thinking he'd go back out the window, but Wainwright had already closed it. Wainwright had also brought his gun along, and had told him that if Duncan wasn't able to rob the family quietly, he'd go in there with his gun and rob them more noisily, and Duncan knew that meant people getting shot. He didn't want to be responsible for that. He moved as quietly as he could to the door, and turned the knob ever-so-slowly so it wouldn't make a clicking sound. The door, though, made a squeaking noise, the hinges needing oil. The squeaking probably wasn't that loud, but it made Duncan jump as if an owl had screeched in his ear.

He opened the door enough to step into the hallway. The dog stood silently waiting for him, its yellowish-orange eyes shining in the darkness. The animal was close enough to Duncan that he could see it was as big as advertised. Before he could react, the dog knocked him to the floor and stood over him, its fangs bared and inches from his throat. Drool from the beast dripped onto Duncan's face, the animal's breath hot and smelling like rotting garbage. Duncan was too scared to cry. Really, too scared to do anything. He remembered the hamburger meat and somehow willed his arm to hold up the meat to the dog. He clenched his eyes shut, expecting his hand to be torn off and chewed up with the meat, but the dog stopped its snarling long enough to take the meat, and it did so without hurting Duncan.

For the next several minutes the dog continued to stand over him and growl fiercely, but the animal otherwise didn't hurt him. The dog's face was close enough to Duncan's that he could see when the eyes began to lose focus, and it wasn't long after that that the dog wobbled drunkenly and then fell to the floor. Duncan wondered at first whether Wainwright had lied to him, and instead of using sleeping pills had poisoned the hamburger meat, but the dog appeared to be sleeping.

Duncan scrambled to his feet. He was too jittery right then to continue on to the bedroom upstairs so he could steal the jewelry hidden away up there. The intense fear he had suffered also left him faint with hunger.

There was enough ambient light in the room for him to see the dog's rib cage rising up and down as the dog slept, and once he convinced himself that the dog wouldn't be any further threat, he went searching for the kitchen.

He found sliced ham, Swiss cheese, mayonnaise, and a loaf of white bread in the refrigerator. Also root beer. He knew Wainwright was outside hiding in the bushes. Well, he could just wait! After what Duncan had just gone through, he deserved to take whatever time was needed to calm his nerves.

He made himself a sandwich, chewed each bite carefully, and drank the root beer from the can. After that, he climbed onto one of the countertops so he could search the upper cabinets, and he found a box of Hostess cupcakes. He ate two of them, licked his fingers clean, and then decided he'd better get the jewelry before the dog woke up.

Duncan's eyes had adjusted enough to the darkness so that he could move around the house without needing to turn on any lights or to use the penlight Wainwright had given him. Sarkosky had told Wainwright that the master bedroom was the first one on the right at the top of the stairs. The door was closed, but this one didn't squeak when Duncan inched it open. The room was darker than the rest of the house, and he considered using the penlight, but after a minute he could make out two large lumps under the covers in the bed. He also heard heavy snoring coming from one of the lumps.

Sarkosky had drawn a rough map of the room so Duncan would be able to find the wife's jewelry box with his eyes closed, if needed. Duncan, being careful not to make a sound, headed toward a dresser where the box was hidden in the second drawer. He was halfway there when the sound of someone stirring in bed froze him. The noise grew louder, and he turned to see the darkened shape of the husband sitting up.

Duncan dropped to the floor and crawled on his belly until he was under the bed. If the man had heard or seen him, it was going to be bad. Earlier, when they were waiting for it to get late enough, Wainwright sat in the car, drinking rye whiskey from the bottle, and when he drank, he got meaner than his usual ornery self. Wainwright wanted that jewelry, and if he heard trouble inside the house, he'd be climbing through the broken window and he'd use the gun. Duncan had no doubt about that.

The husband must not have seen him, because Duncan saw him plodding out of the room. Minutes later he heard a toilet flushing, and then the plodding footsteps of the husband returning. The bed sagged as the man climbed back into it, and Duncan held his breath until he thought he was going to pass out. Soon, though, he heard snoring again, and although his heart was racing even faster than before, he crawled out from under the bed and found the jewelry box. He also took the man's wallet and the women's pocketbook, both of which had been left on top of the dresser. As far as he could tell, as he made his way down the stairs, the man and his wife were still sleeping. As he had arranged with Wainwright, he left through the front door and found Wainwright in the bushes in the back of the house. He handed him back his penlight and everything he had stolen. Wainwright seemed impressed that he had had the foresight to steal the wallet and pocketbook also.

Wainwright used the penlight to make sure everything he was expecting to find was in the jewelry box.

"You did good, boy," Wainwright said after his inspection. "No problems in there, huh?"

"I thought that dog was going to rip my throat out."

"He didn't, so quit your complaining."

Whatever good mood Wainwright had temporarily slipped into was gone. He headed back to where he had parked the car three blocks away, and Duncan followed along behind him, making sure to keep his distance.

Chapter 33

Lindsey Bushnell looked miserable as she sat in one of the interrogation rooms at the Wilcox Avenue precinct and told Morris about the circumstances that led to her finding George and Meagan Campbell inside their house earlier that morning.

"George and I work together, and for the last year we've been involved—"

"Involved, as in you two having a romantic affair?"

"That's right." She sat slumped in her chair and chewed on her lower lip. Several times already she had tried to make eye contact with Morris and failed each time. She tried once more and was once more unable to meet his gaze. "Six months ago his wife found out about it and moved out right afterwards. George promised me after his divorce we would get married, but it turns out he was just stringing me along. A week ago out of the blue he broke it off with me. No explanation. Nothing."

"That must've pissed you off."

"I was too stunned to be angry. I didn't know what was going on with him, and thought it was only a phase he was going through. To be honest, I'd convinced myself he'd be calling me back later and apologizing. When George wasn't at work yesterday, I wormed it out of Bob what was going on."

"Bob?"

"Sorry. Bob Doltrice. He works with us and is buddies with George, and he told me that George was spending the day with his wife, and that he'd been trying to reconcile with her ever since she moved out on him."

"Now that must've pissed you off."

Her expression turned bleaker, but she was able to meet Morris's gaze then.

"I felt like I'd been punched in the face," she said. "I realized that I had been his backup plan. That if he couldn't win his wife back he'd settle for me. For most of the day I was in a daze and couldn't think or feel much of anything, but by the evening I started to get angry. I was at my friend Sam's. The two of us were drinking wine and having a bitch session, and I borrowed her phone so I could send George some pretty mean texts."

Morris had seen them and agreed with her assessment. "Sam?"

"Samantha Rigby. My best friend since college."

"Why'd you use her phone?" he asked.

She gave him a puzzled look as if she couldn't understand why he'd ask something so obvious. "George had blocked my number."

Morris already knew the text messages had gone unanswered. "What happened next?"

"I hung around with Sam until one, then went back to my place, but I couldn't sleep. I just kept thinking about how George had lied to me over the last six months. I know I was only being spiteful, but I wanted his wife to know about his lies. So I went to his house this morning, hoping to confront them, and that's when I found them."

The memory of what she found caused her to shudder.

"How'd you know Meagan Campbell would be there?"

"I didn't know she'd be there. It was just something I felt in my gut." She winced, almost as if she were experiencing a small part of what Meagan Campbell had gone through. "It was so awful what was done to her. I almost fainted."

Annie Walsh's partner, Greg Malevich, had already met with Bushnell's friend, and she confirmed that Bushnell had been at her apartment until one. If it weren't for that, Morris might've thought Bushnell had been stalking Campbell, and if that had happened she could've seen the killer enter the house.

"How'd you get inside the house?" he asked. "Was the front door left unlocked?"

She gave a miserable attempt at smiling. "I handed George back his key when he broke up with me, but I had made a copy."

Morris gave her a hard look as he considered whether she could've been involved in the murder. They already knew from the first victim's fiancé, Alex Frey, that the killer was a man and even with a ski mask on nobody could've mistaken Lindsey Bushnell for a man, but there was still a chance she had paid for the killings—and it wouldn't be the first time someone tried to hide a murder by orchestrating what looked like a serial killer at work. Nor would she be the first person who hired a killer who'd want to see up close and personal what she had paid for.

That scenario only made sense, though, if she found out about Campbell getting back together with his wife before Saturday, which was when Alex Frey and Jill Kincade were attacked. It was possible that Campbell told her the truth when he broke up with her. Or she could've stalked him. And if that was the case, she could've hired a killer to watch Campbell's house for Meagan Campbell's return. Morris didn't think this scenario was likely. In fact, he thought it was far-fetched, but during his years as an LAPD homicide detective, he'd seen even more bizarre scenarios turn out to be what happened. And even though she seemed genuine enough, he had over the years interviewed other killers who had seemed genuine enough. They were going to have to dig into Lindsey Bushnell's background and her banking and phone records before they'd be able to completely eliminate her as a suspect.

"I've been here for almost three hours and have been cooperating fully." Bushnell smiled tragically, the events of the day leaving her face puffy. "And if it wasn't for my stupid impulsiveness, George and his wife still might not have been found. I'd really like to go home, smoke some weed, take a long bath, and try to forget what I saw in that kitchen. How about it? Please?"

"Not quite yet. I have a few more questions."

Chapter 34

The Grace Warren missing-person's investigation was put on hold, and at three o'clock a large gathering filled up MBI's lone conference room. Morris, Charlie Bogle, Philip Stonehedge, Dennis Polk, and Adam Felger were joined by Roger Smichen, Doug Gilman, FBI profiler Gloria Finston, Annie Walsh, Greg Malevich, and three other LAPD homicide detectives. And of course, Parker, who after he excitedly made the rounds and greeted many of the people in the room, lay like a lump under the table at Morris's feet.

Annie Walsh gave a rundown of what the LAPD had so far. The first victims, Alex Frey and Jill Kincade, had an engagement party at a ritzy Bel-Air hotel that ran between 2:00 p.m. and 5:30 p.m. on Saturday. That night, at roughly 7:20, a deliveryman for Roma's Pizza named Joaquin Alvarez was knocked unconscious when he was delivering a pizza to a Santa Monica apartment building. His attacker left behind Alvarez's wallet and other valuables, including a cell phone, and only took one of the pizzas from his car. Twenty minutes later a man claiming to be from Roma's Pizza rang the buzzer for Frey and Kincade's apartment. He was buzzed into the building and soon knocked on their door. According to Frey, he looked out the security peephole and saw a man holding a Roma's pizza box—

Bogle interrupted Walsh, asking whether they knew for a fact that it was the same pizza taken from Alvarez's car.

"We do. The pizza box had an order number scribbled on it, and the box was left behind after the murder."

Polk asked, "Was any of it eaten?"

Walsh shot him an annoyed look, as if he were wasting their time with that question.

"Why would that be important?" she asked.

Polk's eyelids lowered a fraction of an inch as he gave her a deadpan look. "I heard they make a good pizza there," he said.

Gloria Finston cut in. "It's not a bad question. It would tell us something about the killer if he ate any of it at the apartment."

"The pizza was untouched," Walsh said. She continued with her report, describing what happened to Alex Frey and Jill Kincade after the killer forced his way into their apartment. Finston's eyes lit up when she heard about the offer Frey was given, but she held off asking any questions.

"Kincade's mother was worried about not being able to reach her daughter and she drove to the apartment the next morning and found Jill dead and Frey duct-taped to the chair and suffering a severe concussion," Walsh continued. "There's no video surveillance at the apartment building; we haven't found any witnesses yet who saw anyone entering or leaving the victims' apartment, same with no one seeing anyone masquerading as a pizza deliveryman in or outside the building. None of the neighbors heard anything unusual. A complete dead end so far. The description we got of the killer from Frey is suspect, since he claims his concussion left him unable to focus, but he told us the perp wore a Dodgers baseball cap pulled almost to his eyes when he forced his way into the apartment, and later after he woke up the killer was wearing a black ski mask to hide his face. Frey insists the killer had blue eyes and a tattoo of some sort on his right wrist—"

Morris's pulse picked up a beat. He asked, "A wolf baring its fangs?"

Walsh gave him a puzzled look. "How'd you come up with that?"

"A long shot. I'm working a missing-person's case where a suspect was identified by that type of tattoo on his wrist."

"I couldn't tell you what type the perp had. Frey claimed his vision was too blurry to make it out. He did, though, insist that the perp was in his twenties, even though he never got a good look at him without the ski mask. Also that the perp was somewhere between five ten and six feet in height, and with a lean body type."

"Which describes half of the hopeful actors who work as waiters and Uber drivers in this town," Bogle commented.

"Exactly." Walsh turned the floor over to Roger Smichen so he could go into more detail about what was done to Jill Kincade. While LA's chief medical examiner gave his findings, Morris glanced over at Gilman. His future son-in-law had tightly clenched his jaw, but otherwise appeared to be holding it together as he listened to the grisly details. After Smichen finished, Walsh went over the second attack. As with the first, there was no surveillance video and they didn't find any neighbors or other witnesses who saw the killer forcing his way into the victims' home. The assumption was that the killer either followed them from the Beverly Hills restaurant or waited for them outside their home, and viciously attacked George Campbell when he opened the door for him. Charlie Bogle looked incredulous when Walsh further explained how the victims were found that morning by Campbell's jilted lover.

"Damn suspicious, if you ask me," he said.

"It sounds bad," Morris agreed. "But I think it's only an unfortunate coincidence. Whether Lindsey Bushnell was wearing a ski mask, a Dodgers cap pulled down low, loose clothing, or any other disguise, I can't imagine Alex Frey or anyone else mistaking her for a man. I tracked down their coworker, Bob Doltrice, and he was convinced that Bushnell didn't know about Campbell trying to reconcile with his wife until Doltrice let it slip Monday afternoon. If this was some sort of convoluted revenge idea involving a hit man, it wouldn't fit with the first couple being attacked Saturday night. But maybe Gloria might have other ideas?"

Gloria Finston had worked with MBI on three previous serial killer investigations and had Morris's utmost respect, also the rest of the team's. The FBI profiler was a slight, dark-haired woman in her forties, and when she smiled her thin lips made a sharp V-shape. With her narrow face and longish, thin nose, she often reminded Morris of a sparrow. At that moment her small, pale blue eyes were deep in thought as she considered Morris's question. She turned to Roger Smichen and asked whether Meagan Campbell's torture and subsequent murder was similar to Jill Kincade's.

"Pretty much. Campbell suffered more cuts and stab wounds and her torture lasted longer, but that was only because her heart lasted longer."

"Were any of the wounds done postmortem?"

"Not that I can tell."

Finston next asked Walsh whether Campbell was offered the same unholy proposition as Alex Frey.

"We won't know for certain until Campbell is able to speak to us, but given the forensic evidence, there's a good chance that happened. Most likely in his case, he accepted the deal and tried to fight his attacker after he was cut free."

"That was when he was knocked unconscious?"

Smichen answered that. "For the second time that night, yes."

"What exactly was done to him then?"

"He was struck once in the jaw with a club of some sort. The blow knocked him off his feet and he struck his head when he fell. He's now in a coma, his condition critical."

Morris had earlier placed photographs of the murdered women on the conference room table. Meagan Campbell's photo was taken on her honeymoon and showed her in shorts and a T-shirt, smiling brightly. Jill Kincade's was taken a month before she was murdered, and in it she was smiling wickedly, as if she were dying to give the punch line to a joke. Both women were petite, around five feet one, although Kincade was curvier. While Kincade was a blonde and Campbell had reddish-brown–colored hair, they both had very pretty faces that were shaped similarly. Finston shifted her gaze to study the photos and as she did this, she rubbed her slight jaw, her eyes once again showing she was in deep thought. Polk interrupted the silence that had crept into the room.

"Gloria, you know I think you're tops in this profiling racket, but you're making this more complicated than it is," he said, his thick lips set in a shit-eating grin. "I'm no expert, but this looks textbook, if you ask me. Our killer's got mommy issues. Clear as day."

Polk was able to get away with that only because Fred Lemmon was out on assignment. While Lemmon was a former homicide detective now working as an investigator at MBI, he also took on the added responsibility of putting Polk in his place whenever he acted too obnoxiously. If he were in the room, he would've no doubt told Polk that nobody was asking for his opinion.

Finston, for her part, showed Polk one of her V smiles. "Dennis, I believe we must've read different textbooks. That's not what this is. The killer's targets were the men."

"Huh? That's why he stabbed two women to death?"

"Sadly, yes. Each cut and stab wound and disfigurement were meant to inflict psychological pain to the men who were forced to watch as they sat only feet away, bound and helpless. And the cruel deal that he offered them—"

"Assuming that he made that same offer to Campbell," Bogle pointed out.

"Until we learn otherwise, we should continue under that assumption, and that the killer's purpose of offering such a hopeless deal was so these men would suffer for years to come no matter which choice they made. Yes, Morris?"

Morris had scrunched his face into a pained expression, like he had a toothache. "If the men were who he really wanted to hurt, why didn't he follow through with his threat and break all of George Campbell's bones?"

"An excellent question, and I'm afraid I don't have a good answer. There's a piece to this puzzle that I'm missing," Finston said. "The offer he made to Alex Frey was just so sadistically cruel—either choke to death the woman he loved or watch her die an even worse death. This type of personality should've reacted with rage and violence over being defied, and he should've badly hurt Campbell afterwards, even if the man was unconscious, but there's something motivating him beyond wanting to make these men suffer."

"So we need to figure out what's motivating him."

"Correct. And to do that, we need a dialogue. We need to induce this killer to reach out to us. Or if not to us, to the media."

Morris saw several ways that could be done. Under his direction, Gilman's noon press conference provided little information other than two women were murdered, their addresses, and a hotline phone number.

"Let's see if we can frustrate this guy and give him as little media attention as possible," he said.

Gilman looked skeptical. "What if this psycho doesn't care about making headlines?" he asked.

"Then we'll try something else."

Chapter 35

Fred Lemmon followed his target, Wayne Hardacher, to a Van Nuys motel that advertised 59-dollar rooms and from the outside looked like the type of place where you'd need a tetanus shot immediately after entering any of the rooms. Hardacher's wife, Wendy, suspected that her husband was cheating on her, and she had hired MBI to find out. After four days of tailing Hardacher, it looked like Lemmon was about to hit pay dirt and it was about time! Morris had told him earlier about the serial killer investigation, and Lemmon was itching to get off this cheating-spouse case and onto something where he could do some good. Maybe he'd even get to spend some time with Annie Walsh…

He shook his head, angry at himself. How pathetic was it to daydream about something like that? But he couldn't help it. He had a hopeless crush on Annie—hopeless, because he wasn't yet prepared to walk away from his marriage, even though he and Corrine barely talked to each other anymore. Not that it would make much difference if he did end his marriage. He had over twelve years on Annie, which was just too much, especially given that she was such a knockout. Besides, Corrine was his high school sweetheart and the only woman he had ever dated. If he were single, he wouldn't know how to begin with Annie and would probably only humiliate himself. He gritted his teeth hard enough to make his jaw ache and resolved to quit thinking about anything as far-fetched as he and Annie ever becoming romantically involved. Besides, he had a target to keep an eye on.

Lemmon had parked half-a-block away on the other side of the street from the motel. He had a clear view of Hardacher's door, and with the high-performance telephoto lens attached to his Nikon camera, he'd have no problem taking a clear shot of Hardacher's girlfriend when she showed up. He knew it wouldn't be long. There wasn't much chance the girlfriend (or prostitute or whoever it was that Hardacher was planning to meet at the motel) would notice Lemmon in his car, but he still wanted to appear as inconspicuous as possible. He picked up the sports section of the *Los Angeles Times*, unfolded it, and all but disappeared inside of it. Now he was just some guy killing time instead of a private dick watching a motel room and waiting to take a photo.

He was right about it not taking long. He was camped out less than ten minutes when an older-model Oldsmobile drove into the motel parking lot and pulled into a spot near Hardacher's room. Lemmon had his camera ready and he snapped a couple of shots when the person left the car. It wasn't a woman, but a guy in his thirties with dirty blond hair wearing biker boots, faded jeans, a long-sleeved knit shirt, and a scuffed-up leather jacket. Lemmon watched as the man knocked on the door. It quickly opened and the man slipped into the room.

The shots Lemmon took were side views. He'd get some front shots when the guy left the room, but the photos he took were good enough for him to see that Hardacher's visitor had a definite hardness about him. The way the guy swaggered as he approached the motel-room door confirmed this. A tough bastard. Lemmon was sure the guy wasn't there for sex, but to do business. A bookie? Drugs, maybe?

Lemmon wanted a photo of the license plate, but the Oldsmobile was angled so that he couldn't get a clear view from where he was sitting. He left his car and jogged to a spot where the license plate was fully visible through the telephoto lens. After he snapped a shot, he headed back to his car before Hardacher or his visitor could notice him.

It was eleven minutes after entering the motel room that the tough-looking dude with the dirty blond hair left. Lemmon took three photos from the front as the man emerged from the room, and captured him smirking as he shoved a large envelope under his leather jacket.

Lemmon had a decision to make. Stay on Hardacher or follow this badass-looking mystery man. If he had come to the room to sell Hardacher drugs, there was a good chance Hardacher's girlfriend (or whoever he was seeing) would be arriving soon, and Lemmon hated the idea of throwing away four days of surveillance. He was torn. He knew that some sort of business had been conducted in the motel room, and if this guy had showed up to sell drugs, he wouldn't have needed to be in the room for eleven minutes unless he and Hardacher sat around shooting the bull for ten of them. Likewise with placing a bet. Lemmon also had an uneasy feeling about that envelope. There was probably cash in it, but also photos and other papers. Was it possible that Hardacher had hired a hit man, or was Lemmon jumping to conclusions?

Indecision froze him. He watched as the Oldsmobile left the parking lot and then drove off in the opposite direction from where he was sitting.

Well, he had several photos of this dangerous-looking dude. He also had the license plate. If necessary, he'd be able to track him down. For now, he needed to stay put and see whether Hardacher was meeting anyone else at the motel.

He called Morris to tell him about this latest development. "I know you're hot on the heels of a serial killer—"

"Not that hot," Morris said. "Barely any fumes yet. Right now we're just trying to pick up whatever lead we can."

Lemmon told Morris about Hardacher's visitor. "I don't want to sidetrack you, but my gut's screaming at me that Hardacher has bad intentions for whatever he paid this guy to do."

"You're thinking he hired the man to kill his wife?"

"I don't know. But it will help to find out whether Hardacher is having an affair, so I'll keep watching him for now and text you the photos. How about pulling some strings with Annie or whoever else owes you a favor inside the LAPD and find out from organized crime whether this guy's known as a contract killer? Also, ask if our friends at the LAPD could look up his plate and get me a name and address?"

"Will do."

Lemmon used the camera's built-in Wi-Fi to transfer the photos to his phone and then sent them to Morris. With that taken care of, he picked up a cup of coffee he had bought an hour earlier, worked off the lid, and made a face when he realized it was now lukewarm. What the hell. Lukewarm coffee was better than nothing. He was still drinking it when a late-model Prius pulled into the motel parking lot. Lemmon took several photos of the driver after she got out of the car. A skinny woman in her thirties with frizzy red hair. He only saw her through the telephoto lens in profile and from behind, but he thought she looked pretty. She was also dressed nicely, like she worked in a bank. If Polk was around, Lemmon would've offered the lummox ten-to-one odds the woman wasn't a prostitute and knowing Polk, he would've taken the bet.

He watched as she knocked on the motel-room door and took more photos when Hardacher greeted her with a passionate embrace and kiss. This wasn't a casual hookup. The two of them knew each other and were involved in a relationship.

After Hardacher and the woman disappeared into the motel room, Lemmon took a two-foot long lockout tool that he kept in his car and headed across the street. When he started on the force, he could slide a lockout tool—or as it was better known, a slim jim—through the driver's side window and get into any locked car in seconds. These days, most of the luxury cars were built to be impenetrable. But he could still get into a Prius with one, and it took him all of six seconds to unlock the passenger door. He found the registration in the glove compartment, and used his phone to snap a photo of it. He now had the girlfriend's name and address: Lauren Estleman, and she had a Sherman Oaks address.

Lemmon walked back to his car and called Morris to inform him that the client was right about her husband having an affair. "I've got photos, a name, and an address, but I'm worried about the dude who showed up earlier."

"I've already talked with Annie," Morris said. "She's got a request in to pull the registration for the license plate. Organized crime promised to call me back about whether the guy in your photos is known to them."

"Good. I know you want me on your serial killer investigation, but I need to stay on this for now. I'm going to tell the client my suspicions and see if she wants me to keep working on this until we know she's safe."

"That sounds like the right play. Let me know what she says."

Lemmon promised him he'd do exactly that. He next called Wendy Hardacher and arranged to meet her at a coffee shop near where she worked. She tried to get him to tell her over the phone what he found out, but this needed to be done in person. As he drove to their rendezvous point in Glendale, he couldn't help feeling somewhat envious of Morris. He had heard Annie in the background when he had Morris on the phone. So she was teamed up with him. What Lemmon would've given to change places with his boss right then, not that it would've done him a whit of good. Any feelings he had for Annie would need to stay bottled up and remain unrequited.

Chapter 36

Alex Frey sat in his hospital bed, his face swollen and bruised, his skin an unhealthy grayish pallor. The TV was off and when Morris, Walsh, and Parker entered the room, Frey was staring unblinkingly at the opposite wall and didn't acknowledge them, not even after Morris and Walsh pulled chairs up to his bed, or when Parker licked his hand. According to Frey's doctor, Frey was still suffering from concussion symptoms, but they wanted him to remain in the hospital under observation because of signs of severe depression.

During his years as an LAPD homicide detective, Morris learned early on that he needed to wall himself off from becoming emotionally involved with any of the victims; that otherwise he'd lose objectivity and it would adversely affect the investigation. This wall was breached almost the moment he saw Frey. Anger welled up within him as he thought about what the killer had done to this man and his fiancée. As he struggled to get his emotions under control, Frey turned to him and told him that his dog was getting his hand wet.

"Sorry about that." Morris pulled Parker back and introduced himself. Frey stared at him blankly before turning to look at Walsh. A glimmer of recognition showed in his eyes.

"I remember you." Frey's voice sounded heavy, stilted. He turned back to Morris. "I'm not sure I minded it. In fact, it might've actually felt comforting in a way to feel something other than grief. If you wouldn't mind, I think I'd like to pet your dog."

"Sure thing. His name's Parker."

Morris let the bull terrier edge forward, and Frey's hand found the top of Parker's head.

"His fur is very bristly," he remarked. "Like a hairbrush."

Morris said, "We're doing everything we can to find the person who hurt you and Ms. Kincade, but I need to ask you some questions, if you're up to it."

Frey's expression remained unchanged as he continued to lightly pet Parker. He said, "I don't know if there's anything more I can tell that I haven't told Detective Walsh, but I'll try."

"Was it you or Ms. Kincade who buzzed in the pizza-delivery guy?"

"You mean the piece of human garbage who attacked us and murdered Jill?"

"Yes."

Frey's mouth weakened. "I did."

Morris tried not to sound accusatory as he asked him why.

"Because he said he was from Roma's Pizza. That was Jill's and my favorite pizza place."

"But you didn't order a pizza. Why buzz him in?"

"He said that my brother Todd bought the pizza for us." Frey turned to look at Walsh. "I didn't tell you that before, did I? I wonder why I didn't remember that then?"

Walsh said, "It's understandable, given the circumstances." Her tone, though, showed she wasn't happy with herself for not ferreting that out earlier.

"It wasn't just that he knew about Roma's Pizza and my brother Todd, but he told us he brought a fig jam and prosciutto pie," Frey said. "He knew what our favorite pizza was."

Morris had a good idea why that was: The killer was at the engagement party. He asked Frey if he remembered seeing anyone he didn't know at the party. In response, Frey began sobbing. Parker let out a soft whimper and jumped up so that his front paws rested on the bed, and he pushed his nose toward Frey's face so he could lick him. Morris started to pull Parker back, but Frey, through his sobbing, asked him not to. After several minutes, Frey's sobbing came to a haltering stop and he gave Morris a look of pure, abject misery. Morris lifted Parker off the bed.

"I expected to live with Jill my whole life," he said, as if in a daze. "I could've saved her and I didn't even try."

"He put you in an impossible situation," Morris said. "You couldn't have done anything to help Jill."

More tears welled up in Frey's eyes. He gave Morris a beseeching look. "I could've had him cut me free. I could've tried fighting him. That's what you would've done."

"I would've done exactly what you did," Morris said. "I wouldn't want that person hurting my wife any worse than he was already doing, and I'd want to hold out hope that someone would come by to stop him."

Walsh placed a hand on Frey's shoulder. "This psycho killed another woman last night," she said. "It was the same circumstances as what happened with you and Jill. This time her husband had the psycho cut him free and tried to fight him. This is a guy who's big and athletic, and he didn't stand a chance. You wouldn't have had a chance either."

Alex Frey gave Walsh a pained look. "Did that poor woman suffer worse than Jill?"

"Yes."

"Oh, dear lord." Frey appeared stunned, then his face crumbled. "I should've been stronger. I should've ended Jill's suffering. Because of me she suffered worse than she had to."

Frey appeared to disappear into himself after that. Morris never got an answer to his question about whether Frey noticed any strangers at the engagement party. He knew there had to have been at least one, but he didn't press any further. He was concerned that his questioning might push Alex Frey into a worse place, if that was even possible. Walsh was concerned enough also that she got Frey's doctor, who, after a quick examination, sedated his patient. The doctor then asked for Morris and Walsh to leave. Parker was stubborn about doing so and Morris had to coax the bull terrier out of the room.

"That psycho crashed their engagement party," Walsh told Morris as they took the elevator to the lobby. A redness peppering her cheeks showed her anger over that happening.

"I'll get Polk looking into that," Morris said.

"That was kind of sweet the way Parker acted in there."

Morris was surprised by Walsh. Usually she was tough as nails, and he would've thought she'd be more annoyed than anything else that he had brought Parker into the hospital room.

He said, "The little guy's a sensitive soul, at least when he's not mooching food."

He wasn't sure Walsh had heard him. She appeared deep in thought and chewed silently on the inside of her gum as the elevator descended to the lobby. It wasn't until they were outside and walking to his car that she let him in on what had been absorbing her.

"If that had been you, would you have really been able to watch Natalie being cut and stabbed with a knife without doing anything?"

The truth was Morris couldn't say what he would've done. He blew out a lungful of air. "God knows," he admitted.

Chapter 37

Jack Readinger walked into the downtown LA bar feeling good about how his day had gone so far. Earlier at the Van Nuys motel, he saw a scam he'd been working on for over a week come to fruition when he ripped off the mark for two grand, but that was only the beginning. He was going to take so much more from that soft white-collar fool before he was done. The sucker, a guy by the name of Wayne Hardacher, thought he was making a down payment on a hit on his wife, expecting to pay another two grand when the job was done. While Readinger had no problem icing anyone for two grand, he didn't need to do that now. He had placed a pocket-sized digital voice recorder in the inside pocket of his leather jacket, and Hardacher had a big mouth and incriminated himself enough inside the motel room that Readinger would now be able to use the threat of sending the recording to the police to squeeze Hardacher dry. It might take months, because something like this needed a slow, patient hand, but before he was done he was going to empty Hardacher's bank accounts and make the idiot murder his wife himself for the insurance money so he could keep paying Readinger off. It was going to be the gift that kept on giving.

Yes indeed, an outstanding day so far! And as further proof that things were once again going his way, the Mountain Man was working behind the bar. Readinger might've been the only one who called him that, but the name fit. The Lumberjack wouldn't have been a bad name either. A big, stocky barrel-chested man with long, unruly red hair and an even unrulier beard and mustache who always wore a red-checkered flannel shirt and jeans. Odds were that he was also wearing his steel-toe work boots so he could stomp the bejesus out of any misbehaving patrons.

Readinger stood until his eyes adjusted to the dimness inside the room, and then took a seat at the bar. When the Mountain Man looked his way, he sniffed loudly and made an exaggerated motion of rubbing his nose. He waited until the bartender approached him before telling him that he was looking for an eight ball.

"Pool table's in the back," the bartender deadpanned.

"You're a funny guy and you know damn well that's not the kind I'm looking for." Readinger lowered his voice and edged closer to make sure no one else could hear him. "You still got Petty on call, right?"

Wilfred Petty was a skinny-assed punk who had the type of ravaged look of someone who had done way too much crack at one point in his life: Long, greasy blond hair, hollowed-out face, terrible complexion. But the guy could always be counted on to deliver coke that wasn't cut on too severely, and the Mountain Man had hooked Readinger up with Petty on a number of occasions. This time, though, the bartender stayed silent. Readinger made a disgusted face as he worked his wallet out of his back pocket, plucked a twenty-dollar bill from a thick stack of others, and placed the bill on the bar. The bartender picked it up, slipped the twenty into his shirt pocket, and asked Readinger what he wanted to drink while he waited for Petty's arrival.

"Jack and Coke."

Readinger normally didn't like diluting his whiskey with anything, but he was in the mood for something refreshing, and he also wanted to drive home the point of what he was really there for. He'd been feeling sluggish since leaving the Van Nuys motel and he could use the pick-me-up that a couple of snorts would provide. The Mountain Man poured the drink and gave him a suspicious look when he asked Readinger if he wanted to start a tab. That was just plain rude. Readinger had always paid his bills there and the bartender had seen that he was loaded. He didn't have a good reason for thinking that Readinger would skip on his tab today, other than long ago sizing Readinger up and knowing full well what type of person he was. Because of that and his good fortune so far that day, Readinger decided to be generous and not take too much offense after all.

He was working on his third Jack and Coke when Petty arrived. Readinger caught the drug dealer's eye, gave a head signal, and the two of them went to the men's room, where they did business. Readinger waited until Petty finished counting his money before suggesting that Petty give him his phone number so that he could buy coke from him directly without having to go through the Mountain Man. Petty gave him a glazed, dead-eyed stare back in response.

"That's not going to happen," he said.

Readinger decided he couldn't blame Petty for that. If he ever got Petty alone and didn't have to worry about the Mountain Man and his steel-toed work boots doing a number on him, he probably would tie him up and torture Petty to get the location of his stash. Why not? He'd done the same to other coke dealers in the past who were foolish enough to meet him privately.

Petty left the men's room. Readinger locked the door once Petty was gone and tested out the coke, doing four hits. Damn, what a truly exceptional day he was having! He still had over 1800 dollars in his wallet and he was going to be squeezing so much more out of Hardacher. He planned to utterly ruin the man's life, and there was nothing Readinger liked better than sharing the pain.

He snorted one more hit of coke, made sure his nostrils were clean, and left the men's room with a bounce in his step. A nice-looking dish was occupying the barstool next to the one he'd been sitting on earlier. The woman was in her twenties and had kind of a hippie look about her, with long, dark-brown hair that fell well past her shoulders, darkened granny-style glasses, and several cheap glass earrings sticking in each earlobe. She was wearing a flower-patterned sundress and as he got closer, he could see that she was skinnier than he usually liked and had small tits, but she also had soft, full lips and was more than pretty enough, even with a heavy despondency that showed in her eyes and in the way her shoulders slumped. He felt his pulse quicken as he noticed that. A possible honeypot? He wasn't sure, but even if she wasn't one, she looked like she'd been having a bad few days, which left her vulnerable and ripe for the picking—at least as long as Readinger played his cards right. Whichever it turned out to be—a full-fledged honeypot or a quick hookup—he planned to give it his best shot.

He caught her glancing his way when he sat back on his barstool. He lifted the glass he had left on the bar that held half of a Jack and Coke, and made a show of examining it.

"You didn't drink any of this, did you?" he accused, a glint of violence in his eyes.

She looked too startled by the accusation to respond. Readinger broke out laughing.

"Just messing with you," he said. A hard grin etched on his face. He held out his hand. "Jack," he said.

Somewhat reluctantly, she took his hand and told him her name was Audrey.

His grin turned wolfish. "That was pretty mean of me, huh?" he said. "Scaring you like that."

Some hurt showed on her gorgeous, pouty lips. "It wasn't very nice," she agreed.

"I know," he conceded. "But you can't really blame me. It's just been one of those near-perfect days where everything just seems to be going right and it's put me in a playful mood."

He waited for her to ask him about everything that had been going right for him that day. When she didn't, he volunteered the information.

"First, a bet I made paid off big, leaving over eighteen hundred dollars burning a hole in my pocket. Second, I come back from the men's room, and the hottest-looking babe I've seen in months is sitting on the barstool next to mine."

That melted her a bit, at least enough for her to blush. "You're quite the bullshitter," she said.

"I can be," he admitted. "But not about the money I got in my wallet, and not about how delicious-looking I find you."

He gave her a look like he wanted nothing more than to lick every inch of her body. She should've gotten off the barstool and walked away then, but she was too damaged and instead stayed where she was, her blush deepening. He leaned toward her so he could put his lips right against her ear and whisper into it, and he felt the hotness of her skin when he did this.

"In my other pocket I got a bag of something white and powdery that will make us both feel wonderful. Are you game?"

He pulled enough of the baggie out of his pocket so she could see what it had inside.

She nodded. It was a slight movement. Almost imperceptible. But he knew right then he had her. Later that night, after she was drunk and out of her mind on coke, he would bring her back to his apartment and he'd spend hours, possibly even days, humiliating her and doing whatever was necessary to transform her into a full-fledged honeypot. Assuming she wasn't one already.

The irony. He didn't need a honeypot now that he had a cash cow like Hardacher to milk, but life was so much more pleasurable whenever he had a honeypot squirming under his thumb.

He got off the stool, offered her his hand, and led her to a back room where they could have some privacy.

Chapter 38

Morris stood in the kitchen of the Marina del Rey apartment and looked over the room in which Jill Kincade had been brutally murdered. The chairs Frey and Kincade had been bound to with duct tape were seven feet apart and positioned so that Frey would have been facing his fiancée throughout the ordeal. It was the same setup as the Meagan Campbell murder.

When they first arrived at the apartment, Walsh walked Morris through the attack, explaining how it was almost a carbon copy of what happened to the Campbells; the killer first surprising and incapacitating Alex Frey, then chasing down Jill Kincade. The savageness unleashed in both attacks made Morris think of a kill-crazy mountain lion that had found its way into a sheep pen. Later, after the victims were bound and helpless, the killer's actions became more methodical, as if he were following a script as he cut and stabbed Kincade. The very first thing he did with Jill Kincade, and most likely also with Meagan Campbell, was cut off her nipples. Was there an underlying reason for that, or simply to shock and horrify Frey? After the initial mutilation, the cut and stab wounds were mostly superficial at first, at least according to Roger Smichen's examination, but by the end became vicious and disfiguring.

Morris wondered about that also. Was the killer hoping that Frey would take him up on his offer and end Kincade's life before she suffered the worst of her gruesome injuries? Or was it to give Frey false hope that Kincade might survive if he tried waiting out the attack, and to inflict the greatest amount of psychological pain?

They had come to the apartment for two reasons: First, so that he could get a sense of the murder site and pick up vibes about the killer, and secondly to find a list of the engagement party attendees, because it seemed likely that the killer had crashed the engagement party. At least that scenario could explain how he knew about Frey's brother and the couple's favorite pizza.

Morris's train of thought was interrupted by Annie Walsh calling out to him from the bedroom. He left the kitchen and brought Parker with him to the apartment's only bedroom. The look on Walsh's face showed that she'd found something.

"The invitation list?" he asked.

"Not yet. But worst case, we should be able to put one together from the gift cards. Take a look at this."

She pointed out the two cheesy coffee mugs for the "world's cutest couple" that had been left on a small pile of wrapping paper.

Morris frowned as he looked at them. Parker seemed interested in them also and Morris had to keep the bull terrier on a short leash to stop him from grabbing one of them.

"It could've been a gag gift," he said.

"There's the box they came in," Walsh said, nudging an empty box on the floor with her toe. "I didn't find a matching gift card. Frey had told me during our first interview that Jill, being a highly organized person, had scribbled the matching present in all the opened cards, and none of them mention any ugly-ass coffee mugs."

Morris's frown deepened. He took a photo of one of the mugs and texted it to Gloria Finston, then got the FBI profiler on the phone and put it on speaker so Walsh could listen in.

"Did you see the photo I sent you?" he asked.

"Of a sickeningly-sweet chintzy coffee mug?"

"Yep, that's the one. Would our killer bring a matching set of these to Frey and Kincade's engagement party?"

"Was a card attached?"

"Not that we could find."

"My professional opinion, yes. He wouldn't want to crash the party empty-handed and risk undue attention, and he'd find the gift a perverse joke, given what he was planning to do to the engaged couple."

Walsh grumbled under her breath, "Funny, I thought I said the same, but in fewer words."

Parker grunted in sympathy.

Morris ignored both of them. Earlier, he had arranged with Margot Denoir for Finston to appear that night on a special prime-time *Hollywood Peeper*, since Finston thought if she were to put out a bogus and insulting motive for the killer, he might contact them to correct the record, and Margot thought having a scoop on the new serial killer plaguing LA would bring in massive ratings, so it was a win-win for both sides. He asked whether she should mention the coffee mugs on TV tonight.

"If we show a photo of it, someone might remember selling a pair to our killer and save us a day or two," he said. "It could also put the killer in a panic and make him think we're breathing down his neck. I just don't know if that's what we want to do with him. It could make him more cautious."

"Or it could have the opposite effect," Finston said. "I still don't have that missing puzzle piece I need to better understand what's motivating him, but if he starts feeling cornered he might strike out more violently than he's been doing. That's my sense with the limited information I have. I believe for now we're better off proceeding quietly, and that the most we want to push him is to see whether we can coax him into contacting us."

"You're the expert," Morris conceded. "Be careful with Margot tonight. She's more ruthless than she looks. I adore her and have known her for years, but when the camera's rolling, you should think of her as a blond piranha in high heels. The woman's a pro and no one's better at going for the jugular once she smells blood."

Morris could imagine Finston smiling her tiny V-shaped smile as she told him she'd be on the lookout for any traps Margot might try laying for her. After he got off the phone, he told Walsh they needed to find the stores in the area selling these mugs.

"I'll get Greg on it," she said, referring to Greg Malevich. "This psycho screwed up buying them. He screwed up even worse if he had them gift-wrapped at the store. The employee doing it would remember that."

"The store might also have video surveillance."

"Which means we need to get right on this," she said.

If anything, she was downplaying the urgency of the matter. Many of the stores with video surveillance only kept their video for a few days before erasing it. This meant the team would be working late into the night, tracking down the stores in the area that sold these godawful mugs with the hope of finding video of the killer while it still existed.

While Walsh got Malevich on the phone, Morris had Parker lay down and he then started collecting the cards from the unopened presents. Some were taped to the outside of the gift, others were left inside the box. Each guest needed to be interviewed and all photos taken at the party needed to be collected. Walsh finished talking with Malevich and joined him.

"How'd you get Parker to behave himself?" she asked. "I would've thought he'd be trying to muck around in this mess you're making."

It wasn't that much of a mess. Morris was carefully unwrapping the gifts, digging out the cards, and flattening out the wrapping paper in a single pile. Still, that was exactly the type of thing a curious bull terrier would want to stick his nose into, and instead Parker was lying on his side. The dog lifted his bullet-shaped head at the sound of his name.

Morris said, "It's getting close to d-i-n-n-e-r-t-i-m-e, so the little guy's going to be on his best behavior. The one time of day when he actually listens to me."

Parker dropped his head back to the floor and let out a low groan, as if he suspected he was being unfairly maligned.

After they successfully collected all the cards, Morris called Natalie to tell her he would be working late, but promised to be home by midnight.

"This killer made a mistake," he told her.

"You picked up his scent."

Natalie didn't say this as a joke. She thought of him as having a sort of bloodhound instinct—that once he picked up the right clue, the perpetrator was as good as caught.

"Almost," he said.

Chapter 39

Margot Denoir took her seat five minutes before airtime. She offered a sleek, well-manicured hand to Gloria Finston and breathlessly apologized for not being able to chat more before the show.

"Morris, bless him, scheduled this at the last possible minute," she complained, her words tumbling out in rapid-fire. "It will be a miracle if we're able to pull this show off without a major catastrophe. God, I must look a mess. I barely had any time for makeup."

The stage crew was rushing around the set, but as far as Finston could tell, things were under control. The show's producers had gotten their hands on a wedding photo of George and Meagan Campbell and also a photo of Alex Frey and Jill Kincade beaming happily with their arms wrapped around each other's waists, and had blown them up so they'd be prominently in the background. As far as Margot Denoir looking like a mess, quite the opposite. She was stunning in a brilliant red dress and high heels that showed off gorgeous calves. Her makeup had been expertly applied, and her big, blond poofy hair looked almost shellacked so that not a single strand would fall out of place, not even if a hurricane struck. Denoir was in her late forties and had at least five years on Finston, but she also had a lithe, size-two dancer's body and an ageless beauty about her, and Finston looked downright frumpy by comparison. Of course, that was the point of the comment. To make sure Finston recognized how frumpy she looked in her dark gray suit, sensible shoes, unstylish haircut, and no makeup other than a small amount of blush. Anything to gain a psychological edge.

Finston smiled thinly. It was never a good idea to engage in psychological warfare with an expert. "I'm sure we'll have your TV audience so enthralled that they won't notice the laugh lines."

Alarm flashed in Denoir's eyes over the prospect of an imperfection showing through her layers of makeup, but then she caught on to what Finston was doing. She looked suitably impressed, as if she was realizing how badly she had underestimated Finston earlier.

"I'm sure you're right," Denoir said, straight-faced. "But what matters is that we inform the public about this horrible Cupid Killer. And, of course, do what we can to aid in his capture."

Finston hadn't heard that name before. "Why the Cupid Killer?" she asked, genuinely curious.

Denoir seemed pleased with herself. "I came up with the name myself, and will be unveiling it tonight. Quite fitting, don't you think, given how this animal targets such attractive young couples who are so deeply in love?"

"The Campbells were separated."

"I heard they were in the process of reconciling," Denoir stated, casually brushing off Finston's comment. "Besides, the name tested off the charts with our focus group. By tomorrow, that's what everyone will be calling this psychotic monster."

The director interrupted them, signaling that they would be going live in thirty seconds. Denoir picked up a sheet crammed with notes so she could give it one last look, while Finston was left pondering the accuracy of that name. Even though Jill Frey and Meagan Campbell were a similar type—both short, petite and very pretty, with similarly shaped faces, she was convinced that the killer's true targets were Alex Frey and George Campbell; that he was torturing and killing the women only to inflict mental anguish on the men. Because of that, she'd been trying to figure out what Frey and Campbell had in common besides being in their twenties, well-off, and good-looking. She hadn't considered that the killer chose them also because they appeared to be happy and in love with a certain type of woman. The killer might not have known that the Campbells were separated, or about George Campbell's recent affair. He might've simply seen them at the Beverly Hills restaurant where the couple dined Monday night and picked them because Campbell fit his other requirements and that the couple seemed happy together, or he might've latched onto them earlier that day for the same reason. If that was what happened, it meant the killer acted impulsively, quickly choosing his victims, as opposed to stalking them over a period of days. Which meant he'd be killing again soon...

The cameraman began using his fingers to count down from five. Finston's mind was racing with these thoughts and she barely paid attention as Denoir introduced her and launched into her spiel about the Cupid Killer. She felt as if she could almost grasp onto the missing puzzle piece that would allow her to see what was truly motivating this person.

"Is it true that this fiend tortures the woman with a knife while he forces her partner to watch?"

Denoir asked this innocently enough, but Finston caught a trace of a *gotcha* look from her. The police hadn't released that detail to the media yet. It was possible that the *Hollywood Peeper* staff had gotten it from a hospital worker who had overheard Alex Frey, or even from a family member. It was also possible that it had been leaked by someone within the LAPD. Morris had warned her that he suspected Commissioner Hadley of feeding Denoir information in exchange for favorable treatment. Anyway, she couldn't see any harm in admitting the truth about this, and when she did, she caught a glimmer in Denoir's eyes that told her there were more leaks.

Denoir leaned toward Finston, a look of horror coming over her face as she asked whether this fiend cut the nipples off both women. Finston had to admit to herself that Morris was right. This woman was good. The tremble in her voice was impressive, but even more so was the way her face seemed to drain of color, and how she appeared to be waiting with bated breath for Finston's answer.

"The salacious details of what this killer does aren't important," Finston said. "What is important is understanding what motivates him. That's what will help us to build a profile that will lead to his capture."

If Denoir was disappointed by the answer, or lack of such, she didn't show it. Not even a blink. Instead, she continued her bated breath act as she played along and asked what motivated this animal.

"I'm afraid it's rather cliché. He's got mommy issues." Finston's smile sharpened as she thought about how Dennis Polk would react if he were watching this special edition of *Hollywood Peeper* and heard her say that. *That's right, Dennis, this one is for you.* "He needs to murder his mother over and over again."

Finston was rather pleased with that answer—not only because Polk would be spitting coffee out of his nose (or beer, or whatever he might be drinking) if he were watching, but that it served two other purposes: One, it was so off base and flat-out wrong that it would cause the killer to think they were incompetent, and lead to overconfidence and him making mistakes; and two, it might tempt him to reach out to set the record straight.

Her answer also caused Denoir to blink—both figuratively and literally. She couldn't have been happy that it contradicted the Cupid Killer name she invented.

Denoir made a sour face and said, "That sounds a bit clichéd."

"Clichés exist for a reason."

"You don't think that he's doing what he is because he can't stand seeing these couples who are madly in love and have their whole lives to look forward to?"

Finston was impressed with Denoir's insight, but while that was partially true, there was still a missing piece to the puzzle that would explain the killer's true motivation, because there was something else driving him.

Finston smiled sadly at the TV host and lied, saying, "Sorry, but it's the mommy-issue thing."

Denoir didn't want to give up that easily. "Why did he tie up the men and make them watch?"

"Because of his impotency, which he blames on his mother."

Denoir's jaw dropped. "He's killing these women because of a limp dick?"

"Exactly."

Denoir's cheeks reddened as she realized she had accidentally said *limp dick* on the air. That was a no-no. Instead of arguing any further about how implausible she found Finston's theory about the killer, she asked whether Finston had been able to deduce anything else about the Cupid Killer. Denoir wasn't willing to give up on the name, even if it no longer fit based on what the FBI profiler claimed.

"From a witness description, he's in his twenties, has blue eyes, is six feet tall, and between a hundred and sixty and a hundred and seventy pounds." Finston didn't mention the tattoo on the underside of the killer's right wrist, because Alex Frey was not able to describe it due to his concussion. It was possible it was a smudge or birthmark instead, and besides, without being able to describe the tattoo, she'd be drawing suspicion upon potentially hundreds, if not thousands, of millennials living in Los Angeles, which could have the added consequence of sending the police on numerous wild goose chases. "As I have already mentioned, he's impotent and rages about his mother, which he carefully hides from others. He can appear charming and can fit into a social gathering without raising suspicions. He's also impulsive and violent. This is a very dangerous individual and people need to stay alert."

Denoir asked, "How are they supposed to do that?"

"He'll be looking for more couples to victimize. People need to pay extra attention to whether anyone is stalking them, and if you believe someone is, do not approach this person. Instead, go into the nearest store or restaurant and call the police. People need to exercise extreme caution."

Finston purposely didn't explicitly warn people about not opening their doors to strangers. She knew if she did that and the killer was watching, he would stop gaining entry into his victims' home by knocking, and instead would be breaking his way in. At least now there was a chance the next time he knocked on a door, the intended victim would call the police.

"This person's a monster," Margot Denoir said with a shiver that Finston could tell was genuine and not part of her act. "If you let him into your home, it's like you're letting in a wild, savage animal."

The FBI profiler couldn't disagree with her.

Chapter 40

It was after two a.m. when Jack Readinger, with Audrey in tow, pulled into the parking lot of one of the ubiquitous twenty-four-hour convenience stores dotting the Los Angeles landscape. Audrey's full name turned out to be Audrey Zairn, and Readinger liked the symmetry of her initials. From A to Z. That was how he planned to mess up her life: From A to Z.

After loosening her up with shots of tequila and hits of coke, he learned her whole sad story, which wasn't all that different from thousands of other young women moving to Los Angeles with dreams of stardom. She had arrived from her hometown of Des Moines, Iowa, two years earlier, and since then had gotten small roles in a handful of commercials, but not enough to work steadily or to quit her waitressing job, and had become jaded after being turned down for TV and movie roles because her tits were too small, or her legs were too skinny, her eyes were the wrong color, or any other number of arbitrary reasons. At least, that was what they were telling her, but she understood that it was because she was refusing to take their hints and get on her knees for the decision makers, and more and more the hints weren't all that subtle.

She had reached her breaking point yesterday when a producer, who all but promised her the role for a new sitcom after two callbacks, invited her to his hotel suite so they could further discuss the part. He insisted then that he needed to see her naked from the waist down before he'd be able to make a decision. Fighting back tears, she took off her jeans, but fled the suite while she still had her panties on. On top of all that, she found out only a few days before that her creep boyfriend was cheating on her and she was absolutely sick of the tiny one-bedroom roach-infested apartment in K-Town she was sharing with two other hopeful actresses, both of whom were cold fishes. She had gone to the downtown bar that night to decide once and for all whether to give up on her dreams and take a bus back to Des Moines. But then she met Readinger.

Jack fished out of his pocket what was left of his eight ball. Audrey was already coked to the gills, but as they sat in the car he coaxed her into taking another hit.

"Ready?" he asked.

She giggled. "Ready, Freddy."

He grinned at her. "Girl, you're going to be an outlaw soon."

"I already am!"

Sometime around nine that evening they left the bar after Audrey kept insisting that she was a good girl who had never even stolen a stick of gum. She even crossed her heart and hoped to die over that fact. "Well, that just ain't right," Readinger insisted, and he took her to a department store so she could shoplift a couple of scarves. She was drunk and coked up enough that she agreed to do this, and the theft excited her. She grabbed the two scarves Readinger told her to take and they ran out of the department store, Audrey acting like a giddy teenager, her skin flushing bright pink. Readinger put a hand to her cheek and felt like he was touching a furnace. She didn't ask what the scarves were for, and instead joined him in a motel room where they silently shed their clothes and went at each other like a couple of dogs in heat. When they were done and had their clothes back on, Readinger made sure not to pour any more booze into her. As it was, she was going to have a wicked hangover the next day, and he didn't want her passing out on him. Instead, they stuck with the coke. Later, after they had left the motel, he made two stops before driving to the convenience store; the first so he could steal license plates and put them on his car, the second so he could buy a .32 caliber pistol.

He tied a scarf around the lower half of his face like he was a bandit, and gave Audrey the other one so she could do the same. He checked the pistol to make sure the safety was off and that there was a bullet in the chamber, and then slapped the gun into Audrey's hand.

"You follow my lead in there, okay, tough girl?"

He left the car and Audrey followed after him, giggling like a schoolgirl. Once inside, Readinger barked at Audrey to point the gun at the startled employee working behind the cash register, and to shoot him in the head if he moved a muscle. Audrey giggled crazily, too coked-up to question him or care, and she lifted the gun so it was aimed at the employee's face. There was no one else in the store. Readinger bolted for the counter and cleared it as if he were vaulting a pommel horse. The employee, a skinny man in his forties with a thick five-o'clock shadow and a mop of dirty unruly black hair, had his hands up.

"Take the money," the man said. "No sweat to me. It's not mine—"

Readinger hit him in the nose with a hard jab, dropping the man like a sack of bricks. The man had a woozy look in his eyes as he stared up at Readinger, blood oozing from his busted nose.

Readinger flexed his hand. *Sharing the pain*, he thought with a hard grin. He ordered Audrey to get closer so she could hold the gun on the man as he lay on the floor.

"You see him move, you shoot him," he growled at her as he emptied the cash register.

Audrey's eyes became pinpoints as she stared at the man bleeding on the floor. In her coke-fueled haze she must've been looking at him as if he were every sleazy Hollywood producer who'd been trying to make her suck their cocks for her big break. She might not have even realized that her finger was tightening on the trigger—it could've been only a physical reaction from the adrenaline rush, but Readinger could see it happening and he kept quiet. The gun sounded like a cannon when it went off, and the bullet made a bloody mess of the man's left shoulder. The man started moaning like he was dying, and Audrey began laughing hysterically.

Readinger had noticed the surveillance cameras and he also spotted the closet where he knew the surveillance equipment would be kept. He could've gotten into the closet and destroyed the videotape or the disk drive, depending on when the equipment was last updated, but he left it, and instead jumped the counter and dragged Audrey out of the store.

At some point she would be crashing hard, and when she woke up she might think this was all a bad dream. Or at least she would hope that was the case. But Readinger would find the video of the robbery and shooting online, and he'd make sure she'd watch it.

She might not have been a full-fledged honeypot when he met her earlier that evening, but she was now. And he owned her ass.

Goddamn, what a hellaciously fantastic day he was having!

Chapter 41

Oakland, the present

Charlie Bogle took a six a.m. flight to Oakland, rented a car, and after a stop for doughnuts and coffee found the Pill Hill address where Clay Shelby lived. Eighteen months earlier a man had forced his way into Shelby's apartment, tied up Shelby and his girlfriend, and proceeded to torture the girlfriend with a knife that he found in the kitchen. The girlfriend, Suzanne Markin, later died from her injuries. Bogle and Felger had spent yesterday searching for other murders that matched the profile of the two recent home invasions and murders in Los Angeles, and after talking with the Oakland police and getting a copy of the police file, he called Shelby last night and Shelby agreed to meet with him this morning.

The apartment building where Shelby lived looked like it could've once been a small Spanish mission. White stucco walls, clay-roof tiles, an iron gate out front. The gate was unlocked. Bogle walked through it and continued on through the vestibule door, which was also unlocked. He climbed the stairs to Shelby's third-floor apartment and knocked. A skinny man in his thirties with sunken cheeks and long blond hair tied into a ponytail answered the door. He didn't look particularly happy to see Bogle, but he let him in. A skinny woman the same age as Shelby, who had her red hair pulled into a ponytail, was sitting at a small butcher-block kitchen table reading something on a digital tablet.

"That's Cynthia," Shelby said with a weak smile. "We've been together for a year now. What happened to Suzie was terrible, but life goes on."

Cynthia got up from the table and headed for the door. Bogle offered her a doughnut and one of the coffees. She shot him a cold look and told him she drank tea and wouldn't poison her body by eating gluten. Bogle watched as she let the door slam shut behind her.

"Not a morning person, huh?" he said.

Shelby made a *what-are-you-gonna-do* gesture with his eyebrows and shoulders. "She's pissed," he explained. "I told her she had to get out of here when you came over, and she didn't like that. But I'm not about to talk about what happened to Suzie in front of her. Eh, she'll get over it."

They sat at the butcher-block table where Cynthia had been sitting, and Shelby told Bogle that he had no problem drinking coffee or eating gluten, especially gluten that had been deep-fried and coated in sugar. Bogle handed him a coffee and the box of doughnuts, and Shelby chose a lemon crème. Bogle selected a chocolate glazed for himself.

Bogle took a long sip of coffee, then asked, "This is the same apartment where the attack occurred?"

"It is," Shelby admitted. He showed an apologetic smile. "It must seem kind of strange that I stayed here after what happened, but I had too many good memories of Suzie here to want to leave. As time passed, the idea of leaving the little I had left of her just got harder, and then I met Cynthia, and… well…you know how that goes."

Bogle had no idea, but he kept that to himself. When he had talked with Shelby last night on the phone, he told him about the murders happening in Los Angeles, and that he was looking for similar crimes that might've been committed by the same perpetrator. Shelby hadn't been able to talk much on the phone last night—he claimed he was too stoned at the moment to remember details of that night, but he promised he'd refrain from any toking this morning so he'd be more clearheaded when Bogle arrived. He did, though, tell Bogle how the attack happened. There was a knock on the door for someone looking for Dave. Shelby's apartment was 3D, but there was a Dave in 3A, and when he opened the door to explain that the guy had the wrong apartment, he was punched in the jaw with brass knuckles and knocked out. When he came to, he and Suzie were tied to chairs and their tormenter began cutting Suzie with a knife.

"I read the police report," Bogle said. "There wasn't much of a description of your attacker."

"There wasn't much I could say. He was wearing a ski mask. Average height, average weight. That was it."

"You didn't look through your security peephole before opening the door?"

Shelby's expression turned bleaker. "You don't think I've been torturing myself about that ever since? But you have to remember, it's ten at night,

I got what I think is a drunk guy yelling out for Dave, and I just want to send him on his way."

"None of your neighbors heard him yelling."

"I don't know what to tell you. It's what happened."

Bogle let it drop. There were only four units on a floor and the building appeared to be solidly constructed. Shelby had an end unit that was in the back of the building, and it was possible no one would have heard the perp, especially if they had their TVs or stereos on.

He asked, "How old would you guess the perpetrator was?"

"I couldn't tell you."

"If you had to guess."

Shelby munched on his lemon crème, his eyes glazing as he searched for an answer.

"Thirties. That's the best I could tell you."

"Perp's eye color?"

"I don't know."

"Were his eyes covered by the ski mask?"

"No, but it wasn't something I noticed."

"Could they have been blue?"

Shelby made a face to show he had no clue. "They could've been anything," he said.

"Any tattoos?"

"Not that I saw. But I don't think any would've been visible. He was covered up pretty good."

"Did you see anything on the underside of his right wrist?" Bogle pointed to a spot on his own wrist. "Bruise, birthmark, anything?"

"Uh-uh. The bastard was wearing a black long-sleeve shirt and black gloves. If there was anything to see, I wouldn't have seen it with what he had on."

"Did you pick up any vibes or thoughts about him?"

Shelby took another bite of his doughnut and chewed it slowly as he considered Bogle's question.

"A vicious prick. Someone who gets a kick out of dealing out pain. When I opened the door, it was like unleashing a bloodthirsty, savage beast into my home."

"Any idea why he chose you and Suzie?"

"No idea."

Bogle had been a cop for over twenty years before joining MBI, ten of those years as a detective. After all that time on the force interviewing suspects, he could feel it in his bones when someone was lying to him, and Shelby was lying to him right then. Probably earlier, also. At least to a degree.

"I thought you were going to help me," he said.

Shelby opened his eyes wide as if he were surprised by what Bogle was insinuating, but there was something a little off about the gesture. Maybe most people wouldn't have picked up on it, but Bogle did.

"What do you think I'm doing?" he asked, trying a little too hard to sound offended.

"You're holding out on me."

"I agreed to meet you this morning because I want that sick bastard caught for what he did to Suzie. You think I'm lying about that?"

Shelby was trying to hold his gaze steady on Bogle's, but he faltered. It was only for a heartbeat or two, but it was long enough to betray what he had said.

Bogle took a long drink of coffee until Shelby began wilting under his stare.

"If you're doing stuff you don't want the police to know about, that's your business, not mine," he said. "The only thing I care about is catching the perp who tortured and murdered Jill Kincade and Meagan Campbell. I also know damn well you're not leveling with me, at least not completely. I'm giving you one last chance to come clean. If you don't, I'll stay right here in Oakland and keep watch on you twenty-four-seven until I figure out what you're hiding, and I'll take you straight to the Oakland PD afterwards. Why did he choose you and your girlfriend?"

Shelby shifted his gaze to a spot on the wall to the right of Bogle. "He wanted my stash," he muttered under his breath.

"Weed?"

"No. A kilo of coke."

Bogle thought he'd heard everything during his years on the LAPD, but this was something altogether new. Incredulously, he asked, "The perp's stabbing your girlfriend to make you tell him where your drugs are hidden, and you let him do that?"

"It was a kilo, man," Shelby said in a dead, flat voice. "The guy I work for is a violent dude. Paranoid like all fuck. If I didn't sell that coke and pay him sixty grand from the proceeds, he would do worse to me and Suzie than stabbing us with knives. I thought if I waited this guy out, he'd quit and leave Suzie alone. That maybe he'd panic about someone dropping by. But he didn't stop, and it got to where I couldn't take what was happening to Suzie. I told him where the kilo was hidden."

"He stopped then?"

Shelby's mouth weakened. "Yeah."

"Suzie was still alive when he left?"

"Yeah, it was later, maybe an hour, when she died. I saw it in her eyes when it happened. They just went blank, like a light being turned off." Shelby looked up from his folded hands and gave Bogle a beseeching look. "I was left tied up and gagged and I couldn't do anything to help her. It wasn't until almost a day later that we were found, and I had to spend that whole time looking into the face of my dead girlfriend. Suzie was the only person I ever loved and I have to live with what I did, but I swear, everything else I told you is the truth. This sick bastard might've done what he did to get the coke, but he enjoyed every second of it."

Finally, the truth.

Bogle asked, "Did he gain entry to your apartment the way you said earlier, or did he come here to buy coke?"

"Exactly what I said. He was pounding on the door, yelling out for Dave, and I just wanted him to shut up."

Bogle decided that was the truth also. "Okay. I'm going to need a list of your customers, and anyone else who knew about you holding coke."

"Uh-uh. It wasn't anyone local. My clientele are high-end, professionals. It wasn't any of them, not any other dealers either. I looked into it; so did the badass dude I work for. Whoever did this was some sicko passing through Oakland who overheard something."

"I'm still going to need that list."

"You're not getting it. You'd only be wasting your time if I gave it to you."

"My time to waste." Bogle finished his coffee and stood up. "If I have to bring Oakland PD into this, I will."

Shelby smiled thinly. "You do that and I tell them I sold you a work of fiction, and they don't get another word from me. Neither do you. And you know what else probably happens? Within a week my boss cuts my throat—Cynthia's also—which would be really unfair, since she thinks I only drive for Uber. My getting ripped off was strike one, my talking to you would be strike two, and he doesn't usually give any strikes."

Bogle didn't like not getting that list, but he could also see the determination in Shelby's eyes. Bringing OPD in wouldn't help. Instead, he would find a detective within OPD's narcotics task force and get a list of drug dealers from a year and a half ago who had since gone missing. He made an executive decision. He'd let this slide, at least as far as Shelby was concerned.

He asked, "Anything else you can tell me?"

Shelby's smile turned more genuine as he realized that Bogle was going to give him a break. Then his eyes went distant as he gave the question deep consideration.

His eyes shifted back to meet Bogle's. "There was something," he said. "I hadn't even thought about it until just now. He called me *champ* a few times. That's a funny thing to call someone."

Bogle asked Shelby to call him if he thought of anything else. He left the apartment and waited until he was in his car before he called Morris.

"There are some stark differences, but this might be the same guy," he said. "There was a ski mask and the same level of violence, although he left the woman's clothes on and he didn't cut off her nipples or mutilate her like he did our two victims. The motivation here was also different: a kilo of cocaine, and he stopped the torture after the coke was given up. But this was a year and a half ago. Maybe the perp found that he liked using a knife on a helpless woman while the boyfriend was forced to watch. Maybe after thinking about it for eighteen months, he decided to start killing again, but this time for fun and so he could do all the things he wished he had done with the first victim."

"Christ," Morris swore under his breath. "Did this guy have a wrist tattoo?"

"The perp kept himself covered up, so if there was one, Shelby wouldn't have seen it. I didn't get much of a physical description, but also nothing that eliminates our perp. One thing: He liked to call Shelby *champ*. You could give that to Felger and see if that helps with his computer searches. Do you know if the perp called either Frey or Campbell that?"

Morris said, "I'll ask about Frey. It's too late to find out about George Campbell. I got a call an hour ago that he died without regaining consciousness."

"Shit."

"Yeah, I know."

Chapter 42

Los Angeles, the present

Stevie from the boarding house was following him. Ten minutes ago, Duncan had caught a glimpse of the meth head skulking behind him. Something caused him to look back, and that was when he spotted Stevie half a block away. The raggedy-looking meth head stepped into a doorway to keep from being seen, but just a fraction too late.

This time Duncan stopped to tie his shoelaces, or at least make it look like he was tying his shoelaces. He had turned sideways, his foot on a door stoop, and he surreptitiously caught the meth head darting behind a parked van. Duncan gave no indication that he had seen him and after finishing his shoelace act, continued on his path. At the end of the block, he turned right, acting casual about it, and then sprinted to an alleyway. He took several steps into it and flattened himself against the building so that he was mostly hidden in shadows.

He wondered if Stevie had followed him yesterday when he walked to the garage where he kept his car. If he did, then Stevie would've learned that he had a Caddy, and Duncan would've preferred that nobody at the boarding house knew about that. Even if Stevie didn't know about the Caddy, he had to be convinced that Duncan had something of value in his backpack, and was determined to get his hands on it. Stevie was right, of course. There was quite a bit of cash stuffed inside it, as well as enough evidence to convict Duncan several times over for the recent gruesome murders he committed. Which meant that Stevie needed to breathe his last breath…or at the very least, be dissuaded from this reckless course he was on. Duncan hadn't yet decided which it was going to be. While he had no problem philosophically with ending Stevie's miserable life, he also didn't want to bring any police heat to the boarding house. So if he killed him here, the body would have to be close to impossible to identify, and that would be both a tricky and messy thing to do in this alleyway. Not impossible, though, at least not with the dumpster that could provide some cover.

Stevie came huffing past the alleyway entrance, looking wild-eyed and bewildered as he searched for Duncan. The idea must've popped into his head that Duncan had stepped into the alley, because he backtracked and took a tentative step into it. Duncan stepped out of the shadows and punched Stevie in the proverbial breadbasket. An *oomph* escaped from Stevie's mouth and his rail-thin body bent almost in half and sagged at the same time. Even before the punch, Stevie's complexion was something awful with his pockmarked cheeks and cystic acne, and the blow left his skin the same grayish-white as a three-day-old corpse. The man was over six feet tall, but he couldn't have weighed more than 130 pounds, and Duncan grabbed him by his long, greasy hair and dragged him behind the dumpster. If the blow to the stomach hadn't left the meth head desperately sucking in air, he would've screamed.

Duncan didn't give him a chance to recover. He pushed him face-first into the side of the dumpster and punched him twice in the kidneys. There was a brick lying nearby that he could've used to turn that face into a bloody mess that nobody would be able to recognize, but instead he whispered into Stevie's ear.

"All the meth you're smoking turn your brain to goo? If I ever see you again, it will be for the last time, capisce?"

Duncan didn't wait for an answer. Instead, he threw another hard jab, this one landing smack in the middle of Stevie's back, and then he grabbed him around the knees and hoisted him up so that the man tumbled headfirst into the dumpster. Duncan looked to see whether anyone had witnessed this, and as far as he could tell, nobody had. He brushed some dirt off his clothes, left the alley, and continued on his way.

He walked another mile before picking up a newspaper. There was a front-page story with the headline CUPID KILLER STRIKES AGAIN. *Cupid Killer*, huh, he thought. He guessed the name fit, even though he wasn't killing anyone named Cupid. But he was being too literal and he had to admit it was a clever name. The truth was, he didn't much care what they called him.

As anxious as he was to dig into the paper and see what they wrote about George and Meagan Campbell, he exercised some restraint and found a diner on the next block, walked in, and took a seat at the counter. He had been planning to sit at a booth so he'd have a little more privacy, but a TV was playing and it was showing a clip from last night's *Hollywood Peeper*, which had an FBI profiler talking to the host about the Cupid Killer murders. Duncan had no idea that show had been on last night. The boarding house didn't have a communal TV, and he'd been busy yesterday—first hunting for possible victims, then taking a trip to Pasadena. It was six o'clock before he'd got back to LA, and he was feeling kind of beat, so he bought some food at a market and stayed holed up for the rest of the night in his room.

The woman hosting the show looked like an aging Barbie doll. She also had a pretentious-sounding name that must've been fake. The FBI profiler was a very different type. A small, dark-haired woman in her forties who reminded Duncan of a sparrow—not just in the way she looked, but in her quick, flitting movements. She also looked intelligent, which was why her pronouncement that the killer was doing what he was because of mommy issues was so surprising. She couldn't have been further from the truth, although when he thought about it some more, he realized she might've been right. Not about him, but about what really was behind all of this.

Anyway, he didn't much care what reason she gave. What he did care about, though, was that she didn't mention the snarling wolf's-face tattoo. What was wrong with these people?

The clip ended and the newscaster came back on to talk about new updates in the Cupid Killer murders, and Duncan soon understood why there was no mention of the tattoo. He had put Campbell in a coma after he hit him that second time, and Campbell died this morning without ever waking up. *Shit.* The first one, Alex Frey, should've been able to tell the cops about the tattoo, but either he didn't see it, or for some unexplainable reason the cops were holding back on telling the public about it.

Shit.

He had another attack planned for later that night, and he'd make damn sure the guy got a good look at the tattoo. This time he'd also make sure not to kill him.

A grandmotherly-looking waitress who reminded him of Ella Hubble from long ago stepped in front of him holding a coffeepot.

"Hon, what can I get you?"

Duncan blinked several times, his thoughts so jumbled up with what he had just learned from the TV and his plans for the next two days that he had forgotten he was sitting in a diner.

"How about I start you up with some coffee?" she said sweetly enough that he again thought of Ella. She even had the same red apple cheeks as

Ella. It had been years since he had thought of her and eighteen years since he'd last seen her. By now she'd be dead or rotting away in a nursing home.

"Sure thing," he said.

She filled up a coffee mug for him, then suggested he get their lumberjack special, their most popular breakfast and their best value. "You could use to put some meat on your bones."

"That sounds great."

She winked at him. "I'll have them make the eggs scrambled."

"Perfect."

She topped off his coffee and walked off, and Duncan sat lost in a jumble of nostalgic thoughts. These faded and he was left with a steely resolve to finish what he had started.

Which meant he needed to find more victims. Not that he much minded the idea of finding more privileged, oh-so-happy people to hurt.

Chapter 43

The cashier at the tacky Hollywood gift shop told Morris he had one cool dog.

Parker grunted. His tail wagged slowly.

Morris told her, "You're going to give him a swelled head."

Detective Annie Walsh looked exasperated. "How about we get back to the matter at hand? Were you working here last Saturday?"

The cashier, a blonde in her twenties who wore dark-purple lipstick and had a raccoonish look because of the thick mascara around her eyes, admitted that she worked then. "My shift ran from nine to six, but I took a half hour off at twelve-thirty for lunch." She winked at Parker and smiled at Morris. "That's always when I take my lunch break."

Walsh showed her the cheesy coffee mug for the "world's cutest couple."

"Those are so adorable," the cashier said. She wasn't chewing gum, but she looked like she could've been. One could imagine her blowing a bubble.

"They're something," Morris agreed.

Parker grunted out his opinion.

"The store manager already confirmed that a pair were sold here at four-eighteen Saturday afternoon," Walsh said, her cheeks beet-red from her growing exasperation. She took from a bag the small, empty box and gift-wrap paper that was found in the Marina del Rey apartment that Frey and Kincade had shared, and placed them on the counter. "The mugs were wrapped in that."

"It looks like the type we use," the cashier said, her brow wrinkling as she studied the box. "Although I think they're standard, like every shop around here uses. Is it okay if I pick up the paper so I can get a closer look?"

"Knock yourself out."

The cashier opened a cabinet behind the counter and took out rolls of gift-wrap paper and tried matching them to the muted silver paper. None of them seemed an exact match.

"We're always replacing the wrapping paper with different types," the cashier explained. "You'd have to ask Edwin if we were using that type last Saturday. Although I don't think he pays much attention to the paper he orders for the store."

Edwin McGill was the store manager. Morris had called him earlier from a list Felger had put together of the stores in LA that sold the "world's cutest couple" mug. The store's single cash register was computerized, and it automatically updated the inventory records when purchases were rung up. Because of that, McGill was able to tell Morris the exact time two of the mugs were sold last Saturday.

"We'll talk to Edwin," Morris said. "For now, can you remember who bought these?"

The cashier showed a constipated look as she tried to remember. A woman in her thirties walked around Walsh so she could place a ceramic Marilyn Monroe cookie jar on the counter. "Miss, I'd like to buy this," the woman said, her tone curt, strongly implying she didn't plan to wait around for the cashier to remember anything.

The cashier smiled apologetically at Morris. "I need to take care of this," she said. Morris stepped back from the counter and nudged Walsh to do the same, which she did after she collected the box and gift-wrap paper. While he waited, he scratched Parker behind the ear as a reward for being so well-behaved that morning. Walsh stood, seething.

"Take a deep breath," Morris said. He spoke softly so only Walsh could hear him.

"What I'd like to do is arrest this ditz for impeding an investigation," Walsh said angrily under her breath. "Or at the very least, for annoying the hell out of me."

"It won't help any if you rattle her."

Walsh knew that as well as Morris, but it didn't help her temper. She must've also known, as Morris did, that since the store didn't have surveillance cameras they weren't going to get anything useful here. In real life, you seldom came across a witness with a photographic memory who could describe someone they saw four days ago unless they had a damn good reason for paying attention to the person—and even then, any description would be suspect. A roomful of people could witness a robbery and if each of them were interviewed an hour later, you'd end up with vastly different descriptions of the robber. One or two of them might be accurate, but most would be worthless. If you brought them in for a lineup with the perp or showed photos, some would have their memory jarred enough to pick out the right person, but not all of them.

The cashier finished up with the woman buying the Marilyn Monroe cookie jar. Morris waited until the customer walked away before stepping back to the counter. Walsh stood where she was and continued to seethe.

"I'm sorry," the cashier told him. "I've been trying to think back to Saturday, but I can't remember who bought the coffee mugs." She leaned toward him and confidentially added, "I had plans to go clubbing with my girls, and that's where my head was at."

"Can you tell me the hair color of the woman you just waited on?"

The cashier stared blankly at Morris before a look of chagrin came over her.

"I can't," she admitted. "Is that awful of me?"

"Human nature," Morris said. He dug a business card out of his wallet and handed it to her. "If you remember anything, give me a call, okay?"

The cashier promised she would. She wiggled her fingers in a wave-type motion to Parker, and the bull terrier responded by grunting and wagging his tail at a slightly faster beat.

The coffee mugs were looking like a dead end, but maybe not. There was a chance that a nearby store's surveillance camera captured the killer when he walked past it to the gift shop. The next step would be to check the businesses on the block, and maybe they'd get lucky. At least they knew the time the mugs were bought. If they found video that captured pedestrians walking on the sidewalk around that time, they could print out photos of possible suspects and one of them might jar the cashier's memory. They could also show the photos to everyone who attended the engagement party. If they crapped out with that, they still had other avenues they were working on. Bogle was kicking around in Oakland to see if the Oakland Police Department could give him anything useful, and the rest of the team was busy interviewing the engagement party attendees and collecting photos. It was a shame that Frey and Kincade hadn't hired a photographer for the occasion, but there would be other photos taken on guests' phones, and maybe one of them captured their killer.

Walsh had wandered to the front of the store, no doubt thinking Morris would have better luck with the cashier by himself. He made an empty-handed gesture, letting her know that he had gotten nothing from the cashier, which had to be what she was expecting.

Anger flashed in her eyes, but otherwise she controlled herself and withheld any comments about the uselessness of the cashier. She asked,

"Should we talk to the store manager and see if he recognizes the gift-wrap paper?"

"A waste of time," Morris said. "This is where our killer bought the mugs."

"So we check the other businesses on the block for surveillance video?"

"We might get lucky," Morris said.

"And I just might start crapping out gold bricks," Walsh grumbled with disgust.

"Annie, this killer's making mistakes. Big ones. Maybe we'll have a photo of him from the engagement party. We're going to catch him."

"Before he tortures and kills another woman?"

That was the million-dollar question. Morris wished he had an answer for her, or more specifically, he wished he had a different answer than what he knew in his gut.

Chapter 44

Lemmon swore he spent 70 percent of his time on the job at stakeouts, but at least technology was making it easier. Or at the very least, more comfortable. As an example of this, he had earlier followed Hardacher to his office, watched him park his leased Audi, and now Lemmon was sitting in a coffee shop two blocks away, eating a lemon raspberry scone, sipping a latte, and waiting for his target to get back in his car. He could do this because he had Hardacher's car and home office bugged. He could also track the car's location on his cell phone, thanks to the GPS tracker planted on the car's undercarriage, and as soon as the car moved, Lemmon would know it.

Yesterday he had met with the client and showed her the photos of her husband warmly greeting Lauren Estleman at the motel.

"So I'm not crazy after all," she noted bitterly. "The bastard is cheating on me."

"It's worse than that." Lemmon showed her the photos of the man Hardacher met earlier at the motel. She didn't know who the person was, and he explained his suspicions about what her husband had hired the man to do. Her face crumpled as she made sense of what he was saying. It tugged at Lemmon's heart to see that.

"Do I go to the police?" she asked.

"A police contact is trying to identify the man from the photos, but so far no luck. Unfortunately, the police won't be able to do anything unless you're able to give them evidence of a crime, which we don't have yet."

Lemmon suggested a course of action, which she agreed to. She would call her husband and tell him that she needed to go to San Diego right away on an emergency business trip, which was plausible, given her job.

She would also give him a motel address that Lemmon provided, and he would hire a freelance operative to stay there as a decoy while he kept watch on Hardacher. It seemed likely that Hardacher would make contact again with the suspected hit man. Having his wife killed in a San Diego motel room would be an ideal solution for both Hardacher and the man he hired. The only question left was where the client would stay while this was going on, and Lemmon decided to put her up in his home. Polk would give him holy hell if he found out, no doubt making cracks about Lemmon opening up a home for wayward clients.

Corrine wasn't too happy when he brought Wendy Hardacher home yesterday. While she didn't go so far as make him sleep on the couch, she made sure there was no physical contact between the two of them last night, clinging to the edge of her side of the bed so their bodies wouldn't touch. If they had, Lemmon probably would've gotten frostbite.

Lemmon casually read the day's sports section as he chewed on another bite of scone and sipped more of his latte. He had his cell phone on the table, and the app Felger loaded on it was configured to beep when Hardacher's car moved. His thoughts drifted from what the Rams needed in the upcoming NFL draft to how frightened Wendy looked when he asked whether she had any friends she could stay with while he continued the investigation. She was scared to death this suspected hit man would track her down, and so he offered to put her up. He wouldn't have been able to live with himself if he hadn't done that. If Corrine wanted to be mad at him, fine. If it wasn't this, it would be something else. And the hell with Polk and any cracks that jackass might want to make about it!

Lemmon smiled grimly, thinking of how Polk was pissing him off about something that the guy hadn't even done yet. He needed to take some time off from work when this assignment was over. No question, he was going a little nuts in the head. Or maybe it was from thinking about Annie yesterday. The truth was he still couldn't stop thinking about her. He made a decision. When this was done, he was getting in his car and driving somewhere remote and spending a week or longer away from stakeouts, cheating spouses, and insurance-fraud cases. Whether or not Corrine would want to accompany him would be a separate issue.

He took another bite of scone and settled in for what he expected to be a long day of waiting for his smartphone to beep.

Chapter 45

Natalie strategically took a sip of her iced tea to give her time to regain her composure. Never let them see you sweat, and that was especially true of Rachel. She loved her daughter with all her heart, but she could be so infuriatingly stubborn, even more than Morris. The only one she could think of who might have the edge on Rachel in the stubbornness department was Parker. A bull terrier!

The two of them were having lunch outside at a quaint bistro three blocks from UCLA, and Rachel had just dropped the bombshell that she didn't want an engagement party. And of course now she was smiling pleasantly, as if she had only commented about what a perfect sunny April day they were having.

If Natalie showed any sign of weakness, she'd be lost. She took an extra few seconds to pat her mouth with a napkin, and commented about how she thought the engagement party question had already been decided.

Rachel pursed her lips as if she were searching her memory. "I'm not sure that's true," she said. "You did mention that you wanted to throw me one, but I don't believe I agreed to it."

"You're going to make an excellent prosecutor one day," Natalie said. "What exactly would your objection be to having one?"

Rachel made the same face she used to make when she was six and Natalie insisted she eat her broccoli. Nine years later she would become a full-fledged vegan with broccoli a staple in her diet.

"An actor I don't know throwing a big, gaudy party at his Malibu estate," she said. "No thanks."

"I see. Interesting," Natalie said. "My plan was to only invite relatives and friends and anyone else you wanted. And the party would be understated, not gaudy."

"Sorry, no, it's not for me. I don't even understand the point of having an engagement party. I think a small wedding will be sufficient, assuming we don't elope."

Natalie opened her mouth to argue with her daughter, but closed it again as the waitress arrived with their food—a garden salad with extra chickpeas for Rachel, and a Caesar salad with grilled salmon for her. As the waitress arranged the plates in front of them, Natalie caught the wisp of a smile that flitted on Rachel's lips. She understood then what her daughter was up to.

She waited until the waitress left, then said, "I'll make you a deal. If you let me throw you the engagement party, I promise to be hands-off on the wedding plans. Not a peep from me about it."

Rachel's wisp of a smile showed briefly again. She asked, "Including the invitation list?"

"Yes."

"Deal."

Natalie took a small bite of her lunch and chewed it carefully before addressing Rachel again.

"Well played, Daughter," she said.

Rachel's wisp of a smile expanded into a full-out grin. "Thank you, Mother," she said.

Duncan sat at a nearby table, eavesdropping on their conversation. He had followed another couple to the restaurant thinking they might be what he needed, but shortly after the waitress had taken his order he decided they wouldn't be right. He was disappointed, of course. He had invested over an hour spying on them, but after a promising start, he realized they weren't married or engaged or didn't have even have any interest in each other, besides easy hookups. But he needed to eat and this place seemed as good as any, so he ordered a roast beef and cheddar sandwich. His ears perked up shortly afterward when he heard the woman nearby ask her daughter about an engagement party.

He had noticed the two of them earlier, when the hostess brought him to his table. How could any guy not notice them? They were obviously mother and daughter, given how much they looked alike. Both slender, dark-haired, and beautiful, the mother dressed professionally in a blouse, skirt, and flats, and the daughter in a polo shirt, jeans, and tennis sneakers. He had a special reason to notice them—or at least the mother, given how much she looked like his mom, although her hair was darker and she was older than his mom was when she died. But she had similar delicate features and a softness in her brown eyes that flashed him back for a heartbeat to when he was a nine-year-old boy and his mom was kissing and hugging him good-bye for the last time. It was spooky in a way.

Since hearing the word *engagement* Duncan started thinking about making the daughter one of his victims. She was more than just beautiful—a knockout, and it would have to destroy any guy lucky enough to be her fiancé to watch her being stabbed and cut to death. There was something else about her that made him want to choose her as one of his victims. One way that she was very different from her mom was her flinty gray eyes. They showed a certain strength, toughness, and self-confidence. They were the eyes of someone who knew she had a happy life ahead of her, and Duncan found himself wanting to see those eyes weak and pleading for him to spare her. Whenever he could, he snuck peeks at her, and soon found himself thinking he might enjoy killing her even without needing to force her lover to watch her die.

The waitress brought over his food and he ate leisurely, wanting to make sure he finished after the mother and daughter he was eavesdropping on. They were circumspect in their conversation, talking in soft tones, and Duncan had to strain to hear what they were saying and at times he missed not only words, but whole sentences. He wanted to catch their names, but if their names were said, he missed it. Out of the corner of his eye, he caught them leaving the table. If they noticed him glancing their way, they didn't show any indication of it. He waited until they left the patio area before dropping enough money on the table to cover his bill, then stood so he could follow them. A look at their table showed that they paid their bill with cash instead of a credit card, so he wasn't able to get either of their names that way.

He spotted them on the next block hugging, and watched as the mother got into a car and the daughter stood waving good-bye, a big grin on her face. Duncan turned away and acted as if he were studying the bistro's menu that was posted outside. He didn't want the woman to see his face when she drove by. He couldn't shake the thought that if she did, she'd know what he was planning.

Once the car drove past him, he continued after the daughter. She had a two-block lead on him, but he made up the distance quickly, staying thirty yards behind her. If she was driving he would've been out of luck, but the fact she was walking told him this was kismet. That she was meant to be one of his victims. The idea of it fixed in his mind, and he found himself wondering what her fiancé was like. No doubt one of life's most fortunate and beautiful people. He had his plan and all that, but he was going to enjoy himself with these two, especially watching the flinty look in her eyes crumble to dust. Nobody had the right to be that damn cocksure of their future!

He followed her to the UCLA campus and then to the law school building, and he watched as she jogged up the stairs and went inside. He thought of several schemes he could use to get her name, but decided they'd be too risky. He took a deep breath and stood motionless, trying to calm the thoughts ricocheting through his mind. As much as he wanted to claim her as one of his victims, he had his plan, after all. He had to be smart about this.

He'd come back to the campus. If it was meant to be, he'd find her again; if not, he'd move on to other victims. C'est la vie.

For now he would do more hunting. Later, he'd get ready for tonight.

Chapter 46

Dan Skerrit hustled the three beers back to the booth, then slid in so that he sat across from Duncan and Wainwright. Wainwright didn't hesitate to pick up the beer that had been left in front of Duncan. He guzzled down half of it before setting the glass down.

"The boy ain't of legal age," he explained.

Skerrit laughed. "Frank, you suddenly become a paragon of virtue?"

"Damn straight." Wainwright licked his thick, rubbery lips, then picked up the glass and finished off what was left of the beer Skerrit had bought for Duncan. He wiped a jacket sleeve across his mouth. "The boy's my grandson. Someone's gotta look out for him."

That was rich and it should've been enough to get anyone who knew Wainwright as well as Duncan did to bust a gut laughing, but it didn't even crack a smile from him. He sat as serious as could be.

Skerrit leaned halfway across the table and, keeping his voice low, said, "Tell the truth, Frank. You just want to keep this boy skinny enough so he can wriggle his ass through broken basement windows."

Skerrit broke out laughing so hard that he had to wipe a tear from his eye. He wrestled his wallet from his back pocket and offered Duncan a twenty-dollar bill.

"Just 'cause your grandpa is a cheap bastard don't mean you should suffer," he said. "Buy yourself a shot, a beer, or whatever you want. Nobody here will bother carding you."

Duncan took the money and shoved it into his front pocket. He knew Skerrit was right. There wasn't a single person in this dive bar who would care about a sixteen-year-old buying himself an alcoholic beverage, but

Skerrit wasn't handing him the money out of the goodness of his heart. He was doing it so he could talk over the nitty-gritty details of the job without Duncan around.

"I'll stay," he said.

"The boy's all business," Wainwright remarked with a note of pride in his voice.

Whatever disappointment Skerrit might've felt, he kept in check. He didn't even ask for the twenty dollars back. Instead, he sat back and took a drink of his beer. Wainwright picked up the beer that had been bought for him and took a long drink. Duncan suggested they quit lollygagging and get down to business.

"Might as well," Skerrit agreed. He leaned halfway across the table again, and keeping his voice low, he told them that he knew about a coin collection he wanted them to steal. That he would pay them 5000 dollars to do the job. He didn't have to keep his voice low. Conversations from other booths and at the bar—both heated and otherwise—had collected into a loud clamor that would've drowned him out even if he were talking in his normal voice.

Duncan asked, "How much are these coins worth?"

Skerrit made a face as if Duncan had just insulted him. "Five grand's not enough for you?"

"Depends how much they're worth. You've been taking advantage of us, Dan. I think it's about time we start getting twenty cents on the dollar for what we steal for you."

Skerrit was a skinny man with a long nose, pointy eyes, a weak chin, and a generally unkempt appearance, all of which made Duncan think of a sewer rat. Anger shrunk Skerrit's eyes to even tinier dots, and he bared his teeth the way a cornered rat might. He turned to Wainwright.

"Can you believe the nerve of this punk kid?" he demanded, his voice strained. "Frank, don't tell me you want to walk away from five grand?"

Wainwright had gotten quiet. He had also taken his switchblade from his pocket and opened the blade. Skerrit didn't see that, but Duncan had. While Wainwright couldn't have used the knife from where he was sitting, he could if he got out of the booth and sat next to Skerrit. Duncan didn't put it past him to do that. Wainwright had been in an exceptionally ornery mood the last couple of days.

"I think the boy's got a good point," he said, very quiet-like. "The money you paid us for those other two jobs seemed kind of light. Why don't you tell us what the coins are worth?"

"It doesn't matter what they're worth." From the way Skerrit started eyeing the exit he must've seen the open switchblade in Wainwright's hand. "The fence I'm using is paying twenty-five cents on the dollar of the appraised value. I can pay you six grand, but that's it."

"Ten," Wainwright said in his soft, murderous tone.

Sweat had beaded up on Skerrit's forehead and under his nose. "All right, eight grand," he agreed. "That's as high as I can go. As it is, you'll be cutting my own margins down to almost nothing, and I'll be lucky to make a grand out of this myself."

Duncan was convinced Skerrit was lying. He probably had a private buyer already lined up, and would be bypassing a fence altogether. Wainwright should've stuck firm to his ten-grand demand, but it was evident from the smile on that wrinkled his face that he was satisfied with what Skerrit was offering. Eight grand, along with what they made from the other two robberies, would keep Wainwright in booze and whores for months. Wainwright closed the blade with his thumb and put the knife away. He relaxed back in his seat.

"Why don't you tell us about this job?"

Skerrit handed over a sheet of paper that had all the information. What he had joked about earlier with Duncan needing to stay skinny so he could get through a small window hadn't been a completely random thought. The latch for one of the basement windows had been broken by one of the local tradesmen who got paid by Skerrit to break window latches, and that was how Duncan was to gain access into the house.

"Any dogs?" Duncan asked.

"There are no dogs."

"There was one on the last job you sent us on."

Skerrit's nostrils flared to show his annoyance. He crossed his bony arms over his even-bonier chest. "So I made a mistake with that one," he stated stubbornly.

Duncan said, "You weren't the one bit on the ankle."

"You're walking around just fine now. And I paid you an extra five hundred for that scratch."

It was more than a scratch. Wainwright didn't want to bring him to a doctor and stitched Duncan up himself. The wound had gotten swollen and pussy, and Wainwright broke into a doctor's office to steal antibiotic samples. It had only been the last three days that the swelling had gone down and Duncan was able to put any weight on the foot.

Wainwright asked, "Any guns in the house?"

"None."

"All right, then." Wainwright finished up his second beer, sucked in his gut, and squeezed himself out of the booth. Six years ago when Duncan met Wainwright, the man had been lean and lanky, but over the last year he had grown thick around the middle. Age catching up to him, as well as all the booze he'd been drinking.

Duncan followed Wainwright out of the bar. He got behind the wheel and as Duncan drove them back to the motel where they were staying in Madison, Wainwright commented that if this job went well, they would be flush with cash.

Wainwright sat back in the passenger seat and drank rye from a bottle, his thick eyelids closing fast. "We'll spend another month or two doing jobs around here," he murmured, his voice drifting as if he were about to fall asleep. "Come winter, we'll head to Florida. I got a contact there who'll set us up on jobs. If things keep going well, we'll even drive to Orlando and spend a week or two in Disney World and let you play around there. How's that sound, boy?"

Duncan knew it was as worthless a promise as all the others Wainwright had made over the last six years. He didn't bother answering since Wainwright had fallen asleep, the half-empty rye bottle cradled in his arms.

Chapter 47

Maple Bluff, Wisconsin. October 2006. Three days later.

They found the latch for the basement window broken as promised, and Duncan was able to shimmy himself through it. He held onto the upper frame of the window and lowered himself so he would only drop three feet to the floor, but his injured ankle was still tender, and to keep from crying out when he landed he bit his bottom lip hard enough to make it bleed. Once the pain in his ankle subsided enough for him to put weight on it, he hobbled upstairs. Fortunately, he didn't encounter any dogs on his way to the front door. He let Wainwright in and after they put on cheap plastic Halloween masks, they headed upstairs to the bedrooms. One of the bedrooms had been converted into a home office, and the coin collection was kept locked away in a closet inside that room.

Wainwright was good with a lockpick, but Duncan was even better, and they probably would've been able to unlock the closet door and take the coin collection without waking anyone, but Wainwright didn't like the way Skerrit had looked when he said there were no guns in the house. As far as he was concerned, Skerrit was just telling them what they wanted to hear, which meant they needed to tie up the married couple and their two children before they went for the coin collection.

Skerrit had provided a crude map of the upstairs, and so they had no trouble finding the master bedroom. The husband was sleeping on his belly, and Wainwright covered the man's mouth with his hand while he pushed the blade of his knife hard enough against the side of the man's neck to draw blood. He whispered into the startled man's ear that his family members would all die if he didn't keep his mouth shut. The man didn't make a peep, and Duncan tied his hands and ankles together without the wife waking up. They next did the same to the wife, although Wainwright didn't bother holding a knife against her. After that, Wainwright searched the bedroom and found a fully loaded .38 caliber revolver in a night-table drawer on the husband's side of the bed.

"Damn that turd," he muttered, referring to Skerrit. "We could've gotten our asses shot off tonight."

Wainwright wedged the barrel of the gun in his pants behind his back. They next tied up the fifteen-year-old daughter without any fuss, followed by her ten-year-old brother.

The lock on the closet door for the converted study turned out to be trickier than they expected. After ten minutes of fiddling with the lockpick, an exceedingly exasperated Wainwright declared he'd find an ax to use on the door, but Duncan asked to see if he'd have better luck. Three minutes later he had the door picked and unlocked. Inside was a stack of loose-leaf notebooks filled with plastic sleeves, each sleeve holding twenty coins in carefully arranged pockets. Wainwright whistled as he flipped through the pages.

"This page is filled with gold coins," he said. He squinted as he read the date on one of them. "Says here it's from 1804. Never seen anything like it."

While Wainwright was looking at the coins, Duncan searched through a file cabinet in the same closet and found an appraisal report that was dated three months earlier. So that's how Skerrit knew about the collection. Whoever appraised the collection must've sold the information to him. Duncan flipped through the report and on the last page saw that the coins were worth over 300,000 dollars. He told Wainwright that.

Wainwright acted as if he hadn't heard him, but from the way his eyes dulled, Duncan knew he had heard him just fine.

"What's that's, boy?" he asked.

"This report says that's how much this collection's worth."

"That chiseler was going to pay us eight grand?" Wainwright's thick lips twisted into a hard smile. "Hell with that. We're taking these coins straight to Florida and find a buyer there, and maybe for good measure I put a bullet in that turd's ear for thinking he can cheat us." A hot intensity burned in Wainwright's eyes as he mulled over their good fortune. "But goddamn, boy, we should clear a hundred grand easy. You and me are soon gonna be living high off the hog. You take all this to the car and I'll meet you in a little while."

Duncan didn't like the look in Wainwright's eyes, nor the brutal way he was smiling. He asked, "Where are you going to be?"

Wainwright winked at him. "I got some business with that hot little honey we tied up."

The old man mistook the disgust on Duncan's face for jealously. "I don't blame you, boy. That yellow-haired girlie is one hot piece in her short little nightie and long, skinny legs. I bet her tight ass is as juicy as any fresh-picked peach. We got time. No reason you can't have a crack at her. But you just got to wait your turn."

Duncan didn't see the girl tied-up and helpless in her bedroom as a *hot little honey*, but instead as a scared fifteen year old, and he hated the idea of what Wainwright planned to do to her. He could see the orneriness burning in Wainwright's eyes, and he knew if he spoke up all he'd get for his trouble would be a backhand across the mouth. He'd been hit in the mouth hard enough to loosen teeth a few times already for talking back and not showing proper respect, and he didn't much care to have that happen again. So he kept quiet and watched as Wainwright hurried into the girl's bedroom and closed the door behind him, but not without giving Duncan a particularly ugly wink. After several minutes a resolve hardened within him. He'd be damned if he would let Wainwright victimize that poor girl in there any further.

Duncan, being as quiet as a mouse, opened the door and snuck inside the room. Wainwright had the girl on her knees with her nightgown hiked up, his wrinkled bare ass on full display, his pants and shit-stained drawers pulled down to his ankles. The booze he had drunk earlier that night had its effect, and he was working to get himself hard so he could penetrate the girl, whose sobs were muffled by a gag. Duncan spotted the revolver lying on the carpeted floor by the foot of the bed. In his haste to take advantage of the girl, Wainwright hadn't bothered keeping the gun within reach, and instead let it fall where it may when he lowered his pants.

Duncan held his breath as he retrieved the gun and made sure the safety was off. Wainwright was so caught up in what he was trying to accomplish that he had no idea about this until the gun barrel was jammed into his left ear.

"What the hell!" he bellowed.

"You're going to get off her right now or I'm pulling the trigger," Duncan said, his voice surprisingly calm.

It took Wainwright a few seconds to catch on to what was happening. "You that impatient you can't wait your turn?" he snarled, his upper lip curled to reveal his canines.

"Neither of us are having turns with her. I ain't joking. I count to three and you ain't off her and putting on your pants, your brains will be leaking out your other ear."

Duncan started to count to three. Wainwright nearly fell off the bed in his haste to get his pants pulled back up.

"We're blood, boy," he said with genuine hurt. "What in the world has gone wrong with you to do this to your own blood?"

"Shut up."

For the first time since Wainwright had taken guardianship of him, Duncan had the upper hand, and the old man knew he meant business. He finished buckling up his belt and zipping up his pants.

"Looks like you calling the shots for now," he said, his face crinkling with a forced good humor that didn't reach anywhere near his eyes. "What next?"

"You're gonna carry that coin collection to the car, then we're driving away from here."

Duncan kept the gun trained on Wainwright, and if the old man did anything other than what he was supposed to, Duncan would've shot him dead. But Wainwright collected the binders and carried them out of the house while Duncan trailed behind him.

They had left their car in a driveway four blocks away. Skerrit had told them the owners were away on a trip, and that the driveway went far enough back that nobody would notice the car parked there. After a block, Wainwright was huffing badly.

"These coins got to weigh over fifty pounds," he grunted. "I'm gonna have a heart attack, you make me carry these all the way back."

"You can put them down. I'll get the car, but if you ain't here when I get back, I'll be leaving without you."

Duncan thought there was a chance that Wainwright would head back to the house and have his fun with the girl just to spite him, but when he returned with the car, Wainwright was sitting where he left him. Duncan turned off the engine, took the keys, and waited until Wainwright finished loading the trunk with the loose-leaf notebooks before he got out of the driver's seat and moved over to the passenger side.

"You're going to drive," he said.

Wainwright made a sour face. "You know I got bad night vision."

"It will be good enough for now. You know I gotta keep a gun on you."

The old man didn't argue the matter, and did as Duncan ordered. Once he was in the driver's seat, Duncan tossed him the keys.

"How long you gonna point that gun on me?"

"Don't know."

Wainwright showed a bare-fanged smile. "All right boss, so where we going?"

"Florida. Like you said."

For the next hour they drove without either of them saying a word. If Wainwright was waiting for Duncan to tire out and fall asleep so he could grab the gun, he soon realized there wasn't much chance of that happening. Duncan was as wired as if he had drunk a gallon of high-octane coffee, his right leg nervously bouncing up and down.

Wainwright broke the silence, saying, "You know what disappointed me even more than you not letting me have a good ol' time with that sweet little girlie? That you ain't learned the lesson I've been trying so hard to teach you."

Duncan was sincerely confused by the idea that Wainwright had ever tried teaching him anything, and he asked him what possible lesson that could be.

"You take what you want in this life. You see a girlie you want, you take her. You see a sucker with money, you take his money. You don't feel sorry for them. You just laugh in their faces while you take what they got. Boy, why do you think I came for you and took you out of that house?"

Duncan's first thought was because Wainwright was a mean prick who wanted to ruin his life, but he said the second thought that came to his head.

"Because you'd gotten too clumsy to pick pockets yourself and too old to climb through windows. You needed me to do the heavy lifting."

Wainwright's face crinkled like a bloodhound's who'd just bit into something nasty-tasting.

"That's just foolishness," he said. "I was doing just fine on my own robbing banks. The reason I got you out of that home was because you're family, and I couldn't let you grow up soft like your daddy. Look what that life got him. A slave to a paycheck and a mortgage and ending up no better than roadkill. Thanks to me you don't got to live that sucker's life. You got freedom to live like a man's supposed to."

Duncan felt exhausted all of a sudden. "How'd you know where to find me back then?" he asked.

"I was passing through St. Louis when I saw a story on the news about a tragic car accident that claimed the life of a young couple from Jasper." Wainwright had said this with a sneer, but his sneer soon faded, and a flicker of regret showed in his bloodshot eyes. "Tommy might've changed his name, but I recognized him from the pictures they showed of him and your ma. The news story mentioned an orphaned boy, and so I contacted the authorities. They made me give them some of my blood to prove Tommy was my kin, and that was a dangerous thing for me to do, but I couldn't abandon my only living grandson."

"Because otherwise I'd grow up soft."

"Damn straight."

Duncan mulled all that over. "It will probably be hours before that family is discovered," he said.

"Could be a day or longer," Wainwright agreed.

"And that yellow-haired girl is just lying there going to waste."

"A damn shame."

"How about you pull over?" Duncan suggested. "I'll take over behind the wheel before you kill us, and I'll turn us around and drive back there. We'll both have our fun."

Wainwright rubbed away a tear that had leaked from his eye. "Boy, I've never been more proud of you."

The old man pulled the car over to the side of the highway. His back had gotten somewhat creaky over the last six years, and he had just worked his way out of the car when Duncan approached. He showed Duncan a wide grin. "It took a while, but I finally got you seeing things straight," he said.

Duncan shot him in his right knee and Wainwright fell to the ground.

"You shot me," he said as if he didn't quite believe it.

"If you don't get on your knees I'm shooting you again."

"Goddamn you, boy! I'm your flesh and blood. Your grandpa!"

Duncan aimed the gun so it was pointed square in the middle of Wainwright's forehead. He started to pull back the trigger and only stopped after Wainwright struggled to get on his knees.

"I'm in pain," he cried.

"That's a shame. My dog, Buster—did he really run off or did you drive him miles away and abandon him?"

"You shoot me in the knee and that's what you ask me?"

"You better answer me, old man, or I'll shoot you in the balls next."

A meanness edged into Wainwright's eyes. "It would've been cruel for me to do that," he said. "It would've also been a damn waste of gas. I put that flea-bitten mutt in a sack and I drowned him in the creak that ran behind your house."

Duncan reversed his grip on the gun and hit Wainwright in the jaw with it, putting every ounce of strength he had in the blow. Wainwright's dentures flew out, as did several of his remaining molars. The old man collapsed on the ground. Whether he was unconscious or dead, Duncan didn't care.

He got back in the car and drove away.

Chapter 48

Los Angeles, the present

Matt Kammer was scheduled to fly out of Omaha and land at LAX at 9:15 p.m., but he got himself on an earlier flight after seeing a story about the Cupid Killer. He had called Hannah that morning to tell her he would be arriving earlier.

"Of course, there are no nonstops from Omaha," he complained. "The flight has a stop in Minneapolis-Saint Paul, but at least I'll be back in Los Angeles at three."

Hannah, without missing a beat, said, "I'll pick you up at the airport."

"Don't. I have an errand I need to do downtown, but I'll be home by six."

"You're being ridiculous. I'll join you."

"It's better that you don't."

That got Hannah curious. "How come you're acting all mysterious?" she asked.

"I'll explain when I see you."

She was even more curious now. "You can't give me a hint?"

"No. Sorry."

Hannah's cheeks blew up like a chipmunk's. She could usually get Matt to spill the beans, but every once in a while he got stubborn like this, and when he did, she'd have better luck prying open a clam with her fingers than getting him to talk.

"Okay. I guess. How come the change in plans?"

"Yours truly swooped in like Superman and saved the account. If I stick around today, it would only be for additional wining and dining, and they don't need me for that. The sales folks here can handle that part just fine." His voice lowered as he added, "I got onto the *Times* website and saw a story about that psycho killing women. I've been worried sick since then. I just want to be home with you."

"You know I'm a big girl. I can take care of myself."

"You're not that big. Barely a smidgen."

She laughed at that. "You have to admit, a feisty smidgen. And one who knows how to use her elbows and knees."

"That might be true. But it won't stop me from worrying. And if I don't get home soon, I'll probably give myself a stroke."

"Now you're getting me worried. Take deep breaths and try to relax."

"I'll try. Promise."

Hannah asked, "You won't tell me about this errand?"

"It has to be a secret for now."

She didn't like the way that sounded, but didn't push him to divulge his secret. He came home at six o'clock as promised, and after meeting him at the door with a kiss, she raised her eyebrows and asked about his secret mission.

"I'll tell you," he said. "You just have to promise me to keep an open mind."

She didn't like the way he said that. Like he was guilty of something. But she didn't say anything as she followed him to the kitchen. He swung his travel bag onto the counter, then rooted inside of it and pulled out a gun. She knew nothing about guns and had no idea what type this one was other than it was big and deadly-looking.

"You got to be kidding me," she said.

Matt tried smiling, but it came out sickly. "Hannah, I know how you feel about guns—"

"If you did, you wouldn't have brought one into my home!"

"Our home." He pushed a hand through his hair, which was something he did whenever he got flustered. "I saw photos of the two women that maniac killed. They both resembled you. We need this gun until they catch him."

Hannah was going to argue that he was acting insane. They didn't even live in Los Angeles, but in Pasadena, and there were millions of women in the greater Los Angeles area for the Cupid Killer to choose from. But she had also noticed how much those two poor women had looked like her, and it freaked her out a bit. Instead, she asked how he got the gun.

His sickly, forced smile turned sheepish. "I called my buddy Albert. He arranged it."

A coolness filled her head as she stared at her husband. "The gun's not even legal?" she asked incredulously.

"It will be. I'll apply for a permit tomorrow."

"I don't care what you do with it, but I want it out of the house."

Matt clamped his mouth shut and jutted out his jaw: the look he showed whenever he was going to put on his stubborn-mule act.

"I'll keep it in my underwear drawer for now," he said. "I'll buy a lockbox for it tomorrow."

So that was it. As far as he was concerned, the discussion was over.

The other night Hannah had made his favorite dinner—lasagna with sausages—so that it would be waiting for him when he got back from his trip. Without saying another word, she took the pan from the refrigerator and put it in the oven to reheat, then walked out of the kitchen, giving him the cold shoulder.

An hour later they ate dinner together, but Hannah's cold shoulder had become an icy one. Matt made several half-hearted attempts to chip away at the iciness before slipping into his own sullen mood. After dinner, he marched off to his man cave in the basement while she opened a bottle of wine. An hour later he came back to confront her. He'd had enough of her nonsense!

"You're acting like a child!"

She was sitting at the table, a half-empty bottle of wine in front of her. She turned to face him, and her eyes grew as large as saucers and the color drained out of her face. Seeing her like that made the short hairs on the back of his neck stand up, especially once he realized she wasn't looking at him but past him. He was reacting purely on instinct when he turned around to see what it was she was staring at that had her too frightened to talk. If he had a moment to think he would've known better than to do that.

Right before he was hit, Matt caught a glimpse of a man dressed in black with a ski mask covering his face. Then his world went black.

Hannah made a mad dash out of the kitchen and Duncan ran after her. Yesterday when he drove to Pasadena he could've gotten into their house with a lockpick, but they made it easy for him by keeping a key hidden in a fake rock by the side of the house, and when he broke in he found a note with Matt's return flight information. He came back tonight thinking he'd find the house empty or Hannah alone; either one working nicely. Instead, twenty minutes ago when he used that same key to gain access to the house, he heard Matt downstairs in the basement and spied on Hannah while she sat in the kitchen sipping a glass of wine. If he tried sneaking down the basement steps, Matt would hear him, so he hid in the hallway closet and waited for Matt to come upstairs. It didn't take too long for that to happen, and seconds later he knocked the guy unconscious. Duncan just had to hope this time he didn't kill the sucker...

He chased Hannah to her bedroom. She was a speedy little thing, but not quite fast enough to lock the bedroom door on him. He was prepared to put a shoulder into it and knock the door back into her face, but she didn't even try to close it on him. That surprised him. He would've expected her to try that in her panic.

When he stepped into the room, she was rummaging through a dresser drawer. He should've been a little faster on the uptake about what she was looking for, and it surprised him when she spun around holding a 9mm pistol in both hands and pointing it dead center at his chest. This happened too fast for him to react, and his shoulders dropped as he waited for her to pull the trigger and send him to hell.

She pulled the trigger, but nothing happened. No loud noise. No bullet firing and blowing a hole through his chest. Nothing other than an empty *click*. Hannah looked dumbfounded by this.

Duncan stepped forward and took the gun from her hands. He gave it a quick look.

"You had the safety on," he explained.

He shoved the gun in his waistband and in a quick, fluid motion, he swung the leather sap down on her as if he were swatting a fly. The lead-weighted end of the sap struck her flush on the collarbone and left her in a crumpled heap.

Chapter 49

Morris Brick was grabbing some coffee before the eight a.m. meeting when he sensed a person approaching him from behind. He had a good idea who it was from Parker's excited grunts and the way the bull terrier's ropy tail began wagging at a fast clip.

"Good morning, Phil," he said without turning around.

Stonehedge didn't bother to ask how he had figured out it was him. Maybe he assumed Morris had caught his reflection in the coffeepot.

"What did I do to piss you off?" the actor asked in a low voice.

"Why do you think you pissed me off?"

"Easy answer. Because you assigned me to Polk." Stonehedge further lowered his voice and said, "I swear, the inside of his car smells like bad cheese."

Morris chuckled at that. He handed Stonehedge the cup of coffee he'd just poured and grabbed another mug for himself. "It's the liverwurst and limburger sandwiches," he said.

"Huh? Limburger cheese is still something people eat?"

"Apparently. Years ago when Fred and Polk were partners, Fred made the mistake of complaining about the smell of a sardine sandwich Polk had brought on a stakeout, and after that Polk started bringing liverwurst and limburger sandwiches to be even more annoying. Either he grew to like them or is just too stubborn to admit why he started eating them in the first place. Whichever it is, he still brings them on stakeouts and the stench has saturated the interior of his car."

Stonehedge frowned. "He also picks his teeth."

"He does do that," Morris agreed. "Just be thankful you weren't on a stakeout with him. Those sandwiches give him gas. But to answer your question, you did nothing. The work required me to team up with Annie, as simple as that. But we'll see where we are after this morning's meeting. Maybe I'll be able to take you back under my wing. Anyway, spending time with Polk should've toughened you up and helped you get ready for that role."

"Toughen me up, maybe. Help me get ready for my role? Not unless David Lynch were directing the movie. He's not."

The thought of that made Morris smile. He finished adding milk and sugar to his coffee, and the two of them walked to the conference room, with Parker staying close beside Morris.

Morris checked his watch. Ten to eight. Everyone who was going to attend was already seated around the table. Roger Smichen and Doug Gilman were bowing out, since they didn't have anything to contribute and were busy with other work. Bogle also wasn't going to be there. He was flying to Boston to look into a murder that happened a year ago. Felger likewise was skipping the meeting, since Morris wanted him instead to keep searching for other crimes around the country that could've been done by the Cupid Killer.

Morris took a seat next to Gloria Finston and Parker trotted under the table and lay down between the two of them so that his head rested on Morris's shoes. The dog often lay like that, and Morris never understood how that could be comfortable for him. Across the table, Polk sat sullenly, giving him the evil eye.

"I thought there would be food here," Polk grumbled.

"Greta called in an order at Fresca's."

Fresca's had maybe the best breakfast sandwiches in West Hollywood, and the thought of the food arriving soon seemed to mollify Polk. At least he stopped sulking.

"Did she order any of their steak and egg on toasted brioche?"

"Enough so you can have two."

Polk crossed his thick arms over his chest. "All right, then," he said.

Morris reported on what he knew about the murder in Oakland and the little that Bogle and Felger had been able to find out about the one in Boston, which according to the detective Bogle spoke with was also drug-related.

He asked the FBI profiler, "Suzanne Markin was killed in Oakland eighteen months ago, Julia Swan in Boston a year ago, both presumably tortured with knives to make their boyfriends divulge where their drug stashes were hidden. Is this the same guy we're dealing with now?"

Finston had already seen Bogle's notes and the police report on Markin's murder. She hadn't seen the Swan police report yet, because the Boston detective was reluctant to send Bogle a copy, but that would change later today. Finston had already put a call in to the Boston FBI office, and was promised Bogle would be given the report and that the detective in charge of the case would cooperate fully.

"I don't know," she admitted. "The Oakland perpetrator used a knife on Ms. Markin, not just to make the boyfriend, Clay Shelby, comply, but because he enjoyed it. But he also kept her clothed and stopped after he got what he was after. There are enough similarities between Ms. Markin and our recent victims to make me think it's possible, and enough differences to think otherwise. Perhaps what Charlie finds in Boston will help make this clearer. Did this so-called Cupid Killer use the term *champ* to Alex Frey?"

"I don't know. Frey was heavily sedated when we went back to ask him that. We'll try again when his doctor gives the okay."

"Frey didn't say anything about the perp calling him *champ* the first time I interviewed him," Walsh added.

There was a knock on the door, then Greta stuck her head in to tell them the order from Fresca's had arrived. Polk volunteered to help Morris carry over the two large bags filled with breakfast sandwiches that had been left by the reception area. He also made sure to be the first one to rummage through the bag he brought back to the conference room, and grabbed two of the steak and egg brioche sandwiches. He was a happy camper when he took a big bite out of one of them.

Stonehedge asked, "No liverwurst and limburger?"

Polk gave him a suspicious look. He said, "Put that on a bun with a fried egg and that would be a dream come true."

They took a break to eat, and Parker pushed himself to his feet and focused all of his mooching on Stonehedge, who he was perceptive enough to realize was a soft touch. Once breakfast was finished, Morris asked Polk to give them an update on their efforts to identify the Cupid Killer from the Frey and Kincade engagement party.

"So far nothing but a massive headache," Polk said as he brushed several crumbs from his lips.

"Huge headache," Greg Malevich agreed.

Polk said, "It took almost half a day, but we compiled a list of everyone at the engagement party; at least everyone who was supposed to be there."

Malevich thumbed through a notepad until he found the page he was looking for. "A hundred-and-fifty-nine guests, eighteen employees, and three members of a security firm that were guarding the presents."

"It was a royal pain in the ass, but we were able to match up all the gifts to the guests on the list, and we were left with one extra gift."

"The *cutest couple* mugs," Morris said.

"Yeah. I was hoping the security personnel collecting the gifts would've remembered who gave him the box holding the mugs, but he didn't. I can't blame him. He was focused on looking for threats and not on trying to match the guests to the boxes they were giving him."

"Where are you with interviewing the guests?"

"We're up to our necks, that's where we are," Polk said. "We interviewed the eighteen employees working the party—waitresses, waiters, bartenders, and musicians, and none of them noticed anyone acting suspiciously. We talked with Frey's brother, Todd, and he didn't have a conversation with any strangers there. We also talked with both sets of parents. Brett Kincade, the dead girl's old man, threw out three guys who had crashed the party, but his descriptions were worthless. Other than that, we've interviewed forty-seven other guests so far and collected a shitload of photos."

Malevich found another page in his notepad. "A hundred-and-thirty-six," he said.

"Most of these photos are of the happy couple," Polk said. "But they all have people in the background, sometimes as many as a dozen. We need to blow up each one and identify everyone in them. So far, it's been a long, painstaking process."

Morris said, "I'll give Doug Gilman a call and see if the LAPD can loan us more bodies."

Polk scratched lazily at the back of his neck. "You could also pull Fred off whatever he's fooling around on and get him to do some real work like the rest of us."

Walsh's phone vibrated loudly enough to draw Morris's attention. She gave the caller ID a quick glance before answering the phone. Her eyes slitted and her expression grew tense as she listened to whatever the person on the other end had to say. A half-minute later she put her phone back down on the table and looked angry enough to spit nails.

"We've got another victim," she announced.

Chapter 50

Fred Lemmon wished he had been able to plant a bug in Hardacher's phone, but sometimes you just have to make do with what you have.

He finished his fourth coffee of the day, then turned his wrist so he could check the time. Not even 9:30 yet. He was dragging badly that morning, and would be needing a lot more coffee that day. If he could only attach an IV bag directly to a vein, but even that might not be enough.

He closed his eyes and pictured a giant vat of steaming coffee. The high-octane stuff. He imagined diving headfirst into it and doing a backstroke.

He had good reason for being tired. He hadn't slept well in weeks. Months, actually. It was all the uneasiness and bad vibes he picked up from Corrine, and it had only gotten worse since he had brought Wendy Hardacher into their home. Wendy had been quiet, unobtrusive, and really the perfect guest, mostly keeping to herself in Alexis's bedroom (his daughter was away at college), but that hadn't stopped the accusing looks from Corrine, as if Lemmon had ulterior motives. Now, if it had been Annie Walsh instead, Corrine would at least have had just cause for her suspicions...

But enough feeling sorry for himself. He was sitting in his car a mile from Hardacher's house, and so far that morning Hardacher's car hadn't moved and he hadn't picked up any sounds from Hardacher's home office. Lemmon didn't even know whether the target was still home. Someone could've picked him up. Or he could be in bed. Maybe his girlfriend came over last night for a booty call, and they were still screwing around in there.

Lemmon should've bugged the bedroom also. If he hadn't been so sleep-deprived, he would've suggested that to Wendy. Well, he needed to find out whether Hardacher was home or not. He started up the engine and pulled away from the curb. He would bring a briefcase to Hardacher's door and ring the doorbell. If Hardacher answered, he'd act as if he were selling siding, and if Hardacher didn't come to the door, Lemmon would use the house key Wendy had given him.

His cell phone beeped. He pulled over to the curb and saw that it was the app Felger had installed. He fiddled with the display so that it would show where Hardacher was heading.

* * * *

Lemmon followed Hardacher first to LA's fashion district, and then to a public parking lot for the Santee Alley flea market. The parking lot had a second entrance on the other side of the block and Lemmon headed to it so that he wouldn't be following Hardacher into the lot.

He found a spot on the street. The app showed that Hardacher had parked his car. Lemmon listened in on the bug planted inside Hardacher's car, and could hear the car running and country music playing over the radio. Aside from Johnny Cash and Waylon Jennings, Lemmon didn't much care for country music. Polk, though, loved that stuff.

He used field glasses and spotted Hardacher sitting in the car. Five minutes later, Hardacher turned off the engine and radio, then stepped out of the car. He looked bewildered as he stood for a minute, and then started walking a slow loop around the parking lot, as if he were searching for someone. He returned to his car and got back inside.

Lemmon settled in for what he thought could be a long wait. The Santee Alley flea market was about as opposite to Rodeo Drive as you could find in Los Angeles. The flea market was filled with cluttered kiosks selling cheap clothing and other merchandise, just like the stores lining the area. This wasn't a bad place to set up a meeting. It would be easy enough for someone to run out of the parking lot and get lost in the flea market crowd or hide in one of the surrounding stores.

It was maybe fifteen minutes after Hardacher pulled into the lot that Lemmon spotted a woman wearing a long trench coat, a big floppy hat, and dark sunglasses that hid half her face, approaching the car. Lemmon had his camera ready on the passenger seat and took several photos of her before she ducked into the back of Hardacher's car so that she was seated directly behind him. Lemmon turned the volume up on his phone in order to hear everything they said. The app would also be recording their conversation.

Hardacher started to twist around to get a look at her. She told him to keep facing front and he followed her order.

Hardacher: I thought I was meeting Spenser.

Woman: That's not even his name.

Hardacher: I don't understand. (He sounded genuinely confused.) *Is the... um, job done?*

Woman: (mocking Hardacher) *You mean... um, did Jack kill your wife like you paid?*

Hardacher: Jack?

Woman: You're not too swift, are you? Jack's the guy you thought was Spenser. And no, your wife isn't dead. That's not why I'm here.

Hardacher: (wising up) *What do you want?*

Woman: Listen up, genius.

The mystery woman must've pressed a button for a digital recorder to play back part of a conversation between Hardacher and Jack/Spenser. The voices were tinny and Lemmon had to strain to hear it.

The recording the woman played captured Hardacher making a 2000-dollar down payment for this Jack character to kill his wife, and agreeing to pay him an additional two grand after the job was done. The woman pressed a button to cut off the recording after these salient points were made.

Woman: You're going to pay us ten-thousand dollars Saturday—

Hardacher: The deal I had was for Spenser—I mean Jack—to kill Wendy for four grand. I'm not paying anything more than that!

Woman: Look, genius, Jack's not killing your wife. We're blackmailing you, okay? You don't pay us ten grand and the recording goes to the police and you go to prison, got it?

The woman must've been sneering when she said that. Lemmon could just about hear it in her voice. Neither of them spoke for the next thirty seconds, then Hardacher broke the silence.

Hardacher: (distraught) *I can't get ten grand by Saturday.*

Woman: You better figure out a way. I'm leaving a flash drive on the backseat with directions of how you're going to pay us. And don't be a dumb-ass and try to take this recording from me. It's a copy. Jack has the original.

The woman left the car and took off toward the opposite entrance. Hardacher didn't bother chasing after her and neither did Lemmon. If he followed her, she'd lead him to the man Hardacher met at the motel room, the same one who was now blackmailing him. But Lemmon's concern was

Hardacher, not the blackmailer, and he now had more than enough for a solicitation-to-commit-murder charge to stick.

Hardacher hadn't moved, and from what Lemmon could tell the man appeared to be deep in thought, no doubt struggling to figure a way out of his mess. Lemmon drove into the parking lot and pulled up directly in back of Hardacher, blocking him in. He got on the phone with Morris and told him what had happened. He asked whether Annie or one of Morris's other LAPD contacts could send the cavalry pronto.

Hardacher had noticed Lemmon blocking him in and he stormed out of his car, his face contorting into an ugly mask of blind rage. It was bad enough his wife wasn't being killed like he had expected. Bad enough also that he was being blackmailed! But now this? Some joker rudely blocking his car!

Hardacher pounded on Lemmon's window and spittle flew out his mouth as he demanded to know what Lemmon thought he was doing. Lemmon rolled down his window and showed Hardacher the badge deputizing him.

"Relax," he said. "Police cruisers will be here soon and when they arrive you'll be arrested for soliciting a murder. For now, just sit in your car and wait. And try not to be a total jackass and make a run for it. You won't get anywhere doing that."

Hardacher stumbled backward as if he'd been punched in the face. His eyes took on the shifty look of someone who was thinking about making a run for it, but then his face just sort of collapsed as a look of utter defeat took over.

Hardacher got back in his car and waited.

Lemmon was mildly disappointed by this. He wouldn't have minded the opportunity to chase after Hardacher and tackle the guy, and maybe knock out a few of his teeth in the process.

Chapter 51

Morris had left Parker back at the MBI office with Greta, and he and Annie Walsh drove to Pasadena and found Matt Kammer inside the Davis Street precinct with a chicken egg–sized bump over his right eye. A detective had told them they wanted to take Kammer to the hospital to be checked out, but Kammer insisted on going to the station house, telling the detective if he was taken to the hospital they'd probably give him a sedative, and he wanted to be clearheaded when he talked with the police.

Morris was about to introduce himself to Kammer, but realized that he had met this man before. Then he remembered where and when.

"I met you and your wife Sunday at the Santa Monica Pier," he said. "Your wife wanted to pet my dog."

A glimmer of recognition broke through Kammer's dull, glass-like eyes. "You were the one with the bull terrier," he said, as if coming out of a trance.

"That's right. Your wife impressed me as being a very sweet woman. I can't possibly understand how difficult this must be for you—"

Kammer interrupted him. "It would be so much worse if I wasn't doing what I could to get justice for Hannah." He clamped his mouth shut as he choked back a sob. It was a struggle, but the moment passed and he continued, "It's all I have left that I can do for her."

A grim determination had hardened Kammer's feature, but his eyes remained liquid and Morris knew that the man was barely holding it together. That once he finished talking with them he'd be breaking down. Walsh got Kammer's attention, asking if he could tell them what happened. He told them in a near-lifeless voice how the Cupid Killer had found the spare key they kept hidden in a fake rock outside their house and snuck up on him when he was in the kitchen.

"He hit me with a club of some sort before I could do anything about it. The next thing I knew he was using something harsh to wake me."

"Do you remember smelling ammonia?" Walsh asked.

"Yeah. It had a strong chemical taste. It made me feel like my nostrils were being burned." He rubbed at his nose as if he were trying to dislodge the memory of that odor. "When I came to, I was in the kitchen tied to a chair, a gag in my mouth, and Hannah was across from me."

He seemed to lose himself in his thoughts. Morris and Walsh had already talked with the detective in charge, and they knew that the killer wore a ski mask and the same black clothing he wore with Alex Frey. They also knew that Hannah had been stripped naked before she was tied up and gagged, and like the other two women, she had her nipples sliced off and was stabbed and cut over a hundred times. They didn't need to hear any of this from Kammer, but they wanted to hear what he had to tell them in case something new popped loose.

Morris nudged him along by asking what happened next.

"That sick bastard did terrible things to Hannah with a knife." Kammer's mouth weakened and he had to stop for a moment before he could add, "The sick bastard kept cutting and stabbing Hannah until she died."

"Did he say anything to you?"

"Yeah." A hard grimace tightened Kammer's lips. "I remember he called me *champ* a few times."

Morris asked, "Champ?"

"That's right. He was taunting me, saying stuff like, *Lucky you, champ, having a front-row seat for this* and *Champ, how'd an ugly fuck like you end up with a beauty like her.*" Kammer jutted out his chin, a resolve hardening his features. "At the end—and I'll never forget this—this psychopath told me *Now you have yourself an especially wonderful rest of your life.*"

Morris waited for him to say something about him being offered the same cruel Faustian bargain that was offered to Alex Frey. When it became apparent that Kammer had nothing more to say, Morris asked, "Is that all?"

Kammer's mouth fell open and he goggled at Morris as if he had three eyes. "Isn't that enough?" he asked incredulously.

"He didn't offer you a deal?"

"Like what?"

"That he would let you end your wife's suffering."

The baffled look that spread over Kammer's face appeared genuine. "How would he have let me do that?" he asked.

"By cutting you free so you could strangle your wife."

"That's what this sicko offered those other two men?"

"We know he did with the first victim, and we think so also with the second."

Kammer's eyes glazed as if he were staring at something far away. He broke out of his trance, blinking several times and then looking back at Morris. "If he offered me that I would've taken him up on it, and I would've found a way to kill him and Hannah would be alive now. Why didn't he make me that offer also?"

"I don't know. Did you notice any marks, bruises, or tattoos on him?"

Kammer frowned as he considered that. "He wore a ski mask," he said. "A long-sleeve knit shirt also." He squinted badly as if he were trying to pull a stubbornly elusive fact from his memory. All at once he smacked his right fist into his open palm, making a loud enough noise that an uniformed officer standing in the hallway stuck his head in the room to make sure there was no trouble. "He had a tattoo right here," he said excitedly.

Kammer pointed to the underside of his right wrist.

Morris asked, "Do you remember what it was?"

"Yeah. A wolf's face."

Morris wasn't sure he heard that right. It couldn't be that, could it? "Please repeat what you just said?" he asked, trying to keep his voice calm.

"A wolf's face," Kammer insisted with absolute certainty. "Its fangs were bared. Like it was snarling."

Morris's cell phone rang. Fred Lemmon. He answered the call.

Lemmon asked, "What do you call a bunch of canaries?"

"I know a large group of crows are called a murder," Morris said, frowning. "I think with peacocks it's a muster. I don't know what you call it with canaries."

Walsh, who was driving, volunteered that there was nothing special about canaries, and a large group of them was just a flock.

Lemmon asked if that was Annie Walsh.

"Yep," Morris said.

"Tell her I said hi."

Morris's frown deepened. He suspected that Lemmon had a thing for Walsh and the way Lemmon sounded just then, as if he were embarrassed by what he had just said, made Morris suspect that even more.

"You can tell her yourself," he said gruffly, and he put the cell phone on speaker.

Lemmon said, "Annie, I thought it's a flock of seagulls?"

Walsh made a face at that bad joke referencing the 1980s new wave band. She said, "Are you sure that's Fred and not Polk?"

"Ah, I'm wounded deeply," Lemmon responded.

Morris asked Lemmon why he was calling.

"Hardacher ended up singing more than any flock of canaries, and he said something interesting about the hit man he hired. Or really the con man who masqueraded as a hit man and is now blackmailing him. Two things, actually, and they sounded familiar, so I called Felger to confirm why they sounded familiar. This case intersects with your Grace Warren missing-person's investigation."

"How so?"

"First, Hardacher met Jack at the High Spot Lounge in Inglewood, the same bar where Grace Warren was last seen. Second, Jack has a wolf's-face tattoo on the underside of his right wrist."

Morris found the photos that Lemmon had sent him of the man Hardacher met outside the motel room. A real badass-type who also fit the description Trey Johnson gave of the man who took Grace Warren from him. Was it possible that he was also the Cupid Killer?

"Did Hardacher by any chance give you a phone number or address for Jack?" he asked, his voice echoing faintly in his own ears as if it were coming from a distance away.

"Not quite. But he told me how we might be able to make contact with him."

Chapter 52

There were benches outside UCLA's law library, but Duncan chose instead to sit on the lawn under a tree. He had a copy of *Crime and Punishment* that he had picked up for $1.98 from the discount rack at a used bookstore and he assumed, given the way he was so neatly dressed and his carefully groomed appearance, that if he sat where he was and looked like he was reading the book, people would think he was a college student and they'd leave him alone. He'd been mostly right, other than a horny law student whom he caught an hour-and-a-half ago staring at him with obvious interest. Tall, long blond hair, large bust, narrow waist, big-toothed grin. She looked like she could've been a *Playboy* model from an earlier era, and was what Wainwright might've called *statuesque* if the old man had had a better vocabulary. Not Duncan's type, though. After he caught her eyeing him over, she grinned, walked over to where he was sitting, and asked if he wanted to exchange briefs with her. The stunned look on his face caused her to break out laughing.

"I'm sorry," she said. "A bad law school joke."

"I wouldn't know. I'm an English major," Duncan said with a big *aw-shucks* grin. "At least you didn't make a crack about us exchanging oral arguments."

He had decided earlier to play nice if anyone approached him. Less chance he'd draw unwanted attention by doing that. All he'd been able to think about was that flinty-eyed dark-haired beauty he'd seen having lunch with her mom yesterday—even when he was torturing Hannah Kammer last night, he found himself drifting into thoughts about that other woman. He was hoping if he camped out by the library he'd spot her again, and it would've been idiotic of him to intentionally piss off anyone and give them a reason to call security on him.

The statuesque blonde giggled at what he said. "That's actually not a bad idea. I'm up to it, if you are."

He deadpanned, "You mean right out here in the open?"

"We'd get arrested, especially if we did all the things I'd like to do to you. But no, let's go back to my apartment. I live less than a half mile from here."

"My dear, are you propositioning me?" Duncan said with an exaggerated, wide-eyed innocence.

"You bet I am. Life's too short not to go for what you want. And after hitting the law books for the last four hours, I could use a naked tumble in the sack." She held out a hand whose fingernails were painted a deep blood-red. "Sandra."

Duncan reached up and took her hand. "Connor," he said. "As gorgeous as you are and as much as I'd like to take you up on your offer, I have to finish this book today or I'm toast."

She looked both disappointed and relieved. At a subconscious level, she must've realized the mistake it would've been to bring a predator like Duncan into her home, even if she couldn't exactly articulate that insight.

"Another time, perhaps?"

"God, I hope so," Duncan said.

He watched her start to walk away. The poor girl just wasn't in tune enough with her subconscious, because after she'd gone only twenty yards, she turned to give him a questioning look. After all, he'd gotten to watch her delicious rear end wiggle for the last ten seconds, and that had to be enough to change his mind. He raised his hands in a helpless gesture, and she gave him a *too bad* look and continued on her way. After that, he went back to staring at a page in the book, the words just seeming to blend together.

It wasn't so much that Dostoyevsky's more complex writing style had him stymied, but that he would've had trouble that day concentrating even on Dr. Seuss. At times, his thoughts drifted to that flinty-eyed slender cutie and how much he wanted her to be one of his victims—or more precisely, how much he wanted to enjoy making the lucky bastard who was her fiancé suffer. Other times, he'd wonder about whether the police had found the Kammers yet, and what they would think about him deviating from his routine. He'd done everything to Hannah that he had to the other two women, but he didn't offer the husband a deal to stop her suffering. He could see in Kammer's eyes that if he made him that offer, Kammer would've taken him up on it, but instead of doing what he promised he would've tried saving his wife, and Duncan might very well have killed him then and he couldn't afford to do that. He needed to make sure Kammer got a good look at his temporary snarling wolf's-face tattoo so he would later be able to tell the police about it.

If Duncan were being completely honest about it, there was more to it than that. Kammer might've been a member of the fortunate-few club, and he might've been well-off and happily married to a beautiful woman, but he wasn't like the other two men. He wasn't *GQ*-model good-looking, that was for sure. At best he was a lumpy, average-looking guy who got lucky marrying a woman as gorgeous as his wife. Most lottery winners never got that lucky. While Duncan didn't actually feel sorry for him, he nonetheless didn't find himself as rage-filled as with the other two murders. This killing was purely because his plan needed it, and not so that he could unleash his inner demons.

Duncan was making a concerted effort to decipher the meaning of what he was reading, and he almost missed it when the flinty-eyed dark-haired cutie left the library. It startled him when he noticed her on the pathway right across from him. She saw him looking startled.

"Is anything wrong?" she asked, her eyes narrowing and looking especially flinty.

He felt his stomach flip a little. How crazy was that? Up until a year ago he would've simply admired how beautiful she was and left it at that. There was even a time when he would've wanted to introduce himself, talk her into a date, and someday marry her. Now he just wanted to slowly torture and kill her in front of her bound and gagged fiancé.

He smiled apologetically and held up the paperback so she could see what he was pretending to read. "No, nothing," he said. "I was just trying to make sense of a particularly dense passage in this."

Her eyes narrowed further as she read the book's title. "That's a difficult one," she agreed. "Good luck."

He nodded thanks, and waited until she cut through the trees and shrubs so that she could get onto Hilgard Avenue, and then took off after her. There were plenty of trees lining the sidewalk that he could dart behind if she looked back, but he was careful to hang far enough back to keep her from suspecting she was being followed. He had his backpack with him, which had everything he needed, and his plan was to follow her home (she had to be going home, right?) and to catch her unaware as she unlocked her door. Then he would tie her up, draw the snarling wolf's-face tattoo on his wrist, and wait for the fiancé to show up. He slowly narrowed the gap between the two of them. The anticipation of what was coming left his mouth dry and his pulse thumping loudly in his temples.

There were only fifty yards separating them now, and when she turned to head into a large apartment complex, he began sprinting so he could catch the vestibule door before it closed behind her. Odds were she wouldn't notice him, and would instead be too busy heading toward the elevator. If she did notice him, well, he'd change his plan. Maybe he'd knock her out, drag her into the elevator, and go through her pocketbook for her keys and driver's license so he'd know her apartment number. One way or another, he'd be alone with her in her apartment very soon.

He had timed it perfectly. The vestibule door was just about to close shut and he rushed forward to keep that from happening, but someone from inside the building stepped forward and pushed the door open. He looked up and saw a statuesque blonde staring back at him. Duncan blinked several times, wondering why she looked so familiar. Then he remembered: Sandra.

She recognized him immediately and gave him an odd smile, then looked back at the woman Duncan had followed, the same one who at that moment was stepping into the elevator.

"Were you following Rachel?" she asked.

"What?" Duncan asked, looking as confused as he felt at that moment, his mind racing over this unexpected development.

"Rachel Brick. My fellow law school student who just walked into this building."

"No, of course not. I realized what an idiot I was for not taking you up on your offer. I mean, damn, you're absolutely luscious. So I asked about you at the law school and got your address. And here I am, hoping your offer still stands."

She didn't look at all convinced he was telling the truth. "I could've sworn you were following Rachel," she said.

He took hold of her hand and held it against his cheek. "Feel how feverish I've gotten thinking of you."

He knew he'd gotten feverish over his anticipation of what he hoped to be doing to the woman who he now knew was named Rachel Brick (and why'd the name Brick sound so damned familiar?). He manufactured a wolfish grin and her suspicion weakened. He caressed her cheek with his other hand, and he felt that she was beginning to heat up also. Squeezing his eyes closed, he bent forward to kiss her, and tried to imagine she was Julia. Her tongue, hot and thick, was soon probing his throat, breaking any illusion that she could be Julia, but thankfully he didn't shudder or give any indication of how much that disgusted him. She pulled her tongue out of his mouth so she could whisper in his ear that they should go to her apartment and get naked, her voice husky and full of expectation.

She took him by the hand and led him to her apartment, which was on the first floor and in the back of the building. Once they were inside, she was on him, her tongue once again pushing into his mouth. He shoved her away. There was no point dragging this out. If he was going to make Rachel Brick one of his victims, Sandra had to die. There was no way around it, and he so much wanted to make that flinty-eyed girl one of his victims, especially after he realized why the name Brick had sounded familiar.

Sandra mistook his reason for pushing her away, thinking that it was so that they'd both get out of their clothes. But then she saw the look in his eyes and froze. Before she could scream for help, Duncan stepped forward and punched her hard enough in the stomach that he could swear his knuckles pressed against her spine. She collapsed onto the carpeted floor, nearly folded in two as she desperately tried to gasp for air. He got down on the floor with her and forced her onto her stomach, then grabbed her by the chin with one hand as he held the side of her head with his other. He put his shoulder into it and twisted her head until her neck snapped.

He got to his feet and looked at the way her head was unnaturally positioned.

That should shut her up for good, he thought.

He put on the leather gloves that he kept in his backpack, then hefted Sandra over his shoulder, carried her into the bedroom, and stuffed her into the closet.

Rachel Brick had to be in her apartment at that moment. He sat down on the bed and tried to think of a ruse he could use to get her to open her door to him, and he couldn't think of anything that had a reasonable chance of working. If he tried picking her lock, she'd hear him and call the police. If he waited outside her apartment door for her to leave so he could surprise her, there would be too great a chance that someone would see him. As badly as he wanted her, he had to show some patience and come back later.

He hadn't touched anything since entering the apartment, so he didn't have to worry about wiping off prints. The blinds were closed on the two windows in the bedroom. He pushed a pair of slats apart. There was a walkway running along the back of the building, and a dense copse of trees separating this building from the one behind it. He could climb out the window and the odds were no one would see him do so. That was a better option than walking out of Sandra's apartment, past the elevators, and out the vestibule door.

Duncan was about to open the window when he remembered Sandra's pocketbook. He found it not too far from where he had killed her and searched for her keys since one would open the vestibule door. He then brought the pocketbook back to the bedroom so he could leave it in the closet with Sandra. With that accomplished, he left through one of the windows.

It wouldn't be long before he came back for Rachel.

Chapter 53

Showtime.

Philip Stonehedge took a deep, cleansing breath. He was about to give the performance of a lifetime, except this time it wouldn't be for a film, but to catch a serial killer. The thought of that was staggering.

He stood outside the High Spot Lounge and concentrated on arranging his facial muscles to show a tough, hard grin; the type a scumbag, chiseling crook would show. The building, a squat, cement structure painted black, looked more like a bunker than a place for people to gather for a drink, although it did have a small movie marquee–like sign with gold letters spelling out its name and a cardboard sign in the darkened window advertising $2.00 draft beers. Stonehedge opened the door and walked in.

The Inglewood bar looked every bit as much a dive inside as it did outside: A dark and dingy space with a musty, stale-beer smell lingering in the air. On the right, a dark-stained oak bar ran halfway down the room, booths lined the left side, and a pool table, jukebox, and a scattering of tables were in the back. Creedence Clearwater Revival's "Who'll Stop the Rain" was playing on the jukebox, so the place at least had that going for it.

Stonehedge was in disguise and had on the same grungy clothes he'd worn when he met Trey Johnson. He stood in the doorway, pulled a comb from his pants pocket, and ran it through his scruffy, blond wig, but this was only to give his eyes a chance to adjust to the darkness of the room. He spotted Fred Lemmon and Detective Annie Walsh camped out at a table in the back. They had gone to the bar a half-hour earlier to look for the Cupid Killer, and if they had seen him the cavalry would've been called in. Lemmon and Walsh were also dressed casually, and Stonehedge thought they made quite the couple. Besides them, there were an elderly couple in a booth and a middle-aged man huddled at the end of the bar nursing a gin and tonic.

Stonehedge took a seat at the bar and the bartender gave him a bland, welcoming smile. "How about a two-dollar draft?"

"Friend, that's only during happy hour," the bartender said apologetically. He was a balding, short, thick-bodied man in his fifties with a square, fleshy face and a flat nose.

"But I'm feeling happy now," Stonehedge said.

"Sorry, but rules are rules."

"Bureaucracy is a beautiful thing, isn't it?" Stonehedge said, letting his grin turn sour. He wrestled his wallet from his back pants pocket and rummaged through it for a fifty-dollar bill, which he laid out in front of him. If this made the bartender at all curious, he didn't show it, and instead he maintained his bland expression.

"A Bud, then," Stonehedge said. "And you can keep the change if you get a message to Jack."

"I know several Jacks, but I don't have a clue which one you're talking about."

"He also likes to use the name Spenser."

The bartender finished pouring Stonehedge a draft, placed the beer in front of him, and picked up the fifty.

"Friend, I don't think I know anybody by that name. What do you want me to do with your change?"

"How about you keep it for now? See if it helps jog your memory. If it doesn't, you can buy a round for the house on me."

The bartender's bland smile began to show some strain. "Let's say I make a few calls and figure out who this Jack/Spenser fellow is. What message do you want me to leave him?"

"Tell him I'm giving him until five, and if he's not here by then I'll be messing up the game he's running and sending his ass to prison."

The bartender's smile was gone and his eyes darkened as if a veil had slipped over them. "That's quite a stick, friend. What's the carrot?"

"Simple. He pays me a small percentage of his game and I leave him alone, maybe even cut him in on an even more lucrative game I'll be starting soon. If he shows up, I also pay you another two hundred."

"Awfully generous." The bartender's smile was back. "In the rare event that I locate this fellow, who do I say wants to meet him so badly?"

"I don't believe he needs to know that."

Stonehedge picked up his beer and made sure to show an overly-confident swagger as he sauntered over to an empty booth. An Oscar-worthy performance. It was a shame he couldn't send it in for consideration.

He had the bartender hooked and was certain that the Cupid Killer would be making an appearance within the hour. Or at least trying to. Morris, Dennis Polk, and a dozen LAPD officers were in position to arrest the Cupid Killer once he showed his face. In the unlikely event this sicko killer eluded them and got inside the High Spot Lounge, Lemmon and Walsh would be cuffing him before he even realized what happened.

Stonehedge would've liked to have been part of the team arresting the Cupid Killer, but even so, this was going to be a wet dream for his publicist. He took a sip of beer and tried to keep from showing the excitement he was feeling. The fact was, he found this absolutely thrilling and quite a departure from the drudgery of acting in a movie. When he was on set, he'd sit around for an hour or two waiting for the next scene to be set up, then the same scene would be shot over and over again until he wanted to scream.

He bit his tongue to keep from laughing over what a prima donna he was being. Yeah, sure, he led such a tough life making all that money with a bullshit acting gig, and poor, pitiful him having to do the same lovemaking scenes a dozen or more times with beautiful actresses like Claire Rose. Still, though, he wasn't joking as much as Morris might think about giving up the acting life to work for him as an investigator. He soon found himself fantasizing about the Cupid Killer making his way past Morris and all the others so that he could deal with the psycho himself.

Now that would be something!

Chapter 54

Boston, Massachusetts. October 2014

Duncan found Wes Cafferty sitting in a booth with a pint of Guinness and a shot of whiskey waiting for him. He slid into the seat across from Cafferty, nodded thanks as he lifted the shot glass, and swallowed down the whiskey, feeling it burn the back of his throat.

"What do you got for me?" he asked.

Cafferty, his expression inscrutable, said, "Family's fine. Thanks for asking."

"Why would I care how your family is?"

Cafferty's thick eyelids lowered as he took a healthy drink of his beer. It had to be a Heineken. Cafferty was on a Heineken kick this year and that was all he'd been drinking. After he placed the half-empty glass back on the table, he wiped a hand across his mouth and gave Duncan a pitying look.

"Because we're both human beings and that's what human beings do. They inquire about what's important to each other."

"What's important to me is that you tell me about the job."

"There's no helping you," he said with disgust. He leaned forward and lowered his voice so that only Duncan could hear him. "Unless you're really good with safes, this job will require some rough behavior, but you'll be nicely rewarded as your take will be twenty-five grand."

Duncan met Wes Cafferty three years ago, and since then Cafferty had set him up with dozens of burglaries in which Duncan was able to get the job done without hurting anyone. He was inclined to turn Cafferty down on this one, but the opportunity to make twenty-five grand on a single score was enticing. He was averaging three grand apiece on the jobs Cafferty put him on, and the most he had gotten from any of them was $7,200.

"How rough?" he asked.

"There's fifty grand sitting in a safe. However rough you need to be to get the target to open it."

"Are you sure about the fifty grand?"

"I can guarantee it."

Cafferty wasn't one for bluster and he wouldn't guarantee something unless it was true. Still, there was something about the way he looked at Duncan that made him wary.

"Is the guy I'll be hitting connected?"

"Not with the mob. A different crime syndicate. He's a cop, but you won't get any heat from this. There's not a damn thing this asshole will be able to do about being ripped off, except take his lumps."

"A dirty cop, huh?"

"As dirty as a sewer rat."

Duncan smiled thinly. "You know what? I think I like the idea of that."

Cafferty's own smile was broader and he showed all his teeth, even his broken and cracked ones. "Why isn't that a surprise?" He reached under the table and handed Duncan a sheet of paper that had been folded into a thick, two-inch square. Duncan slipped it in his pants pocket without looking at it. He didn't need to see it to know that every relevant detail for the job would be written on it.

He asked, "The job's not scheduled for tonight, is it?"

Cafferty sat back in the booth and polished off the rest of his beer before mouthing the word *tomorrow* to Duncan.

Duncan winked at his associate. "In that case, there's still drinking to be done tonight. I'll get us another round."

Duncan, at twenty-three, was still as lean as a rail and had little trouble slipping out of the booth and squeezing his way through the crowd that had gathered at the Blue Rose, a bar in East Boston that was popular among the local blue-collar crowd and a certain unsavory criminal element that he and Cafferty were part of. As much as the police would've liked to have planted an undercover cop inside the Blue Rose to listen in on conversations like the one he had just had, any stranger showing up would be noticed and made to feel unwelcome.

Duncan was working his way through the crowd surrounding the bar, when he noticed a big gorilla-type harassing a blonde wearing a light-brown suede jacket and designer jeans. He couldn't see much of her because she couldn't have been more than five feet two and was slight in stature and the big, drunken oaf was all over her. From what little he could see, she seemed scared and was trying desperately to get away from the Neanderthal who had her cornered. Duncan didn't know the guy's name, but he had seen him before in the neighborhood: A big bruiser who worked as a leg-breaker for a local loan shark by the name of Jimmy Jordan.

Duncan wasn't planning to get involved. This East Boston neighborhood was slowly becoming gentrified, but still there were rules in place. If someone who didn't belong, like that woman, tried slumming it at a place like the Blue Rose, they were going to take their lumps. But when the leg-breaker grabbed the woman by the upper arm and started dragging her toward the back of the bar, he got a look at her horror-stricken face, and he couldn't help himself from veering off course to intersect them.

He got in their way and told the big lummox, "Buddy, how about you leave the lady alone?"

The leg-breaker gave Duncan a drunken, confused look, as if he didn't understand what Duncan had said. Then his eyes got piggish and mean.

"How about you mind your own business?" the leg-breaker said, his words badly slurred. He let go of the woman's arm and threw a wild haymaker. Duncan ducked under it. He bent the leg-breaker over by rabbit-punching him below the belt, then straightened the man up with an elbow to the nose, which left his face a bloody mess. The woman looked like she would've screamed if she weren't so shocked by this sudden flurry of violence.

"Ah, I'm sorry," Duncan told the leg-breaker. "I got you all bloody. Let's take you back to the men's room and clean you up."

The crowd gave Duncan and the leg-breaker a wide berth as Duncan rushed the man toward the back of the bar, but instead of heading to the men's room, he pushed the oaf through the fire door and sent him falling face-first into the alley behind the bar.

"You *sumabitch*," the man slurred badly as he pushed himself up. Before he could get to his feet, Duncan kicked him in the chin and sent him tumbling backwards. He crouched next to the drunk and warned him about what would happen if he ever showed his face at the Blue Rose again.

The drunk tried giving Duncan a cold stare, but his eyes were too unfocused to manage it. "You know who I work for?" he grunted out as a threat.

"You think I give two fucks?"

Duncan grabbed him by his big, floppy ears and slammed the back of his head onto the pavement. The blow knocked him out for good.

Duncan went back inside and was surprised to find the woman he had rescued waiting near the fire door. He caught her staring at his bruised knuckles.

"What did you do to him?" she asked.

Duncan rubbed his knuckles. "I convinced the big gorilla that he had too much to drink and it would be better if he went home and slept it off. Surprisingly—because usually drunks aren't all that agreeable—he did as I suggested. This bruise was from when I gave him a little tap to the nose."

A sigh of relief escaped from her. "Thank you," she said. "I was scared to death about what he planned to do to me."

Duncan had seen the look in the leg-breaker's eyes and he knew that the man was planning to rape her once he got her into the men's room, and maybe worse than that. He also got his first good look at her and it startled him to see how beautiful she was, even though her face was still tense from her earlier fright. She was his age, as slender as he first thought, and with a peaches-and-cream complexion and shoulder-length curly hair that was more golden than blond. It was her almond-shaped hazel eyes and the way she looked at him that made him feel funny in the chest.

"You need to be more careful," he said, his voice turning gruff and heavy and catching in his throat. "The Blue Rose isn't a place for someone like you."

She saw the effect she was having on him and any tenseness in her face was replaced by a burning curiosity. The thought that she might be curious about him left him feeling light-headed.

"And what type of person am I?" she asked, smiling impishly.

He could've simply said that she was someone with a bright future, at least as long as she stayed out of places like the Blue Rose, but instead he said she was someone who wasn't from the area.

"*Au contraire.* I moved to the neighborhood three weeks ago." She held out a small hand that was as delicate as the rest of her. "Julia Swan."

The surname Swan didn't fit. A woman with that name should be tall and graceful with a long neck. Someone like Gwyneth Paltrow. The top of Julia's head barely reached Duncan's chin, and while she might not have had a long, graceful neck like a swan or Gwyneth Paltrow, Duncan found her far more desirable than any woman who would've more closely fit the name Swan—or to be honest about it, any woman he'd ever seen. He'd had more than his share of drunken hookups and one-night stands, but he also accepted long ago that it wasn't in the cards for him to ever have more than that. How could he, given the type of person he was? The type of person Wainwright had made him into? But when he looked at Julia, he felt a longing that he earlier wouldn't have believed possible.

"Duncan Moss." He took her hand and felt how perfectly it fit in his own. The look in her eyes made his heart skip a beat. He couldn't speak right away, and when he finally did, his voice cracked as he suggested that he escort her around the neighborhood and show her more suitable establishments than the Blue Rose.

The smile on her lips had lit up her eyes. "That would be lovely," she said.

Classy and breathtakingly gorgeous. Duncan realized that for the first time since before his parents died, he was feeling genuinely excited about what might be happening next. He couldn't keep the grin off his face as he led Julia out of the Blue Rose.

It was only hours later, while he and Julia were sitting in an Italian coffeehouse in the North End neighborhood of Boston, drinking cappuccinos and sharing a tiramisu, that he remembered he had left Cafferty stranded at the Blue Rose and never bought the round of drinks he had promised. The thought of that made him smile.

"What?" Julia asked.

For the umpteenth time that night he found himself nearly breathless as he looked into her soft, hazel eyes.

"I'll explain it someday," he promised.

Chapter 55

Boston, Massachusetts. October 2017

Duncan's arms were loaded with packages, and he had to do some juggling before he could free up his hands and unlock the door to the Jamaica Plain apartment he shared with Julia. He called out her name even though he knew she wasn't home. He could tell not just by how quiet it was, but because whenever she was around he could feel her energy.

Good. If he hurried, he should have time to get everything ready.

He had made a trip to the North End to pick up *linguine alle vongole* for Julia (her favorite) and lasagna and meatballs for himself, and of course, an order of tiramisu from the same coffeehouse they went to the first night they'd met. After all, it was the three-year anniversary of that night! After he placed the food in the oven to keep it warm, he trimmed the stems on the dozen red roses he'd bought, arranged them in a vase, then placed it in the middle of the small oak table off to the side of the kitchen. He needed to make a decision about the gift-wrapped box holding the pair of delicate gold and freshwater pearl earrings that Julia had remarked about three weeks earlier when they were window-shopping. Should he leave the box next to the flowers or choose somewhere else? He decided to leave them on Julia's pillow. He smiled, thinking about that. When she came home she'd think he'd only bought her the flowers and she would act as if they were enough, but later, when they went to bed, she'd find her real present.

Once all that was taken care of, he stripped off his clothes and headed to the bathroom. He had spent the day repairing an oil burner at a West Roxbury office building and he needed to scrub off the grime and sweat. He also needed to pay some additional attention to the soot under his fingernails and see if he could surprise Julia by coming to dinner with clean nails for a change.

Usually the water in their shower was lukewarm at best, but his timing that evening was perfect and he got a nice blast of hot water. As he soaped himself up, his thoughts drifted to that night three years ago when they spent hours talking in a North End coffeehouse. It was a magical night. That was the only way to explain it. Hell, it transformed him from a criminal with no future beyond his next robbery to what he was today. That night Julia had asked him what he did for a living and he told her odd jobs, and he saw the disappointment in her eyes as he confirmed her worst suspicions. She wasn't an idiot—far from it, and she knew what he meant. But she didn't press him. She didn't want to know about the crimes he was committing to get by.

He didn't see her the next night—he had that job to do and he wasn't about to go back on his word to Cafferty. He never wanted to see Julia disappointed in him again, so he planned on it being his final job, which meant he was going to need that twenty-five grand to ease him into the straight life. The job went smoothly enough—he was able to get the cop out of bed and down to the basement where the safe was kept without waking anyone else, and Duncan only had to slash the guy in the face a few times with the gun barrel before the dirty cop gave him the combination. As Cafferty had promised, Duncan found fifty grand waiting for him, and no blowback happened from the robbery.

After that, he started seeing Julia religiously every evening. Some nights they'd go out to dinner and talk for hours, other nights they'd spend quietly listening to music. Those nights were as magical as their first night together, but Duncan could sense that something was troubling her and after two weeks he couldn't ignore it any longer. He knew what it was. *His odd jobs.* He promised her that those days were over.

"I never had a reason to leave that life before," he said. "I do now."

She had her doubts about what he had just told her. He could see that from how tired she looked all of a sudden.

"Duncan, the only thing I ask is that you never lie to me," she said.

"I won't and I'm not lying now."

She still wasn't fully convinced. "What are your plans?" she asked.

"Over the last two weeks I've been thinking about that and making calls. I found a vocational training program in Dedham that will train me in six months to install and repair heating and air-conditioning systems. After that I'll get a job and work eight-to-five, or whatever hours HVAC technicians work. Not the most glamorous work, I know, but at least it will be honest work."

Her eyes moistened with tears and she once again took his breath away. She was just so heartbreakingly beautiful.

"You're serious about this?" she said.

"I told you, I'm never lying to you and I'm never bullshitting you either."

That evening they were at a Chinatown restaurant, sharing an appetizer platter and a highly-potent drink called a lover's bowl that tasted as innocent as fruit punch. She took hold of his hand with both of hers.

"I only want you changing your life if it's what you want, and not just for me."

"Julia, trust me, I badly want to do this." His expression turned pained as he broached a different subject. "We need to consider moving out of East Boston. That knuckle-dragger who bothered you at the Blue Rose is named Duane Gerkan, and he works for a lowlife by the name of Jimmy Jordan. Jordan's a low-level guy, but still dangerous, at least in that neighborhood. I heard whispers over the last two days that he wasn't happy about what I did to Gerkan and he wants payback. Before I met you I wouldn't have cared about a threat from someone like him, but as you know, my situation is different now. The thing is, I can't leave while you're still living in that neighborhood. I don't think that meathead Gerkan would do anything if he ran into you in the street, but I can't take that chance."

Julia looked alarmed by this. "Where could we go?"

"I'm thinking Jamaica Plain. The rent's cheaper there and it would be a quicker commute for you than where you're living now. And as far as East Boston lowlifes like Jimmy Jordan are concerned, Jamaica Plain could just as well be a different country. I'll find a place to rent and you can crash with me until you find your own place."

Julia let go of his hands and shifted her gaze from him. She looked so small as she sat pensively, her hands clasped in front of her. The silence soon became unbearable to Duncan. He was afraid he had lost her—that his criminal past (even though he had refused to give her any details) had become too real for her. A panic gripped him and an unbearable pain welled up in his chest, because he knew right then that he'd sooner die than not have her in his life. When she looked into his eyes again, he realized that nothing had changed between them. He hadn't cried since he was nine and his parents died, but he had to fight then to keep his emotions from bursting loose. It surprised him in a way that crying from joy was a real thing.

"What?" she asked, her face scrunched into a puzzled look.

He wiped away a tear that was threatening to leak from his eye. "Allergies," he said. "What were you going to say?"

"I was about to suggest that we look for an apartment together."

He broke out laughing. He couldn't help it. He had undergone a complete whirlwind of emotions in a matter of seconds.

She gave him a cross look. "Did I say something funny?" she asked.

"No, nothing. I'm just happy, that's all. But us moving in together after only two weeks of dating? Is that even allowed?"

She showed him her best poker face. "I'm not aware of any laws prohibiting it."

"You know what I mean. Dating etiquette. As you know, I haven't had much experience in that regard."

Her poker face broke as she showed a trace of a smile. "And yet you've displayed quite a mastery in bed."

"That's a different matter, as you well know."

"True," she acknowledged. "But to answer your question: Have you had any interest in us moving in together?"

"Only since the first night I met you."

"Same here, bub. So I guess the question's been answered."

The rest, as they say, was history.

* * * *

Duncan turned off the water, grabbed his towel, and dried himself off. He wrapped the towel around his middle and stepped out of the shower. His nails were mostly presentable, but he used a brush on them until he heard Julia entering the apartment. Or maybe he felt her energy before he heard the door opening. He wasn't sure which. He left the bathroom and met her by the table where he had left the roses. She moved into his arms for a passionate kiss, her eyes dazzling.

"The flowers are beautiful and the food smells wonderful," she said once they separated. "From Carmine's?"

"Where else?"

"Let me guess. There's also a piece of tiramisu from Piccolo Café?"

"I'm getting too predictable," Duncan complained.

"Well, it is our three-year anniversary."

Duncan leaned in for another kiss, this one lasting longer than the first one. Afterward he showed her a guilty smile. "I wish I could've taken you out tonight instead, but that boiler emergency last week at that condo complex screwed up my plans for taking the GED exams, and I really need to knuckle down and study the next three nights if I'm going to pass them."

"Tonight will be perfect," she said. "We'll have a nice, romantic dinner, and then I'll help you study. I can't think of anything I'd rather be doing."

The amazing thing was, he knew she meant it. "I picked up a bottle of chianti," he said. "I've got it decanting in a carafe and it should be good to go. Why don't you pour yourself a glass while I get dressed?"

Julia must've been a ninja in a previous life, because she could move as quietly as a cat when she wanted to, and Duncan didn't realize she had followed him into the bedroom until she asked about the small, gift-wrapped box on her pillow.

"I have no idea what that is," Duncan said with mock surprise. "Someone must've broken into the apartment while I was taking a shower."

"I see."

Julia pulled the towel away from his midsection, and then put both of her small hands on his chest and pushed. Duncan complied and fell backwards onto the bed. He watched as Julia stripped off her clothes.

"I've got my gift to give you," she said, her eyes half-lidded.

"But I've got to study for my GEDs," Duncan said, putting up only a token resistance as Julia climbed on top of him.

"You'll have time for both," she breathed into his ear. "I promise."

As usual, she was right.

Chapter 56

Boston, one year ago

Julia lounged on the couch, a pillow wedged between her back and the armrest, her knees pulled up so the bottom of her feet rested against Duncan. She became consciously aware that it had been a while since she heard the *click-clacking* sound of him typing. She looked up from her book to see him scowling at the laptop.

"I'm too old to be applying to college," he grumbled.

Julia knew him well enough that when he got into one of these moods she shouldn't argue or placate him. That if she gave him a little time, he'd tell her what was really bothering him. Sure enough, after a minute of more intense scowling and biting his thumbnail, he told her the problem was the essay question.

"How am I supposed to write an essay about why I want to go to college when the answer can be summed up in four words: *To make you proud.*"

"That would certainly be a succinct answer," she said.

"Damn straight."

"How many words do they want?"

Duncan made a face like he'd been punched in the gut. "Six hundred," he groaned.

"That's not so bad."

"It's a lot more than four. And that's all I have."

"Hmm. Can I make a suggestion?"

"Go ahead." He heaved out a sigh with an exaggerated sense of despair. "But the damn thing is hopeless."

"Maybe not. I would start with your original thought, since a short and concise answer seems like the right mindset for someone wanting to study mechanical engineering."

Duncan groaned. "If I spell out your first and last name, that will give five words. But I'll still be five-hundred-and-ninety-five words short."

"Very true." Julia stroked her delicate chin, which was a habit she had whenever she was deep in thought. She soon stopped and looked quite pleased with herself. "You could write about how your life changed so suddenly when you were nine and your parents died and an abusive grandfather took guardianship of you. How he kept you out of school and that for you to survive you had to do things you weren't proud of, but through strength of character you turned your life around. Duncan, darling, it's impressive what you've done and it should impress any college-admissions board. You could further write that you're engaged to be married, and that you want the best possible life for yourself and your future family."

Before Duncan proposed to Julia six months ago, he decided she deserved to know the whole unvarnished truth, and so he told her all of it. He knew in his heart they were soul mates, but even so, he was worried sick that once she knew about Wainwright and his robberies and other crimes that she would look at him differently. That didn't happen. If anything, the fact that he trusted her with these sordid details only brought them closer together.

"Damn, you're brilliant," he said.

She tried her best to look humble right then, but she couldn't stop smiling that pleased-with-herself smile. "I wouldn't say that. I had plenty of experience writing college essays back in the day. And the grant letters I write now for the nonprofit aren't all that much different."

"You're still the smartest person I know. The cutest too. But I am going to make one change to your brilliant suggestion and write about how the love of a good woman is what's been motivating my better impulses."

"Only a *good* woman?"

"If I told them how amazing you really are I'd make them too jealous to want to accept me."

The look Julia gave him right then made him blush. "Put your laptop down," she said.

He did as she ordered, and she scooted over on the couch so that she fell into his arms as she sat on his lap, her hands locked around the back of his neck and their lips pressed together. Duncan didn't want the moment to ever end, but of course it had to. When she pulled away, she breathed into his ear that that was only a coming attraction for later. "I should let you get back to working on your essay," she said, her voice soft, but with an unmistakable huskiness.

"I could work on it tomorrow instead. The application's not due until next week."

"You should type up the essay now while what you want to write is fresh in your mind."

"You can be a cruel woman sometimes."

Julia laughed. "Show a little patience. Good things come to those who wait."

She scooted off his lap and positioned herself the way she was earlier on the couch and picked up her book again. Duncan made a show of his unhappy grumbling, but opened the laptop and went to work fast and furiously on the essay. He figured if he applied himself, he could have it done in an hour, and afterwards he'd be racing Julia to the bedroom. That was motivation enough to buckle down. He was ten minutes into it when someone knocked on their door, and then a man's voice saying, "It's Dave. Open up."

His boss at work was named Dave Connelly. The voice was muffled, but it could be him. Duncan was old-fashioned for a millennial in that he relied on a watch. He gave it a quick look. Almost 10:30 on a Tuesday night. It was possible there was a boiler emergency, maybe a water heater in a building nearby blew up, but would Dave really drag him out of his apartment at that hour? There were other workers on call for that.

More knocking and that same muffled voice calling out, "Open the door already. It's important."

The last thing Duncan wanted right then was to leave Julia so that he could instead spend hours repairing a busted boiler. He mouthed to Julia that he thought it was his boss. He whispered, "Should we pretend we're not home?"

Julia showed him a helpless gesture.

Duncan, resigned to the situation, pushed himself off the couch, but he couldn't help feeling annoyed at the situation. He'd go out on the job—this was the life he signed up for, after all—but he was still going to give Connelly a piece of his mind. They had him scheduled at work to be on call two nights that week, and this wasn't one of them!

He opened the door prepared to complain bitterly to Connelly, but it wasn't Connelly at the door. Instead, it was a guy hiding his face with a ski mask. Before Duncan had a chance to react, he caught a glint of metal flashing toward him, and then something much harder than knuckles smacked him in the jaw.

* * * *

Before waking up, Duncan's consciousness ebbed in and out like an ocean tide. At some level he was aware of how badly his jaw and shoulders ached, and that his arms felt numb and disconnected from him. With a start, he remembered a stranger wearing a ski mask who punched him in the face with brass knuckles.

He tried screaming out for help, but only a muffled, whimpering noise escaped from him. He couldn't move his arms or legs, and as he struggled to open his eyes, he realized he was sitting on one of the wooden chairs he and Julia kept by the table, his arms pulled behind him, his wrists tightly bound with duct tape, and his ankles tied to the chair legs. With a concentrated effort he forced his eyes open, and the light in the room hit him like broken glass slashing deep into his corneas, the pain driving all the way into his brain. He fought through the pain and soon he could focus and see that Julia was sitting naked in a chair opposite him, also gagged and bound.

He tried again to scream, but the gag had been shoved into his mouth and it once again stifled him. He fought to bolt from the chair, but the duct tape wrapped around his wrists and ankles refused to let him budge even a fraction of an inch.

"Settle down there, champ, or you'll give yourself a stroke."

Duncan turned toward the voice. The guy in a ski mask from earlier was standing off to the side, holding something behind his back. Duncan fought again to break free, but only accomplished exhausting himself and making his head hurt even more.

"You're not too swift, are you, champ? There's not a damn thing you can do to help your sweet little thing, not the way I got you tied up. But let me tell you something—if I had found a decent score here, I would've left you two with only that little love tap to the jaw. But thirty-eight stinking dollars? A worthless laptop I can't fence? Nothing else here but junk? It really pissed me off, enough so I decided to get my money's worth another way."

The creature (because that was how Duncan thought of him) showed what he was a hiding behind his back: A carving knife he had taken from the kitchen. Duncan tried again to scream and break free before slumping back in his chair. The creature made a *tsking* noise as he moved over to Julia.

"I want you to remember this is all your fault. If you had kept a few hundred dollars in your apartment, sweet little thing here would've been left untouched."

Jacob Stone

Julia had small breasts, but as far as Duncan was concerned they were beautiful and perfect. He watched in horror as the creature sliced off her right nipple and then her left. Blind rage exploded inside him. He fought like a wounded animal to free himself, but it was futile and accomplished nothing but draining the little energy he had.

"Champ, you're one stupid muthafucka, aren't you? Get it through your thick skull you ain't moving."

The creature said this as if it were something funny. Duncan stared into the creature's eyes and saw only cruelty. Whatever hatred he might've once felt toward Wainwright was only a drop in the ocean compared to what he felt for this person.

What happened next was worse than any imaginable nightmare. Duncan watched helplessly while the creature repeatedly stabbed and cut Julia. The creature stopped after a while and came back to him. His shirtsleeve had crept up enough so that Duncan saw the tattoo on the underside of his right wrist. He tried to keep that fact hidden, but the image of the snarling wolf's face would forever be burned into his memory.

The creature crouched in front of him so their eyes were level.

"I'm making you a once-in-a-lifetime offer. No matter what you do, your sweet little thing is dying tonight. But if you agree, I'll cut you free and let you end her suffering by choking the life out of her. I gotta warn you though, champ, if you don't live up to your end of the deal, I'm going medieval on her, and she'll die so much uglier than otherwise. So what will it be?"

What he was asking was impossible. Duncan couldn't possibly agree to something like that, not while there was a chance someone could rescue them. But if he were cut free and tried fighting off this creature and failed, he knew this creature would keep his word and ramp up the torture. Forget that he had a broken jaw—what chance would he have when he couldn't even feel his arms anymore? Little to none? Was that even too high?

God help him, he shook his head, turning down the offer.

The creature's eyes showed his disappointment. "Don't say I didn't give you a chance."

The creature moved back to Julia and used the knife in even crueler and more disfiguring ways. Over and over again, until it became a mantra running in Duncan's head, he made silent promises to a God he didn't believe in about what he would do if Julia could be spared any further pain, but there was no divine intervention. It took hours before she finally succumbed.

Before the creature left the apartment, he told Duncan, "Now you have yourself an especially wonderful rest of your life."

Chapter 57

Boston, the present

Charlie Bogle was not having a particularly good day. First, it was announced that his flight to Boston was delayed forty minutes, then the plane was stuck on the tarmac for an additional fifty minutes while he was stuck in the middle seat between two beefy alpha males who were determined to take control of the shared armrests. After they landed, he found himself in thirty-eight-degree weather with freezing rain slashing into his face as he waited in line for a taxi. He didn't care how good the chowder was here—if this was what the locals had to deal with in April, they could keep it! Finally, or what he thought was the final cherry on top of a craptastic day, he was stuck in what seemed like interminable traffic for what should've been a four-mile ride to the New Sudbury Street police station so he could meet with Detective Lloyd Bracken.

"This is worse than driving on the LA Freeway," Bogle observed, trying to be philosophical about it. "Is it always this bad here?"

"Russia, yeah. Always," the cabdriver mumbled in a mushed-mouth Slavic accent.

That answer made no sense to Bogle, and he puzzled over it until he realized the cabdriver said *rush hour* instead of Russia. His phone *dinged* to notify him about an incoming text message, and he saw that Morris had sent him a photo of the suspect. Bogle thought the man looked like Kurt Russell from *Escape from New York*, except with shorter hair and no eyepatch. He called Morris and asked how certain he was this was the Cupid Killer.

"He's got a wolf's-face tattoo on his wrist and he likes to pose as a hit man so he can blackmail suckers who hire him."

"That's all?"

"I got a feeling," Morris said.

"A feeling you can't hide," Bogle said, slightly altering a line to the same Beatles song.

"Are you okay?" Morris asked with concern. "You're sounding a bit loopy."

"Just all the traveling. Do you have a name for this suspect?"

"Not yet. We've got a stakeout going on. Hopefully he shows. If he doesn't, we'll blast his photo tonight all over the internet and TV."

Bogle could understand Morris hoping he wouldn't have to do that. Not only could it cause the guy to rabbit, but other than the tattoo, they didn't have anything yet connecting him to the Cupid Killer, and there had to be more than one person in LA with that tattoo. If Bogle were setting odds, he'd give it no more than fifty-fifty at this point.

He asked, "Did you send his photo to the Oakland PD?"

"Yep, and I talked to the detective in charge of the Markin homicide investigation. OPD will be showing it to their CIs to see if anyone knows him."

"I'll try to get the Boston PD to do the same here. Right now, I'm in a taxi creeping along at one inch per minute." Bogle squinted as he tried to look past the cabdriver to see what was in front of them. He groaned. "It looks like there are five lanes merging into two, so I'll be sitting here for a while. If you get a handle on your Cupid Killer suspect and he confesses, call me so if I'm still stuck in this godforsaken traffic, I can bail from the cab and walk back to the airport."

Bogle had gotten an earful earlier from Bracken when he called him about his plane being late. After he got off the phone with Morris, he called the Boston homicide detective again to tell him he would be even later, thanks to this horrendous airport traffic, and Bracken cut him off in mid-sentence to give him another earful.

"Bad enough you ratted me out to my bosses, now you're going to keep me at my desk all night!"

"First of all, I didn't rat you out to anyone," Bogle said, his temper flaring. "I'm working a serial killer case in which four people have been murdered so far and two other victims brutalized. An FBI agent assigned to the case called her office for assistance. Second, it's only five-thirty. You cops in Boston have pretty short days, huh?"

"I've been on the job since five a.m., asshole."

Bogle had to count to three before he trusted himself to speak. It had been that kind of day so far.

"How about we start over?" he suggested. "I've been traveling all day, I'm hungry, and I don't want this ending with us having a fistfight, which is the way we're heading—"

"I'd kick your butt if that's how it turns out."

Bogle took a deep breath. This guy was more irritating than Polk. "That might or might not be true," he said. "Regardless, how about we meet at a nearby restaurant. You pick the place as long as we don't need a reservation and I can get lobster, and I'll pick up the tab."

There was a distinctive change in Bracken's attitude when he asked if drinks were to be included.

"Hell yes," Bogle said.

* * * *

With a shaved square-shaped head, thick neck, and body to match, Detective Lloyd Bracken looked like a Marine drill sergeant. He had chosen an Italian restaurant in Boston's North End, and after several beers and littlenecks sautéed in garlic and Pinot Grigio, he had become downright chummy. He also brought a copy of the Julia Swan homicide file, and handed it over to Bogle without any fuss. Bogle thumbed through it, stopping when he got to the crime-scene photos. Swan had been stripped naked and her body suffered the same grotesque injuries as the LA victims. He flipped past the photos and found the witness statement from Swan's fiancé, Duncan Moss. According to Moss, the killer had a wolf's-face tattoo on the underside of his right wrist, and Bogle let out a short whistle when he read what the killer told Moss before leaving the apartment.

Bracken was in the process of tilting back a bottle of Sam Adams. He made a face as if he thought Bogle couldn't possibly be serious.

"It's the Cupid Killer," Bogle volunteered. "Same wolf-face tattoo, and what he said to the witness—*now you have yourself an especially wonderful rest of your life*—matches what he said to one of our witnesses. This guy also killed Suzanne Markin in Oakland twelve months ago."

"The perp in Oakland had that same tattoo?"

"We don't know, but he called the poor guy he was tormenting *champ*, same as he did Moss. Why'd you think Julia Swan's murder was drug-related?"

"We got a tip that an apartment in Jamaica Plain was about to be hit for a heavy amount of coke. Word was five or more kilos, but we weren't given an address. Then this happened and when I looked into Moss, I found out he was all wrong."

Bracken took a long pull on his beer, emptying it. He waved over the waitress and ordered another round, and this time added bourbon shots. When the waitress walked away, he told Bogle he heard on the street that Moss was well-known for pulling off serious heists.

"He built himself a nice cover working a nine-to-five job, but that was only to scout out more robberies. He must've found the five kilos that way and someone figured out he took it and wanted those kilos back. A shame about Julia. A beautiful young woman, and by all accounts a good egg. But that's the type of collateral damage someone like Moss can cause."

The story made sense to Bogle. The same guy tortured and killed Suzanne Markin in Oakland and Julia Swan in Boston for no other reason than to rip off kilos of coke from their boyfriends, and now he was doing the same in Los Angeles purely for kicks. A shiver ran down his spine. This psycho discovered with Markin and Swan just how much he enjoyed using a knife on a helpless woman while her significant other was forced to watch. He texted Bracken the same photo Morris had texted him earlier.

"It's not a hundred percent, but we think he's our Cupid Killer."

Bracken peered at the photo before looking up at Bogle. "What odds would you give it?" he asked.

"Earlier I was thinking fifty percent, now I'm closer to ninety-nine."

"You got a name for this asshole?"

"We're working on it."

Bracken gave the photo another look. "I'll make sure this gets passed around to our CIs, see if anyone knows him." Somewhat accusingly, he asked, "Anything else you're holding back?"

"Not a thing."

The waitress returned with their food and drinks. Bogle had ordered the Lobster Fra Diavolo and Bracken the veal chops. Bogle took a bite of his food and had to admit it was damn good. Maybe not quite good enough to make up for dealing with this nasty April weather, but still very tasty. For the next forty minutes the two men concentrated on their food, drinks, coffee, and small talk about Boston weather and the odds of the Red Sox and Dodgers meeting next fall in the World Series. When they were done with dinner, Bracken offered his hand and told Bogle he wasn't as big a jerk as he thought earlier.

"Same here," Bogle said, grinning. "Now that I've gotten to know you, I'm only slightly tempted to kick your ass."

Bracken returned the grin. "Which I'm sure is just that much less than I'd like to kick yours."

Before separating, they promised to keep each other informed about any developments, and Bogle caught a taxi to take him to a hotel near the airport. He called Morris, who told him they were still waiting for the Cupid Killer to show.

"We'll give the stakeout another hour and then go to plan B," Morris said.

"Plastering the guy's photo everywhere.'

"Exactly."

Traffic to the airport flowed easily, and in less than ten minutes the cab was pulling up to the hotel. Charlie Bogle had a change of heart. It wasn't even 7:30 yet, 4:30 LA time, and he felt like doing a little exploring—namely, find Julia Swan's fiancé and see if he formed the same opinion of him that Bracken did.

Bogle told the cabbie that he wanted to go someplace else and to keep the meter running. He searched through the file Bracken had given him and found Julia Swan's Jamaica Plain address.

* * * *

On one side of the street was a large cluster of fairly ugly four-story brick buildings that looked like they were constructed in the sixties, and on the other side was what looked like the boundary to a small forest, which had to be why the street was named Forest Hills. Bogle found within the cluster the building that matched Swan's address. The front door was left unlocked and he climbed the stairs to the third-floor apartment. After a knock on the door and no answer, he tried again, this time banging harder. A white-haired woman in her seventies stepped out of a neighboring apartment and gave Bogle a bug-eyed stare before asking if he was police officer. Bogle told her that he was.

"Is this about what happened to poor Julia?"

"Yes, ma'am."

"That was terrible," she said, her face aging a decade as she reflected on Swan's fate. "She was such a nice, young woman. If you're looking for Duncan, he hasn't been home for at least a week."

That was a surprise. "Do you know where he went?"

"Sorry, I don't. Only that I haven't heard a peep over there and his mailbox hasn't been emptied in at least that long."

"You two been neighbors for a while?"

"Oh golly, since they moved in. That would be over four years now."

"What's your impression of Mr. Moss?"

Her raisin-sized eyes hardened as if she didn't like the insinuation that there would be anything wrong with her neighbor.

"Duncan is a fine, young man. Hardworking, and he was deeply devoted to Julia. If you think he had anything to do with what happened to her, you're badly mistaken."

"Ma'am, I'm not thinking anything. We have what we hope is a break in the case, and I need to discuss it with Mr. Moss, that's all."

"Duncan will be so pleased to hear that. I know this has been tearing him apart. I wish I could tell you how to reach him."

She nodded hesitantly at Bogle, as if she wasn't sure about the proper etiquette in this situation, and then stepped back into her apartment. Bogle could've looked for the landlord to let him into Moss's apartment, but the guy or gal could be a stickler wanting a warrant, and he had brought a lockpick set with him and the lock looked like a garden-variety one. After less than a minute of fiddling around, he had the apartment door unlocked.

He had hoped to find a letter, note, or something that would help him find Moss, but there was nothing in the small one-bedroom apartment. No mail stacked up in the kitchen, no notes attached to the refrigerator with magnets, no papers in the bedroom or the room that served as a combination living room-dining room, nothing useful in any drawers. Wherever Moss had gone, he made sure to clean up the apartment before he left. From the stale, musty smell in the apartment, no one had been in there for at least a couple of weeks.

In the bedroom, Bogle came across a framed photo of the couple. Julia Swan was beaming with happiness while Moss was smiling in a more self-conscious way. Bracken's file didn't include any photos of Moss, and the only ones he had of Swan were the crime scene and autopsy photos, and it was impossible to tell from those how absolutely stunning she was.

Bogle took the photo from the frame, figuring he'd add it to Julia Swan's homicide file.

Chapter 58

Los Angeles, the present

The stakeout's going to be a bust.

It was a quarter past five, no sign of the Cupid Killer, and Stonehedge was feeling a sense of deflation as he nursed his fourth beer since he'd been there, trying to drag out the process. The guy must've smelled a setup and wasn't coming; Stonehedge was sure of it. He'd stick around until Morris gave the signal for them to clear out, but at this point he was wasting his time, and feeling awfully foolish about it—especially after the ultimatum he'd made to the bartender.

Out of the corner of his eye he caught a woman sitting at the bar, staring at him, and he turned to smile at her. Twenties, long brown hair, slender body, cute face—at least from what he could see with a third of her face covered by a pair of oversized sunglasses. There was something familiar about her. Did he ever work with her? She had the looks to be an actress, but he couldn't place her. If she had recognized him through his disguise, she could blow his cover, not that that would matter much anymore; but still, as a matter of pride he'd prefer it not to happen.

Well, he needed to have a chat with her!

He pushed himself out of his booth, approached the bar, and asked the bartender to get the lady whatever she wanted. She seemed surprised by this, but told the bartender she'd have a vodka martini. While the bartender was busy mixing the drink, Stonehedge leaned toward her so he could whisper, "You recognized me, huh?"

The expression that froze her face took Stonehedge aback. A panicked flight-or-fight look. Her voice caught in her throat as she asked, "How'd you know I was with him?"

This confused Stonehedge even more, but he asked her to join him at his booth so they could talk privately.

The bartender brought over the vodka martini, Stonehedge handed him a twenty, telling him to keep the change, and as he led the way back to the booth he wondered what she meant by that. It was only after he sat back down that he understood why she looked so familiar. She wasn't wearing the trench coat or floppy hat he had seen in the photo Fred Lemmon had taken of the woman who approached Wayne Hardacher at the Santee Alley flea market parking lot, but those were the same sunglasses, and Stonehedge gulped as he realized she was the same woman.

The woman's eyes narrowed and she reached across the table, grabbed his prosthetic nose, and yanked it off.

"You're wearing a disguise?" she hissed at him, a wild panic in her eyes as she rose to her feet. "Who are you?"

Stonehedge was flabbergasted as he made sense of the fact that the Cupid Killer had sent a proxy to the bar instead of showing up himself. The woman's panic had become so palpable that he could feel it in his own gut. She turned to flee the booth and ran into a waiting Annie Walsh. Fred Lemmon stood behind Walsh and remarked that she was the same woman from the flea market. "I can't believe I didn't recognize her when she came in," he added with disgust.

The woman tried to fight her way past Walsh, but that didn't go particularly well for her and she was slammed face-first into the table and cuffed. The bartender ambled over as if he were going to stick his nose into the situation, and Walsh barked at him to back off.

"LAPD," she growled. She showed him her badge. "Fred, make sure Curly over here doesn't make any phone calls."

"Will do."

The woman who'd been cuffed and still bent over the table began sobbing, insisting she hadn't done anything.

"We've got you on tape delivering a blackmail demand to Wayne Hardacher earlier today."

"Jack made me do that!" she sobbed, strands of saliva dripping from her mouth and pooling on the table.

Walsh lifted the woman to her feet and turned her around so she could look in her eyes. "Jack, your blackmail partner, is the Cupid Killer. Did you know that?"

Audrey stopped her sobbing. "That's not possible," she said.

"The guy, Jack, he's got a wolf's-face tattoo on his wrist, right? Where is he?"

She stared at Walsh as if she were waiting for a punch line. When she realized one wasn't coming, she reacted as if she'd been slapped.

"I swear, I had no idea," she insisted, her eyes filling with tears. She gave Walsh a look as if this was all some big misunderstanding. "Two days ago I was ready to give up on my dreams of being an actress and fly back to Des Moines, but then I met Jack at a bar and he got me drunk and coked up and made me do things I didn't want to do, but I had no idea about him being the Cupid Killer—"

"Unless you want to be charged as an accomplice, you better damn well tell me where he is right now!"

Walsh's words cut through her crippling fear.

"I'll tell you," she promised.

* * * *

Morris received a call from Walsh telling him that the Cupid Killer had sent a woman named Audrey Zairn into the High Spot Lounge, and that Zairn was supposed to take Stonehedge into a block-long alley behind the lounge.

"Did you get the Cupid Killer's name?" he asked.

"Jack Readinger."

"And he's waiting somewhere in the alley?"

"Supposedly."

"Does he have a gun?"

"She says no. A knife only."

Morris had the police block off both ends of the alley and then he, Parker, Greg Malevich, and two uniformed officers started from one end, while Polk, Ray Vestra, and three officers started from the other. When Parker began growling at a dumpster, Morris kicked it as hard as he could, making a thunderous racket.

"Jack, it's all over. Come on out, unless you want a headache to go along with being arrested."

Parker's growling grew louder, but not a peep from the Cupid Killer. Malevich and the other officers drew their guns, their faces tense.

"Jack, this is going to get serious real fast. I suggest you get out from behind there before you get something far worse than a migraine."

Morris picked up a brick and slammed it against the dumpster.

A man's voice yelled out, "All right, all right, just don't shoot me."

Readinger crawled out from behind the dumpster. In person, he had a ratlike, feral look, and didn't resemble a young Kurt Russell much at all.

Malevich cuffed him behind his back and after patting him down, removed a switchblade from one of his boots.

Readinger wore a red long-sleeved knit shirt—most likely choosing it so it wouldn't show any of the blood he expected to get splattered on it. Morris pulled the right sleeve up and saw the wolf's-face tattoo on the underside of his wrist.

"You've been keeping us busy the last four days," he said.

Readinger gave him a puzzled grin, as if he had no idea what Morris meant. Morris didn't much care for that look—it was as if Readinger knew all they had was the tattoo, and that he'd been careful enough at the murder sites not to leave behind any DNA or prints, or any other evidence for them to find.

Malevich's voice became a dull monotone as he read Readinger his rights and Readinger played dumb, claiming he dropped a quarter and it rolled behind the dumpster. "I went back there to pick it up. That's all. You're telling me there's a law against doing that?"

That was about the most idiotic story Morris had heard from a perp during all his years on the force and as an investigator. From the screw-you grin twisting Readinger's lips, he had to know it was idiotic, but it didn't stop him from glibly using it. Morris had no doubt they were going to need shovels to dig out from all the bullshit Readinger would be serving them later.

If Malevich was insulted by Readinger treating them like idiots, he didn't show it as he maintained a bored countenance while informing Readinger they were arresting him for solicitation to commit murder and attempted blackmail.

"I got no idea what you're talking about," Readinger claimed, still playing dumb and still showing a hint of his screw-you smile. "Did some crazy, brown-haired bitch put you up to this? I hooked up with her last night, and she was hell on wheels this morning, accusing me of shit that made no sense. I wouldn't put it past her to make up this kind of bizarro story."

Morris said, "We got a confession from Wayne Hardacher."

"I got no idea who he is," Readinger insisted without missing a beat. "Maybe he and that crazy bitch are working some angle together. Who knows?"

The smirk he flashed Morris told him that Readinger must've realized the real reason they arrested him. He would've had to—there were too many cops on the scene for it to be only what he was told. From the way he was grinning he must've believed they didn't have enough to hold him on the Cupid Killer murders, but he didn't know they knew about Boston and Oakland. If they could place him in those cities when Suzanne Markin and Julia Swan were killed, the DA would have enough circumstantial evidence for a grand jury indictment, possibly also a conviction.

Hell with him, Morris thought. They weren't going to tell Readinger about Boston and Oakland. Let him think he had a chance of getting away with those murders.

A police cruiser arrived and Readinger was still grinning when he was put in the backseat. From the way Parker continued to growl at him, he would've bitten him if given the chance.

For Parker's sake and not Readinger's, Morris kept a short leash on the bull terrier. He didn't want his dog getting ptomaine poisoning.

Chapter 59

Doug Gilman's cell phone rang. He glanced at the caller ID and told Rachel her dad was calling, then had a quick, mostly one-sided conversation in which he only muttered the words *wow* and *okay* before getting off the call. A glint of excitement shone in his eyes as he told Rachel that Morris had arrested a suspect for the Cupid Killer murders.

"They don't have any physical evidence yet tying him to the murders, but he's got the same unusual tattoo on his wrist."

"That doesn't sound like a lot," Rachel said.

"Your dad feels strongly about this guy."

Gilman and Rachel were at a table at their favorite Chinese restaurant and had placed their order ten minutes earlier. He smiled apologetically at his fiancée and told her he needed to head back to their apartment so he could put on a suit before meeting Morris at the Wilcox Avenue Hollywood precinct, where the suspect was taken.

"Here's another idea," Rachel said. "Instead of spending a half hour driving back and forth to change your clothes, we could spend the time eating dinner, and then you could go to the precinct wearing what you have on. As far as I'm concerned, you look every bit as dashing in your cargo shorts and polo shirt as you do in your suit."

Gilman cleared his throat, a slight blush tingeing his cheeks. "That may be true, my dear, but I've got a certain image to uphold." Then, more seriously, "Depending on how your dad wants to handle this, I might need to talk to the media later. How about you stay and enjoy dinner? You can take an Uber home later?"

"That's okay, we'll have them pack up the food." She showed him her best inscrutable flinty-eyed look and added, "Somebody's got to help you pick out the right tie!"

Gilman made an exaggerated harrumphing noise and waved over their waiter so he could pay the bill and get their food to-go. Once they were in the car driving back to their apartment, Rachel told him she'd make him a sandwich to take with him. "You're not waiting until midnight or later to eat anything," she decided.

He agreed, as long as she made him a roast beef and cheddar on sourdough, which he knew they had in the fridge. Since Rachel was vegan, it was up to him to keep track of buying deli meats and cheeses.

"As long as it's with mustard and not mayonnaise."

"Deal," he said, knowing better than to argue this point with her. The Bricks considered putting mayonnaise on roast beef sandwiches an unnatural act.

After that, they drifted into a comfortable silence. Gilman found himself hoping Morris was right and they had taken the Cupid Killer off the streets. The murders had struck a deep chord in him, and he found it simply unimaginable what the victims went through—both the men and women. All he knew was he'd rather die than ever see Rachel hurt like that. A shiver ran through him, his body convulsing as if he'd been hit with an electric current. Rachel placed a delicate, slender hand on his arm. Out of the corner of his eye he could see her concern.

"Are you okay?" she asked.

"My mind drifted to something unpleasant," he admitted.

"Well, don't let that happen. Think instead of what we'll be doing when you get home."

He arched an eyebrow. "You're vegan. Why would you be joining me in heating up the Sichuan-spiced chicken?"

She gave him what was supposed to be a playful tap on the shoulder, although he still winced. The Bricks were a tough breed, even when they were only five feet one and weighed less than a hundred pounds like Rachel.

"What we'll be doing after you eat."

"Brushing our teeth?"

"After that."

Gilman's tone turned more serious as he said, "You've got an eight o'clock class tomorrow. I'm sure you'll be asleep by the time I get home."

"If I am, wake me. I mean it."

"You'll be too tired tomorrow morning."

Her hand moved to his thigh. It was a loving gesture only, but it still gave him an instant erection. Rachel had that effect on him. His cargo shorts always bunched up at the crotch when he sat, so there was a good chance she hadn't noticed it. But if she did, she didn't let on to the fact.

"Nothing an extra cup of coffee won't fix," she said.

He nodded, not trusting himself to talk. Since they'd become a couple they'd had many moments like this, where he wanted her so badly it caused him physical pain. He probably had time for a quickie and he was sure Rachel would be up for it, but the thought of meeting Morris right after having sex with the man's daughter frightened him. He could imagine the way Morris would look at him, knowing what he and Rachel had done, and that thought was as effective on his libido as a cold shower.

He pulled into the parking lot behind their building, and Rachel's hand found his as they walked into the apartment building, their fingers interlacing.

"Sorry about ruining our date night," he said.

She bumped him with a very slender hip. "And yet I still love you."

"What can I say?" he said, struggling to suppress a grin. "I'm a lucky guy."

"I'd have to agree."

The grin he'd been fighting so hard to keep hidden broke free. They walked hand in hand into the elevator and once they had some privacy, he tilted Rachel's chin upward and stole a kiss. Since their apartment was only on the third floor, the kiss was unfortunately a short one. They were all business as they left the elevator, acting as if the kiss had never happened.

When they approached their apartment door, Gilman felt Rachel's body stiffen. He turned toward the fire stairs to see what she was looking at. A man dressed in black clothing and wearing a ski mask was approaching them at a fast clip, a gun stretched out in his right hand. Gilman saw a tattoo of some sort on the underside of the man's right wrist. A wolf baring its fangs?

"I'll shoot both of you if either of you move," the man growled, his voice muffled by the ski mask.

Gilman froze, his legs becoming blocks of ice. Rachel might've tried running back to the elevator, but she wasn't about to leave him, and whatever slim chance they had was gone. The man was on them in seconds, the barrel of the gun pressing against the side of Rachel's head.

"Champ, you have five seconds to unlock the door, or you'll be wearing your fiancée's brains. Either of you make as much as a whimper, the same thing."

Oh Jesus, Oh Jesus, Gilman whispered to himself. He fumbled with his keys and somehow kept his hand steady enough to fit the key into the slot and turn it.

"Slowly," the man ordered in the same soft, menacing tone. "You try closing the door on me, you both die."

Gilman willed his legs to move forward and he stepped into the apartment. Rachel followed him, and the man kept pace so the gun barrel never budged from the side of her head.

Gilman's focus was only on the gun and everything else melted into a red haze. A roaring in his head drowned out any other noise. Without conscious thought, he shoved Rachel forward so that she fell into the apartment and away from the gun. He then seized the gun with both hands and tried to wrestle it free. The man in the ski mask was thinner than he was, but he had a wiry strength, almost like his arms were steel bands, and the barrel of the gun forced its way toward Gilman until it pushed into his stomach and backed him up several steps. Gilman could see the man's eyes through the eyeholes in the ski mask. Blue, cold, unforgiving. They exploded into a blind rage. It was a startling thing to witness, and before Gilman could move the man pulled the trigger. The blast rocked Gilman's body and he fell like a rag doll to the floor.

Rachel was picking herself off the floor when she heard the gunshot. An iciness filled her head, and she bit her lip to keep from crying out in pain at the sight of Doug lying on his back and bleeding from the bullet wound. She could see the surprise in the masked gunman's eyes as she rushed him. It had to be the last thing the bastard expected, and she delivered a roundhouse kick to his left leg that dropped him to his knees. She roared out in her pain as she drove her knee into his chin, knocking him onto the floor. The gun tumbled out of his hand and she dove for it. Her fingertips were grazing the gun's grip when he grabbed a fistful of her hair and slammed her head into the floor. The world disappeared on her.

* * * *

Duncan pushed himself to his feet and tested his jaw, moving it from side to side to make sure it wasn't broken. Damn, she had nailed him good.

He pushed her body with the toe of his boot. She was out cold. He felt a grudging admiration for her. Stunningly beautiful and as fierce as could be. The way she went after him was really quite something, and Duncan knew in his heart she did it to save her fiancé's life and not her own. He shifted his gaze to Gilman and he felt nothing but loathing. Fucking weakling. The guy had gotten both hands on the gun, and he still couldn't keep Duncan from forcing the gun barrel into his stomach, even though it would've meant saving the life of the woman he loved. Absolutely pathetic. If Duncan had been given that same chance, Julia would be alive now.

Gilman was still breathing, but he wouldn't be for much longer. The plan hadn't been to shoot him, but the hatred he felt for the guy became so overwhelming that he couldn't help it. Gilman could've been the president of the oh-so-happy privileged-few club with his tanning-booth tan, perfect hair, perfect teeth, perfect fiancée, and perfect life. Before today he would've believed the kind of senseless, random violence someone like Duncan could bring would never touch him. Well, he'd just been proven wrong.

Duncan needed to think this through, and he decided it didn't matter that Gilman wouldn't be alive to tell the police about the snarling-wolf tattoo. Even though there hadn't been anything on the news about the tattoo yet, the last guy, Kammer, must've told the police about it.

He reached behind and stuck the gun in his waistband. Gilman had dropped his keys and Duncan picked them up. Earlier he had tried picking the door lock, thinking he'd wait inside the apartment and surprise them when they returned, but he couldn't pick the damn lock. As he examined the four small magnets built into the key, he realized it wasn't a matter of him losing his touch, but that they had installed a space age–type door lock that was impenetrable. In the end, it didn't help them one bit. Tough luck for them.

He tossed the keys onto the floor, bent his knees, and lifted Rachel into his arms so he could carry her into the kitchen area. He'd undress her there and then bind her with duct tape to one of the chairs. Even though Gilman was too out of it to realize what would be happening to his fiancée, Duncan was still going to kill her exactly the same way he had the others. While he wouldn't get the release from tormenting Gilman through Rachel's torture and pain, it still needed to be done. He knew that Rachel's dad was Morris Brick, and that Brick was the one in charge of the Cupid Killer investigation. Duncan needed to make damn sure Brick was left highly motivated to catch the guy responsible for these killings.

"Sorry, lady," he murmured under his breath. "I'm not going to get any pleasure out of this. I can promise you that. If we had only met under different circumstances..."

He stopped in his tracks, wondering why he was suddenly smelling a funky, rotting-garbage odor, and why it seemed familiar. Then he remembered in all the excitement he had forgotten to lock the apartment door.

He turned to see that Stevie the meth head from the rooming house had snuck into the apartment and was the source of the unpleasant odor. He tried ducking the ancient-looking rusted crowbar Stevie swung at his head, but it struck him above the ear and knocked him and Rachel to the floor. He scrambled to get to his knees, but the meth head kicked him in the ribs, knocking him over.

"You think you can throw me into a dumpster?" Stevie seethed, his voice sounding like a badly rusted garbage disposal. "Who's the one with goo for brains now?"

Duncan had his arms up to protect his head, and Stevie was breathing hard as he battered Duncan with the crowbar, hitting him repeatedly on the arms, all the while ranting about how he had followed Duncan from the rooming house and that Duncan was too stupid to realize it. That he watched while Duncan hid in the bushes, and later followed him into the apartment building and onto the back staircase.

"When I saw you put on your ski mask, I knew what you were up to," Stevie exclaimed excitedly. "You're that Cupid Killer freak. I'm gonna beat your skull in and hand you over to the police, and I'll be living large on the reward I get. So who's the dumb-ass now?"

Duncan tried once more to get to his knees. This time when the meth head tried to kick him over, Duncan caught his foot and lifted it up, sending Stevie crashing to the floor. Duncan crawled on top of him and hammered him in the nose until it was a bloody mess. He picked up the crowbar and drove it down with two hands as if he were driving a stake into a vampire, striking the meth head's mouth, splintering his ruined teeth and pushing the piece of metal halfway down his throat.

Duncan's voice was something guttural as he swore, "Choke on that, you dumb fuck."

He watched Stevie struggle feebly for a few seconds, and caught the moment his life bled out of his wide-open, panicked eyes.

He rolled off the dead meth head and gingerly held his head in his hands. Goddamn, did he hurt! His head, jaw, arms, back, ribs, and the back of his leg where Rachel had kicked him. It felt like he'd crawled away from a car crash. He was carefully working his way onto his feet when he heard a rustling behind him. He looked back to see that Rachel had woken up and picked up the gun that had fallen out of his waistband during his struggle with Stevie. She was woozy and listing a bit to one side, but she was still aiming the gun at his face. He watched as the knuckle of her trigger finger began turning bone white, and he dove to the floor as a gunshot rattled the apartment.

Shit. Shit. Shit.

He crawled toward the door, zigzagging the way he'd seen actors do in war movies. Another shot rang out and he thought he'd been hit, but realized what bit into his thigh was a jagged piece of the hardwood floor splintered off by the bullet.

He reached up for the doorknob and felt the heat from a bullet zipping past his cheek. Somehow he swung the door open, fell out of it without being shot, and pushed the door closed behind him. He wobbled as he got to his feet, and nearly fell over before he steadied himself. Several of Rachel's neighbors had opened their doors to see what the commotion was about, but none of them tried to stop him as he hobbled for the back staircase.

* * * *

Rachel gasped as she saw that Doug's skin color resembled curdled milk. Any thought she might've had of chasing after the Cupid Killer disappeared once she saw that. She also noticed the dead man with a piece of metal sticking out of his throat, but she didn't have time to wonder who he was and how he was connected to the Cupid Killer. Doug was still alive and she needed to do whatever she could to save him.

First things first, she locked the door so that psycho bastard couldn't return. Next, she needed to put pressure on the wound to stanch the bleeding. She grabbed a throw pillow, got down on her knees, and pressed it against the wound.

She fought back tears as she saw how close Doug was to death. Crying was for later. For now, she needed to call 911, but where was her pocketbook? She had no idea where it had ended up during the melee. But Doug kept his phone in his pants pocket. While pushing down on the pillow, she searched one pocket, then the next, and pulled out his phone, using his index finger to unlock it.

She called 911 and her voice had an eerie calmness to it as she told the operator to send an ambulance and the police to her address. It was almost as if she had left her body and was only a spectator to what she was now doing and saying. "The Cupid Killer shot my fiancé in the stomach and he needs immediate medical attention."

The operator sounded unconvinced as he asked whether Rachel was sure it was the Cupid Killer.

"Yes. He ran out of my apartment less than a minute ago. If you send the police right now they can catch him."

"Miss, how do you know it's the Cupid—"

Rachel hung up and called her dad and told him what happened. "Please, get an ambulance here," she pleaded.

"I promise, honey. Right away."

Rachel felt too numb all of a sudden to hold onto the phone; her hands and arms icy cold, like she might pass out. She dropped it. She needed to concentrate on pushing down on the pillow and putting enough pressure on the wound to keep Doug from bleeding to death. He was still alive, but his skin had gotten unnaturally gray and his eyelids were fluttering.

"You're not leaving me," she told him, her voice breaking up, tears suddenly streaming down her face. "You promised me we'd have a life together. You're keeping your promise!"

She heard sirens off in the distance and they were coming fast. "Help's coming," she told him through her sobbing. "We're having babies together. We're growing old together. Don't you forget that!"

His eyelids stopped fluttering and she knew he had died.

In her grief, she barely noticed that someone was pounding on the door.

Chapter 60

Jack had paid off a waiter to find out who the big winner was at the Hopper's backroom poker game, and after the game broke up at midnight he followed the guy to a Hollywood hotspot and took a photo of him so Grace would know what the mark looked like—pear-shaped, sweaty, balding. For the last ten minutes she sat at the bar at this same hotspot, watching him act like a big shot, buying good-looking women drinks and being shot down by all of them. If these women knew he'd left Hopper's backroom game with over eight grand stuffed in his wallet, maybe they wouldn't have been so quick to tell him to get lost.

Grace was wearing what Jack had picked out for her: A dress so short you'd be able to see her panties if she were wearing any and knee-length red leather boots. "Sexy as all hell, Grace," Jack had told her. "Pillsbury Doughboy won't be able to resist you." No kidding. From what Grace could tell, that butterball would be drooling over any woman in the place willing to give him the time of day no matter how much leg or cleavage she was showing, and she was showing plenty of both. Well, time to get to work.

She caught his eye, took a sip of her watermelon vodka, and made a show of slowly licking her lips. Just like Pavlov's dog, he came running over. Well, as much running as a pudgy guy could do in a crowded bar. He gave her a crude look up and down, all the while grinning like an idiot.

"That's got to be the shortest dress I've ever seen," he said.

What a toad! Still, she had a job to do. She manufactured a look as if she were actually interested in him, and said, "You like it, then?"

"With your legs? Oh, yeah." He licked his lips, but on him it just looked grubby. "I'm trying to figure out if you're wearing any panties."

She had her legs crossed. If she uncrossed them, he'd know the answer. "Smooth line," she said.

His doughy face deflated as he realized he might've just blown it with her. "I stuck my foot in it again, didn't I? I just never saw a dress so short and your legs are just so... *wow*, but I didn't mean to insult you. Let me buy you a drink to make up for it."

His move, she thought. *Act like a jerk so he could apologize by buying a drink. Actually, not bad. It might even work every blue moon.*

Grace signaled the bartender for another drink. "Mr. Smooth here is buying."

The butterball beamed at the nickname. "I like that," he said. "Mr. Smooth. Maybe I'll get business cards with it." He leaned closer to her and said with a dim-witted grin, "Would you hold it against me if I told you you have a beautiful body?"

"Wow," she said. "That is just so unbelievably clever. Did you just think of it?"

His face turned red, not sure whether she was making fun of him or actually meant it as a compliment.

"I might've heard it before," he admitted. He held out a hand that felt every bit as pudgy as it looked. "Scott Wallaban."

"Lulu Palooza."

He gave her a look as if she were putting him on. "That can't be your real name," he said. "Is it?"

She laughed. "As bright as you are witty. It's my stage name. I'm an actress."

The last part was almost true. There was a time when she hoped to be an actress, but she was never able to get her big break, and then she met Jack, and well, that was that.

"An actress, huh? Have you been in anything I know?"

"Doubtful, but I've got an audition tomorrow afternoon." She crossed fingers on both hands. "Wish me luck."

"Hang out with me, Lulu, and I bet my luck rubs off on you."

Grace tipped her martini glass back, finishing her drink. "So you're a lucky guy?"

"Tonight I was." He lost himself reminiscing about his earlier victories than night. "Drawing inside straights. Taking three cards and picking up a full boat. Yeah, tonight was something special." He gave Grace a hopeful look. "Who knows? Maybe it will get even more special."

She laughed. "Don't hold your breath."

"Hey, I'm a hopeful guy."

"So how much did you win?"

He got cagey then. "Enough."

The bartender brought over a fresh watermelon vodka for Grace and Wallaban, realizing his glass was empty, asked for another scotch. "Make it a Dewar's this time," he said. After the bartender left, he asked Grace about the role she was auditioning for.

"It's a small part. A love scene."

That got his interest. He edged closer to her and gave her a wolfish leer, which looked obscenely idiotic on him.

"I wouldn't mind helping you practice for it."

"It's a nude scene," she said.

"I could do that."

She gave him a look that made him blush. "We might have to run through the scene a few times. You think you're up to it?"

"I carry around a little blue pill for this very reason."

She laughed at that. "Just in case an actress asks you to practice a scene with you, huh, sport?"

"You know what I mean." He started to look antsy, as if he were afraid if he didn't move fast she'd change her mind and he'd see his fantasy blow up on him. "What do you say, babe? We blow this popsicle stand?"

"*Blow this popsicle stand*? What are you, an extra from the forties?"

"I don't know. Maybe. I must've heard the line from an old movie." He yanked up his jacket sleeve to glance at his watch and see that it was already 2:30 in the morning. Last call in Los Angeles was supposed to be two o'clock, but this hot spot paid off the right people and was known to serve until four each morning. "So what do you say, ready to go practice for your big audition?"

She teased him with a smile. "What about your scotch?"

The bartender was at the other end of the bar chatting with a couple of skimpily-clad blondes. Wallaban tossed forty dollars on the bar to cover the drinks—the one Grace was sipping and the scotch he was never going to have.

"The bartender can have it." He grinned at her. "For the best. Another scotch might affect my performance, and we can't have that. We've got hours of practicing to do, right, honey lips?"

"Call me that again and I'll break your nose."

He looked taken aback as he realized she wasn't joking. "Sorry, Lulu," he said, meekly.

"Just don't let that happen again."

She got off her barstool and halfway to the door realized Wallaban was where she'd left him, looking chagrined. *What a schmuck*, she thought. She gave him a wave and he came running after her like a puppy dog.

"My motel's on Sunset Boulevard," she said. "You want to drive, sport?"

"Sure, thing, Lulu." He looked tongue-tied, as if he were trying to make up his mind about something. "I've got a nice place on the outskirts of Laurel Canyon, complete with hot tub and pool if you want to go there instead."

If she had noticed Jack anywhere around so he'd be able to follow them, she would've taken him up on the offer, but Jack must've been waiting back at the motel.

"That's sweet," she said, "but I left the script in my room."

He gave her a confused look. "We're really going to be practicing a scene?"

"Oh yeah. But it *is* a nude scene." She moved in close and nibbled his earlobe. "And we'll be doing a lot of improvisational work."

He grabbed her in his arms and tried to kiss her, but she pushed him away, laughing. "Wait until we're in the motel room, sport."

"You're going to give me a heart attack," he complained.

"If you're lucky."

His BMW sedan was only a few steps from the door, and he ran every red light on the way to the motel. "Some nights you just keep drawing aces," he said, as if marveling over that fact. Grace pointed out her room and Wallaban pulled into the empty spot in front of it. Once they got inside and had the door closed behind them, he remarked that he didn't see a script anywhere.

"Whoops," she said, exaggerating the gesture as she innocently touched the tip of her index finger to her lips. "I must've left it back home. No problem, though. I've got all the lines memorized. Sport, you're overdressed for the part."

He grinned and kicked off his shoes, then hurried to strip off his pants, showing off that he was a tighty-whitey guy. Even though he was a pear-shaped chunk, he had spindly legs. When he took off his sports jacket, he revealed a shoulder holster that was being put to use.

"You're packing?" she said, surprised by this.

"More ways than one, babe," he said with a wink. He started to remove the holster, but she surprised herself by suggesting he keep it on.

His grin disappeared. "Why's that?"

She lowered her voice to a whisper, because Jack was in the adjoining room and the motel had thin walls. "Because if you were half as smart as you think you are, you'd know I brought you here only so me and my man can rob you of the money you won tonight."

All of his good-natured goofiness from before faded. He no longer looked quite as pear-shaped and harmless either.

"How exactly was that going to happen?" he asked.

"My man's in the next room," she said. "Once we start screwing, I'm supposed to make enough noise for him to hear me. That's his signal to come in here and bust you up with a pair of brass knuckles. He likes busting up guys with brass knuckles almost as much as he does taking their money."

"Why are you telling me this?"

She shrugged more with her eyes than her shoulders. "I'm a complicated person."

Wallaban pulled his pants back up and put on his shoes. He took a 9mm pistol from the holster and moved so he'd be standing by the door. He turned off the room lights and told Grace to signal her partner.

"I'm supposed to make sure the door's unlocked before taking you to bed," she said.

Wallaban checked the door and unlocked it.

"Oh baby, oh baby," she moaned loudly as if she were in ecstasy, "give it to me harder, harder."

She repeated this until the door eased open. Readinger stepped into the room, a glint from an outside light showing off the brass knuckles he wore on his right hand. Wallaban stepped out from where he was hiding and slugged him on the back of the head with the gun, and Readinger slumped to the floor.

If Wallaban had asked Grace to join him, she would've left with him, but the look he showed Grace before he stepped out of the room showed he'd rather drive away with a carful of rattlesnakes. So instead, she watched as Readinger reached blindly for the back of his skull to see if he was bleeding, and then as he struggled to get back onto his feet. He looked groggy and in pain as he rubbed the back of his head.

"What happened?" he asked

"The mark figured out the game."

Readinger squinted at her as if he were having trouble focusing. "Yeah? How'd he do that?"

The frightened little-girl look she was showing turned into a brazen smirk. "Because I told him."

"Why'd you do that?"

"I thought it would be funny and I was right. It was downright hilarious!"

Readinger reached back with his right fist and, putting all his weight into the punch, hit her flush in the eye. If he hadn't been wearing the brass knuckles (and to be honest about it—she pissed him off so much he had forgotten he was wearing them) he would've only knocked her out, but he felt her eye cavity caving in, and he knew she was dead before he knelt next to her and searched for a pulse that no longer existed.

He fumed as he thought about how she'd not only cost him eight grand, but set him up to have his head bashed in. Goddamned crazy bitch. Yeah, she got what she deserved, no question about it. That was the thing about honeypots: They didn't last forever. Sooner or later they ran dry and when that happened you had to get rid of them, because they were nothing but trouble then. This one had showed a mouth on her from the very start, and it was only a matter of time before something like this happened.

He tried to be philosophical about it, telling himself there was no use crying over spilled milk, but that was easier said than done. Eight grand! That was what she stole from him. More than that, actually. He had paid the waiter at Hopper's two bills and slipped the desk clerk at the motel another 300 so he'd be given two rooms off the books. And now he had to clean up this mess.

He pulled the sheet off the bed, used it to mop up the small pool of blood by Grace's head, then laid the sheet on the floor and wrapped her in it. Most of the blood came off the cheap industrial-type carpeting used in the room, and the small stain that was left wouldn't draw attention. He got his car and backed it up into the spot in front of the motel-room door, and then hustled Grace into the trunk. He had already moved the shovel he usually kept in the trunk into the backseat. Readinger always kept a shovel in his car. You never knew when you were going to need one.

He spent the next two hours burying Grace in a secluded spot off Mulholland Drive. He was dirty, tired, and in a rotten mood by the time he got back to his apartment. He filled a plastic bag with ice, got a beer from the refrigerator, and sat on the couch holding the bag of ice to the back of his head and drinking the beer. He couldn't stop thinking about what a clusterfuck tonight ended up being, his mood darkening by the minute. Yeah, it was a bad one, all right, almost as bad as that night back in April when he was in Boston. Goddamn, that was one screwed-up night.

He had paid a grand to get the address for where five kilos of coke was supposed to be stashed, and had played his usual game that night, pounding on the door and claiming he was Dave. (Sometimes instead he'd knock on the door and yell for someone named Dave—it was amazing how often both of these simpleminded schemes worked.) The second the door swung open, he stepped forward and broke the guy's jaw with a pair of brass knuckles, and before the guy hit the floor he realized he had the wrong address. The drug dealer had been pointed out to him earlier that week and this wasn't him. Readinger could understand the mistake. The apartment building was in a complex of identical brick buildings, and he'd been given the wrong number. He should've left then. If he had, he might still have had time to get the right address and score those five kilos. But that pretty little blonde had to start screaming, which meant he had to shut her up.

She was a pretty little thing, no question about it, and he thought he might as well have a little fun with her—mostly of the harmless variety, but the way she looked at him, as if he were lower than a cockroach, made him change his mind about the kind of fun he would have.

Even after he had stripped her and bound her to the kitchen chair, he still wasn't planning to do what he did. He was just going to cut her a dozen or so times and watch her boyfriend squirm, but it just became one of those nights. It was really the boyfriend's fault. It was the way he acted—as if he'd do anything to save that pretty little thing's life, even if it meant giving up his own. To be fair, it also pissed him off, realizing that while he'd have crazy, messed-up bitches he could take advantage of, he'd never have a pretty little thing like that, and it was never good when he got pissed off.

So things happened that night, and when he was done he had to forget about those five kilos and get out of Boston. He decided he'd go back to the west coast, this time choosing Los Angeles.

As he remembered that night in Boston, the boyfriend's name popped into his head: Duncan Moss. He even remembered Moss's address and an evil thought came to him.

He pushed himself off the couch. He'd have to clear out all of Grace's belongings, but he could wait until later to do that. For now, he pulled out from under the bed the box of souvenirs she collected. He rummaged through it and found what he was looking for—a *Welcome to Hollywood* postcard. He brought the card to the kitchen table and very carefully wrote on it *Now you have yourself an especially wonderful rest of your life*, and admired his handiwork.

The idea of mailing the postcard to Moss lifted his spirits.

There was nothing he enjoyed more in life than sharing the pain.

Chapter 61

Los Angeles, the present

Morris learned how dire the situation was during his ride to Ronald Reagan UCLA Medical Center. Before the paramedics arrived at the apartment, Doug Gilman's heart had stopped and while they were able to resuscitate him, he was hanging on by a thread and would be in surgery for hours, if he survived that long. "Miracles do happen," a trauma surgeon had told Morris, but the woman didn't sound optimistic that would be the case this time.

Morris had brought Parker with him and the dog sensed something bad had happened. Instead of the bull terrier's normal, rambunctious self, he was subdued, and as they walked through the hospital corridors to the room where Rachel was waiting, Parker sensed Morris's growing anxiety and became more agitated.

It broke Morris's heart when he saw Rachel looking grief-stricken and lost. Parker must have felt the same way. The bull terrier let out a painful whine as he padded over to Rachel, and was surprisingly gentle as he attempted to lick her face and do whatever he could to comfort her. Rachel hugged the dog around his thick neck and began sobbing, which only made Parker more persistent in his attempts to lick her face.

Morris wanted to say something to comfort his daughter, but he was at a loss for words. There was only a slim chance at best that Gilman would survive the night, and if he said something like "everything will be all right" it would sound trite and unconvincing. As he stroked Rachel's hair, his voice broke into a gruff rumble and he told her that her fiancé was a good man. "I know he loves you with all his heart."

She looked up at him, her eyes a sea of pain. "Doug saved my life," she said. "If he hadn't done what he did, that psychopath would've done to me what he did to those other women."

"Doug's a hero. Thank God for that. Were his parents called?"

"They're on their way."

Morris wanted to be there only to comfort his daughter, and hated the idea of questioning her right then, but what he had to ask was too important to hold off until later. His voice became gravel as he asked whether she saw any tattoos on her attacker.

She pointed to the underside of her right wrist. "He had a wolf's face right here, the fangs bared."

Morris showed her the photo on his phone of Jack Readinger's tattoo. "Did it look like this?"

"Exactly like that." She gave him an exhausted look. "What does this mean? Is the guy you arrested working with the psycho who attacked me and Doug?"

"I don't know," Morris admitted. Annie Walsh had already shown the blond cashier at the Hollywood gift shop a photo lineup with Jack Readinger's picture, and the woman insisted that she never saw any of them so she couldn't have sold their suspect the "cutest couple" mugs. Polk and Greg Malevich were off to show Jill Kincade's parents the same photo lineup, and Morris was expecting the same results, which just made no sense. His gut was screaming at him that Readinger was involved somehow, but how?

Parker's ears perked up and he turned toward the door, his tail wagging a beat faster as Natalie walked into the room. Rachel disentangled herself from the bull terrier, got to her feet, and stumbled toward Natalie. The two women embraced, both of them quickly teary-eyed. Morris felt a growing unease as he watched them, knowing that the only thing he could possibly do to help his daughter was catch the bastard responsible. He cleared his throat and told Natalie and Rachel he had to get back to work.

"I don't think it's likely, but an unmarked patrol car will be watching the house just in case this sonofabitch tries something."

"I'm not budging from here until I know Doug's okay," Rachel insisted.

Natalie was using her thumb to wipe away tears from her daughter's face. "And I'm not leaving you," she said.

That was pretty much what Morris expected. "In case you need to go home for any reason, you'll be safe," he said. He knew Parker wasn't going to budge. While the bull terrier was ostensibly his dog, he was nuts about Rachel, and there wasn't any chance he'd leave her side while she was in such distress. He was glad Parker would be there to protect them in case the Cupid Killer tried something desperate.

Morris thumped the bull terrier on the side. Before he left, Nat showed him a tragically sad smile and then turned back to their daughter. Morris had never wanted to catch any bad guy more than this Cupid Killer.

He would've bet almost anything earlier that Jack Readinger was their guy, and he still couldn't let go of the idea that Readinger was somehow involved, even though that no longer made sense. Was it possible that two men were committing these murders? It would be diabolical if that were true. If they caught one of the killers, but only had a heavily circumstantial case, the other could set up an airtight alibi by continuing the killings.

Morris shivered involuntarily over that awful thought. But even if they had to cross off Readinger, at least they weren't starting from scratch: They now had a 9mm pistol from the killer, and they had the dead man left inside Rachel's apartment. Rachel had told the first officers at the scene she had never seen the dead man before; that when she woke up the Cupid Killer had just killed this person. For some reason, this man had followed the Cupid Killer to Rachel's apartment and confronted him there. He didn't have any identification on him, and from photos that were texted to Morris, the man looked like a meth addict and could've been living on the streets. But there had to be a connection between him and the Cupid Killer. The first step was to check the shelters, drug clinics, meth dealers, and skid-row boarding houses, and figure out who this man was, and maybe that would lead them to the killer.

Morris got a call from Polk, first asking about Rachel, then telling him that Jill Kincade's parents didn't recognize Readinger. "They're both sure he wasn't at the engagement party. I could try showing the dirtbag's photo to other guests, but I think I'd be wasting my time."

"I'd have to agree," Morris said. "I'm heading back to the office. Let's regroup there and see if we can come up with any ideas while LAPD works to identify our dead guy."

"Makes about as much sense as anything," Polk agreed.

Later, when Morris was pulling into his spot at the MBI office building, he got a call from Walsh to let him know the gun was a dead end. "On a hunch, I called Matt Kammer and asked if the Cupid Killer had taken a gun from his house, and he told me he had bought an illegal nine-millimeter because he was worried about his wife. He looked in the drawer where he'd left it, and it was gone."

Morris said, "We got to find out who that dead man is."

"Hadley has made it a departmental priority. We've got a small army working on that right now. Should I still try to pull a warrant on Readinger's apartment?"

"Yeah. I still think he's involved somehow. Both he and the killer having those same tattoos are too big a coincidence." Morris wasn't sure he entirely believed that, but he also wanted Readinger's apartment searched to see if they could find a connection between Readinger and Grace Warren. "Let me know when you get the warrant; I want in."

"Sure thing."

Morris felt emotionally and physically drained as he made his way into the building and took an elevator to MBI's office suite. Blind rage flared up inside him whenever he let himself think about what had happened to Rachel and Gilman, and he knew he had to fight harder to keep those thoughts at bay. If he was going to catch this psycho, he would somehow have to keep a clear head.

He checked his watch. It wasn't even seven yet. It felt so much later. He was dragging the same as if it were four a.m. He'd have Greta order pizza for the office. He planned on being there however long it took to get a lead on this killer, and he knew the rest of the team would be doing the same whether he asked them to or not.

He walked into the office and saw Greta behind the reception desk, and Lemmon leaning against it, immersed in a thick file. Greta's face melted into a look of concern as she asked about Rachel and Gilman.

"Rachel's hanging in there, trying to stay positive. Doug's battling. It's going to be a long night."

Lemmon walked over to him and put a hand on Morris's arm. "Doug's tougher than he looks. And they got him at Ronald Reagan, right? That's one of the best trauma centers in the country."

Morris felt his eyes misting up. He choked back a sob, then said, "He saved my little girl's life."

"That's what I'm talking about. And with a beautiful, smart, and loving girl like Rachel waiting for him, nobody's got more incentive to pull through than he does. Keep the faith, okay? And in the meantime, take a look at this." He handed Morris the file he'd been reading. "The Julia Swan homicide. Charlie faxed it over earlier, and this has to be our killer. Maybe you'll be able to glean some other nugget from it."

Morris took the homicide file and asked Lemmon and Greta whether they preferred pizza or something else. Both of them gave the thumbs-up for pizza and Greta volunteered to call in an order. Morris took Swan's homicide file back to his office, put his feet up on the desk, and resisted the urge to close his eyes. The last thing he felt like doing was immersing himself into another of this psycho's murders, but Fred was right—it might spark an idea. He was thumbing through the pages when he came across the photo of a smiling Julia Swan that Bogle had taken from a picture frame.

He was sure he had recently seen the guy in the photo with her. Then he remembered where. It was Sunday at the Santa Monica pier. Parker had growled at him and this was only minutes after Hannah Kammer had approached Morris about petting the bull terrier.

This guy from the photo had been stalking Matt and Hannah Kammer.

Morris searched through the file to get the name of Swan's live-in fiancé. He fought to hold back his excitement when he called Bogle to ask whether the guy in the photo was Duncan Moss.

"I assumed so," Bogle said. "I found the photo in their bedroom."

"Could you check with the Boston police? I need to know positively whether that's Moss."

"Okay," Bogle said. "What's your reason?"

"He's our Cupid Killer."

"Wait a minute," Bogle stumbled out, as if he were trying to collect his thoughts. "Moss had a broken jaw and was hysterical when the police found him bound and gagged inside the apartment. He couldn't have been responsible for Julia Swan's death."

"I know that."

"So why is he the Cupid Killer?"

"Somehow he found out that the guy who killed his girlfriend was in LA, and he's been killing these women here in the same way and with the same tattoo on his wrist, so we'd find the guy who killed Swan."

"That's pretty messed up," Bogle said. "Any frame-up would fall apart if Swan's killer had an alibi for when any of the Cupid Killer killings happened."

"He doesn't care about that. He just wants to know who the guy is so he can take care of matters himself."

"You're telling me he killed four innocent people to do this?"

"More than that. He attacked Rachel earlier today and shot Doug in the stomach."

"Oh hell. I'm sorry, Morris. How's Rachel?"

"Some bruises. Emotionally distraught."

"Is Doug going to make it?"

"They don't know yet."

"I'll light a candle for him tonight. That's got to be Moss in the photo, but I'm off now to the BPD to rattle some cages."

Morris drifted into a Zen-like trance while he waited for Bogle to call him back. A short time later Lemmon walked into his office and asked him what was up.

Morris said, "You came into my office, not the other way around."

"That was to tell you the pizza's here. But something's up."

"Why's that?"

"You're way too calm."

"Fred, when you're right, you're right." Morris pointed to the photo of Julia Swan and Duncan Moss. "I'm waiting for Charlie to identify this guy."

Lemmon gave him a suspicious look. "You already know who that is. The fiancé of the woman who was killed in Boston."

"I'm waiting for confirmation."

"Why's that?"

"He's our killer."

Lemmon didn't look convinced. "You were able to divine that from the homicide file?"

Morris pushed himself to his feet. "I'll explain over pizza."

"You better get a move on it, then. Greta ordered five pies, which should've been more than enough, but Polk—aka 'the bottomless pit'—showed up five minutes ago. If we're lucky we might still grab a slice each."

Lemmon had exaggerated. Only half a pie was gone by the time Morris and Lemmon joined Polk, Greta, and Felger in the conference room. As promised, Morris explained how he'd figured out that Moss was the Cupid Killer—or at least, the man from the picture who he assumed was Moss. He was working on his third slice when he received a text from Bogle with Moss's driver's-license photo and the message *I rattled some cages and it's Moss.*

Morris showed the text to the others in the room. "It's been confirmed," he said. "We know the sonofabitch's name."

"So that's it?" Polk asked. "You'll give that to the LAPD and we're done?"

"Not quite yet," Morris said. "But for now, all of you go get drunk or stoned, or go home and get some sleep, or whatever it is you want to do. We'll be busy tomorrow, though."

"How's that?" Lemmon asked.

"I'll tell you tomorrow. Nine sharp."

Lemmon said, "A free night, huh? In that case, I'll be heading over to UCLA Medical Center. There's someone I'd like to stand vigil for."

"Not a bad idea," Polk said.

"Agreed," Felger added.

Lemmon asked Morris, "How about it? Would you like a ride over there?"

"You go on without me," Morris said. "There are a few things I need to take care of first."

Chapter 62

Morris wanted additional confirmation regarding Duncan Moss, and he got it when he texted Moss's photo to Missy Alderberg, who was the cashier at the Hollywood gift shop, and then called to ask whether she'd ever seen the man before. She asked him to wait. He heard her humming for a minute or so, and then received a text with a photo of Moss that was taken inside the gift shop, apparently surreptitiously.

"Sometimes I take pictures of cute guys who come into the shop," she said. "It helps with the boredom. But if he had bought the 'cutest couple' mugs, I would've remembered."

"What time was the photo taken?"

"Let me look." More humming, then, "Saturday at three-thirty-six."

Morris thanked her. Given this confirmation, he tried calling the mayor's office and was promptly given the runaround. He tried again and got the same result. On the third try, he was shuffled off to a low-level assistant, and this time he told the assistant that if the mayor didn't call him back in five minutes he'd be holding a press conference and would claim the mayor wasn't giving him adequate assistance to solve the Cupid Killer murders. Three minutes later, he got an angry call from the mayor demanding to know whether Morris was threatening him.

"Damn straight," Morris said. "You weren't making yourself available."

"I've been busy," the mayor snapped back. "My deputy assistant was critically wounded earlier this evening."

"In case you've forgotten, Doug is my daughter's fiancé, and she was attacked also."

"I did forget," the mayor said contritely. "It's been a madhouse here since word came down about Doug. I have, of course, been in touch with the medical staff, but I haven't had a chance to get over to the hospital yet. Morris, what can I do for you?"

"I know the identity of the Cupid Killer."

The mayor sounded nonplussed as he asked, "Did you give this information to Commissioner Hadley?"

"Not yet. I still have a few t's to cross first. But I do have an unusual request for you."

"Go ahead."

Morris told him his request and his reason for making it, and the mayor agreed that it was unusual, to say the least. "You really believe this is needed?"

"I don't know. The LAPD might be able to pick him up on their own, but my gut is this is our best chance to catch him before he hurts any more innocent people."

"I noticed that you were careful to qualify that with the word *innocent*."

"I'll also try to keep him from killing the less-than-innocent, if possible."

"I'll take care of your request," the mayor promised. "If there are any problems, I'll call you."

Morris knew that with the mayor handling what he needed there wouldn't be any problems. He next called Margot Denoir. She answered on the first ring, sounding breathless.

"Morris, darling, I was so hoping you would call. Rumor has it that you arrested a suspect for the Cupid Killer murders earlier this evening."

"Not our guy. But, Margot, I can give you the scoop of a lifetime."

"I'm all ears."

"What I'm about to tell you is off the record. If you burn me, you don't get the exclusive. Do we have a deal?"

"Yes, of course."

"There will be conditions, but nothing you won't be able to handle."

"Morris, sweetie, you've got me on the edge of my seat. Spill it already before I burst!"

Morris smiled at the thought of Margot ever getting that worked up. No one in the business was cooler and calmer than her, but she could be quite theatrical when it suited her.

"We arrested someone today that I pegged for the Cupid Killer. A lowlife named Jack Readinger and we picked him up on a criminal-conspiracy charge. I was wrong about him being the Cupid Killer. We have a new suspect and this one is a hundred percent."

Margot asked incredulously, "This isn't the scoop?"

"No. The scoop is why the Cupid Killer is doing what he's doing, and the story is a doozy."

"It better be, with what you're giving me off the record! When are the police releasing details about your new suspect?"

"I don't know. I haven't given them the name yet, and they'll have to figure out how they want to handle it. They might decide to keep the information quiet until they pick him up."

"Do you have an address?"

"Nope. No clue where he is."

"But you're sure he's the Cupid Killer?"

"As sure as I've ever been about anything."

"Can you tell me what you have? We're still off the record, after all."

"Not yet. So let me tell you my conditions. Jack Readinger will have his bail hearing tomorrow morning at nine-thirty. Bail will be set at ten grand—enough so he can't raise it. You, however, will step in and offer to have your station put up the bail in exchange for an interview that morning. And you need to make sure to give out his apartment address in the interview. And run the interview enough times so it gets picked up by the national media."

Margot's voice had a chill in it as she asked why she would want to interview Readinger.

"Because he was a suspect in the Cupid Killer murders."

"Why was he a suspect?"

"He has a wolf's-face tattoo on the underside of his right wrist. Fangs are bared, very unique."

"And the Cupid Killer has the same tattoo!" Margot exclaimed angrily. "I knew the FBI profiler you sent on my show was holding out on me!"

"Margot, it couldn't be helped. One last condition: When you interview him, I want you to sandbag him and ask him if he was in Boston on April twelfth, 2018, and in Oakland on October eighteenth, 2017. And when you end the interview, I want you to wish him an 'especially wonderful rest of the day.'"

"What's the significance of all that?"

"Patience. All in good time."

"You want me to help you use this Readinger as bait," she said accusingly.

"Are you in or not?"

"This scoop better be as big as you're saying it is."

"It's bigger."

"You bastard," she said, laughing. "I'm in, as you damn well knew I'd be. When am I getting this scoop to end all scoops?"

"Soon. With some luck, tomorrow."

"Until then. Ta-ta, darling."

"Whew!" Morris said after Margot got off the call. He made the motion of wiping imaginary sweat from his brow. He knew that if she had heard about what happened at Rachel's apartment, she would've been relentless in calling him that evening, but still, it was a relief that their call ended without her asking about it. Just like he knew he could count on the mayor, the same was true of Margot. She'd climb Mt. Everest with the four-inch heels she liked to wear on her show if it meant getting a story as big as the one he was offering.

Now that he had finished crossing his t's, he had no good reason to delay calling Hadley any further. Unlike Margot, Hadley didn't sound at all excited to hear from him.

"How come we're not getting anywhere with this Readinger character you like for the Cupid Killer?" he demanded, his voice raspier than usual.

"Because he's not the guy. But he's involved in a way. Indirectly."

"What are you talking about?"

Morris breathed in deeply, filling his lungs before letting the air out slowly through his nose. He knew this wasn't going to go smoothly, but he dove in, telling the police commissioner everything he knew about Duncan Moss and why Moss was the Cupid Killer. From Hadley's impatient grumbling, the police commissioner did not sound impressed.

"Let me see if I got this straight," Hadley said. "Every few hours you plan to send us on a wild-goose chase after a new prime suspect? That your plan, Brick?"

"This is our guy, Martin."

"Yeah, and why is that? Because of a cockamamy story you tried selling me? Or because you saw someone at the Santa Monica Pier who you thought might look like Moss?"

"Because it makes sense, and nothing else does."

Hadley let out an angry snort. "It makes sense, huh? Then maybe you can explain to me why Moss came to LA to hunt for Swan's killer? What are you going to try selling me next, that the killer sent Moss a postcard telling him he was here? Face it, Brick, you're grasping at straws here."

"Martin, the cashier from Hottest Hollywood Gifts took a picture of Moss inside the store within a half hour of when those 'cutest couple' mugs were bought."

Another snort of derision. "And you also told me she claims she didn't sell him the mugs."

"Moss was cautious. He had someone else buy them for him, probably convincing the person that he wanted them for himself and the cashier working inside the store. When you identify the dead man in Rachel's apartment, you'll find another link to Moss, and I can guarantee guests from the engagement party will recognize him."

"You're Nostradamus now, huh?"

Morris had had enough of Hadley. He rubbed his eyes with his thumb and index finger and stifled a weary groan.

"Look, Martin, it's late," he said. "I need to get to the hospital and be with my wife and daughter. Moss is our guy and with a little bit of legwork LAPD will be able to prove it. You might even be able to pick him up before he ditches his ski mask and knife, and I've got a few ideas of how you can do it—"

"Can it, Brick. As far as I'm concerned, you and your team of misfits are now off the investigation, and we'll be handling it from here." Hadley's raspy voice softened. "I'm sorry about your daughter."

Hadley disconnected the call before Morris could thank him.

Will miracles never cease, he thought. The call went pretty much as he had expected. Hadley would always have a twenty-pound bug squirming up his butt where Morris was concerned, so his expressing any concern for Rachel was a nearly earth-shattering event.

Morris shut off the lights inside MBI on his way out. What he had in mind for tomorrow was so damned delicate, and even a slight wind could tear it apart. He didn't want to just catch Duncan Moss, he also wanted to tie Readinger to the Swan and Markin murders, and for that to happen, Readinger would have to agree to be interviewed by Margot, and Margot would have to catch him off guard enough for Readinger to say something incriminating. But that wasn't the only reason he wanted Margot interviewing Readinger. As she had guessed, he wanted to use Readinger as bait.

He waited until he was in the car before calling Natalie to tell her he'd be there soon.

"The MBI cavalry arrived with pizza a half-hour ago," she said. "Awfully sweet of them to come here to show their support. Me and the little guy are appreciative. Thanks!"

"I'm sure Charlie would've been there too if he wasn't still in Boston. And I'm glad to hear Polk didn't polish off the pizza on the way there. I'll be stopping at Five Star to pick up some vegan food for Rachel just in case we can coax her to eat something. Any word on Doug?"

"Nothing yet. He'll be in surgery most of the night."

Morris picked up the worry in Natalie's voice, and he knew the thought she was trying hard to suppress. *This would only be true if poor Doug lived that long.* He cleared some frogginess from his throat, then asked how Rachel was doing.

He heard shuffling noises, and knew that Natalie was moving to the hallway so she could talk to him more privately. Even so, her voice was barely a whisper when she told him Rachel wasn't doing well.

"Morris, she's trying so hard to be strong, but this is tearing her apart, and it's tearing me apart to see her suffering like this."

Morris heard a big inhale from Nat, and he knew she was struggling to keep from crying—not so much to be brave for his sake, but so Rachel wouldn't see that she'd been crying. He pictured how worn-out and miserable she must've looked right then and he never felt more helpless. His voice was barely a croak as he asked about the Gilmans.

"Rachel got a call from them a few minutes ago. Traffic from Santa Barbara was more brutal than usual, but they should be here soon. I can't imagine what they're going through."

Morris could imagine it. When Rachel called him earlier, he let those terrible thoughts enter his mind of how he would've felt if Moss had taken his daughter's life. He prayed he was wrong about what he believed to be inevitable with Gilman. When he pressed the trauma doctor earlier, she reluctantly gave him odds of one in a hundred of Gilman surviving the surgery, and he got the sense she was exaggerating for his benefit. Blind rage surged inside him and he punched the steering wheel before realizing what he was doing.

"What was that?" Natalie asked.

"I punched the steering wheel," he admitted. .

"Don't do that again," she said. "It won't help anyone if you break your hand."

"I know." Morris flexed the fingers on his right hand. "Nat, I know who this psycho is and I'll be catching him soon. I promise."

"Good," Natalie said.

Chapter 63

Morris waited until midnight before urging the MBI team to go home, telling them they would be having a busy day when they returned to the office in the morning. There was absolutely no chance of getting Rachel to leave until she saw Doug after the surgery and knew he would be okay, which meant Natalie and Parker weren't about to budge from the waiting room.

The Gilmans were a good deal older than Morris and Natalie, and maintained a mostly stoic countenance as they sat vigil for their son, although when Mrs. Gilman explained that Doug was her baby—the youngest of four boys—she looked for a minute as if she were on the verge of weeping before choking it back and regaining a stiff upper lip. At two in the morning a surgeon came in to inform them that there had been complications and the surgery would be continuing on into the next day.

"Tell me straight," Mr. Gilman demanded. "Will my son be surviving this?"

It looked as if the doctor was about to tell him something trite, but had a change of heart. "I don't know," he admitted. "The internal damage is more severe than we had anticipated. But we're doing everything we can."

Both Gilmans looked crestfallen from this news. Rachel looked frightened to death.

"What are my boy's chances?" Mrs. Gilman asked, her voice a ghost of a whisper.

"I can't say. Sometimes it's up to the patient. On how badly they want to live."

The doctor excused himself, and after some coaxing from Morris, the Gilmans agreed to let him take them to his house so they could rest. When

Morris returned, nothing had changed and seeing Rachel and Natalie looking so miserable and frightened made him want to punch a wall.

What good would it do? he thought. *None.*

He plopped down next to his daughter and put his arm around her thin shoulders. Parker was lying by Rachel's feet and he looked up at Morris and slowly wagged his tail once, but the bull terrier looked every bit as miserable as Rachel and Nat.

Over the next several hours, Morris kept his arm around Rachel while Nat held her daughter's hand and Parker maintained his vigil by Rachel's feet. A little after 7:30 Morris received a call from Annie Walsh to let him know she had pulled a warrant to search Jack Readinger's apartment.

"Hadley sent out a memo last night that you and MBI are off the Cupid Killer case, and that the department is not to share any further information with any of you, but the hell with him. You want to join me in executing the warrant?"

"Sure thing. Any luck identifying John Doe?"

"A meth dealer gave us a first name. Stevie. That's all we have so far."

"How about Duncan Moss's photo? Please tell me Hadley is having it shown to the guests who attended the Frey-Kincade engagement party?"

"That started last night and it hasn't been going so well. Photo lineups were shown to eleven of the guests, including Kincade's parents, and two of them think they saw Moss there and five pointed to other photos. We've got a trace on Moss's credit cards to see if we can place him in LA and patrol units have his photo, but otherwise Hadley ordered us to shut this down until we can link John Doe to Moss. How sure are you that he's our guy?"

"I'm sure of it."

"Then let's hope John Doe leads us to him. Or we find something in Readinger's apartment."

* * * *

The apartment was littered with dirty clothing, food-encrusted takeout containers, empty bourbon and vodka bottles, and other assorted garbage. But there were no trophies from Julia Swan and Suzanne Markin, nor were there any cutout newspaper articles about their murders, brass knuckles, or photos. There really was nothing at all to show a personal connection between Readinger and another person. It was the apartment of someone who had no intention of establishing any roots. No past or future could be divined from any of Readinger's belongings, only a sordid present. Walsh found a baggie that likely held cocaine residue when she dumped out a trash can, but that was it.

"This has been a bust," she said.

"Nothing in his car?" Morris asked.

"Nope. If he's got anything incriminating, he's keeping it hidden elsewhere."

Morris called Natalie. Doug was miraculously out of surgery and still clinging to life, but unconscious and on a respirator.

"Rachel's with him now. I've called Doug's parents and they're on their way. The doctor told us the next twenty-four hours will be key."

Morris said, "Let's keep the faith."

Natalie laughed tragically. "I'm trying. Anyway, I'm in the waiting room with the little guy, and he's beside himself that he had to leave Rachel's side."

Morris had heard Parker whining. "I've got to be in court soon, but I'll pick him up afterwards. Maybe a change of scenery will help."

After the call, Morris headed to the courthouse and had a quick strategy session with Margot. The police had done a good job keeping a lid on what happened at Rachel's apartment and even Margot, with all of her sources, hadn't caught a whiff of it. She did, of course, try to wheedle out of him the identity of the Cupid Killer and the big scoop that he had for her later.

"Do you have any idea how painful this has been?" she asked. "Not a single one of my so-called friends at the LAPD will return my calls about whether they have a suspect for the murders. Not one! I know we were off the record, but you're making me sit on a ginormous story that a suspect has been named—"

"By me, not by the LAPD, evidently."

"That by itself would be huge!"

"Patience," Morris said.

Margot puffed up her cheeks in frustration. "When you're finally ready to give me your exclusive interview, you're bringing your adorable four-legged partner with you. My audience loves him. But this time you better keep him from getting to first base with me!"

Morris grinned at that memory. The last time he'd brought Parker with him on the *Hollywood Peeper*, he had given Parker a rawhide bone to keep the bull terrier entertained. Margot, bless her, thought the visuals would be better if there was no bone, and she arranged to have it snatched away from the dog right before they went on air. This backfired badly, as it caused Parker to become overly excited and leap onto Margot's lap. End result: He made a mess of her makeup by licking her face a dozen times before Morris was able to drag him off of her.

"As long as you don't pull any more stunts, Parker will be just fine."
He spotted Readinger being escorted into the courtroom, and pointed
him out to Margot.

"A weaselly-looking individual," she said with distaste.

"That he is."

They followed him into the courtroom, and Morris took a seat in the
row behind Readinger so he could listen in on Margot's conversation with
him. As they had arranged, Margot approached Readinger and offered to
have her station pay his bail if he'd agree to an on-air interview at noon.
Readinger seemed genuinely baffled by the offer, and asked why she would
want to interview him.

"Because the police considered you a suspect in the Cupid Killer
murders. In fact, they searched your apartment this morning, looking for
evidence to tie you to those murders."

"Why would they think that?"

"Because of your wolf's-face tattoo."

"Yeah?" His voice became tight, angry. "They're trying to railroad me
because of a tattoo?"

"My thoughts exactly, which is why I want to interview you."

"You got your interview, honey."

Margot had him sign a contract, and when the bail hearing started
promptly at 9:30, Readinger was called first, as Morris had arranged, and
the bail set at ten grand. Margot paid the bail and winked at Morris before
leaving the courthouse with Readinger. Her crew, which included Dennis
Polk, was waiting for them outside.

First step accomplished, Morris thought.

Chapter 64

Duncan Moss felt battered and bruised as he lay on a bed in a North Hollywood motel room and watched the local news. Stevie had worked him over good with the crowbar, his leg ached where Rachel had kicked him, and his jaw even more so from her kneeing him. He was lucky nothing got broken and he was able to extricate himself from that shitstorm in one piece. After leaving the apartment, he ran for two blocks before hiding behind a building and changing into the clothes he had brought in his backpack. Then he continued on until he was a mile away from Rachel's apartment building and called for an Uber to take him to a North Hollywood strip club. He had no interest in going inside the club; he just didn't want the Uber driver to know his real destination, and he later walked a mile to the motel. He figured once the police identified Stevie it would bring too much heat to the boarding house, and besides, feeling as beat-up as he was, he could use a real bed. He also needed to do some thinking.

In a way, he was glad things worked out the way they had last night. It woke him up, in a sense. The first killing was satisfying, at least to a degree. He was like a steam valve that was ready to explode if pressure wasn't released, and watching a soft and spoiled member of the privileged few like Alex Frey suffer just as he had suffered when Julia's life was snuffed out helped release that pressure. The second killing, though, wasn't satisfying at all, and the third left him feeling disgusted with himself. Gilman represented everything he had grown to hate, and even when he shot the man in the stomach and could see in his eyes that he was going to die, it didn't make Moss feel any better.

Of course, making himself feel better wasn't why he needed to kill those people. The real reason was simple: He needed Julia's killer caught. If the guy ended up getting convicted of the murders Moss was responsible for, Moss could live with that. If the guy was arrested and later released, even better. If that happened, Moss would track him down and spend hours torturing him with a knife, but he'd leave him alive, and make the miserable prick live out his years in agony. Because of that, Rachel didn't need to die. She saw his temporary snarling wolf's-face tattoo, and because of that her dad would be properly motivated to catch Julia's killer.

A revelation Moss had had last night was that he had another reason for what he'd been doing. Subconsciously, he'd been needing to recreate that terrible night from a year ago as a way to prove to himself that there was nothing he could've done to save Julia, and he finally accepted that. No matter what he had tried doing, he wouldn't have been able to stop Julia's killer.

Moss was done. Whatever nightmarish fever had gripped him over the past year had finally broken. He'd rest up for a few hours and then get in his car and head back to Boston. He knew it was just a matter of time before the police found the monster with the wolf's-face tattoo who murdered Julia. If the courts released him, Duncan would come back to LA one last time.

He was drinking a can of Coke when the local anchor announced there would be a special *Hollywood Peeper* at noon with Margot Denoir interviewing a just-released suspect in the Cupid Killer murders, and Duncan snorted a mouthful of Coke out of his nose. There'd been nothing on the news about the police picking up a suspect or about Duncan turning that apartment into a slaughterhouse. He'd been wondering about that and somehow he knew those two were tied together.

His stomach had been rumbling and he'd been planning to get something to eat, but he forgot about his hunger and barely blinked as he continued watching the TV. When the interview started, he knew that the scumbag Margot was interviewing was Julia's killer even before they showed his tattoo—the same one he'd been recreating and that had forever been burned into his consciousness. He could barely believe the lousy timing of everything—that the police picked him up yesterday afternoon, but dropped him as a suspect for the Cupid Killer after the brutal attack yesterday afternoon in Rachel Brick's apartment. They mentioned Doug Gilman being shot and now in critical condition after over twelve hours of surgery, and they showed a photo of Stevie's corpse with the crowbar removed from his throat, asking the public for any information about the dead man.

When the interview started, Duncan moved himself to the edge of the bed only three feet away from the TV. Near the end of the interview he sat blinking, not quite believing what he had just heard: Denoir asking this murderous prick where he was on April 12 of last year. She knew about Julia! The police knew about Julia. And the bastard's reaction was a dead giveaway. There was no doubt about it when the interview ended with Denoir wishing him an *especially wonderful rest of the day*. That wasn't quite the end: Denoir faced the camera and told the audience that this interview had taken place in Readinger's apartment, and she gave the address!

It was almost as if this interview had been done for Duncan's benefit.

He realized that that was the case.

Brick was laying a trap for him.

Chapter 65

Hadley sounded over the phone like he might pop a blood vessel as he demanded to know what that was all about.

Morris calmly said, "I have no idea what you're asking."

"No idea?" Hadley sputtered. "Margo's interview, dammit! And don't you dare say you weren't involved! You were seen palling around with Margot at the courthouse!"

"Martin, I'm not a mind reader. How was I supposed to know you were calling about that?"

"Damn you, Brick, I'll have your license pulled for this stunt! You had no right releasing any of that information to the press!"

"Au contraire. Read the contract I signed when I took on the investigation. It gives me free reign to handle matters as I see fit."

There were several seconds of heavy breathing in which Morris pictured Hadley gnashing his teeth. A quaint phrase and maybe a bit clichéd, but one that seemly highly appropriate in this case.

"I fired you, Brick," Hadley finally forced out. "Your contract was voided then."

"Technically, you can't fire me. My contract is with the mayor's office, not the LAPD. But that's beside the point. I arranged the interview with Margot before our talk last night. My visit with her at the courthouse was just a social call."

The call ended abruptly with Hadley disconnecting from his end. If he were talking on an old-fashioned landline, he would've slammed down the handset with enough force to break it, but since he was calling on a cell phone, all he could do was press a button.

Morris didn't bother sticking the phone back in his pocket. He expected more calls to be coming in. He coaxed Parker along on the walk. The bull terrier had been moping ever since Morris picked him up from the hospital. "Soon," Morris promised, knowing the dog wanted to get back to Rachel. "But you need to go on more of a walk first, buddy."

Ten minutes later a call came in from Polk.

"I wanted to let you know I'm in position," Polk said. "Fred will be taking over at six?"

"Yep, he's got the six-to-midnight slot, and I'll be there after that until six in the morning."

"And then I'm there again, huh?"

"Correct."

Polk let out an unhappy grumble. He wasn't exactly a morning person, and he'd have to roll out of bed by five for a six a.m. shift, and no matter how much high-octane coffee he drank, he'd be dragging at that early hour. "What about Charlie?" he said, a note of petulance in his voice. "I mean, you should be with your family, not working a stakeout."

"He's still in Boston looking into a loose end. Just us three for now. Unless you want me to rope Greta into this."

There was enough of a pause to show Polk had taken Morris's facetious comment seriously. "Nah, probably better not. Everything's set?"

"Should be. I talked with Adam earlier and he gave a thumbs-up."

"I got to tell you, I'm sick of this Cupid Killer already. Let's hope it ends soon." Polk let out a heavy breath, then asked, "Any change with Doug?"

"Still unconscious. But at least he's survived this long."

"That's got to be a good sign," Polk said, although he didn't sound particularly confident about it. "Give my best to Nat and Rachel when you see them later."

"Will do."

For the next fifteen minutes, Morris tried to convince Parker to walk another block, but the dog had become adamant that he wasn't going any further. Morris gave up the fight. The dogs were called bull terriers for a reason. No other breed was more bullheaded. They were halfway back to the car when Morris's cell phone rang. Caller ID showed it was Annie Walsh.

"Hadley blasted out another memo after the *Hollywood Peeper* aired," she said. "It's our jobs if any of us talk to you."

"That sounds un-American if you ask me," Morris said.

"True that," Walsh agreed. "Anyway, the hell with him."

"You said that this morning."

"The sentiment still holds. I thought you'd like to know the interview got us a lead on John Doe. The dead guy's name was Steven Hicks and he was staying at a rooming house on Crocker Street. Guess what?"

"Moss was staying at the same place."

"That's right. The office manager recognized him from the photo. We've got an officer sitting tight in Moss's room, but something tells me he won't be showing up again."

"Anything left behind?"

"Nothing. They use a communal bathroom, so no point in having crime scene examine the shower and sink for any of the victims' blood—if we found any evidence it wouldn't hold up."

"What's the next step? LAPD advertising Moss to the press?"

"That's Hadley's call," Walsh said. "But I'm thinking it would be better to pick him up quietly than give him a reason to ditch evidence."

"In that case, Hadley will definitely be advertising it."

Walsh laughed. "The eternal optimist."

Morris had returned back to his car by the time his call with Walsh ended, and Parker was pawing at the passenger door, making sure Morris knew that he wanted in.

"Yes, sir," Morris told the dog.

Chapter 66

Yet another stakeout.

This one was different than most. Than any other, really. Instead of the tedium Fred Lemmon usually felt, the night zipped by as his thoughts kept drifting to the other day when he and Annie Walsh were on a stakeout together at the High Spot Lounge. He knew they were just playacting as a couple, but it felt so right. He kept thinking of how she laughed at his jokes, and the way her eyes just seemed to sparkle so brightly. It seemed like she felt the same connection he did. Like she might even be attracted to him…

He shuddered as the truth of the matter slapped him hard in the face. Of course Annie was acting that way. She was a professional. They were supposed to act as a couple inside the bar, so she was simply doing her job, nothing else. What an idiot he was to get caught up in these fantasies that had no chance of ever happening. And even if by some miracle Annie felt a fraction of what he felt, he was still married to Corrine.

For better or worse.

A beep from his phone alerted him that Jack Readinger's car had moved. He glanced at the dashboard clock. Twenty to midnight. The night wouldn't be a complete dud after all and sure enough, seconds later the car came rolling down the driveway from the apartment building and the moonlight provided enough light for Lemmon to see that it was Readinger behind the wheel. The GPS tracker attached to the undercarriage of the car would give him the location in case he lost the tail, so he had the luxury of waiting until Readinger was two blocks away before pulling away from the curb.

Thunk-thunk.

Lemmon got out of the car to see that both his rear tires were flat. A quick examination showed they'd been slashed with a knife. He took out his phone and called Morris.

"Target's on the move and I can't follow him," Lemmon said.

"Why not?"

"Someone sneaked behind my car and slashed my rear tires."

"No kidding?"

"Would I kid about that?"

"No, you wouldn't," Morris said. "I'm fifteen minutes away. I'll pick up the tail. The GPS tracker working?"

"It was when Readinger drove away. The car is still moving and heading toward Inglewood. A silver older-model Cadillac, I think an Eldorado, drove past me after I came to an abrupt stop. California plates, but I'm guessing they were stolen. Driver was a male, late twenties, wearing a baseball cap. I didn't get a good-enough look at him to say definitively it was Moss. At least this looks like it's coming to an end soon."

Morris sounded tired as he said, "I sure hope so."

* * * *

Readinger's car hadn't moved in ten minutes. Morris knew there was a bar at the address the GPS app was giving him, and he was guessing Moss had followed Readinger there. So Moss would've either parked outside waiting for Readinger to leave, or would've followed him inside so he could watch him more closely.

Except that wasn't what happened.

Morris approached the address and saw three police cruisers with lights flashing and a small mob of onlookers. It wasn't until he pulled up to the scene that he saw Readinger's car had crashed into a tree. A patrolman was about to tell Morris to keep moving, but he recognized him.

"What happened here?" Morris asked.

"Another car rear-ended this one and pushed it into the tree. According to witnesses, the driver of the car doing the rear-ending hit the other driver with a club, pulled him out of the car, got him into the trunk of his own car, then drove off."

Morris thanked him and pulled back onto the road. Earlier that day, Polk had placed the GPS tracker on the underside of Readinger's car, but Morris had also requested that the mayor get a court order to put a tracking chip in the sole of one of the biker boots Readinger was wearing when he was arrested. It was possible that Readinger wasn't wearing the biker boots when he left his apartment, and Morris held his breath while he fiddled with his phone and brought up the app to trace the location of the boots. The app gave him an address five miles away and in the opposite direction of Readinger's apartment. When Morris drove to it he saw it was a shuttered school scheduled for demolition, soon to be townhouses.

He circled the building and spotted a silver Cadillac parked on the street. He called Walsh. It rang through to voice mail and he tried again. This time she answered, sounding groggy as she complained that he had woken her from the most beautiful dream. "I was in the ring with Hadley and I had him on the ropes and was tenderizing his midsection with a flurry of jabs. It felt better than sex. What's up?"

"Something's going down right now between Readinger and Moss." He gave her the address of the shuttered school. "I'm heading inside," he told her. "Bring whatever sized army you can muster."

"Morris, don't go in," she ordered. "I'll have units there in minutes."

"Too much static," Morris said. "I can't hear you."

He disconnected the call and turned off the phone. He unholstered the .40 caliber pistol he had brought and flipped off the safety. He didn't need to check whether it was loaded.

Morris found a fire door with a busted lock. He moved quietly down a hallway with his gun in one hand and a flashlight in the other. A rustling noise startled him, and he swung the flashlight to show a rat scurrying away. He stood still and focused to stop his heart from racing, then held his breath and tried to listen for other noises. He heard an eerie, inhuman cry—except he knew in his heart it was very human. A muffled scream from someone who was gagged and being tortured.

He heard the noise again and followed it to one of the classrooms. He swung the door open with his gun stretched out in front of him. Readinger was facing the door. He was bound naked to a chair, a rag stuffed in his mouth, and Duncan was using a knife on him. Both of them were illuminated by a heavy-duty flashlight. Morris's intrusion sent Duncan ducking behind Readinger with the edge of the knife pressed against Readinger's throat.

Readinger was bleeding from his forehead to his groin and Morris realized Duncan had carved out words in Readinger's flesh. *Now* was carved out on his forehead; underneath was *you*; *have* ran down his left cheek; *yourself* along his right cheek; *an* at the base of his throat; *especially* across the full length of his chest; *wonderful* in big letters and split in two on his stomach; and the words *rest*, *of*, and *your* above his groin. The word *life* was missing, but Morris was sure Duncan was planning to carve it somewhere.

"Duncan, it's over," Morris said. "Put the knife down."

Morris was standing in darkness, while Duncan faced the heavy-duty flashlight he had set up. He blinked several times as he tried to make out who was interrupting him.

"You're that detective in charge," he said. "Brick."

"That's right."

"Then you know why I'm doing this."

"You don't know Readinger is the one that hurt Julia."

Duncan laughed bitterly. "I recorded this coward confessing to it. All it took was the word *now* and he was ready to spill his guts, and he gave me details only Julia's killer would know. When I demanded more proof, he confessed to killing another woman in Oakland the same way. Just give me an hour to finish up here and I'll make things easy for everyone. I promise."

"I can't do that."

Duncan looked dumbfounded, as if he couldn't understand why Morris couldn't give him an hour.

"Julia was the sweetest and most innocent person who ever lived. She saved me in ways you'd never be able to understand, and this piece of garbage butchered her for kicks."

"The same as you did to Jill Kincade and Meagan Campbell and Hannah Kammer. And the same as you wanted to do to my daughter."

Duncan looked close to tears as he blinked at Morris, the knife digging deep enough into Readinger's throat to draw blood. "That's not true and you know it," he said. "You know why I did what I did. What would you have done if your wife was butchered like Julia was, and the homicide detective in charge acted like it was your fault?"

"Not what you did."

"Bullshit. You would've done whatever was necessary to find the animal who hurt your wife so cruelly."

Police cars had arrived at the school. They had kept their sirens and flashing lights off, but car doors could be heard closing and so could a police radio. Duncan grew increasingly agitated as he realized he wouldn't have an hour with Readinger.

"I'll kill him, then," Duncan said.

Morris fired a shot past Duncan's left ear. He didn't much care whether Readinger died, but he couldn't in good conscience let Duncan kill him in front of him. He did, however, care very much that Duncan live. He wanted Rachel and Doug and every person connected to Duncan's victims to be able to face him in court and to have the opportunity to read a victim's statement.

"If you don't drop the knife right now, the next shot will take off the top of your head," Morris threatened. "I'll then destroy your phone and no one will ever see the recording you made. Readinger will never be punished for Julia's murder."

The sound of policemen could be heard running down the hallway. Duncan blinked several times as he tried to decide whether Morris was bluffing. Either he decided he wasn't, or he wasn't willing to take the chance. He dropped the knife.

"He's unarmed," Morris yelled.

Four officers came rushing into the room. It was over quickly after that. As they were taking Duncan out in handcuffs, Morris's phone rang. Rachel.

Her voice broke apart as she cried, "Daddy." And he braced himself for the worst possible news.

Epilogue

Morris stood at the edge of the cliff overlooking the Pacific Ocean and drank a beer from a small Czech Republic brewery that Philip Stonehedge claimed was his favorite lager. He squinted toward the sun and felt the heat from it warm his face.

A fine day, he thought. *A perfect day.*

Someone tapped him on the shoulder and a familiar voice said, "Morris the booger head."

He turned to see his sister Esther grinning at him. She wore a sheer peach-colored dress, stood barely five feet tall, and at age forty was still as slender as a teenager. With her long red hair, delicate features, and radiant beauty, she looked so much like their mom that it was startling. He grinned back and said, "Esther the pest."

They embraced. "I'm so glad you could come," he said once they separated.

"We're making a habit of meeting face-to-face," she said, her grin stretching wider. "Two times now in two years. Do you think you can stand it?"

Esther had moved to London when she was twenty-four, and while they tried to Skype every month, during the last sixteen years they'd seen each other only three times other than today: thirteen years ago at their mother's funeral, four months later at their dad's, and roughly twenty-one months ago when Morris and Nat were traveling to Italy on a much-belated honeymoon and Esther brought her four-and-a-half-year-old daughter with her to meet up with them in Venice for the day.

"I think so. Did you bring Isadora?"

"Of course. She's with Rachel now, getting better acquainted with her and her beau. She has also become fast friends with that brute dog of yours. Izzy has been so proud of Rachel, telling everyone she meets back home how her American cousin will be getting married." Esther laughed. "She's become downright insufferable!"

Morris scanned the crowd hanging by the pool and food stations and he spotted his six-year-old niece gathered in a small group with Nat, Rachel, Doug, Stonehedge, and Brie Evans. Izzy was wearing a yellow sundress and was a tiny little thing like Esther had been at that age. She was petting Parker while the bull terrier sat on the ground, grinning happily. Nat noticed Morris and waved to him. He waved back.

"Isadora is beautiful," Morris said.

"She is and she knows it, making her all that more insufferable. Very dramatic, that one." Esther's expression turned somber. "It's almost unimaginable what Rachel and her intended went through. I saw the interview you gave on that tabloid show, and it made me want to cry. And to think, you were the one who arrested that demented creature."

Morris briefly flashed back to the phone call he'd gotten from Rachel when the police were removing Duncan Moss from the classroom. She hadn't called him Daddy since she was seven, and the way she burst out crying convinced him the worst had happened. Fortunately, Nat took the phone and explained that the opposite was true. Doug had regained consciousness and promised Rachel he wasn't leaving her. Rachel wanted to call Morris to tell him the good news, but was too overcome with emotion.

He noticeably shivered. Esther took his hand and squeezed it tight.

"The ordeal is over," Morris said. "Doug is already looking like his old self and doctors expect a full recovery. How about we head back to the party? I'd like to spend some time with my adorable niece, even if she is insufferable."

"A splendid idea." Esther peered out at the horizon. "Nothing but clear skies ahead."

She could be excused for thinking that. She had no way of knowing about the evil brewing in the Hollywood Hills.